HUSBANDS *and* LOVERS

"Harris relates the games of love and war in a fast-forward, high octane style, resurrecting 'the nervous '70s' through a welter of accurate detail, from the clothes and books and other cultural artifacts to the sexual mores of the period. A dead-on accurate social critic, Harris has captured the feel of being young and hungry and ambitious in New York."

Erica Abeel, *New Woman*

"An easy-to-read, very contemporary tale of seemingly successful people who would like to sustain meaningful relationships, and could, if only husbands (and wives) were like lovers—always full of fun and flattery."

Library Journal

"With this designer-labeled guide to life in the fast track, Harris is just the novelist to step into Jacqueline Susann's sling-back, gray suede Charles Jourdan pumps."

Booklist

Another Fawcett Crest Title
by Ruth Harris

A SELF-MADE WOMAN

HUSBANDS and LOVERS

RUTH HARRIS

FAWCETT CREST • NEW YORK

TO MICHAEL,
with love

CONTENTS

PROLOGUE

November 1982:
Husbands and Lovers

*C*arlys Webber Arnold *was a woman who never took* anything for granted. She was a woman who had turned herself from a loser into a winner, from ordinary into extraordinary, a woman who had lived through the best of times and worst of times and learned from every minute. At twenty, Carlys had been mousy, invisible, the classic grind. By thirty, she'd even given up on Mr. Okay, never mind Mr. Right. Because she'd had no other choice, she had devoted herself to her career. At thirty-seven, though, she had it all—a spectacular career, a handsome and successful husband, plenty of money, and even a style of her own. Her green eyes were softly shaded and penciled; her flawless skin, always her best feature, glowed; her light brown, naturally curly hair was cut into a flattering, shiny cloud and her body, toned by constant exercise and fanatic self-control at mealtimes, was slim and strong. She dressed for success, but under her expensive, carefully tailored suits, she wore fragile and lacy lingerie. The woman under the executive. Very Carlys. Very attractive. Very eighties.

At a quarter to eight on a Tuesday evening in mid-November, Carlys stepped out of a taxi in front of her expensive Upper East Side co-op. She still remembered her depressing one-room walk-up, and because she did, she appreciated the elegant building in which she now lived, with its handsome limestone façade and solicitous doormen who greeted her whenever she entered or left. She said good evening to the doorman, got into the elevator, and chatted with the elevator man as they ascended to the tenth floor. She stepped out of the elevator and crossed the few steps of thickly carpeted hallway to her own elegantly lacquered front door and, inserting the key into the lock, opened it. She was shocked to see her husband.

"Kirk! What are you doing here!" she exclaimed, her heart stopping. "I thought you were in Los Angeles."

"I *was* in Los Angeles," he said and smiled and put his arms out to her. He was tall, rich, and handsome, a brilliant businessman with a hot hand in corporate affairs, an American aristocrat with a film star's charisma, a younger Prince Philip, a taller Robert Redford. He was blond and tawny and the scar that intersected his left eyebrow only added a mysterious hint of an intriguing past. "I kept thinking about you and I decided to give myself a birthday present and spend it with you!"

"How romantic!" she said, thrilled, glorying in his embrace, his attention. She had been his wife for seven years and sometimes, when she saw him across a room, she still couldn't really believe that she was actually married to him. The Wallflower and the White Knight. "When did you get back?"

"This afternoon," he said as he handed her a small shopping bag from Tiffany. Even though it was his birthday, his forty-eighth, he was the one who gave the present. Early in their marriage, he had forbidden her to mark his birthday. Kirk's hatred of birthdays seemed a peculiar quirk to Carlys, but she had finally accepted it as one of the mysteries in the man she had married.

He watched as she opened the present. Her green eyes sparkled with pleasure and a healthy acquisitiveness as she took the three wide ivory bangles out of their box and immediately tried them on. Carlys's sheer animal pleasure in *things* always delighted him; his first wife had never cared. "Do you like them?"

"You know I do!" she said, holding out her arm, turning it this way and that, the better to appreciate and admire the handsome Peretti bangles. It was just like Kirk to give her a present, she thought. He had trouble putting his feelings into words; he gave gifts instead. Gifts that said *I love you. I'm sorry. You mean everything to me.* Gifts whose meanings he expected her to interpret. "I *love* them!"

She smiled again and, putting her arms around him, kissed him.

"That's no kiss!" he chided. Gently at first, and then

deeply, he probed her mouth, excited by her familiar, slightly spicy taste and the feeling of the familiar sensuous curves of her body against his.

The next morning Carlys made him breakfast and kissed him goodbye at the door.

"I *love* the bracelets," she said, already wearing them, as she held the door for him as he picked up his briefcase to return to the coast and the Silicon Valley negotiations. "Thank you again."

Carlys kissed him, smiled, and let him go. She was a wife used to a husband who traveled constantly on business; a sophisticated woman living a sophisticated life in a sophisticated city; a woman who had it all: a successful career, a loving husband, a passionate lover.

*The apartment on East Sixty-second Street, once photo-*graphed by *The New York Times,* was handsome and invit-ing. The man who lived there was the architect who had designed it. He was an amber-eyed Greek God, olive-skinned and dark-haired. George Kouras was sensitive and passion-ate, a lover, he said, not a destroyer. A giver, he had told Carlys right from the beginning, and not a taker.

"I couldn't wait for you to get here," he said tenderly, later that day. He helped her off with her jacket, his hands caressing the back of her neck. She shivered under his touch.

"When is the magic going to stop?" she wondered out loud.

"Never," he said, silencing her with his mouth, excited just to be with her again. He needed her just the way he needed Jade. He needed them both and he wasn't going to let either of them go.

His lips on hers were gentle at first and then more insis-tent. George was an artist with women, a genius at love and its complexities. He loved love, lived for love and never thought that loving one woman was a reason not to love another.

Gradually, Carlys returned his kiss, still thrilled by the novelty of his taste, by the mysteries of his mouth and hands and body. As he led her into his bedroom she told herself that it was only an affair, and that she could stop anytime she wanted. Besides, Kirk was such a workaholic, so caught up in business, that he'd never find out.

Jade Mullen was an original. She always said that the best thing that ever happened to her was not being born pretty. She had hair the color of wet sand, bronze eyes with gold-flecks, and beautiful hands with almond-shaped nails. She had too much nose and too little chin, but the only thing anyone ever noticed was that she was always the best-looking woman in the room. When a candy-box pretty girl got picked to be Snow White in the fourth-grade Christmas pageant and Jade got to be a dwarf in a lumpy brown costume, she swore on her grungy Grumpy's hat that she would never again be treated as second best just because she wasn't pretty—and she never was.

Jade never did anything the way other people did. She didn't talk like anyone else. She didn't dress like anyone else. She didn't look like anyone else. Being unconventional had always been the secret to her enormous success—with a long line of men who found her irresistible and with a dazzling career in fashion that made her the muse of one of Seventh Avenue's most influential designers. The one and only time Jade had ever done anything conventional, she had failed.

Like just about everyone else, Jade had gotten married and, like half the people who get married, had gotten divorced. Being single suited her; to Jade being single didn't mean alone and it didn't mean lonely. It meant love and independence and, for three years now, it had meant George Kouras.

On Seventy-third Street, just outside the gloomy offices of a well-known Park Avenue physician, Jade Mullen jammed her Borsalino down over her new Paris haircut, slung her suede bag bandolier-style over her quilted Issey jacket, and began to look for a telephone. Park, of course, was too chic for phones. The one at Lexington and Seventy-third was broken. The one at Lex and Seventy-first was busy. She finally found one at Lex and Sixty-ninth that was both functional and available. She even had a dime but, naturally, the line was busy.

She gave up, and as she began to walk downtown, she wondered how he would react to the news. It was, she reflected as she turned the corner on Sixty-second Street, the kind of news that was better delivered face-to-face.

Meanwhile, in the small lobby of the brownstone building, Kirk Arnold searched the nameplates on the buzzer system. There it was, the third name from the top. GEORGE KOURAS, it read. Kirk pressed the buzzer and waited for the answer.

In his hand he carried the small Tiffany bag that hours before had contained the Elsa Peretti bracelets. Now it held a gun, a gun that had already taken two lives. Even as the buzzer sounded in reply, Kirk, knowing he was about to meet his wife's lover face-to-face, his emotions in turmoil, did not know what he was going to do next.

PART ONE

The Married Woman

"I always thought I was doomed to be on the outside looking in. To me, getting married was just like all the other good things in life. For other people. Not for me."

—CARLYS WEBBER ARNOLD

CHAPTER 1

Carlys Webber never understood what was supposed to be so wonderful about being single. When she first met Kirk Arnold in the spring of 1971, Carlys was twenty-six and unmarried, alone and lonely, vulnerable and unhappy, the survivor of go-nowhere jobs and go-nowhere men. The sixties had happened to everyone except her. The sexual revolution had freed everyone but her, and the women's movement seemed to apply to everyone except her.

Her father was Jewish; her mother, Lutheran. As a girl, Carlys had attended synagogue on Saturday and church on Sunday, the recipient of a double dose of guilt. Her mother had had multiple sclerosis and Carlys had spent her childhood being good at school and being good at home where she was her mother's nurse, her father's housekeeper. It took multiple sclerosis seven years to kill Eleanor Webber, who died when Carlys was sixteen. Jacob Webber lived on, clinging to Carlys for dear life.

"I want my own apartment," Carlys told him seven years later, her heart pounding guiltily, almost drowning out her words. "I found a nice studio on East Eighty-first Street."

"Please don't move out! You're all I've got! I'll be all alone!" Jacob Webber pleaded. He was a sad and gray man whose own life had ended with his wife's death. In the year after her death, he retired not only from business but, so it seemed, from life, abandoning his interests in the stock market, his Tuesday night poker game, and his Sunday morning round of golf. He told Carlys that he had given up everything to devote himself to her. He refused to go out; he refused to meet new people; he refused to travel; he refused to go to temple; he refused to go to the movies. He even refused to have the apartment painted. He didn't want to change anything from the way his wife had left it seven years before. "If you go, you'll kill me."

9

"I'm twenty-three," Carlys said, aware of the hammering of her heart. Part of her was afraid that if she left, he *would* die, the way her mother had died. What gave her courage was the terror that more years of living with him would snuff out the little spark of life that still flickered in her. "I'm grown up. It's time I was independent."

"Please stay! Please don't go! I'll do anything you want!" he bargained, clutching her hand, physically trying to stop her from leaving.

"No, Daddy," she said, sounding firmer than she felt. There were tears in her eyes. "I'm entitled to a life of my own."

Even as she spoke Carlys had no idea of whether or not she was capable of creating a life of her own. The little confidence she had lurched and threatened to slip away.

On the same day that Carlys moved out of her father's apartment Jacob Webber had a heart attack. His face turned ashen and he clutched his chest, his hands clawed with pain.

"Carlys! Don't go!" Jacob gasped. "You can't go!" He slumped onto the dining table in agony. "It's my heart! I'm dying."

Carlys called 911 and Dr. Barlow and for the next few days she raced back and forth between West End Avenue and East Eighty-first Street, between her new apartment and Roosevelt Hospital. Maybe he was right, she thought. Maybe she *was* killing him. Maybe she shouldn't move out, shouldn't get her own apartment. She was tormented by guilt. She was terrified that his prophecy was coming true. She had moved out and it was killing him!

She accused herself of being selfish. She told herself that her father's heart attack was her fault, and that she was wrong to want to make a life of her own. She should stay with him, care for him, put him first, herself second. She should be a good daughter.

Her father's doctor convinced her that she was wrong.

"Don't let him blackmail you," Dr. Barlow said. *"You're* not the selfish one. He is. You're a young woman, Carlys. You're entitled to a life of your own."

Without Gordon Barlow, Carlys would still have been living with her father but, ironically, the farther she got from West End Avenue in time and distance, the more closely she seemed bound to it. She was always the good girl, always the dutiful girl, always the girl who put others first and herself last. She was so accustomed to taking care of others that she often had difficulty taking care of herself. It was the reason she was so grateful for Norma Finkelstein's friendship and good advice; it was the reason she was so vulnerable to Winn Rosier, who swore he loved her but was breaking her heart instead.

Only at school and work did Carlys ever seem to shine. The summer after her graduation from Hunter (she majored in liberal arts, which qualified her for exactly nothing), she took a basic secretarial course at Katharine Gibbs and found a job in the typing pool in the public relations department of the telephone company. Always a straight-A student in English, she was shocked at the semiliterate press releases she was handed to type. Very tentatively she began to "fix" them, and the copywriters soon began to hand Carlys "rough copy."

"Fix it up, would you?" they'd say and Carlys would dutifully "fix it up." Except that the "fixing" was more like rewriting, and soon enough, she was writing press releases herself. All the copywriters were men and they were being paid $225 a week; Carlys was getting $110.

"You're getting screwed," said Norma, the office agitator. She was one of the two assistants to the office manager and had access to the personnel files. It was Norma who had discovered that Carlys was getting paid less than half of what the men, whose work she'd been doing, were getting paid.

"I know," said Carlys.

"You have to stand up for your rights," said Norma.

"I know," said Carlys.

The first time Carlys asked for a raise and a promotion she was nice about it and got nowhere. The second time she asked, she wasn't, and she got what she wanted.

"I'd like a promotion and a raise," she told Mr. Ryan, her supervisor, her heart thumping, her hands shaking, her voice shaky but determined. "I think I've earned it. I want to be a copywriter. I've been doing the work for almost two years and everybody in the office knows it."

"I'll see," said Bob Ryan with a sigh. Bob Ryan was bald and moon-faced. He lived with his sister and mother in Queens and his only ambition was to sneak through life unnoticed. The thing Bob Ryan hated most was change, particularly change in his own department. "But you'll have to be patient."

Carlys agreed to be patient. She always agreed to what other people wanted. Two months later, though, nothing had been said or done. Carlys was still doing a copywriter's work for a typist's pay. Egged on by Norma, inspired by massive media coverage of employers' unfairness to female employees and President Nixon's proclamation of Women's Rights Day, Carlys went back to Mr. Ryan and reminded him of their conversation. This time she had come prepared with a threat.

"If you don't do anything," she said angrily, "I'm going to *your* supervisor and if *he* doesn't do anything, I'm going to *his* supervisor. And if *he* doesn't do anything, I'm going to *The New York Times*. I'm doing a man's work and getting a woman's pay and I'm not going to put up with it anymore."

"Be patient," Bob began, sighing heavily.

"I've been patient," said Carlys. "Now are you going to pay me what I'm worth or not?"

He sighed again. "I'll talk to my supervisor," he said and swiveled around in his chair, turning his back to her, a signal that the meeting was over. "Ballbreaker," Carlys heard him mutter as she left his office. She wanted to kill him but she pretended not to hear. She wanted the raise and the promotion and told herself that it was better to shut up for the time being than tell him what he could do with himself and his precious balls.

Within two weeks Carlys was promoted to junior copywriter and got an office of her own, an office that consisted of semiopaque glass partitions that cut off air but not noise in the middle of the huge open-plan floor space. Every Monday she bought a single rosebud at the subway entrance and kept it in a bud vase on her desk.

Her small triumph at work seemed a good omen to Carlys.

"Maybe my love life will perk up," she confided to Norma as 1970 turned into 1971. Her last date had been six months ago.

"Not as long as you work at the phone company," Norma said.

Norma was right. As long as she stayed in her cubicle at

the phone company, she'd stay invisible. A job, if it was the right job, could be socially invaluable. Even Carlys knew *that*. Since she had had no luck meeting men through blind dates or in singles' bars, at resorts or in museums or art galleries or all the other places that seemed to work for everyone else, she decided that she might as well try to meet one through a job. If she didn't, at least she might have a chance to work her way up to a decent job and a decent salary. Carlys began to read the *Times*'s want ads every weekday, and every Saturday afternoon she went to the all-night newsstand on First Avenue near her apartment. She waited for the back sections of the *Times* to come in and bought the Sunday Help Wanted section the minute it arrived. In February she found an ad, placed by the Arrow Personnel Agency, that seemed to speak directly to her: CHALLENGE; PRESTIGE; STATUS FOR THE RIGHT COPYWRITER WITH MAJOR LEAGUE PR BACKGROUND.

On Monday morning she got off the subway at Grand Central Station and walked over to the Forty-second Street and Fifth Avenue office of Arrow Personnel. It was a quarter to nine. The receptionist's desk was empty, and Carlys timidly walked back into the office area.

"I'm here about the copywriting job," Carlys said, clearing her throat. She stood outside the open door of the first occupied office, unsure whether or not to enter without an invitation, awed by the handsome executive inside.

"Which job?" he asked, looking up from his emery board and wondering where the hell the receptionist was. Winn Rosier was a few years older than Carlys and had fine olive skin and comely, even features, the most striking of which was a strong, cleft chin. Winn was well aware of his good looks and, at the dawning of the Me decade, was dedicated to making the best of himself. He shampooed his wavy blue-black hair daily and carefully blow-dried it. Every morning and evening he applied a trace of skin cream under his alert brown eyes to forestall premature wrinkling. He took care of his body, exercising regularly and controlling his weight by excluding refined sugar, red meat, and most starches from his diet. He took time and trouble with his clothes and jewelry, and this morning he wore a Giorgio Armani suit with a Ralph Lauren shirt and tie, a good imitation Cartier tank watch (as soon as he could afford to, he planned to buy the real one), and a gold ID bracelet, a gift from one of the many women who pursued him. A Prince tennis racket was propped up against the side of his desk next to a Louis Vuitton carryall that held his tennis clothes. A large jar of organic vitamin tablets stood on the window ledge. "We have a dozen copy jobs."

"There's one in a public relations department," Carlys said, pulling the circled ad out of her purse and handing it to him. He glanced at it, and then at her. She had unstyled, curly, dishwater hair; heavy, unplucked eyebrows; no makeup except a tentative dot of pink lipstick; and an excuse-me-for-being-alive expression on her face. She wore a plaid polyester shirtdress with a white nylon collar and cuffs—a drip-dry number Winn could tell. A real pooch. He couldn't wait to get rid of her.

"I'd like to apply for the job," Carlys said, standing uncertainly on the other side of the desk, afraid of wasting his time. "I work at the phone company. I'm a copy-writer," she said and fumbled in her purse for the sample press releases she had brought along.

"Forget it," he said. "SuperWrite is strictly blue chip. They're not going to be interested in you."

"But you haven't even seen my work!" said Carlys, stunned by his offhanded dismissal. "You don't know what I can do."

"I don't have to," he said, picking up a metal letter opener and rotating its shiny blade to catch different angles of his reflection. As she spoke, he concentrated on his own image. "I've seen *you*. That's enough."

"That's a terrible thing to say," said Carlys, unable to stop the sudden tears that had come to her eyes.

"Don't cry," he said, annoyed. Her hang-dog expression and dumb clothes irritated him beyond belief. "I'm sorry if I hurt you, but I've found it's better to tell the truth. SuperWrite is a fast-track company. You don't look like a fast-track person."

"I don't?" she asked pathetically.

"And it's not just looks," he added, deciding he might as well let her have it. "You're too self-effacing, too tenta-tive, too apologetic." The tears welled up in her eyes again and he immediately felt guilty. Winn wasn't a bastard, just a minor-league sadist. "Tell me, do you have a job now?" he asked in a softer tone.

"Yes," She said gratefully, thinking he wanted to hear about her experience. "At the phone company."

"Let me give you a little advice," he said, leaning forward. He took one more fast peek at himself and, liking what he saw, put the letter opener down. "The phone company is a good place to work. It's secure. The benefits are great. You look like you fit in there."

"You don't have *any* job that I might qualify for?" Carlys persisted hopelessly.

He shrugged his shoulders. "Look, let me level with you. We're a grade-A agency. We deal only with top-flight companies and top-flight personnel. You look like someone who ought to stick with the phone company until you can get that boyfriend of yours to marry you." He winked at her conspiratorially and leaned back again, feeling he had done the right thing by her. "You get me?"

"No," she said stubbornly, "I don't 'get' you."

"All right," he said and sighed. "Have it your way. The fact is that I'm not going to send you on any interviews. You'll screw up my track record."

This time, the tears didn't come to Carlys's eyes.

"What's your name?" she asked politely.

"Rosier," he said. "Winn Rosier."

"My name is Carlys Webber," she said, with sudden, touching dignity. "I'll be back."

"God forbid," he said under his breath, but loud enough for her to hear, as she left his office. He opened his top desk drawer, pulled out a breath spray, and used it before making his first telephone call of the day.

"It was a disaster," she told Norma as soon as she got to the office. She felt crushed and humiliated. "A total disaster. He made me feel as if I'd just stepped off a bus from Nowhere."

"What did he say?" Norma was working on a Twinkie and a Tab. She was fat, aggressive, generous, and, like Carlys, unmarried. She lived alone in a spacious apartment on Seventy-fourth Street between Riverside Drive and West End Avenue with two German shepherds named Bunny and Alice with whom she ran twice daily in Riverside Park. Norma had sought out Carlys's friendship when, after a coffee-break conversation about Bob Ryan's bully-coward syndrome, she had decided that Carlys was the only other person in the place with half a brain.

"That I didn't look like a fast-track person," Carlys said.

"Well, screw him!" said Norma, insulted on her friend's behalf. "One of us has got to get out of this dump and since I have to lose twenty-five pounds before anyone gives me the time of day, I guess you're elected. Fast-track person, huh?" Norma snorted contemptuously. "I'll bet we can make you into a fast-track person in one week."

"What *is* a fast-track person?" asked Carlys, her heart beating faster. Norma always gave her the courage to do things she wanted to do but was afraid of. Norma's great talent was vicarious experience.

"What you're going to be one week from today," said Norma, polishing off the Twinkie and pegging the wrapper into the wastebasket, a perfect two points. Norma was always very definite when it came to other people.

Norma's authorities were Vogue *and* Mademoiselle *and* Cosmopolitan.

"Hair is number one," announced Norma. "*Vogue* says that layered hair is in." She showed Carlys photographs of several different versions of the layered look. The biggest and most prominent photo was credited to a hairdresser named Jules.

"He's famous," Norma said, a connoisseur of beauty hints, gossip columns, and the *National Enquirer*. "I read that he cuts Candy Bergen's hair."

"Do you think you could copy it?" Carlys asked.

"I'll try," said Norma, who cut her own hair and didn't do a bad job. She didn't do a bad job on Carlys either, layering it around the face, cutting it a little shorter in the front than in the back the way Jules had. She was not brave enough, however, to cut the wispy bangs that fringed the model's forehead in the photograph. Nevertheless, both were pleased with the result. Carlys was thrilled to have a haircut *Vogue* said was in. Norma said it showed more of her face.

The right clothes, Norma decreed, were the next step.

That Thursday night, when all the stores were open late, Carlys, under strict instructions from Norma, who was starting with Weight Watchers for the third time and there-

fore couldn't accompany her, went to Macy's, to the Young
Career department. She fumbled through the racks, de-
clining an offer of help from a trendy young salesgirl who
sported an extreme shaggy haircut called The Monkey, a
midi-skirt with a leopard-printed cumberbund belt, and highheeled black leather boots. She waited until an older, more
conservative-looking saleswoman wearing a dark suit and
dark red sweater was free. Pink, plastic-rimmed eyeglasses
swung from a black cord around her neck and rested on her
ample bosom. She polished them assiduously and put them
on, peering at Carlys as she spoke.

"I'd like to see somthing to wear to the office," Carlys
said nervously. "I'm interested in a fast-track job."

"Then you'll want a suit," said the saleswoman authoritatively and showed Carlys three.

"I like the gray," Carlys said, pointing toward it, thinking that gray was a good, safe color.

"You'll do better with the navy," said the saleswoman.
"Navy is a power color."

Carlys had never heard the phrase, but it was exactly the
kind of expression Winn Rosier had used. When Carlys
wrote a check for her purchase, the saleswoman told her
that she'd made a good choice. "It's a copy of a Calvin
Klein," she confided.

"Now you need the right makeup so your features don't
wash out under harsh, fluorescent office light," Norma
advised, quoting *Mademoiselle*.

On Saturday, while Norma took Bunny and Alice to the
vet, Carlys went to Bloomingdale's. At the Ultima counter
a makeup artist was doing free makeovers. He was shorter
and smaller-boned than Carlys, as slim as a leaf and fragile
as a butterfly. He had velvety clear skin and exquisitely
expressive large brown doe eyes that might or might not
have been subtly outlined with gray pencil.

"Wonderful skin and wonderful green eyes," he diag-
nosed, in a soft voice, as Carlys slid onto the makeup stool.
He took her chin gently in his hand and examined her face
from every angle. "Your skin is like velvet and your eyes
are a photographer's dream, huge and wide set. The trouble is they're hidden under those brows. I'll thin them out

and shape them. Then, once you use the right shadow and liner, they'll turn the color of emeralds."

Swiftly and confidently he plucked the stray hairs from Carlys's eyebrows, trimming and shaping them. Next, he applied foundation, shadow and liner, mascara and blusher, and lipstick, pausing now and then to step back and observe his work. When he was done, he held up a hand mirror.

"Do you like it?" he wanted to know, as anxious to please as Carlys always was.

"Oh, yes!" said Carlys, excited by the way she looked. With a few strokes of his brushes and fingers, he had created high cheekbones and interesting hollows beneath Large, mysteriously shadowed eyes that had once been hidden under heavy brows *were*, magically, the color of emeralds. Her mouth was a subtle terra-cotta that made her lips soft and sensuous and her teeth seem blindingly white. "I look so pretty!"

Reluctantly she handed the mirror back and bought fifty dollars' worth of the products and brushes he had used. She would have to borrow the money from Norma until next payday. When he gave her the bag containing her purchases he showed her how to work the magic he had worked. He told her where to place the shadows and the blusher, how to create the hollows under her cheekbones, how to put on mascara so it looked thick but didn't cake, and how to apply the lipstick so that her mouth looked soft and pretty, natural-but-better-than-natural.

"You *are* pretty," he said in his soft, earnest voice when she was ready to leave. "And you have gorgeous eyes. When you do your makeup, be sure you really bring them out." Even though he was obviously gay, Carlys didn't care. She treasured his compliment because she knew he was right. Deep down, she had always known she was pretty. It was just that people never really looked at her. No one else had ever noticed.

On the way home from Bloomingdale's, Carlys bought the next day's Help Wanted section.

The Arrow Agency had run the identical ad that had appeared the week before. Obviously, the SuperWrite job hadn't been filled. At a quarter to nine on Monday morning she went back to the Arrow Agency. Just as she had the previous week, Carlys arrived before the receptionist and went straight back toward Winn Rosier's office. Remembering what Norma had said about acting confidently, and what Winn had said about being too tentative, Carlys knocked firmly on the door and entered his office before he could say anything.

"Mr. Rosier?" she asked.

"Yes?" He'd been brushing his hair, but he put away the brush as soon as he realized an attractive woman was looking at him. The clothes definitely looked like Calvin Klein to him. "Can I help you?"

"I'm interested in the job at SuperWrite," she said, approaching his desk and sitting in the chair in front of it.

"How did you know about *that?*" he asked, startled. She wasn't supposed to know who his clients were. No one was. Personnel agencies keep their listings top secret.

"You told me last week."

"I did?" He looked at her blankly and flipped through his files quickly. "I sent over two candidates," he said, getting out the card and reading his notes. "They were both men. They were both turned down."

"You never sent me," Carlys said quietly. "You advised me to stay at the phone company."

"Oh," he said, inspecting her carefully, now realizing who she was. "What did you do to yourself? Spend the week at Elizabeth Arden's?"

Carlys ignored the remark. "Please make an appointment for me with SuperWrite," she said politely. "You know, it was nice of me to come back to you. I could have gone straight to SuperWrite, and if I had gotten the job, you wouldn't have gotten your commission."

Winn Rosier looked at Carlys again, studying her, impressed by the transformation, impressed by her aggressiveness. He tended to like aggressive women, at least in the beginning.

"What did you say your name was?" he asked.

"Carlys Webber," she replied.

"Well, Carlys, why the hell not?" he said, smiling at her in a way he knew women really went for.

CHAPTER 2

SuperWrite's offices were in a sedate-looking building on Madison Avenue and Forty-eight Street. They were furnished the way Carlys imagined an English men's club would be furnished: dark wood paneling, somber tapestries, heavy mahogany furniture, and faded oriental rugs. They looked as if they had been there forever. The head of the copy department, who resembled an undertaker in his three-piece suit and wing-tip shoes, also looked as if he'd been there forever. He interviewed Carlys as somberly as if she were a relative of the deceased, put her resumé and samples in his "in" basket, and said that he would call her later in the week.

"We'll want to see other candidates," he told her when the interview was over. He shook her hand formally, not giving her a clue as to how she'd done.

When she called Winn Rosier to report, he asked her if she had a particular interest in corporate public relations.

"No," she said, having been put off by SuperWrite's stodgy atmosphere. "Not particularly. I just want a better job at a first-class company."

"The reason I ask is that something new just came in this afternoon," he said. "Another copywriting job. Only it's not client-side. It's an agency. Barron and Hynes. You want to go over?"

If SuperWrite was blue chip, Barron & Hynes was tinsel and glitz. Lennard Barron, the founder, was in and out of fancy drying-out institutions. Currently in. Joshua Hynes had hung on, thanks to Kirk Arnold, the corporate miracle worker Joshua had called in to save Lennard Barron's company from Lennard Barron.

Barron & Hynes represented Cellini, the legendary Italian

leathergoods maker with shops on Fifth Avenue, Rodeo Drive, and Worth Avenue; a motion picture company; and a chain of West Coast newspapers. It also represented individuals, among them an opera star named Sergio Maliterno, who'd become a superstar; and a new client, a stock market pundit named Lansing Coons. Its offices in the Onassis-built Olympic Towers, which housed Halston's glittering headquarters, overlooked St. Patrick's and Saks to the south. Cartier was one block to the north and Rockefeller Center was across the street. It was definitely, Carlys thought, in fast-track territory.

Tom Steinberg, an account executive, interviewed Carlys and, after a brief consultation with Joshua Hynes and Kirk Arnold, called to offer her a job that same afternoon in what was referred to as the "personals." The "personals" were the individuals represented by Barron & Hynes as opposed to the companies. The individuals, Steinberg pointed out, baiting his hook, were either celebrities or about-to-become celebrities.

"Do you think you'd be interested?" he asked. "We see you as a comer."

"Can I have until Monday to think it over?" Carlys asked, hiding her excitement, wanting to talk it over with Norma first. A comer! She liked him already.

"Okay," he said. "But only until Monday."

"You did the right thing," Winn Rosier said on the telephone, his voice warm and intimate, caressing her with approval. "Asking for time. Let me get on the phone to SuperWrite. I'll tell them they'd better make up their minds."

That Friday Carlys had two job offers as a full-fledged copywriter. The salaries were identical and much more than she earned at the phone company. The companies, though, as she told Norma, were as different as day and night. SuperWrite seemed sort of moribund. Not Barron & Hynes. She had the feeling that she might meet some interesting people there. By interesting people she meant interesting men.

"Writing releases about SuperWrite's corporate policies and executive promotions sounds just as boring as the telephone company," she told Norma. "But no one's going to turn away at a party when I say I work for Sergio Maliterno.''

"I know what you mean," Norma said, thinking, as Carlys did, that meeting celebrities would be exciting and glamorous.

"So you think I should take the job at Barron and Hynes?"

"It's what *you* think," Norma insisted loyally, not wanting to sway her friend one way or the other.

"Barron and Hynes!" Carlys said, doing what she'd wanted to do right from the very beginning.

That Monday afternoon, Carlys left work a little early and was a the Arrow Agency at five o'clock. Winn had warned her to drop the crack-of-dawn routine.

"I've decided I want to take the job with Barron and Hynes," she told him.

"You must be psychic," he said, favoring her with an intimate, only-between-us look. "SuperWrite's in trouble. They're in the horse-and-buggy business in the jet age," he confided, making some notes on her application with a Mont Blanc pen he'd gotten wholesale through the stationery salesman who sold to the office. "First thing tomorrow I'll give SuperWrite the bad news and Barron and Hynes the good news."

"I appreciate your help," Carlys said earnestly. She had come to think of Winn Rosier as an ally. "Thank you."

"You don't have to thank me," Winn said, running his hands through his thick dark hair, enjoying the clean, silky feel. "I make my living getting people jobs. I get a good commission. In your case, it's going to cost you an extra month's commission. After all, I sent you to two places. It's not my fault you got two offers and turned one of them down. SuperWrite wasn't too happy. I had to sweet-talk my way, *your* way, out of it."

He pushed a legal-looking agreement across the desk for her to sign.

"Well, anyway," said Carlys, signing the paper, not quite following his line of reasoning, "I appreciate it." Later, when it would be too late to do anything about it, Norma would tell her that Winn was ripping her off.

"Sure," he said, acknowledging her thanks. He glanced at his watch. It was just five-thirty. "I've got an hour to kill until my date tonight," he said suddenly. "Want to have a drink?"

Carlys's face lit up like a Christmas tree as she accepted and Winn was glad he'd done her the favor of asking her out. It made him feel good about himself.

The next morning Carlys gave Bob Ryan two weeks' notice.

"Who'd want to hire you?" he asked, annoyed that his department was being upset.

"Three years ago *you* wanted to hire me," Carlys reminded him, happy to have the chance to be just as nasty as he was. "Don't you remember?"

Carlys looked forward to the first day of her new job the way she used to look forward to the first day of school. Even more exciting was the way Winn had said he'd call her when they'd said good-bye outside the hectic commuters' bar he'd taken her to around the corner from Grand Central. Every time a man said he'd call, Carlys always believed him, even though her experience told her that men never called when they said they would. She believed Winn Rosier, too. Norma told her she was just fooling herself.

That first Monday, Carlys got ready for the office the way she would have gotten ready for a date. She was determined that her new job would change her luck. No one at Barron & Hynes had known her as anything other than a copywriter, she told herself. It wouldn't be like the phone company where she had started out as a pool typist and where, she had concluded, even if she ended up as president, people would still see her as the girl at the third desk from the left in the second row.

As she left to get the bus she took a last look at herself in the full-length mirror on the back of her closet door. The layered haircut, which Norma had trimmed that weekend, was right in style—just like Jane Fonda's haircut in *Klute*. The navy blue suit had the power look the saleswoman had promised and the makeup, which she had conscientiously practiced applying, *did* bring out her eyes. Carlys decided that she looked like a fast-track person. The next step would be *to feel* like one.

*   *   *

Tom Steinberg was a Jewish prince with coronation on his mind, coronation in the form of a Barron & Hynes vice-presidency. He had been in public relations for a dozen years, starting in the NBC Press Department when he had graduated from the Columbia School of Journalism. He had gone from NBC to the NFL and from there to Barron & Hynes, where he had survived the blitzkrieg of firings over which Kirk Arnold had presided in the course of getting Barron & Hynes back on the right track. Tom was pretty smart and fairly ambitious and he didn't mind being nice as long as it didn't cost him anything. He was also, although he refused to admit it, lazy. It helped that he had a very rich wife, the only daughter of a garment center tycoon. Tom—who wore Brooks Brothers suits, Brooks Brothers shirts, Brooks Brothers ties, and a Burberry raincoat even when the sun was shining—got up from his desk as Carlys entered his office, lit a Parliament Long, took a puff, then crushed it out instantly.

"Trying to quit," he explained to Carlys ruefully, picking a lime lollipop out of a bowl on his desk to suck on, a ploy he had learned at Smokenders. "Come, I'll introduce you around."

Tom took her from one office into the next, each one, Carlys noticed, more gaudily and egocentrically decorated than the one before, introducing her to the account executives and assistant account executives she'd be working for and to the copywriters she'd be working with. She noticed that there were a number of women in fairly high positions and she concluded—incorrectly—that Barron & Hynes was an enlightened firm.

Tom walked her through the row of secretarial desks that guarded the outer ring of executive offices and introduced her to people in the typing pool, accounting department, mail room, and Xerox center. Everyone seemed aggressively with-it and they all seemed to accept Carlys as one of them. Michelle Delande, who handled the fashion accounts, invited Carlys to lunch and Peter Salzany, one of the assistant account executives, told Carlys she was the only good-looking woman Barron & Hynes had hired since Kirk Arnold had appeared on the scene. More than ever, Carlys was sure she'd made the right decision when she picked Barron & Hynes over SuperWrite.

As Tom Steinberg completed the circuit of the office, he gave up and lit a Vantage. "Now," he said, inhaling luxuriously, "you've met everyone."

"Not everyone," said a husky voice from the doorway of the large corner office. "She hasn't met me. Hello, Carlys. I'm Kirk Arnold."

The chemistry between them was instant and immediate. Even Tom noticed. Carlys felt it, but she couldn't believe it. In her new clothes, her new makeup and haircut, she felt like an impostor. Men like Kirk Arnold never noticed her. It was the clothes and makeup he was reacting to, she told herself, not her.

Kirk Arnold had blond hair the color of butterscotch, and the year-round tan that Carlys associated with tennis courts, sailboats, country clubs, and expensive winter vacations on romantic Caribbean islands. His dark blue eyes were set under handsomely molded brows, the left of which was intriguingly intersected by a deep, crescent-shaped scar. He wore an impeccably tailored dark pin-striped suit with a subtle, heavy silk tie, and his handmade shoes cost more than Carlys earned in a month. He was impressive, intimidating, and incredibly self-confident.

"How do you do, Mr. Arnold?" Carlys said, remembering Peter Salzany's grudgingly admiring comment about Kirk Arnold, the miracle worker who brought companies back from the dead.

"You're much too good for lightweights like Sergio Maliterno and Lansing Coons," he said in a distinctive, husky voice that, impossibly, almost made him sound as if he'd been crying. "I've got a new job, too. Tell Barron and Hynes to get lost and come work for me."

"Now Kirk," Tom cautioned, trying to insert himself in the crackling electric field he sensed between them. "We got her first. . . ."

"Tell Tom you're quitting," Kirk said, speaking directly to Carlys as if Tom weren't there. "Whatever you're getting paid, I'll raise it by ten percent."

Carlys looked at Kirk, then at Tom, dying to do what Kirk Arnold told her to do. Why should she work for a Brooks Brothers clone when she could work for a man Michelle had called the White Knight of Wall Street? Tom seemed to sense how she felt.

"You pull that kind of shit, you'll never get another job in PR," Tom warned. "Your credibility will be zilch."

"If she goes to work for me, she won't *want* another job in PR," Kirk countered.

They both turned to Carlys.

"Well?" Tom asked.

Carlys's instincts pulled her in one direction; the teachings of the rabbis and the ministers pulled her in another.

"Thank you, Mr. Arnold," she said reluctantly in the good-girl voice she hated, the rabbis and the ministers winning as they always did. "But I *did* accept the job here at Barron and Hynes."

Later she asked Tom about Kirk Arnold.

"Where is his new job?" she asked. The minute he opened his mouth Carlys had a feeling she knew what the answer was going to be.

"SuperWrite," he said indifferently, struggling with a nicotine fit and shrugging. "Typewriters. Who needs it?"

C H A P T E R   3

*E*leanor Webber's illness had robbed Carlys of a childhood and an adolescence. Perhaps it had been the illness, or perhaps it had been something else, but Carlys had also been robbed of an identity. She did not know who she was or who she could be. All she knew was that she wanted to be someone, that she wanted to stop being invisible. She also wanted to be loved and approved of, so she was highly vulnerable to external images. When Winn Rosier had spoken admiringly of fast-track people, Carlys had wanted to be one. When Tom Steinberg called her a comer, Carlys responded.

Carlys took Tom's pep talks to heart. If she wanted the world (and, particularly, the Kirk Arnolds of the world), to notice her—and she did—being a comer was one way to get their attention. So far, being Carlys Webber had gotten her nowhere. She thought of Winn Rosier every week when her paycheck came through with a deduction for the Arrow Agency. Like all the other men who had said they'd call but never did, Winn didn't either. Carlys was more or less resigned to being a loser with men; she didn't think she had to resign herself to being a loser at work, too.

"What did you mean by a 'comer'?" she asked Tom, as always wanting someone else to define her to herself.

"Aggressive," he said.

"Sure," agreed Michelle, a realist who had Uncle Tommed her way to a thirty-thousand-dollar-a-year job. She was lush and blond and looked as if she ought to be reclining on satin sheets in a magazine centerfold. Instead, she was divorced from an off-Broadway playwright, who had gone to Wales to find himself, and was single-handedly raising two small children. Michelle, who had learned about men and jobs and money the hard way, made Norma seem like a Pollyanna. "Just remember that when men say aggressive they mean you should do all the work but let them take all the credit."

Carlys took half of Michelle's advice. She decided she'd do the work first and worry about getting the credit later. She went to every meeting she could, met every client she could, took on all the extra work no one else wanted, and spent evenings and weekends thinking up new ways to publicize Barron & Hynes's clients. "Why not?" she asked herself. She never had other plans anyway.

She almost fainted one afternoon when Sergio Maliterno came into the office carrying a shopping bag full of newly purchased Beatles records.

"I never imagined you liked the Beatles!" Carlys exclaimed.

"The Beatles are fine, fine musicians," Sergio whispered, saving his famous voice for paying audiences. Sergio, who considered himself the living successor to the great Caruso, was, at six-foot-five and 270 pounds, built like a defensive linebacker. He had a massive, barrel chest; thunder thighs; a gargantuan appetite; snow-white hair that he let grow down to his collar; and great, thick, coal-black Mephistophelian eyebrows. He dressed himself in black pants; black turtlenecks, even in the summertime (to protect his throat); and a vast, flowing black cape fastened with gold-braid frogs. His ego easily matched his size and appetite and he was not someone anyone forgot—ever. In his exotic, Italian-accented whisper, he launched into an in-depth analysis of the musical tradition that linked Bach, Brahms, and the boys from Liverpool.

"That would make a wonderful article," Carlys said, impressed by Sergio's knowledge and theories. "Why don't you write one?"

"I'm a singer," Sergio whispered witheringly in the voice that had thrilled millions. "Why would I sit down and scribble?"

"Would you mind if I wrote it?" she asked as the idea came to her. "Maybe we could place it somewhere."

He looked at her, flinty suspicion in his slate-blue eyes. "Would it have my name on it?"

"Of course," Carlys said. "My name is meaningless."

"So be my guest," he said, only a degree or two of doubt leaving those piercing eyes. Nevertheless, as he swept out, he favored her with the smile capable of projecting into the second balcony of opera houses the world over.

That weekend Carlys went to the music library at Lincoln Center and drafted an article on the links between Beethoven, Brahms, and the Beatles under Sergio Maliterno's by-line. The media department came through and placed it in the Sunday *Times*'s drama section in late August, five months after Carlys had first gone to work at Barron & Hynes.

That Sunday turned out to be a wonderful day for Carlys. Not because of the article, which only Sergio, Tom, Norma, Michelle, and her father knew she'd written, but because at five o'clock, when Carlys was doing her laundry, the phone rang. It was Winn Rosier.

"Do you feel like a drink?" he asked.

An hour later she met him at Dazzle's on Columbus Avenue, around the corner from his West Sixty-eighth Street apartment.

"I know you've been waiting for me to call," he told her as he ordered her a glass of white wine without asking her what she wanted.

Carlys smiled at him and tried to hide how excited she

felt. They had a table in the glass-enclosed terrace, right in the front, where Carlys could see other couples, arm in arm, enjoying a Sunday stroll on Columbus Avenue and where, she knew, others saw her, saw that she was with someone very handsome and desirable, saw that she was wanted, saw that she wasn't alone. Being with a man as good looking as Winn made her feel pretty and desirable. As she sipped her wine and listened to Winn talk about his last vacation in St. Maarten, the shinsplints that had temporarily interfered with his jogging, and the expensive new stereo he had just installed in his apartment, she kept telling herself that he had said he'd call and he actually did. Maybe her luck *was* changing.

They stayed for a chef's salad and at eight-thirty, Winn walked Carlys to the bus stop on Sixty-fifth Street.

"I'm not going to make a move on you, so don't be insulted," he told her, fondling his new Merona sweats. "Im not interested in a one-night stand. I'm way past that. I'm only interested in relationships now."

"I know what you mean," Carlys said, wanting to sound as sophisticated and experienced as he was. "Everything else is kid stuff."

"I knew you'd agree," said Winn. "I'm good at psyching out what people are really like," he said as the bus doors opened and Carlys reluctantly moved toward them. "I'll call you this week," he called after her.

Carlys felt she was flying on the brand-new Concorde instead of crossing the park in a filthy, graffiti-sprayed bus. Like a Sanskrit scholar, she kept analyzing Winn's last words to her. "I'll call you this week," he had said. The *this week*, she told herself with heartstopping elation, was a big difference from just *I'll call you*. It meant he really liked her.

The Bach, Brahms, Beatles article led to Carlys's next assignment.

"Cellini is setting up in-store boutiques across the country," Tom told her. Although Carlys had worked for him for only a few months, he already realized she was perfect for all the shit work. She worked like a dog and never complained. If she did, she could be bought off with a smile and a trinket. He thought she was an ideal employee and whenever other women in the office complained about something, he told them that they ought to be more like Carlys. "They need a company history. Go interview old man Cellini, get the scoop, and write it up."

"All right," said Carlys. She had never written a company history, but she didn't bother to say so. One of the things she was learning was never say no. Another thing was that most of the jobs to which men attached importance were fairly easy and basically mechanical.

"And Carlys?" Tom said as she was about to leave his office. "Make it zingy. I'll give you one I wrote a few years ago as a guide. It's one of the best of the genre."

Carlys smiled and thanked him. Something else she had learned was to smile a lot. As Michelle had pointed out, it made men think you weren't a threat.

Carlys read Tom's history of Western Broadcasting. It was about as zingy as a hamperful of dirty laundry. Carlys decided to try to write a company history someone might actually read. She did much more than just interview Giuseppe Cellini, the son of the founder of Cellini. She interviewed his three sons and two daughters, all of whom were in the family business. She interviewed office clerks, leather workers, and salespeople. Using the history Giuseppe had given her, the plans for the future his children talked about, and loyal and flattering quotes from employees, Carlys wrote a lively company history of Cellini leather as a combination rags-to-riches story and multigenerational family saga. The Cellini story got picked up by newspapers across the country.

"Old man Cellini wants to hire you," Tom told Carlys. He'd been a damn fool to tell Giuseppe who'd actually written the damn thing. It was just that Giuseppe had driven him crazy until Tom had decided it was easier to tell the old man than to put up with the constant phone calls. "I told him to keep his hands off you."

Carlys was thrilled at being wanted.

"You're a fool," Michelle said when Carlys told her what had happened. "You should have used the opening to ask for a raise."

Carlys realized Michelle was right. Next time, if there was a next time, she'd do just what Michelle said. She had been at Barron & Hynes for over six months and no one had ever said a word about a raise. At least at the phone company you got reviewed every six months. At Barron & Hynes they seemed to think they were doing you a favor by letting you work for them.

Just as Carlys hadn't been smart about getting a raise when the opportunity had presented itself, she knew she wasn't smart about handling the money she earned. The rent on her Yorkville studio apartment was modest, and so were her living expenses. Carlys was naturally someone who walked when she could, took buses instead of taxis, made all her big purchases on sale, and knew every discount drugstore in her neighborhood. Even so, she was never able to save any money. Every month, her income just barely equaled her expenses. She was doing something wrong but she didn't know what. Her own problem gave her an idea.

"Why don't you write an article about single women and money?" she suggested to Lansing Coons after talking to a dozen women on the subject. She spoke to Michelle, who earned a lot; to Norma, who earned as much as Carlys; and to the secretaries and photo-copier operators, who had more modest salaries. She learned that every one of them was just as inept at handling money as she was. The inability to handle money seemed to be a universal problem among working women.

"Sure. *Cosmopolitan* would eat it up," he said, agreeing instantly. Lansing, who had Scrooge-like instincts covered over by the veneer of an Andover-Yale education, was a fairly obscure financial expert who managed a Merrill, Lynch office in Charleston, South Carolina. At Tom Steinberg's suggestion, he had begun a newsletter, and although it wasn't losing money, it wasn't a world-beater either. Lansing, like many other clients, knew a bit about public relations and was desperate to see his name in print. "When can you get it done?"

Cosmopolitan *bought the article. Lansing got the by-line* and he got the fee. Carlys didn't mind the by-line, but she did think she should have gotten at least part of the fee, not to mention a raise. She remembered Michelle's advice and marched into Tom's office.

"Don't worry about the fee," Tom told her in his Big Daddy voice as he sucked on a licorice stick that was making his gums black. "It's peanuts."

"It's not peanuts to me," said Carlys. "It's not fair that I did all the work and Lansing got all the money."

"Don't worry about it," Tom said soothingly. "We'll make it up to you."

"Does that mean I'm going to get a raise?" she asked.

"It means we'll do something nice for you," he said, turning on the charm and crinkling the corners of his eyes in a buddy-buddy grin. "That's a promise."

"A promise?" Carlys asked, trying to pin him down. "When?"

"A promise," Tom confirmed. "You can take it to the bank."

"So I'll get a raise?" she asked, trying to get a definite commitment out of Tom.

"Don't be a pest, Carlys. I told you we'd do something for you. Believe me, you won't be disappointed," he said. Her face told him that she might be getting mad. He smiled and winked at her. "Be a good girl, Carlys. Believe me, you'll get everything you deserve, and more. Meanwhile, why don't you take an extra-long lunch hour? Go to Saks and buy yourself some perfume. Bring me the bill. I'll put it on my gyp sheet."

"Thanks, Tom," said Carlys, dredging up a smile. She wanted to know when she'd get the money Tom had promised, but she didn't know how to press Tom without getting him mad. "That's nice of you."

"Nothing to it," he said and winked again in ersatz complicity. Carlys got up to leave his office. "Oh, Carlys?"

"Yes?" she asked, halfway to the door. She knew that she had let him get around her too easily, but she didn't know how to get her way without coming across stridently. Although she had let it drop, the incident still bothered her. She told herself that if a similar situation ever came up again she'd handle it differently. How, she didn't quite know.

"On second thought, not perfume," Tom was saying, picking up a second licorice stick. "Better make it toilet water."

*   *   *

Three weeks passed before Winn Rosier called again. It was a quarter to six on a Tuesday, just as the office was beginning to wind down for the day.

"Hi," he said as casually as if they spoke on the phone constantly. Even though he had been dating other women, he kept thinking about Carlys. She wasn't hard the way so many New York women were. "How'd you like to have dinner?"

"I'd love to," said Carlys, all her resolutions about playing hard-to-get going out the window, not to mention the night school class in Public Relations and the Media that she had scheduled for that evening.

"I'm around the corner," he said, surprised at how much he was suddenly looking forward to seeing her. "Ten minutes?"

"Wonderful," she said, reaching down to open the drawer in which she kept her makeup.

He took her to P.J. Clarke's, where he ordered chef's salads and white wine.

"Are chef's salads all you ever eat?" she asked, nervously trying to make conversation. From the moment they'd walked into P.J.'s Winn had been looking around, commenting on which women were attractive and why and which were pooches and why. He seemed oblivious to Carlys's existence. Carlys's remark got his attention.

"Why?" he asked, brushing his hair back with his fingers. "Are you saying I'm cheap?"

"No! Not at all," she said, trying to laugh. His cheapness or lack of it had been the furthest thing from her mind, although he wasn't exactly Aristotle Onassis bearing rubies. All she had wanted was his attention. "I just mean that every time I've seen you we've had chef's salads."

"We've only seen each other twice," he pointed out, and Carlys took it as a warning and allowed him to do all the talking. When they were finished eating, Winn paid the check and they stood at the bar for a while, drinking more white wine and watching the Ranger game.

"Where did you say you live?" he asked at ten-thirty.

"Eighty-first and First," she said. She thought he was going to ask to come up and she didn't know what to say. She was ashamed for him to see her half-furnished apartment. She wouldn't know what to do if he made a pass at her. Half of her wanted him to, the other half didn't. She hardly knew him and even though he was extremely good looking, she didn't feel right about going to bed with a man she barely knew. On the other hand, if she rejected him, he might never call her again.

"Eighty-first and First?" he asked. "Good. That means you can take the Third Avenue bus straight up." He paid the bar bill and walked Carlys to the street.

"I really enjoyed being with you," he said, suddenly anxious to get home so that he could be asleep by midnight. "You're a good conversationalist." He kissed her quickly, waited until she got into the bus, and hailed a taxi for himself.

As the bus made its way uptown, Carlys examined her mixed feelings. She wondered if she'd ever hear from him again. She wondered why she even cared.

On Thursday Winn called.

"How'd you like to have dinner tomorrow night?" he asked.

Tomorrow was Friday and Friday night was almost as good as Saturday night and Carlys, forgetting how lonely and discarded she'd felt going up Third Avenue alone in the bus, accepted.

"Why don't you come to my place? I'm a good cook," he said, not revealing how anxious he was to impress her. He knew she liked him, but he wasn't sure how much. "I'll make dinner."

"Can I bring anything?" Carlys asked immediately, always the well-brought-up girl.

"Wine," he said. "A Bordeaux. First growth."

Carlys spent the next twenty-four hours trying to decide whether or not to put in her diaphragm. Putting it in seemed sort of whorish. Leaving it at home seemed awfully unrealistic. Finally she decided to put it in her purse. If she needed it, she'd have it. If she didn't, no one ever had to know it was there. As she rode the crosstown bus to Winn's apartment on Sixty-eighth Street between West End and Columbus, she kept having the awful fantasy that the clasp on her bag would break and the diaphragm in its telltale pink plastic case would roll out on the floor and everyone would know her shameful secret. She clutched the bag close to her so it couldn't betray her. All she wanted was to be happy. All she wanted was to love and be loved. She wondered whether it was as hard for everyone else.

As it turned out, Winn was an excellent cook.

As it turned out, she needed her diaphragm.

"You know," he said as they lay in his bed, its fake-fur throw over them, "you're really a much better lover than I thought. I figured you might be a little on the inhibited side."

"Thank you, Winn," she said, cuddling close to him, her head on his chest. The trace of an expensive cologne lingered around his body and he smelled very good. She loved the warm way it felt to hold him and be held. The sex hadn't been nearly as good as the cuddling, but she gladly exchanged one for the other. "It's awfully nice of you to say that."

"I always make it a point to give compliments when they're due," he said, kissing her and finding that he was excited all over again.

She stayed the night and the next morning as Winn was putting on his jogging clothes and Carlys was putting on her baggy panty hose getting dressed to go back home, his telephone rang and he sighed and picked it up.

"I know I said I'd call," he said impatiently. "I just didn't have a chance. It was a super-busy week."

He listened as the other person spoke. A woman, Carlys could tell.

"Come on," Winn cajoled, "don't bug me."

As Carlys quietly opened the front door, ready to go, she heard him continue. He sounded aggrieved. "I just don't know what's the matter with you women. What makes you all so demanding? Don't you understand I need a little space?"

Out of the corner of his eye Winn noticed that Carlys was leaving. He put his hand over the mouthpiece, mouthed an "I'll call you," and blew her a kiss as she left. She went home alone in the bright Saturday morning light and wondered if he'd ever call and, if he did, what she'd say.

On the first workday of 1972, as B-52 bombers made the biggest raid yet on Vietnam's DMZ and Richard Nixon announced officially that he would seek reelection, Tom Steinberg called Carlys into his office.

"It's bonus time," he told her, handing her a generous check, as beneficent as if it were his own money he were giving her. Carlys glanced at it. It *was* generous, but not so generous that it made up for the magazine fee Lansing had received. Nevertheless, knowing from experience that the commandments according to Michelle Delande worked, she smiled.

"That's very nice," she said, surprised and disappointed at the same time.

Tom leaned back in his chair and smiled patronizingly. Tom liked playing Big Daddy and thought he did it very well.

"Reward time, too, Carlys," he said, artfully (he thought) teasing her with his air of mystery. "How'd you like to be my assistant?" he asked, letting the secret out of the bag with a shit-eating grin. "Your title would be assistant account executive. And, of course, a juicy raise goes along with it. . . ."

Carlys left Tom's office walking not on the carpet but somewhere in the air above it. The promotion from copy to accounts was very unusual—and a big compliment—but Carlys had shown an ability to oversee an account and to keep in mind the big picture while coordinating all the small details. Along with her new title, she was given an inside office that had walls that went almost all the way to the ceiling, a tan leatherette visitor's chair, and a second telephone line. She was invited to the all-agency Monday morning steering meetings and included on invitation lists to all Barron & Hynes–sponsored functions. Barron & Hynes paid for elegant business cards with her name and new title, and she got to share a secretary with two other assistant account executives.

The raise (it was nice but not juicy) allowed her to buy her first real Calvin Klein, a gray flannel suit, which she bought during Saks's January sale.

"It's really beautiful," Norma said when Carlys modeled it. "But you know what I think? I think you ought to treat yourself to a real Jules haircut."

Carlys's eyes lit up. "Now why didn't I think of that?"

A Jules haircut cost fifty dollars and Carlys, holding her

breath, dialed the number of Jules's East Fifty-seventh Street salon. In her cool British accent the receptionist informed Carlys that Jules's first available appointment wasn't for three and a half months. Gratefully Carlys took the appointment.

"Three and a half months," she moaned to Norma. "How can I wait that long?"

Now that she had made up her mind to spend some real money on herself, Carlys couldn't wait. She kept thinking about her first Jules haircut and one day she told Michelle about it.

"Why didn't you tell me sooner?" Michelle said casually. "We handle the Storrs account." Storrs owned hairdressing franchises in department stores across the country. "Jules has a contract with Storrs as artistic director. Let me see what I can do for you."

Like magic an appointment was arranged.

"Is Thursday all right?" Michelle asked. Thursday was the day after tomorrow. "It's the best they can do."

It was the first time Carlys had ever used the power that came along with her job, and it was even more exciting than the haircut that was, with no near comparison, the best Carlys had ever had in her life.

"What happened to your hair?" asked Winn. "It looks fantastic."

"I changed hairdressers," said Carlys suavely, not telling him that in addition to the haircut, Jules had suggested a rinse to add gold highlights, a suggestion Carlys had accepted instantly. "I've started going to Jules."

"Jules?" asked Winn, openly impressed for the first time Carlys could remember. "He cuts Candy Bergen's hair, doesn't he?"

For a while he treated her like someone special.

CHAPTER 4

The sixties got all the publicity; the seventies were when everyone's life changed. Marriage was out, living together was in and so was sexual freedom. The birth rate dropped, the divorce rate soared, and the self reigned. An apparently infinite range of life-styles—straight or gay, single and committed, married but open, bicoastal and bisexual, unmarried mothers, single fathers, stepfamilies, extended families, and adult households—seemed to promise that everyone could and would be happy. Everyone, that is, except Carlys.

Her relationship with Winn couldn't even be called a relationship.

"It's an exercise in masochism," Michelle said, telling Carlys what she already knew.

"At least you've got someone to mistreat you," Norma said, polishing off a bag of Famous Amos cookies. "I can't even get that far."

They laughed, ha ha, bruised Manhattan women of the seventies.

"I'll call you," Winn usually said at the end of every date. I'll call you—it was his theme song.

Sometimes he did. Sometimes he didn't.

"I'll call you Tuesday night," he said in February 1972, for once being specific. Carlys interpreted it to mean that, this time, he really *would* call. She stayed home that Tuesday evening, skipping her Media course again. The phone never rang. When she complained Winn was annoyed.

"Don't be possessive," he warned. "I can't stand possessive women."

When she pointed out that she wasn't being possessive but that he had caused her to miss a class that was important to her career, he told her that he needed space. When she told him that he was indulging in psychobabble, he accused her of being insensitive. Nevertheless, when he invited her to dinner she accepted.

"I'll meet you at Victor's at eight," he said. Victor's, at Seventy-first and Columbus, was convenient to his apartment. For Carlys it was a crosstown bus trip. Nevertheless, she got to Victor's promptly at eight. Winn wasn't there nor, when she asked, had he left a message for her. Carlys sat alone at a table for two for almost an hour, feeling increasingly conspicuous and miserable. Finally she screwed up her courage and left the restaurant, leaving a message for Winn with the maître d'. She thought Winn would call. He didn't. Not for almost two weeks. When she finally broke down and called him he was still angry.

"What kind of shit was that?" he asked. "I walk in and my date's not there."

"You must have been at least an hour late," Carlys said, feeling that for once she had the upper hand.

"So what?" he said, all righteous indignation and bruised feelings. "You never heard of being tied up in a meeting? I'm leaving Arrow. I'm going to a headhunting firm. It's a big step up for me. I was thrilled. I thought we'd have champagne to celebrate. Instead, I walk into Victor's and I find out my date's walked out."

"Oh, I'm sorry," said Carlys automatically guilty, instinctively retreating to a role that, though painful, was also comfortable in its familiarity. "I didn't know. I didn't realize. I'm sorry—I really am."

Finally he accepted her apology. "I guess anyone can screw up once," he said.

*In April Winn seemed ready to take the relationship an*other step forward.

"Remember I said in the beginning that I was interested in a relationship?" he asked, casually testing the waters. "I've been thinking about maybe living together."

Before she could say a word he continued: *"Maybe,"* he said, emphasizing the word. Even so, Carlys's heart leaped. Being wanted, being accepted, meant everything to Carlys.

In May they were having a drink at the bar at the Sign of the Dove when a striking brunette saw Winn through the open french doors and waved. Winn motioned her in. She arrived at their table in a cloud of Rive Gauche and kissed him hello.

"Genia, this is Carlys," he said, making the introduction. "Genia's an ex."

"Hello," Carlys said politely.

"Hi," said Genia, and Carlys noticed that she had a warm smile. She was tiny and small-boned, an olive-skinned brown-eyed brunette with a vivacious laugh. She was extremely stylish in her head-to-toe Ralph Lauren outfit and inch-long perfectly polished nails. From the conversation Carlys concluded that Genia worked at Bergdorf's as a personal shopper. While Carlys listened Winn and Genia caught up on old acquaintances and reminiscences. The whole time Winn spoke to her, he held her hand, stroking it sensuously. Carlys watched, hypnotized, almost sick with envy.

"Why don't we have dinner?" she suddenly heard Winn ask Genia. Carlys couldn't believe her ears. Winn took his small Gucci diary out of his jacket pocket. "How about Thursday?"

"For old times' sake," Genia said as she agreed to the date.

As she left Genia spoke to Carlys for the first time.

"He broke my heart," she said suddenly, the hurt obvious in her eyes. "I'm still trying to get over him." She spoke as if the emotion were still fresh, still painful, and Carlys realized that under her perfection, Genia was a wounded survivor of a seventies-style relationship that was probably a carbon copy of hers. "Don't let him do it to you."

Carlys didn't know what to say and she glanced over at Winn, who smiled at her and winked, looking almost proud of himself.

Suddenly Carlys's envy completely dissolved and she felt sorry for Genia. She realized that the way Winn treated her was apparently the way he treated everyone. She wondered, not for the first time, what she was doing with someone like Winn. How much, she asked herself, did anyone need to suffer?

"How could you do that?" Carlys asked when Genia was gone.

"Do what?" Winn wanted to know.

"Make a date with someone else while I'm sitting here?"

"What do you want me to do?" he asked blandly. "Go

behind your back? You know, Carlys, we agreed to be upfront with each other, didn't we?"

June 1972 was the month that held the seeds of the disillusion that would ultimately pervade the entire decade. It was the month of the Watergate break-in, a "third-rate burglary" that would change history. It was the month that Carlys observed, but did not celebrate, her twenty-seventh birthday. It was the month that Winn informed her that he had taken a share in a summer house on Fire Island.

"Maybe I'll invite you some weekend," he told her.

For the thousandth time Carlys swore to herself that she'd never see him again. It was just too painful.

Why, Carlys asked herself over and over, did she put up with Winn? Why, like a beaten dog, did she keep going back for more? Her questions had one, inevitable answer: Winn seemed to be the only game in town.

Although Carlys met more men at Barron & Hynes than she had at the phone company, they were always the wrong men. Married men who wanted a little something on the side, gay men who thought they'd give bisexuality a whirl, men who wanted a mommy, men who weren't ready to make a commitment, not even for Saturday night, men who wanted only sex, and men who didn't want any sex and called themselves the new neuters.

Sergio made a pass—if it could be called that—at her one day in the office. He was there to discuss the arrangements for his appearance at the Kennedy Center.

"Are you going to come with me?" he asked her in front of Tom and Peter Salzany in his creepy whisper.

"No," replied Carlys. "I never go out of town with clients." She wasn't high enough on the totem pole for that.

"She can if you want," Tom broke in immediately, shooting an annoyed glance at Carlys.

"I want," whispered Sergio, stroking his white hair absently. "We'll make love before the performance."

Carlys opened her eyes in shock. The thought of getting into bed with the massive and massively egotistical singer was simply beyond her.

"Is good for the lungs. Clears the phlegm," Sergio went on, indicating his throat and chest with a huge, outstretched hand, startlingly white against the black turtleneck. "A fine orgasm just before I meet my audience. . . ."

" . . . is not good for the copywriter," said Carlys, appalled, finishing his sentence.

"Now, Carlys," warned Tom. "We'll talk about this later."

Carlys made it clear to Tom that sex, even for medicinal purposes, was not part of her job. He seemed annoyed at her.

"You don't have to actually screw him," Tom said, trying to get her to see things his way. "Just let him feel you up a little."

Carlys did not accompany Sergio to Washington. She did not even ask which lucky girl got the job.

Carlys didn't know whether there was something wrong with her, something wrong with men, or something wrong with the times. What she did know was that she could do nothing about the men she met or about the times in which she lived. *She* was the only thing she could do anything about.

She read every issue of *Vogue* and *Cosmopolitan* and every book by every self-help guru who promised happiness, confidence, attractiveness, popularity. Faithfully she tried every diet and every new makeup. She read all the articles about how to start a conversation with an attractive man, but all the intriguing and attention-getting suggestions died in her mouth. Following advice on how to give a party and meet new men, she invited everyone she could think of and asked all her guests to bring an unattached man. The party cost her almost three hundred dollars, and when it was over, she found herself alone in her apartment at midnight with a tipsy art book editor, who confided that he thought he might be gay but wasn't sure, and a mutual fund salesman, who asked to borrow money for a taxi home.

Maybe other single women had swarms of eligible men sending flowers and vowing undying love, but Carlys wasn't one of them. Maybe being single was wonderful if you were Gloria Steinem or Jackie Bisset or Catherine Deneuve. It wasn't wonderful if you were Carlys Webber. She once told Norma that she never even got obscene phone calls.

She still thought of herself as invisible. She lived in a city that was electric with power and sex and excitement and she had none of it—no power, hardly any sex, no excitement. Every day in the gossip columns she read about glittering parties to which she hadn't been invited, fabulous openings to which she hadn't gone, celebrity-studded discos in which she had never set foot. She thought she would literally die of invisibility and loneliness and insignificance, and although she never quite gave up, she also never quite seemed to get anywhere.

Just beneath the very thin layer of her brand-new image as a fast-track person, she was still the kind of tongue-tied woman who faded away at gatherings, whose name people had trouble remembering, whose clothes no one ever noticed, whose opinions no one paid much attention to, and, although Carlys was painfully aware of it, she didn't quite know what to do about it except to keep trying. One day, she told herself, something would work, something would be different. One day *she* would be different.

Meanwhile, although she was better off than she'd been at the phone company, she seemed stuck in her life, stuck in her relationship with Winn, unhappy but unable to change.

"I love you," Winn told Carlys when the summer was mercifully over. He had started perceiving her in a new way after they bumped into his friend Dwight Connors walking out of Cinema II. Dwight told Winn later that Carlys was really a knockout and when Winn thought it over he decided she *was* much better looking than the pooches with whom he had wasted his summer at Ocean Beach.

Being a seventies suitor, though, he pleaded guilty with an explanation. "But I'm not sure I'm *in love* with you. Do you know what I mean?"

She assured him that she did.

"I feel the same way," was how she put it, and it did sort of make sense to her except that if anyone had asked, she couldn't have explained why. No one asked.

A whole year more went by; a year in which Winn courted and confused her. He surprised her with a crystal heart on Valentine's Day and her initials in chocolate on Easter. She would see him every night for a week; then almost a month would go by before he'd call again. It was a year of making up and breaking up, a year in which he occasionally told her he loved her, a year in which he now and then talked about living together but usually in the subjunctive.

"What if we lived together?" he'd say, making it clear

that he was just thinking out loud. "Just to see how we'd get along."

"I'd like that," Carlys said, thinking that they'd been dating for over a year. Apparently, as far as he was concerned, they did get along. Still, he never mentioned a specific date or time.

"If we lived together we'd need to get a bigger bed," Carlys said, thinking that doing something together might be the first step toward a commitment. "Shouldn't we go shopping for it?"

"I don't want to get involved with trivial domestic details," he said immediately. "Anyway, we haven't decided where to live. Your place or mine. You probably ought to move into my place. It's a little bigger and a lot nicer. Yours is a dump."

Carlys couldn't disagree.

"What should I tell my landlord?" Carlys asked, thinking that the issue of *where* they'd live had finally been settled. "The lease says I have to give a month's notice. Plus I'll have to get the movers. When should I schedule them?"

"How should I know?" he said, annoyed. "Don't rush me, Carlys."

"I'm not pushing you," she insisted, although she knew that she was. "We've been going together for over a year. It's time we made a commitment or broke up. One or the other."

"I'm ready for a commitment," he said, his sincerity temporarily defusing her ultimatum. "You know that. I just need time to get used to the idea."

Her head told her to stop seeing him, but whenever she told him she wanted to break off, he begged her to reconsider.

"Things will be different from now on," he'd promise. *"I'll* be different."

Her heart always overruled her head and she always relented.

"Okay," she'd say, knowing she was a doormat but not knowing what else to do, knowing she should tell him good-bye once and for all but not having the courage. As she constantly reminded herself, if she didn't have Winn she'd have no one. It wasn't as if she met a lot of men, and Winn *was* single, heterosexual, attractive, and available.

Why throw away the one chance she had? "But only if you mean it this time."

"Of course I mean it," he said, relieved that she had relented. "Maybe we *both* ought to get rid of our apartments and find a place that will be really *ours.*"

Carlys's heart leapt; this time, she told herself, Winn meant what he said. This time things would be different and, for a while, they were. This time he would tell her how much he cared for her and really seem to mean it. He would telephone her at least once a day and take her to dinner at expensive restaurants he couldn't really afford. He would bring her presents—once it was a baby picture of himself that his mother had found while going through some old family albums—making it clear that he never did this with other women. Even when he was ridiculous, he could also be sweet.

But two days later, four days later, a week later, Winn would snap at Carlys for making him feel trapped. It was the same old song with the same old tune, and she was still the same old Carlys.

Even so, she promised herself that one day things would change. She promised herself that one day she would be happy. She would never give up. Never.

Besides Winn and Norma, the only other significant person in Carlys's personal life was her father. Jacob Webber lived alone in the big, dreary West End Avenue apartment in which Carlys had grown up. She visited him every Sunday afternoon and made him lunch. While she was there she paid his bills, balanced his checkbook, did his grocery shopping, and spoke to the super about getting the exterminator, fixing a leaky faucet, or seeing if he could stop the radiator from banging at five-thirty in the morning. What he ate, however, was always on Jacob's mind.

"I've been losing weight," her father would tell her and she could see that it was true. He was a tall man and his clothes hung on him. "The reason is that I'm bored with my food. You're good at things like that. Could you give me some ideas of different things I could have?"

That was typical of her father: a compliment followed by a responsibility. She had heard it since she'd been nine and her mother had first gotten sick and the job of running the household fell to Carlys. You're a good cook, her father had said, you make dinner. You're a good shopper, you go to the A&P. You're good with machines, you take the laundry to the laundromat. Dutifully, Carlys did what he wanted.

His primary obsession was with food, and being a retired widower who lived alone, he focused all his considerable energy and intelligence on what he did or didn't, would or wouldn't, put into his mouth. Jacob Webber refused to turn on the stove, so his meals had to consist of foods that didn't need to be cooked. He didn't like sandwiches from the local delicatessen because the bread was usually too dry. He wouldn't eat Chinese food because it was greasy. He didn't like canned sardines because he was sick of them. He didn't like cheese because after a few weeks in the refrigerator it got a blue mold. He wouldn't eat frozen food or canned food because they were full of additives. He wouldn't eat anything that had to be mixed because then he'd have to dirty a bowl. He would no more consider washing an extra dish than he would consider turning on the oven.

"What about cereal?" Carlys suggested, thinking that cereal would be perfect for her father. It didn't have to be cooked, you didn't have to dirty a dish, you could pour milk over it and eat it right out of the box. "Why don't you try a few until you find one you like."

"Then I'd have to buy milk," he said. "I'm only one person and I can't use it all up before it turns sour."

"They sell it in small containers now," she told him, convinced she had finally thought of something he'd like.

"Small containers?" he said dubiously. "I never heard of it."

Carlys thought that the following week she'd bring him a small container of milk and a few different packages of cereal. That way he could at least try her idea. She was sure he'd like it, sure he'd thank her, sure he'd tell her what a good idea she'd had. Meanwhile he had a week of meals to get through.

"How about canned salmon?" she tried hopefully.

"It's got bones," he said.

"Well, pick them out!" she said, finally exasperated.

"I'll think about it," he said.

He was just as stubborn and negative when he complained about being bored and depressed. No matter what Carlys suggested—that he get together with old friends, go see a movie she thought he might enjoy, or read a book—he would find fault with it. She knocked herself out trying to think of things her father might do to make his life less boring and less depressing. The most he would ever say was that he'd think about it. Every Sunday when she left his apartment and went home, her sad and lonely Yorkville studio seemed like paradise. She struggled constantly for her father's approval just as she struggled to make Winn care for her, and despite the repeated failures she never stopped trying. With her father, at least, she had an excuse. Even though he was absolutely impossible, she knew that deep down he loved her very much and was always on her side. That knowledge made the guilt almost unbearable because the minute she left West End Avenue she felt as if she was getting out of jail.

As the seventies approached the midpoint, though, Carlys began to think she was, finally, finally, finally, making progress. She wasn't *as* hopeless as she'd been, wasn't *as* invisible and insignificant. Sometimes, these days, Carlys thought there were two Carlyses: the tiger and the doormat. Work seemed to bring out one Carlys; her private life, another. Every time her father asked for her advice and then rejected it, every time Winn jerked her around again with his on-off, stop-start, pull-me, push-you courtship, Carlys seemed totally at their mercy. She didn't know how, in a loving way, to put a halt to her father's endless demands; she didn't know how to get Winn to treat her the way she wanted to be treated.

At work, Tom and Michelle and even Mr. Hynes seemed to think the world of her. When she wrote an eight-page special section for a newspaper insert for Cellini leathers for the Christmas of 1972, she got a handwritten note of congratulations from Joshua Hynes.

To Carlys, Joshua Hynes had always been a distant planet, remote, glamorous, influential with vast, unseen power over her and her life. Joshua Hynes worked in a large corner suite guarded by two secretaries and two assistants that Carlys had entered only once when Tom had buzzed her to bring in a file. She had been impressed with the vast office, its handsome modern furnishings and expensive original art. She was also impressed with Joshua Hynes, who was sleek and suntanned and, although only in his early forties, completely bald. He carried himself like a general and had, paradoxically, a smile that could light up a city.

When she got the note complimenting her on the special section for Cellini, she felt as if galaxies of stars shone for her alone. "I didn't know Joshua Hynes knew I was alive," she told Tom Steinberg, naively showing him the note.

"Don't kid yourself," Tom had said, instantly wary of Carlys even though she was his subordinate. "Joshua knows everything that goes on here."

Just as important as Joshua Hynes's approval was the fact that the clients liked her, even the impossible ones like Sergio and Lansing. In fact it was Lansing, one of the true eccentrics of the era, who would, quite literally and unintentionally, be responsible for the first major change in Carlys's life.

C H A P T E R   5

Lansing Coons was one of those people who thought that money made the world go round. Money—and sex. Lansing was obsessed with the state of the stock market, which, he thought, was intimately connected to the state of his penis (with which he was also obsessed). It was a theory Carlys spent much of her time trying to conceal from the financial press and the subscribers to his $750-a-year newsletter. Carlys tried to get Lansing to tell her what his market theory was in printable English and the more she asked the more he raved on about his hard-ons-up and hard-offs-down until, finally, in desperation, she asked Tom what to tell the press.

"Read the gobbledygook in Lansing's newsletter," Tom

advised suavely, "and make up your own gobbledygook to explain it."

Scared to death but feeling she had no choice, Carlys had followed Tom's advice. Her press releases, which she often didn't understand, were faithfully picked up, sometimes verbatim, in columns and articles in financial pages in newspapers across the country. Only the article she had written for *Cosmopolitan*, which she had researched in the public library, made any sense.

Nevertheless, Carlys was doing an excellent job with the penis-crazed financial prognosticator. In the time she'd worked on the account, she'd taken Lansing from an obscure stock market analyst who wrote a newsletter in his home office on weekends to a media star who appeared regularly on "Wall Street Week," wrote a syndicated Beta Trends analysis column (actually Carlys wrote it based on scribbled notes mailed to her by Lansing from wherever he happened to be), and got $2,000 per lecture, traveling around the country speaking to investment clubs. She'd made him a star and now she was stuck with him.

"He needs a title," Tom Steinberg said while he tore matches out of a matchbook one by one, lit them, blew them out, and then arranged the spent matches in a tic-tac-toe pattern on the glass top of his desk. Carlys noticed that giving up smoking was the same to Tom as dieting was to Norma—a way of life. "He wants to write a book. Got any ideas?"

Carlys didn't have Idea One. She shrugged slightly, then thought for a second.

"How to Get Rich?" she suggested, having learned after several years at Tom's knee that the obvious was never a bad place to start.

"Not bad," Tom said magnanimously, "but not great either." He fiddled with the matches, popped one of the synthetic, sugar-free mints he was trying as a nonfattening nicotine substitute, swiveled in his chair, gazed out the window, ran his hands through his hair, cleared his throat, and swiveled back. Carlys could practically see the light bulb go on over his head.

"Get Rich in Your Spare Time?" he suggested desper-

ately in a man-in-over-his-head tone, taking off from Carlys's suggestion.

"So-so," she said indifferently. Tom lapsed into silence, sucking on his mint, waiting for her to save him. She thought another moment. *"How to Make Your First Million?"*

Tom's response was instantaneous. He almost choked on the mint.

"I love it! I love it!" he enthused when he had stopped coughing. "It'll fly. It'll soar," he said, envisioning big success, big bucks, big fees, and plenty of new clients who would want Barron & Hynes to do for them what they had done for Lansing, not to mention a fat raise and promotion for himself. "Now go write an outline. . . ."

"What do I know about making your first million?" Carlys asked, startled. She had thought she was just being asked to suggest a title.

"What do you know about Beta Trends analysis?" Tom countered.

She looked at him a second, trapped.

"Touché," she said, and as she left the room, Tom noticed that, if you looked at her closely, beneath the crisp efficiency, she was quite a looker. Tom, of course, rarely looked *that* closely. Married for almost a dozen years, Tom had never broken his own rule about not getting involved at the office. Besides, Tom's own taste ran to the kind of girl he couldn't take anywhere.

Based on Carlys's outline, Lansing Coons received a one-hundred-thousand-dollar advance for How to Make Your First Million, news that Carlys relayed to the columnists, who dutifully printed it.

Lansing was annoyed.

"Why didn't you say that it was an advance in the six figures?" he asked crabbily, three deep frown lines appearing across his forehead. Lansing was short and stubby and the scars and pits of adolescent acne were scattershot all over his face. He wore the last crew cut in the Western World and brown suede elevator shoes. When Lansing was pissed off, the three horizontal lines appeared across his forehead. When he calmed down, there were only two horizontal frown lines. "That way people might think I got a half a million or more."

Carlys stared at him, speechless.

Later Norma told Carlys that she should have told him to go to hell. Carlys thought Norma was probably right. Instead, just like with her father, she felt guilty that she hadn't done more. Why hadn't *she* thought of telling the columnists that he'd received a six-figure advance? It *did* sound much more impressive.

*At eight-thirty on the morning the announcement of Lan-*sing's book sale made Liz Smith's column, the phone on Carlys's desk rang.

"Don't you dare write it for nothing," Kirk Arnold said, starting the conversation right in the middle. Although Carlys had spoken to him at various Barron & Hynes parties now and then, she had never spoken to him on the phone. Nevertheless, she recognized his distinctive husky voice immediately.

"Don't worry," she laughed, her heart beating faster as it began to sink in that Kirk Arnold had actually called her. "I'm *not* about to write it. I don't know one thing about making a million dollars."

"Neither does Lansing," he said crisply. "But I know Tom. And I know Lansing. You've done everything else for them, they'll want you to do this, too."

"I doubt it," Carlys said, knowing that Kirk and Joshua had lunch now and then. Still, it amazed her that they must obviously have spoken about her. She still had trouble thinking that she or anything she did was of the remotest interest to anyone else. "Anyway, no one's asked."

"Don't worry, they will," he said. "And that's not one of Tom Steinberg's bullshit promises. That's a Kirk Arnold promise. Just remember, when they do, call me. They'll try to screw you, but we won't let them," he said. "We'll figure out how to get you a fair deal."

"By the way," she asked, glancing at her watch just before they said good-bye, "how did you know I'd be in the office this early?"

"I figured you'd be first in, last out," he said. "You're the type."

"I'm not sure that's a compliment," she said doubtfully.

She wanted him to think she was attractive and sought-after, not a nose-to-the-grindstone drone.

"Would you rather I tell you you have eyes like emeralds?" he asked and hung up before she could say another word, leaving her literally shaking with pleasure and excitement. She almost wished Tom *would* ask her to write the book. It would give her a reason to call Kirk Arnold.

Two days later, Tom asked Carlys to come into his office.

"Guess what?" he asked with his friendliest smile. "You're going to write a book."

Carlys stared at him, assaulted by a barrage of conflicting feelings. Fear that she couldn't do it. Anger at his bland assumption that she'd do whatever he wanted. Excitement that she had a reason to talk to Kirk Arnold again. Tom misinterpreted her silence as incomprehension.

"You're going to write *How to Make Your First Million,* dear," he said, the winsome smile gone, speaking as if he were spelling something out to an idiot. "You'll be taken off all your other accounts. You're to devote yourself to *Million.* You'll go to Charleston so that you can have access to Lansing's files. The book has to be finished in three months. The publisher wants to make the fall list. I'll get my girl to make your plane reservation."

Carlys left Tom's office with such mixed feelings that she couldn't think straight. She *knew* she couldn't write a book, but at the same time a little voice said you could *try.* She was flattered, as she always was when someone asked her to do something, but she also resented the fact that Tom hadn't mentioned money. She remembered the *Cosmopolitan* fee. She hated being taken for granted the way Tom took her for granted. One thing she *did* know: She'd take Kirk Arnold up on his offer.

"They asked," she said on the phone as soon as she got back to her office, imitating his habit of beginning a phone conversation in the middle.

"See?" he said. "I told you so."

"Now what?" she asked, panicked.

"Meet me for a drink," he said. "The King Cole Bar. Six o'clock."

*   *   *

The King Cole Bar smelled of money and deals and sex
and power and flirtation. Kirk Arnold sat at a corner table
looking as if he could buy and sell the whole place and not
notice the difference. Seeing him again, Carlys realized that
she had forgotten the enormity of the sheer physical impact
he had on her. Carlys felt almost scorched by the heat of
his presence across the small table. He sipped a vodka
martini and asked Carlys what she wanted. When she said
white wine he turned to the waiter and ordered her a glass
of Sancerre.

"The thing is," Carlys began, trying not to babble, "they
ought to pay me and I don't know how to ask for money.
I'm really terrible at it."

Kirk considered her words for a moment. "That's the
point, then. You don't ask for money. Never show your
weakness."

"But what *do* I do?" Carlys asked, sipping the wine and
thinking of how deliciously dry and cold it was.

"Lansing's cheap and Tom's a bully," Kirk said, looking
right at her, as if he really saw *her,* her uniqueness, her
individuality, her strengths, and her weaknesses. Carlys
loved the way he treated her difficulty in talking about
money as a problem to be solved rather than a fatal flaw. It
made her feel that hopelessness simply wasn't a word in his
vocabulary. "On the other hand, Lansing's desperate to be
famous and Tom's scared. All you have to do is say no and
keep saying it until they get the message."

"What message?" asked Carlys, suddenly lost. "I don't
quite follow you."

"That offering you money might be the way to get you to
do what they want," he explained and Carlys thought he
was brilliant.

"But what if I get fired?"

"You won't get fired," he said. "They need you more
than you need them. Besides, if they fire you, I'll hire
you."

"You will?" she asked. She had no idea of how her eyes
lit up and how her cheeks flushed. She had no idea of how
pretty she seemed to him at that moment. He reached out,
unable to help himself, and traced the line of her chin with
his index finger.

"Sure I will," he said, suddenly withdrawing his finger.

She felt as if the sun had gone in. "But first we'll get them to pay you what you're worth."

She smiled, reveling in a certain kind of glory. That *we* again! At last she had someone who mattered on her side. At last she didn't feel so all alone. They sat for another half hour. He asked her about herself, about her job, about her past. He listened, looking into her eyes all the time, as if he really cared. Reluctantly he looked at his watch.

"I wish I didn't," he said signaling the waiter for the check, which he paid with a crisp new one-hundred-dollar bill, "but I have to go."

As she picked up her bag to leave, Carlys noticed people watch them. She never imagined that it was she who drew eyes; she thought it was entirely the incredibly handsome, nice, and decent man she was with. He walked her out to the sidewalk, stood with her under the awning until the doorman got a taxi and opened the door. Kirk helped Carlys in and, with a crinkly, let's-get-the-bastards smile, gave her a last reminder: "Just remember: 'No' is the only word in your vocabulary."

As the taxi pulled away, Carlys felt she was parting with life itself. She turned around in the cab and looked back to see him getting into a big, shiny limousine. She wondered what it would be like to be Kirk Arnold. She wondered what it would be like to be someone who had a big, shiny limousine. She wondered what it would be like to know what you wanted and just how to get it. In the three-quarters of an hour she had just spent with Kirk Arnold she had been someone who mattered, someone who counted, someone who knew what she wanted and just how to get it. It had been wonderful and she tried to hold on to the feeling.

All her life Carlys had always said yes to everything and everyone. For a change she was going to try no. She was scared and excited at the prospect.

"Because I'm not going to write Lansing's book for him," Carlys told Tom two days later when he called her into his office and asked her why she hadn't picked up her Charleston tickets yet.

"Why the hell not?" Tom was jiggling his feet nervously and sucking on a plastic cigarette. He had to produce for

Lansing—or lose him. Carlys was a big asset and Joshua was giving Tom the credit for bringing her into the company. PR was too often a no-win business. If you did nothing for a client, you'd get fired. If you did well—as they'd done for Lansing Coons—the client often decided that he needed a bigger and better PR firm and you got fired anyway. Lansing was beginning to give off those restless vibes and Tom, who'd spent fourteen years in public relations, was as alert to them as a showgirl to a millionaire. "Give me one good reason why not."

"I'm not a writer," Carlys said. She was speaking with a determination Tom had never seen in her.

"Horse. Shit." Tom made it into two words and made a disgusting slurping noise as he sucked away on his cigarette-substitute. "What do you think you do for a living? Write. Every day of your life."

"Press releases are *not* the same as a book," Carlys said adamantly.

"That's true," Tom said, disarming her by appearing to agree with her. The instant he saw her relax a bit he zinged her; "But suppose you think of a book as fifty press releases strung together? That way it's a cinch."

"It's not a cinch," Carlys said, refusing to be budged or bullshitted. "I don't know how to write a book. I don't *want* to write a book. I don't know one thing about how to make a million dollars and I don't even begin to understand Lansing's off-the-wall theories. I've never refused an assignment. But I'm refusing this one," Carlys said.

"Refusing?" Tom asked in a deceptively pleasant voice.

"Refusing," Carlys repeated grimly.

Lansing kept after Tom and Tom kept after Carlys.

"You know, Carlys, it's company policy to supply ghost-writing for our clients," he told her in his creamiest supersincere, I-wouldn't-kid-*you* voice.

"It is?" Carlys asked blandly. "I've never heard of that policy before."

"Sure," he said. "It's common practice. You don't think celebrities write their own books, do you? When do you think they have the time? Their PR people do it for them, that's what. At Barron and Hynes we do it all the time."

"Give me an example," Carlys said.

"Talk to Michelle," Tom said triumphantly, scoring his point. "She's written a couple."

"A couple is right," Michelle said, rolling her eyes heaven-ward. The memories still pained her. "Two, to be exact. *Be Beautiful, Stay Beautiful* and *Bio-Exercises."*

Carlys had noticed copies of them in Michelle's office. The first was a beauty book that carried the by-line of a famous makeup artist and the second was an exercise book by the doyenne of a chic Fifty-seventh Street exercise salon.

"Make them pay you," Michelle advised. "They paid me."

"How did you get them to do it?" Carlys wanted to know.

"I smiled, stuck out my tits, and told them I wouldn't turn on my typewriter without a check and a contract."

"Write a book?" Winn said, looking shocked. "What makes anyone think *you* could write a book?"

"That's just how I feel," Carlys said instantly, relieved that *someone* agreed with her darkest doubts. Then, and she would never know why, she suddenly heard herself as if she'd been a stranger listening in. She heard how meek and self-effacing she sounded, how instinctively and imme-diately she agreed with an unflattering opinion of herself. It suddenly dawned on her that one of the reasons Winn had such a hold on her was that he saw her the way she saw herself.

Used to see herself, she told herself immediately. Si-lently, she began to ask herself why *couldn't* she write the book and do a damn good job of it? Why *couldn't* she manipulate them into paying her for the work? This time Norma and Michelle and plain justice were not the only ones on her side. This time Kirk Arnold was on her side. She really did think of him as the White Knight. *Her* White Knight.

Still, she sometimes silently agreed with Winn, and some-times her fears *did* overrule her growing self-confidence. Nevertheless, even though Tom was pressing and even threatening her, she stood her ground and she felt good about it. She was reminded of the way she'd felt the first time she'd gone to Jules. The first time she'd done something just for herself. It didn't feel selfish, the way she had imagined it would; it felt good.

She smiled, stuck out her tits, and kept saying no.

Over a ridiculously expensive lunch, Tom tried to get her to work as cheaply as possible.

*La Côte Basque, on East Fifty-fifth Street, was chic, ex-*pensive, exclusive, and fashionable. When Tom invited her to lunch there Carlys realized that, as Kirk had predicted, he was beginning to get the message. Carlys had never been there in her life and she was more than slightly intimidated. She shouldn't have been. With her stylish hair, her well-cut suit, and her becoming makeup, none of the waiters mistook her for a sightseer or a tourist; she was clearly Somebody and she was treated very well. She ordered a glass of Sancerre to start with and the waiter smiled his approval.

"Sancerre?" Tom asked with his patented combination of being impressed and condescending at the same time. "I didn't think you knew anything about wine."

"Why on earth would you think I don't know anything about wine?" Carlys responded and Tom, for once, was fresh out of his usual bullshit answers. He buried himself behind the menu.

"I can't understand why you won't write that book," Tom said conversationally a little later over twenty dollars' worth of smoked salmon.

"If I knew how to make a million dollars I'd be out making it," she told him adopting an equally conversational tone. "I wouldn't be writing a book about it."

"We could make it worth your while," Tom tried.

"Oh," said Carlys. She felt her heart begin to race, but she pretended she was Glenda Jackson in *A Touch of Class* and spoke coolly and crisply. "You could?"

"Yes," said Tom. Just then the busboy cleared away the first course dishes and the moment hung, suspended in time.

"We can give you twenty-five percent," Tom offered when forty dollars' worth of truffled pigeon had been placed in front of them. "Twenty-five percent is twenty-five thousand dollars," he pointed out. "You can't turn it down," he added with a self-confident smile and cut into the pigeon, as sure of the one across the table as he was of the one on his plate.

"Yes I can," Carlys said, amazing herself and almost choking Tom.

"But I need you!" Tom said, his phony cool deserting him momentarily. "You know how Lansing writes. You understand his style."

"I not only understand it," Carlys said tartly, enjoying herself now. She was dying to tell Kirk Arnold about the conversation. "I invented it."

Tom upped the offer over eighteen dollars' worth of Grand Marnier soufflés.

"Fifty percent," he said and then helpfully proceeded to do the arithmetic for her again. "Fifty percent is fifty thousand dollars. You *can't* afford to turn *that* down."

"How do you know what I can and can't afford to turn down?" she asked, wondering if he thought she couldn't add and thinking with amazement that all of a sudden they were talking about fifty thousand dollars! "Just because you thought I don't know anything about wine doesn't mean I don't."

"Now don't get huffy," Tom cajoled and signaled the waiter and ordered a pack of Parliament Longs. He wondered what was wrong with Carlys. Why was she being such a bitch? Then it occurred to him that she was probably getting her period and he relaxed a little. In a day or two she'd be more reasonable. "Don't say no so fast," he said soothingly, patting her hand. "Think it over. It's a good deal."

"Good? So-so," she shrugged, feigning reluctance over bitter espresso and La Côte Basque's special cookies. "But, all right. I'll *think* about it."

She left Tom on the corner of Fifty-fifth and Fifth and tele-
phoned Kirk Arnold from a phone booth in the St. Regis lobby.

"He offered me fifty thousand dollars!" she exclaimed. "He offered me twenty-five first but I told him no. He couldn't believe it! Come to think of it, I couldn't believe it either!"

"Good for you!" he said, and it occurred to her that his

husky voice was the sexiest voice she had ever heard. "You played them perfectly!"

"But I would never have been able to do it without you!" she said, thrilled, glowing, exhilarated. He wasn't Wall Street's White Knight. He was *her* White Knight!

"Well, then," he replied, and she could hear the smile, "aren't you glad you have me?"

Me have *you?* A girl like me and a man like you? Carlys asked herself and she began to laugh. She laughed all the way back to the office and she didn't care one bit that some people stared at her in the street. Strangers, caught up in her exhilaration, smiled at her and she smiled back. She didn't care what anyone thought. She loved the whole wide world and she felt she was sitting right on top of it.

The next time she saw Winn, she made sure the matchbooks from the St. Regis and La Côte Basque were out in plain sight.

"La Côte Basque?" he asked, picking one up. "The St. Regis? When did you go there?"

"This week," she said casually.

"Who with?" he demanded. "Who took you?"

"A White Knight," she said mysteriously. "No one *you* know."

Later he said they could spend Friday together.

"I'll cook," he offered. "You can stay over."

"I'm sorry," Carlys said, suddenly remembering the power of a no. "I can't. I'm busy."

"Busy?" he repeated incredulously, as if he hadn't heard her correctly. "You're never busy."

She let him flounder in her silence.

"Then Saturday," he suggested and remembered the matchbooks. "We could go out. Somewhere nice."

CHAPTER 6

Money had been extremely important throughout Carlys's entire life. Not money, really, as much as the lack of money. Her father's business had been a modest one and her mother's illness had been very expensive. Carlys had grown up learning to deny her material wants. New dresses and trips to Florida and gold charm bracelets had been for others, never for her. She had always repressed her envy of those for whom money was no problem, but she had always wondered what it would be like not to have to look at a price tag, not to have to make do or do without. She had never known what it was to have money or the choices that money meant. She had reacted by telling herself that money wasn't important.

Carlys was twenty-eight now, thinking about thirty. It was time she began acting like an adult. It was time she began to think about taking care of herself. One of the things she had noticed in the office was that the men were interested in money and that the women were interested in praise. The men were constantly talking about how much they earned, how much someone else earned, how much someone was worth, how much money Company A earned versus how much Company B earned. The women talked about who the boss liked and didn't like, they fretted about criticism and preened under approval.

Lansing, of course, was obsessed with money and spoke about virtually nothing else save an occasional detour about the current state of his penis. Tom was crazed at even the suspicion that another of the men on his level might be earning one dollar more than he did. Peter, on the day he learned that a female account executive at another firm earned exactly as much as he did, smashed the glass bottle on the water cooler with the Kalashnikov he said he'd captured from a Russian soldier during the Hungarian revolution. Even Sergio, who proclaimed himself a Star with a capital S, reserved his most awesome tantrums for concert fees and contract negotiations.

In a way, Carlys thought, they were ridiculous. They were like little boys in a schoolyard comparing the sizes of their penises. Yet in another way, Carlys thought, they were right. In business, money was what counted. In life, money counted, too. Money meant freedom and choices; money meant the difference between the original and the copy; money made a difference in what other people thought of you; money could make the difference in the way you thought of yourself. To a great extent Carlys still thought of herself as an impostor. Money in the bank, she decided, might make her feel like less of a fraud. She told Tom that she'd thought his proposition over and that she'd decided to write Lansing's book for him. Fifty thousand dollars was a huge amount of money. It was an opportunity she might never, ever have again. She wanted to handle it just right.

The person she turned to was Kirk Arnold.

"Now that I've got them to do what I want, what do I do?" she asked him over the phone one morning at eight-thirty. She had that panic-stricken, in-over-her-head feeling. Getting what she wanted was a brand-new experience for Carlys, and she was feeling thrown by it. He heard it all in her voice.

"First of all enjoy it," he told her, giving advice he had never been able to follow himself. "Then get a lawyer and make them sign a contract."

"A lawyer? A contract?" Tom asked. "What kind of shit is that? Don't you trust us?"

"I'd prefer that my lawyer handle it," Carlys said politely but firmly.

"For Christ's sake," Tom moaned, but did what she said.

Carlys asked Kirk Arnold to recommend a lawyer and he did—a woman named Judith Rosen. Judith Rosen was pushing sixty but sixty wasn't pushing back. Judith was everything Carlys wanted to be: feminine, strong-minded, assertive, confident, sexy. Tom hated her.

*   *   *

Carlys went to Charleston and spent the next three months writing *How to Make Your First Million* in the comfortable study of Lansing's Tradd Street townhouse. The book was a mélange of rewrites of old columns, transcripts of lectures supplied by Lansing, and several tape-recorded interviews in which Carlys tried to get Lansing to explain his esoteric theories. Writing it turned out to be hard work but, like most work, hardly impossible. In fact it *was* rather like writing fifty press releases and stringing them together. Of course the new, savvy Carlys would never admit that to Tom. She worked twelve-hour days and the worst part was that she found she couldn't remember what she wrote. Every morning she had to reread what she'd written the day before. There was a here-today, gone-tomorrow, totally unreal quality about writing Lansing's book that disturbed Carlys.

"Did you feel that way when you wrote the exercise book?" she asked Michelle on the WATS line, wanting to make sure she wasn't losing her marbles.

"And the beauty book," Michelle said, remembering the temperamental, alcoholic exercise guru who'd had her boobs *and* ass lifted and wanted to make sure no one knew. "The point," she had kept telling Michelle, "is that people should think that exercise is the only reason for my beautiful body." Michelle remembered the barely there beauty expert who wafted through his days on a combination of organic eggs and Valium and only came to fully when he was talking about lipstick colors and blusher placement. She knew just what Carlys was going through.

"Dealing with bullshit like that is just like tap dancing on sand," Michelle said. "A lot of effort and no noise. Just close your eyes and think of the money," she advised.

How to Make Your First Million was vigorously advertised through a massive mail order campaign so that potential buyers could exercise their greed in the privacy of their own homes. Carlys's fifty percent share eventually earned her sixty-two thousand dollars. She had never had sixty-two hundred dollars in her life, let alone sixty-two thousand.

"Sixty-two thousand dollars!" she kept saying, hardly able to believe it. Characteristically she asked everyone and his brother what she ought to do with the money.

"Invest it in the stock market," Lansing said. "Follow my tips and you'll make a fortune."

Knowing the basis of Lansing's predictions and knowing that he was wrong almost as often as he was right (something his publicity *never* mentioned), Carlys wasn't convinced.

"Give it to me," Winn said, wanting to be protective. "I'll invest it for you."

She almost handed it over to Winn except that Norma pointed out that if she did, she'd probably *never* be free of him.

"Thank you, anyway," she finally told Winn, "but I don't understand investments, even when someone else handles them."

Unaccustomed to rejection, Winn sulked for weeks.

"My father-in-law is a genius with investments," Tom said. "Let me ask him if he'd handle it for you."

Carlys had never met Tom's father-in-law and the idea of giving her money to someone she didn't know scared her.

"Put it in the bank," Jacob advised, forgetting the depression that had almost wiped him out. "Banks are safe."

"Spend it," said Kirk Arnold without thinking twice. "That's what money is for."

"I think my father's right," she told Norma. Spending it seemed reckless to Carlys. It had been too hard to earn it. It never even occurred to her that she might earn it again. "I think I'll put it in the bank."

"That's dumb," Norma said. "You have good clothes and a good job. You've changed everything about yourself except that dump you live in. It's time you got rid of that, too. Why don't you buy yourself a decent apartment?"

"Buy?" said Carlys, absolutely shocked at the idea. Buy an apartment by herself? *For* herself? She was single. Who was she to buy an apartment? How could she afford it? How would she furnish it? What if she didn't like it? What would she do if she met someone? The mere thought of buying an apartment actually panicked her.

"I'm too scared," she blurted out and was astounded at the word that had popped out of her mouth. Scared? She was terrified.

*　　*　　*

Carlys had lived in her studio for over five years and it was still only half furnished. The single bed, the table she ate off, and the black-and-white portable television set were leftovers from her parents' apartment. She didn't own a sofa or a desk. The apartment had no night table, no easy chair, no curtains, not even a dresser. She kept her sweaters and underclothes on bookshelves abandoned by a former tenant. Window shades rescued from the basement of Norma's building kept the neighbors from peering in. The Indian cotton bedspread was left over from her old bedroom on West End Avenue, and the folding chairs were the ones her mother's nurses had once used. For years Carlys had told herself that "next year" she'd put up shelves and hang wallpaper. That "when she met someone" she'd get some decent furniture. "Next year" never came and she never seemed to "meet someone."

"That's right," Norma agreed. "You *are* scared, but not of buying an apartment. You're scared of the commitment."

"No I'm not," she said, angry at Norma for one of the few times ever. "After all, I'm the one who wants a commitment. It's Winn who doesn't."

"And you still won't tell Winn to get lost," Norma pointed out.

This time Carlys was silent. This time she stopped and thought about what Norma was saying.

Reluctantly she realized that maybe Norma was right. And maybe she was right about more than just the apartment. For years Carlys had blamed her unhappiness on Winn and his refusal to make a commitment. Now she suddenly asked herself whether she, too, had feared the commitment. It was certainly much easier to make Winn the heavy and blame him for all her unhappiness than to think that the fault might be hers.

Norma's words affected Carlys profoundly and the more she thought about them the more she decided that they must be true. *Had* she been saying and thinking one thing and, in reality, doing another? Could it be that *she* was the one who was afraid of an involvement? Could it be that *she* was the one who was scared of a commitment? Maybe, she thought. Just possibly. But she would take care of first things first. That same week Carlys called three different co-op brokers.

* * *

A month later Carlys bought a sunny three-room apartment on Seventy-fifth Street just off Third Avenue for twenty-two thousand dollars. She spent almost ten thousand more furnishing it with the help of Lord & Taylor's decorating department. Done in blues and cream, the apartment was tidy, tranquil, and comfortable. Carlys had never been so happy with anything material in her entire life.

Norma approved. "Now," she said, "you look as successful as you really are."

Winn didn't like it at all. "No one has their apartment done by Lord & Taylor anymore," he sneered. "All the with-it people go to Bloomingdale's."

"That may be," Carlys said quietly. "But *I* like it."

Winn just looked at her. He was too vain to let his mouth hang open but that was just how he felt. He was speechless.

Her father told her she was crazy. "They saw you coming," he said. "That apartment was on the market for two years. They reduced the price four times before you came along. You should have put the money in the bank."

"I don't agree with you," she told him firmly but nicely. "I love the apartment. I'm thrilled with it. I think I did exactly the right thing."

Jacob Webber, like Winn Rosier, wasn't used to a Carlys who stood up for herself. He was silent for a moment and then he said, in a sweet tone that brought tears to Carlys's eyes, "Well, as long as you're happy, honey. I just want you to be happy."

Money was not her only reward. Joshua Hynes named Carlys an account executive of Barron & Hynes; Tom Steinberg got his long-awaited promotion to vice-president. Word was beginning to get around in the outside world that Carlys Webber was someone to watch. In the next three months Carlys was offered three other jobs. One was with the Corporate Information Office of an enormous manufacturer of drugs and medical supplies, the other two were from competitors of Barron & Hynes. Carlys turned them all down after Tom offered to meet the competing salaries. As a further inducement to get her to stay, he awarded her an outside office. After working for six years Carlys finally had a window.

"Decorate it any way you want," Tom told Carlys in his lord-of-the-manor way. He was a vice-president, she was only an account executive. The lines of command were still clear and Tom still knew how to deal with subordinates. Basically, he treated them like one of the "good" slave owners treated his slaves. Too bad Tom hadn't been born in the Old South. "We like people to express themselves around here."

In Carlys's opinion people at Barron & Hynes expressed themselves *too* much. The ones who didn't run to their shrinks on their lunch hours spent evenings in encounter therapy groups and weekends at EST and Arica seminars. Carlys wondered what had ever happened to discipline and self-control, but kept her opinion to herself. She went straight to Knoll and chose a well-designed desk and desk chair, two comfortable visitor's chairs, a small sofa, and a coffee table. She selected handsome tan carpeting, sleek blinds, and hung a striking blue-and-white Amish quilt on the wall. In an office where rolltop desks, barber's chairs, juke boxes, antique Smith-Coronas, and cut-out, bullet-riddled human figures from police target ranges all loudly proclaimed the individuality of their inhabitants, Carlys's office seemed perversely businesslike.

"Are you *sure* that's what you want?" Tom asked, just trying to save her from a mistake. He had furnished his own office with Sheraton and Hepplewhite antiques. Chintzes, hunting prints, and "ancestor" paintings picked up in Third Avenue shops completed his office furnishings. For a nice Jewish boy from the West Side, Tom gave himself the props of an English lord. Carlys, who was half Jewish herself, always wondered what the Jews saw in the Anglo-Saxons. Not to mention vice versa. "Don't you want to express yourself a little more?"

"But I *did* express myself," Carlys insisted. Tom shrugged and let the matter drop.

"You know," said Joshua Hynes, who occasionally dropped into Carlys's office, "this is the only office in the whole place that looks businesslike."

He meant it as a compliment, and Carlys took it as a compliment.

*　　*　　*

Carlys had not had her new office six months when the telephone on her desk rang one morning at eight-thirty. Only one person ever called that early.

"I want you to meet me at the Regency right now, this minute," Kirk Arnold said.

"I'd like to but I can't," said Carlys. There was an all-agency marketing meeting for Cellini's introduction of a new line of expensive writing instruments scheduled for nine o'clock and, after that, a copy conference for Sergio's forthcoming seven-city Canadian tour. Most important of all, at eleven Carlys was to pitch SportsLine, a television sports film packager that was looking for new PR representation. "Not this minute. Not even this morning. I just can't get away."

"Yes you can. It's easy. All you do is get up from your desk, put on your coat, and walk out," he said and hung up before she could say another word.

Carlys sat there for a moment, not knowing what to do, wondering if she ought to call Norma or see if Michelle was in her office. Then, for the first time, the rabbis and the ministers lost. Decisively, and in full control of her destiny, Carlys stood, picked up her coat, walked out, and headed for the Regency.

The power-broker honchos—the Felix Rohatyns, Hugh Careys, Roy Cohns, and Robert Levitts—were gone, off to change the shape of the city, the country, and the world, and the big, comfortable room was pleasantly quiet. Kirk Arnold sat alone at a big corner table. In a dark pin-striped suit, with impeccably groomed hair and a Southampton tan, he looked like someone who'd been born with a silver spoon, a lifetime subscription to *Town & Country,* and not a worry in the world. He was an extraordinarily handsome man who seemed utterly unaware of his good looks, and no matter how often she saw him, Carlys was still almost physically struck by the aura of absolute confidence and command he projected.

"Carlys," he said, welcoming her with a smile. "You look beautiful."

She flushed and sat down.

She was aware of Kirk Arnold's physical presence, but totally unaware of her own powerful impact. Her beautiful skin, well cared for and skillfully made up, seemed to reflect the light and her large, clear eyes were intelligent and responsive. She had worn a well-tailored suit that morning, along with an emerald-colored silk blouse. The gold shell earrings she had bought for herself at Cartier one lunch hour after weeks of anxious debate cast warm arcs of light that becomingly glittered beneath the fine strands of her gold-shot hair. With her Cellini briefcase, expensive shoes, and conservative watch, she fit in perfectly, no longer an impostor, but someone who was about to belong.

Orange juice waited at Carlys's place and a rosebud in a silver vase stood on the table. She was curious, flattered, and excited—exactly as she knew he intended her to be. She smiled—a real smile, not one of Michelle's Uncle Tom specials—and waited for him to speak.

"You did it," he said, holding her eyes with his.

"Did what?" she asked, her eyes drifting toward the scar that traced its way through his left eyebrow and wondering, not for the first time, how he'd gotten it. On a yacht, the boom unexpectedly swinging across the deck? A fall from a horse going over a jump during a fox hunt? A sudden accident, she was positive, in a terribly glamorous setting. She could see the drops of blood on his yachting whites, could imagine his top hat flying off as his horse caught the top of a jump.

"Quit," he said matter-of-factly. He was being deliberately mysterious. He liked holding her in his power, and she liked being held. Beneath their words an elaborate mesh of unspoken questions and answers, actions and reactions was being silently and fiercely woven.

"Quit what?" she asked, beginning to feel the faint stirrings of alarm. She assumed he meant one of her accounts.

"Your job," he said seriously. "I quit it for you. I just called Tom Steinberg and told him."

"Are you crazy?" Carlys exclaimed, almost knocking over the orange juice.

"No, not at all," he said, suppressing a smile.

"You *quit* my job for me?" Carlys asked, certain that she hadn't heard correctly.

"Yes," he said calmly. "You're going to be publicity manager for the office equipment division of SuperWrite."

"I am?" she asked.

"Apart from a *much* larger salary you'll have more authority, more responsibility, more clout," he said, finally allowing the smile to appear. "Now drink your orange juice."

Thrilled, excited, shocked, mystified, scared, happy, Carlys picked up her glass. As it turned out, it wasn't orange juice, but orange juice mixed with champagne.

"If you think I'm going to get down on my hands and knees and beg you to stay, you can forget about it," Tom Steinberg said when Carlys got back to the office. He was in full Condition Red, absolutely furious, ready to maim and kill. "What the hell kind of trick is that anyway? Having Kirk Arnold call and quit for you?"

"It's not a trick," Carlys said, still in a state of semishock. "*I* didn't know he was doing it myself."

"Bullshit!" said Tom, his cheeks blazing, his eyes popping. He leaned forward and looked Carlys straight in the eye. "So tell me, is there something going on between you and Kirk Arnold?"

"Come on, Tom," said Carlys, offended but not surprised that Tom would leap to that conclusion. When it came to dealing with women, Tom thought that sex was the answer to and the reason for everything. "Kirk Arnold and me? You know that Burt Reynolds and I. . . ."

"Yeah. Okay. Okay," he said brusquely and dismissed her, still beside himself, every single one of his liberal resolutions gone. She was a slave and who the fuck were the slaves to walk out?

"You don't really mean it, do you?" Tom Steinberg asked two days later. He'd calmed down, and, after an encounter with a distinctly displeased Joshua Hynes, he decided he'd sweet-talk Carlys into staying. She'd become invaluable. She handled all the pain-in-the-ass clients and did a damn good job. On top of everything else, Lansing was making noises about leaving if she did.

"Yes, I do," said Carlys. She couldn't wait to leave. She was counting the minutes, the seconds, until she went to SuperWrite, until she could see and talk to Kirk Arnold every single day. "I'll stay here for two weeks and train my replacement. Then I'm going to SuperWrite."

"We'll match your salary," Tom offered. Replacement? How the hell could he find someone with her talent and utter lack of confidence? She was like the perfect appliance. She worked twenty-four hours a day, never broke down, and never shorted out. General Electric should only get the patent! God had created her for him and now she was going!

Carlys shook her head. "Money isn't going to make the difference," she said.

Tom lit an old-style, unfiltered, guaranteed-cancer-producing Camel, inhaled straight down to his toenails, and fixed Carlys with a nicotine-boosted stare.

"The so-called White Knight is crazy. Nuts. Out of his gourd. Did you know that, Carlys?" he said, unleashing the multimegaton ballistic missile he had kept in reserve for just such an emergency.

When she didn't reply, he continued. "Do you hear me, Carlys? Watch out. Stay away. Don't fall for the surface charm. Kirk Arnold is Bananas City."

"Come on, Tom. Just because he quit my job for me?" she said. Tom was desperate. Even *she* could see that! "I admit he's unconventional. But unconventional isn't crazy. He's as sane as you are and as I am."

"I didn't spend any time in a loony bin. Did you?"

"Of course not!"

"Kirk Arnold did," Tom said, detonating his weapon, blast-scorching the earth. He took another fantastically, incredibly satisfying drag on his cigarette and slumped back in his chair the way another man would after an orgasm.

"Why? What happened?" Carlys asked, wondering if there was any possibility, however remote, that Tom could actually know what he was talking about. She remembered—and it ricocheted with an uncomfortable echo—her own, automatic question when Kirk had said he'd quit her job for her. Are you crazy? she had asked. The words had just floated out of her mouth. Had her unconscious known something *she* didn't know? It just wasn't possible. Still, a nettle stung at her, clinging tenaciously just underneath her surface calm and reason. "What's supposed to be wrong with him?"

Tom shrugged. "Ask him about Covington."

"Covington?" Carlys had had a classmate at Hunter

who'd had a nervous breakdown and, for a while, all the talk was about what treatment she'd have, what hospital she'd go to. Carlys had heard of Covington, along with Briggs, Silvermine, Menninger. She simply could not believe that someone as important and responsible as Kirk Arnold had ever spent time in a mental institution.

"Kirk Arnold met his wife there," Tom said authoritatively.

Wife? Carlys felt her heart lurch and sink. Still, somehow, she'd known all along that he was married. Men like Kirk Arnold always were. She locked her emotions away, knowing she would take them out later and examine them, and continued with Tom.

"I don't believe it," Carlys said, knowing that Tom went in for character assassination. She remembered the gleefully malicious way he'd talked about Lennard Barron and his problems with the bottle. She also knew that Tom had almost been fired in the reorganization Kirk Arnold had overseen at Barron & Hynes. Tom probably hated Kirk and didn't care what he had to do or say to get back at him. "I simply don't believe you," she said bluntly.

"Don't," said Tom snottily. "It's just a lie I'm telling you so you'll stay."

"A company like SuperWrite wouldn't make him a special consultant if that were true," Carlys said, trying to bring the conversation back to a rational level. "Neither would Barron & Hynes. Kirk Arnold has enormously responsible assignments. He handles millions of dollars and huge companies. Tough businessmen wouldn't hire him if . . . there were anything wrong with him."

Tom shrugged, inhaled, and tried a new tack. "It's going to be boring, you know. Working for corporate America. They're a bunch of male chauvinists. They don't go for women."

"It's a chance I'll take," Carlys said witheringly. She refrained from commenting on Tom's own cloddish chauvinism and left his office.

Tom lit another Camel with the butt of the first and his eyes followed Carlys as she left his office. From deep within his haze of smoke, Tom Steinberg wondered if little Miss Webber was deeper than he had given her credit for.

He had believed her the other day when she'd said there was nothing between her and Kirk Arnold. He'd fallen for it completely. One thing he'd learned about Carlys: She never lied. But then Tom asked himself why she had been so blindly defensive about Kirk Arnold during their conversation, refusing even to consider that what he said might be the truth? Which it was.

Tom suddenly remembered Carlys's first day at work. A blind man would have seen the sparks between her and Kirk Arnold, and Tom Steinberg was no blind man. Tom began to put two and two together. Kirk Arnold and Carlys Webber? Why not?

C H A P T E R   7

*S*uperWrite *was one great big family. One great big* unhappy family. SuperWrite had its roots back in the postwar 1940s in the Long Island City garage of an army-trained electronics tinkerer named Howard Mundees who invented the first bidirectional typewriter, a machine that allowed typists to nearly double their typing speed. So revolutionary was the invention, a precursor of the first computers, that by the late 1950s almost every office in the United States was equipped with the SuperWrite bidirectional typewriter. Because the invention was locked up by a series of unbroachable patents, SuperWrite had no close competition during the entire upward-growth economy stretching between the end of the war and the beginning of the sixties.

Howard's father, Charles, a disbarred lawyer who'd made a bundle in second mortgages, had originally put up the money for Howie to start the company. The old man named himself president and owned the stock. When Charlie died in the early 1950s, his three children—Howard, Molly, and Faith—inherited all his stock and all his prejudices. On the day of his father's death Howie named himself chairman of the board and told his two sisters to butt out.

Howie, at an even six feet and 150 pounds, was New England lean and Doberman mean. Lank, dark brown hair flopped over his high forehead and fell just short of cool gray eyes that registered the spectrum from mild suspicion to outright paranoia. His business philosophy was simple: Howie was strictly a bottom-line man who cared only that profits were up each quarter. Apart from a certain native shrewdness, the big thing Howie had going for him was his sex.

As for Molly, she was much smarter and even tougher than her brother, and all that stood between her and total control of SuperWrite was a penis. If money could have bought one, Molly would have been first in line with her American Express gold card. She thought that Howie was too narrowly bottom-line-oriented in his outlook for the good of the company and she felt that his son, Ray, current president of the company, was a total wimp. She felt—with good reason—that she would have been a better chief executive. Unfortunately for Molly Charlie had been an old-line chauvinist and the terms of his will were such that, although his daughters inherited stock, they were to play no official part in the running of the company.

Faith, the youngest, had always been the sexy one. Just before the family board meetings she was the one who cruised Bergdorf's in search of just the right ruffled Oscar de la Renta. She had been married and divorced four times and, pushing sixty, still hadn't given up on romance. Faith had absolute faith in love, beautiful clothes, and gracious living. She considered Howie an uncouth grease monkey and Molly a foul-mouthed, money-grubbing disgrace to her sex.

None of them were on speaking terms unless it was absolutely, positively essential.

Lucky Ray Mundees, Howie's son by his first marriage, was in the middle. Ray had been an adequate executive when SuperWrite dominated its market. But then in 1965, the fifth year of Ray's presidency, IBM introduced the Selectric.

"The Selectric?" Ray replied to Molly's question at one of the quarterly board meetings. "It hasn't been proven in the marketplace. I wouldn't worry about it at this point."

"I wouldn't either," growled Howie. "We're outselling them eight to one."

"If I were you, I'd worry about it plenty," Molly told her nephew later in the backseat of the limo on the way home to Locust Valley. Molly wore English Leather aftershave, a scent that made Ray choke.

"I'll have a survey done," Ray said, rolling down the window on his side, relieved that at least she hadn't cut off his balls in front of his father. Maybe, he tried to tell himself, she was mellowing.

So was Genghis Khan.

*Within two years the Selectric had cut noticeably into Super-*Write's market share, and by the time SuperWrite introduced its own version of the ball-element typewriter, in 1968, it was too late. Molly had been predicting for a long time that Howie's shortsighted focus on the bottom line and Ray's unaggressive leadership would get the company into trouble. Molly, unfortunately, was right. SuperWrite's profits—and the value of the family-owned company and its stock—went down and stayed down.

"Now what are we going to do?" asked Ray, literally wringing his hands and looking at his father, who glanced at Molly.

"We're going to hire Kirk Arnold," Molly said. "And we're going to give him whatever he wants to turn the company around."

"Who?" asked Ray.

"The White Knight," said Molly. "I play tennis with Helen Hynes. Kirk Arnold saved Joshua's ass when Barron & Hynes was taking a nosedive."

By the time the board voted to hire Kirk Arnold to turn the company around, SuperWrite was in serious trouble. Unaccustomed to competing, it had forgotten how. Not one of the recent innovations in typewriters—the flying-ball element, the disappearance of the manual return lever, the self-correcting feature, the shift from electric to electronic, the introduction of memory—had originated with SuperWrite. Its physical plants were antiquated; its patents, once its greatest asset, were worthless; its market share was insignificant. Under the passive direction of Ray, management responded rather than initiated, reacted rather than acted.

SuperWrite was an over-the-hill company in the throes of rigor mortis.

"This time I have to do more than just turn a company around," Kirk told Carlys. "This time I have to bring it back from the dead."

She looked at him and wondered, not for the first time, why a man who looked as successful as Kirk Arnold seemed obsessed by failure.

For the next year Carlys lived, ate, slept, and dreamt of Kirk Arnold. She saw him in the most flattering way a woman can see a man—through the eyes of people who need and admire him. Carlys had never worked harder; she had never had more fun; she had never known that work *could* be fun. Kirk Arnold thought nothing of working until midnight—and he thought nothing of having his staff work until midnight. Weekend and holidays did not seem to exist for him—or for his staff. He drove the people who worked for him, but no harder than he drove himself, and his employees were not only in awe of him but fanatically loyal as well—including Carlys.

Sometimes she thought that she and Kirk Arnold were the same person. They quickly got into the habit of conferring on almost everything and, together, coming up with solutions to the series of problems continually faced by a company in trouble like SuperWrite. They could finish each other's sentences; they could almost read each other's minds; they always knew what the other was thinking and feeling. They could never remember whose idea had been whose. So it was with the idea of making Howard Mundees better known to the business community.

Few people remembered that it had been Howie who had invented the SuperWrite typewriter. Those who did thought he was dead. In a series of conversations Carlys and Kirk decided that raising Howie's profile would serve a triple purpose: First, it would make people aware of SuperWrite again; second, it would make them aware that SuperWrite was a company that was being turned around. Third, and not least of all, it got Howie, a meddler and second-guesser, out of the way. Howie, in his blunt, no-nonsense style, was a good speaker and Carlys persuaded the Office Equipment Association to have him give the keynote speech at its annual dinner. Carlys wrote the speech and took Howie shopping for a conservative suit and a manicure before the dinner. Subsequently, she arranged interviews for him with *Business Week* and Dan Dorfman. She briefed Howie beforehand and prepared some good quotes for him. He was both grateful and resentful.

"Putting words in my mouth?" he asked suspiciously as Carlys suggested an angle for a *Wall Street Journal* interview.

"It's my job. It's what you're paying me for," said Carlys politely, not wanting to tell the truth, which was that Howie couldn't get through a sentence without two "fucks" and three "goddamns."

As far as the public was concerned, it was Howard Mundees who represented SuperWrite. As far as Kirk and Carlys were concerned, it was Ray Mundees who was the stumbling block. His indecision and weakness made their long hours longer and their hard work harder. Ray was afraid of everyone—Howie, Molly, Kirk, as well as the people who worked for him. He was also afraid to say no to anyone. Since he said yes to everything and everyone, he was, as an executive of a company that needed crisp leadership, a walking disaster. But when Kirk decided that Edwin Avakian, the treasurer, had to be fired, Ray balked and argued that the man had been with SuperWrite for a dozen years and ought, at least, to be kept on even if in a less important position.

"No," said Kirk firmly. "Edwin has no credibility with bankers and capital markets. He's one of the reasons your credit line is a joke for a company SuperWrite's size."

Ray finally pretended to go along but, behind Kirk's back, assured Edwin Avakian that he would always have a place at SuperWrite. When Kirk fired him Edwin refused to leave.

"Ray told me I could continue," he said stubbornly, literally holding on to his desk. "No matter what you tell me."

Kirk had to call a meeting with Ray and Edwin and tell Edwin in front of Ray, that he, Kirk, had the ultimate authority over hiring and firing and that Edwin was fired. He was to be out of the SuperWrite building by five o'clock.

"Firing people is the worst part of the job," Kirk told Carlys later. He looked drained and exhausted and dark shadows showed under his eyes. "I hate it. Ray made it even worse than it had to be."

When Kirk decided to close down an antiquated plant near Lowell, Massachusetts, and rent the space out to one of the high-tech companies that had sprung up around Boston, Ray had gone to the rental agent and tried to stop the deal. SuperWrite typewriters had been made in Lowell since 1952; Ray thought they should still be made there. The agent, who had a signed agreement of intention with a computer manufacturer, called Kirk in a rage. His commission was at stake.

"What the hell is going on there?" he demanded over the phone, his booming voice causing the lines to crackle in Kirk's ear. "You told me to go ahead and find a tenant. Now this joker comes along and tells me the space isn't for rent. If this deal doesn't go through, I promise I'm suing SuperWrite for my commission."

Kirk calmed the man down, told him to go ahead with the rental agreement, and persuaded him not to sue.

"This guy's an unguided missile," he told Carlys, meaning Ray. Closing the Lowell plant and renting it out had a dual objective: It cut down on operating overhead and generated a dependable cash flow. It was an ingenious way to turn a money-loser into a money-earner and Ray had almost screwed it up. "No wonder SuperWrite's in the shape it's in."

Despite Ray's constant interference, Kirk was completely reorganizing SuperWrite from its manufacturing plants to its sales organization to its financial structure. He had brought in the best manufacturing, engineering, financial, and marketing people he could hire to help him. Some of them had worked for him before—and all of them thought that Kirk Arnold hung the moon. He delegated responsibility, didn't second-guess, and stood behind his people one thousand percent.

Kirk Arnold took care of the people who worked for him. When his staff worked through dinner, Kirk Arnold ordered up. Not a tuna plate from the coffee shop but an elegant dinner from the Silver Palate. He ordered taxis to get everyone home after a late-night work session. He was generous, almost lavish, with compliments, praise, and bonuses, and when the people who worked for him had problems, Kirk was always there to help solve them. Martin Reis was a marketing consultant who had worked with Kirk on half a dozen turnarounds. When Marty's daughter, Barbara Jane, shattered her knee in a playground accident, Kirk had B.J. flown to Houston, where, at the world-famous Houston Medical Center, the kneecap was put back together. Because of Kirk B.J. would walk again without a limp. Bob Rohn, called the Wiz, was a financial genius who had begun his career with Lazard Frères. When Bob's wife complained that she never saw her husband because Kirk demanded more and worse hours than even André Meyer, Kirk arranged dinner, theater, and dancing once a week for the Rohns. Bob always said that Kirk Arnold had saved his marriage.

But what about Kirk's own marriage? Carlys wondered. He worked nights and weekends and in 1974, a dozen months after he went to work at SuperWrite, he moved into the SuperWrite corporate apartment at the Carlyle even though, Carlys knew, he had a home in Armonk. She wondered about Kirk Arnold's marriage and about Mrs. Kirk Arnold. Was she a housewife? Did she have her own career? No one really seemed to know very much about her; apparently she rarely attended business-related social functions with her husband. Michelle had said that she thought Bonnie Arnold was a psychiatrist and Peter Salzany had said that Bonnie Arnold had given up a career as a professional dancer to marry Kirk. All Carlys knew for certain about Kirk Arnold's marriage was that it was a marriage of long standing; that he had two children, a boy and a girl; and that he was, as far as anyone knew, a completely faithful husband.

"Don't get your hopes up. He doesn't screw around," said Tom Steinberg when Carlys had started working at Barron & Hynes and asked curious questions about the man who had tried to hire her away her first day on the new job. "I know because every woman in this office tried. No one even got to first base."

Michelle had a different theory: "He's dying to have an affair. He just hasn't met the right person yet."

C H A P T E R 8

He was, Carlys thought, perfect. He always knew what to do, when to do it, and how to do it. He was always in control, always in command. She never saw him hesitant, uncertain, or doubtful. If he had any weaknesses he followed his own advice and never revealed them. He was used to power, and power became him. When Carlys complained that her intense work schedule had prevented her from doing her Christmas shopping, he told her to take the afternoon off.

"Take my limo," he offered, and placed it at her disposal. As Carlys shopped down Fifth Avenue and up Madison the limousine followed, and the chauffeur helped her with her packages. It was the most headily luxurious experience she had ever had in her life. Having Kirk Arnold's powerful car was like having Kirk Arnold's power, and that feeling was intensely exciting and almost unbearably erotic.

As she left Bottega Veneta, Bill Saperstein, the SuperWrite sales manager, came out of the newsstand across the street where he'd just bought the *Post*. He saw Carlys get into the limousine with the K.A. vanity plates and jumped to the obvious conclusion.

"Nothing like screwing the boss," he told Arnie Holt, the head of Midwest sales who was in New York for two days of meetings, "to get the afternoon off to go shopping while the rest of us work for our money."

Carlys, mesmerized by luxury and comfort, hadn't noticed Bill, but the gossip that he started would ultimately bleed through all twelve floors of the SuperWrite offices. The stories Arnie spread would eventually sizzle through all seven regional sales offices.

"I felt like a movie star," Carlys said when she told Norma about shopping with a limousine in tow. "Or maybe a millionaire!"

"You're almost beginning to look like one," Norma said, painfully aware that Carlys was changing, even more painfully aware that she wasn't. She was still working at the phone company, still twenty-five pounds overweight, still living alone with Bunny and Alice in her crummy two-room apartment. Norma tried not to be jealous of Carlys and, mostly, she succeeded. After all, they were friends and Norma wanted the best for Carlys, just as she wanted the best for herself.

As Carlys began to see herself in the flattering mirror that Kirk Arnold held up, she began to feel different about herself and she began to act differently. She was less inhibited, less desperate to please, less anxious to be liked, less willing to play the role of doormat. The important relationships in her life began to change. Winn stopped taking her for granted, and so did her father.

"I've been thinking about living together," Winn said, off balance because Carlys was no longer available whenever he was in the mood. He noticed the way men were beginning to look at her and the new, confident way she looked and acted. She was exactly the kind of person he thought he had always deserved and ought to have. "What would you say if we made it official and moved in together? I saw a nice apartment on my block. It's big enough for the two of us and the rent isn't bad. The lease starts a month from now."

A year ago she had hoped and prayed for Winn to make a commitment; now, immersed in a challenging job that she was handling superbly, she was no longer desperate. In addition, Kirk's style and air of command made Winn seem more than slightly shallow and superficial.

"I can't," Carlys said, speaking to him as coolly as she now sometimes spoke to people at work. The balance of power between her and Winn had shifted in her favor. She was now almost consciously cruel to him. She wasn't proud of herself, but she couldn't help it. She had been in too much pain for too long. It felt good to see Winn as needy and hurt as she had once been and she couldn't resist her rare opportunity for revenge. "I'm too busy."

He began to call her when he said he would; he even began to send her flowers. The less she wanted him the more he wanted her.

"You're working Sunday afternoon?" her father asked over the telephone. He was surprised, annoyed, uncomfortable. "You can't come this Sunday afternoon? What kind of job is this, anyway?"

"It's an important job," Carlys said in her new, cool "office" voice.

"More important than your father?"

"More important than my father's grocery shopping," she replied, almost exhilarated that the old guilt strings no longer bound her so tightly. "It's a nice day. Why don't you take a walk to the A and P?"

"But I've never been," he said. He didn't want to go to the A&P. He wanted *her* to go. He didn't want to take care of himself. He wanted *her* to take care of him.

"Now's your chance," Carlys said briskly and humorously, but before she hung up she agreed to come over one evening and write the checks. It was one thing to punish Winn; she did not intend to hurt her father, only to make him a bit more self-sufficient.

"Raising Howard's visibility was a brilliant idea. Bankers who wouldn't return his calls do now and SuperWrite's competitors are beginning to take the company seriously again," Kirk told Carlys in the summer of 1974, that historic summer of two presidents—Richard Nixon and Gerald Ford. "What made you think of it?"

"It wasn't *my* idea," Carlys replied. "You thought of it. Don't you remember?"

"No," he insisted, intent on giving her the credit. *"You* thought of it. It was *your* idea."

"You're wrong," Carlys said, just as insistently. "I'm positive you thought of it."

Kirk looked at her and shrugged at their ridiculous "after you, Alphonse" routine. Together they laughed.

"How many times have we had this conversation anyway?" he asked. He felt more comfortable with her than with almost anyone, but Bonnie was wrong to think Carlys had a crush on him. She was too standoffish, too business-like. Bonnie was probably just being jealous.

"I don't know," she said, her eyes sparkling in the unending pleasures of their conspiracy-for-two. "Every day—or at least that's the way it seems."

Kirk and Carlys were together constantly: in marketing meetings; in meetings with other departments; at business lunches. They traveled together: to Omaha when Howie gave a speech to the National Association of Manufacturers, which Carlys had arranged; to Washington, when he testified at congressional hearings about the safety of video display terminals—testimony that Carlys had set up and which got Howard Mundees and SuperWrite invaluable exposure on the network news; to trade shows around the country as they researched the office products market. Kirk was becoming more and more convinced that typewriters were a dead-end business, and he was working on a strategy that would bring SuperWrite into the 1980s.

Hour after hour and day after day Carlys and Kirk found it necessary to be together. Necessary—and increasingly exciting. Whenever they handed each other a report their hands seemed to touch—just for a second. So often, on the way into or out of a restaurant, Kirk Arnold put his hand on Carlys's back or elbow in a protective gesture, and she was as aware of his touch as if he'd burned her. At the office, working together at Carlys's desk, he found himself leaning over her, aware of the scent of her hair and able only with almost superhuman restraint to stop himself from touching it.

"Chemistry," Kirk told Carlys. "We have fantastic chemistry. I knew it the first moment I saw you."

"So did I," Carlys said, remembering how she had felt it and amazed at how she had refused to let herself believe it. The beaten-down, defeated Carlys was someone she now rejected. She shunned all reminders of her former self and, both consciously and unconsciously, transformed herself into a portrait of success.

Kirk and Carlys were right. It never occurred to them, though, that chemistry which was appropriate in a lab might be dangerously volatile in an office.

*　　*　　*

Kirk Arnold was the first outsider ever to attend a Super-
Write board meeting. His presence, regarded by the Mundees
family with suspicion and distaste, had been permitted only
because of the disastrous state of SuperWrite's fortunes.
Kirk Arnold was regarded as a savior and, as such, was
both needed and resented. As he told Carlys: "They're
paying me to tell them what they're doing wrong. Naturally, they hate me for it."

What he didn't add, because he himself didn't see it, was
that he added fuel to their resentment. He considered himself socially superior and barely hid his feelings. He was
comfortable only in positions of authority and control and
treated the Mundeeses as employees instead of the other
way around. His confidence, which seemed to border on
arrogance, covered scars even he no longer acknowledged.
Like Carlys, Kirk was anxious to obliterate a past that
threatened his present. He consistently turned down Howie
and Miriam Mundees's invitations to dinner parties and
cocktail parties. Miriam was not appreciative.

"We're good enough to pay him a fancy salary," she
told Howie, "but we're not good enough to have dinner
with." Miriam, who had come up the hard way, did not
appreciate Kirk's Princeton background, his Park Avenue
style, his patrician born-with-a-silver-spoon attitude.

Howie nodded. He felt the same way but what was he
going to do? Howie, as always, had his cool gray eye on
the bottom line. He needed Kirk Arnold. *SuperWrite* needed
Kirk Arnold.

"What SuperWrite does best," Kirk told the board eight
months after he had been hired, summarizing a long report
Carlys had written that was buttressed with proposed manufacturing, financial, marketing, and advertising plans, "is
help people get words on paper. SuperWrite should get out
of the typewriter business. The machine SuperWrite ought
to make is a word processor."

The word processor, according to Marty Reis's marketing scenario, would be primarily an office machine, posi-
tioned to sell to both large and small corporate accounts.
The advertising, publicity, and promotion would stress
SuperWrite's long experience in getting words on paper
and its unexcelled reputation as a quality manufacturer
with quality products, efficient service, and excellent cus-

tomer support. The word processor was to be called the Alphatec. It had a ten-million-dollar budget and an eighteen-month development, testing, and on-sale schedule.

Howie was negative.

"We're typewriter people," he argued, suspicious of the new, scared by the size of the dollar investment, the largest in SuperWrite's history. "We ought to stick to what we know."

"Even if it's a stagnant business?" Kirk asked. He was, by almost fifteen years, the youngest person in the room, an anomaly to which he was accustomed since his father's sudden death when, at twenty-one, Kirk had taken over and run a family business. "Adjusting for growth, typewriter sales have remained level for almost a decade."

Molly liked the idea of the word processor.

"It's a way to get a jump into the eighties," she said. One thing Molly loved was the future. The future could be different, better. In the future a girl could inherit stock—and run the company. "The paperless office is the office of the future. Computers are the coming thing. Word processors are a specialized form of computer. I think Kirk is right."

"It would take a major financial commitment," Howie said, still resisting. Money, as usual, was on his mind. "The company would have to go into debt for the first time in its history."

Ray had a lot of questions. He wanted to know if a word processor could be developed for less; he wondered whether their pricing should be competitive with Wang or should they try to undersell; he couldn't make up his mind about how to borrow the money, should they go to the banks or should they undertake their first public offering? He wondered if word processing was really the coming thing or just a here-today, gone-tomorrow fad. He really couldn't imagine that computers would be a part of everyday office life. He asked if the original SuperWrite typewriter should be redesigned and remarketed. He wondered out loud about going into the office copier business instead.

All of Ray's questions were reasonable enough, but no one paid the slightest bit of attention to them. Howie scanned the marketing research Kirk had just passed out, rustling the pages loudly. Molly took out a compact and powdered her nose. Only Faith, who always listened when a man spoke, tried to follow.

"Ten million dollars is a fortune!" Faith exclaimed when Ray was done. Her theory was that whatever cash the company had in the till she might be able to glom on to. Whatever it spent was out of her grasp forever. "What if the idea doesn't work? We'll lose the whole company!"

"And if it *does* work you'll be richer than ever!" Molly snapped, turning to her sister. "For Christ's sake, you'll be able to go to Bergdorf's and buy the whole goddamn place, not just the third floor."

At the thought of *that* delicious possibility, Faith shut up.

"Let's go for it." Howie said suddenly. His opinion, he knew, was the only one in the room worth a shit; still, although he never admitted it, Molly's words carried a lot of weight with him. He knew that, except for an accident of birth, *she* would have run the company, and he suspected—although he'd have to face a firing squad before he'd admit it—that she might have done a better job than he. "We'll announce SuperWrite's entry into the word processing field," he said, his mind reluctantly changed by Kirk Arnold's convincing arguments and the fact that the company had been losing money for much too long. "On one condition. . . ."

"Which is?" Molly demanded.

"That Kirk Arnold stay on to oversee the planning, production, and launching of the Alphatec," Howie said, turning to Kirk. So far, Kirk's contract specified only that he oversee the reorganization of the company. "If it works, if SuperWrite succeeds, you get the credit," he told Kirk, his gray eyes suddenly the color of sleet. "If it fails, we'll hang you."

Everyone in the room turned toward Kirk.

"Well, Mr. Arnold," said Molly coolly. "It seems you're on the spot. Do you agree?"

"On one condition," Kirk said, his intense blue eyes now just as cold as Howard's.

"Which is?" Ray asked.

Kirk turned to him and spoke contemptuously.

"That you resign—now."

Ray turned white. Howie turned red and snapped, "Wait

a minute," Faith gasped and even Molly thought that Kirk Arnold had gone too far. They all turned to Kirk, barely believing their ears.

"He's incompetent," Kirk said, oblivious to their shock. If the board wanted him to oversee the development and marketing of the Alphatec, they would have to let him do it his way. Ray Mundees would have to go. "I can't work with him."

Kirk gave the board no choice and Ray's "retirement to pursue outside interests" was announced, although he was allowed to keep an office at SuperWrite. Kirk Arnold was named acting president of SuperWrite. He would serve, Howie made it crystal clear, at the pleasure of the board.

It was the first time Carlys ever thought Kirk was wrong.

"Wrong?" he demanded, stunned that Carlys would disagree with him. After all, *she* knew what an incompetent Ray was. She had complained about him at least as much as Kirk had. "Ray's hopeless. *He's* the one who ran the company into the ground."

"He's also the boss's son," Carlys pointed out, surprised at how oblivious Kirk seemed to be to the potential consequences of his action. He had put a gun to the board's head—they may have done what he wanted, but they couldn't have liked it too much. Even when she pointed it out to him he seemed totally unaware of the family's feelings. It was a side of Kirk Arnold she hadn't seen before. It wasn't like him. It wasn't like the Kirk Arnold she knew.

"Howie Mundees already believes you think you're too good for him," Carlys pointed out. "Firing his son, even if he *is* incompetent, isn't going to make him like you any more."

Kirk seemed utterly amazed to hear it. "What makes Howie feel I think I'm too good for him?"

"You never go to his and Miriam's parties," Carlys said, repeating the office scuttlebutt.

"The reason I don't go to his parties is that my beloved wife refuses to go," he said. It was the first time he had ever talked about his wife, and the depth of his bitterness startled Carlys.

"Oh. . . ." said Carlys, shocked and acutely uncomfortable, not knowing what else to say.

"Well, it doesn't matter," he said, turning to sarcasm. "From now on I can spend the rest of my life kissing Howie's ass and going to Miriam's parties."

"What do you mean?" she asked.

"My wife is having an affair," he said, suddenly turning to her and laying it on the table. "We're getting divorced."

CHAPTER 9

In 1974 very few women had risen as far in business as Carlys had at SuperWrite, and as an explorer in a brave new territory, she had no compass and no maps to guide her. Magazines like *Savvy* and *Working Woman* did not exist. The rules of dressing for success would not be published until 1977. The ins and outs of corporate manners and hierarchies had not yet been studied and defined the way they would be later in the decade. Carlys had never heard of a mentor, although Kirk Arnold certainly was one. She had never heard of networking, because the concept did not yet exist. She did not know about the pursuit of excellence, about Japanese management techniques, one-minute managers, or executive-suite etiquette. She did the best she could; out of ignorance, she made a lot of enemies and a lot of mistakes.

Kirk, who had been in business his entire life, was also blind to the particular problems of high-level executive women for the identical reasons that Carlys was. Since women in high echelons were rare there were no rules for those women. Because he valued Carlys's work so much Kirk assumed everyone else did. Naively, he rewarded her just the way he would have rewarded a male executive.

In September 1974, in the same week that his wife had asked for a divorce and he'd been named acting president of SuperWrite, Kirk named Carlys director of public affairs, a title he created especially for her.

"You earned it and you deserve it," Kirk told her.

"Thank you," she said, thrilled. Her promotions at work had always meant everything to her. They were, after all, the only tokens of acceptance she'd ever received. "It's been fun. It's been exciting."

Working with Kirk Arnold didn't feel like work. His feeling of triumph whenever a problem was solved, his word of congratulations every time she met a challenge, the flowers he sent whenever she had a particularly good idea lit up her days. Carlys loved talking to him, being with him. She loved the way he noticed her, praised her, and appreciated her in a way no one else in her life ever had. Not her father, who had been too preoccupied with her mother's illness when Carlys was younger and too preoccupied with himself now that she was older; not her teachers, who tended to ignore good students and pay attention to problem students; not Bob Ryan at the phone company, who was interested only in maintaining the status quo; not Lansing Coons, who wanted a perfect ghost, or Tom Steinberg, who wanted a grateful slave; not Winn Rosier, who wanted an uncritical worshipper. Working for Kirk was not remotely like working for Tom. Tom had been interested in wringing her out and keeping her down. Kirk was interested in getting the best out of her and then rewarding her for it. Kirk and Carlys both thought that they were businesslike and straightforward. Unfortunately that was *not* what anyone else at SuperWrite thought.

"I'd be director of public affairs, too, if I were having a private affair with the boss," said Charlie Trok, who handled SuperWrite's employee relations. "Too bad I'm not queer."

"He shouldn't have done that," Kirk's secretary, Dolly Fass, told Angie Paderno, Carlys's secretary, when Carlys's new title was announced. "They're getting awfully blatant. I heard they were together every night at that trade show in Atlanta. *Every* night!"

Helen Wallenberg, who had handled the banking liaison for four years, complained to her boss. "I've been here longer than Carlys Webber," she said. "If she's worth a special title, I think I am, too."

Everyone seemed to have something to say:

"Supposedly they were having an affair when they were still working for Barron & Hynes."

"How else do you think she got where she is? By sleeping with the boss, how else?"

"Someone saw them in the King Cole Bar playing kissy-face. I suppose they spent the night there."

"I feel sorry for his wife."

Kirk Arnold and Carlys Webber were Topic A in the halls and corridors, offices and rest rooms, elevators and conference rooms throughout the SuperWrite building. Branch offices talked and speculated, factory floors were rife with jokes and wisecracks—and it wasn't idle talk. The talk undermined people's confidence in SuperWrite's future, in Howard Mundees's judgment and ability. It spread outside the company to business reporters, to bankers and investment bankers. The company was losing credibility. Kirk and Carlys were deaf and blind to the gossip, rumor, and innuendo that swirled around them. No one was brave enough or foolish enough to warn them; if anyone had been, there was little that either Carlys or Kirk could have done about it anyway. They were successful, they were young, they were attractive. No one felt sorry for them. No one was on their side. Especially not Ray Mundees.

"Everyone thinks you're tolerating it because you and Miriam were in the same situation once," Ray told his father. Howie's own scandalous affair with the woman who was now his wife had been an office affair in excelsis. It had ended with the tight-lipped, cadaverous Howard divorcing his wife of thirty-two years to marry the blond and voluptuous Miriam. "Well, Dad, *are* you sorry for them or do you think you're playing cupid?"

Howard Mundees was caught between a rock and a hard place. SuperWrite stock was worth something again—and Kirk Arnold was responsible. Howie was rich and getting richer. He was also becoming famous—and Carlys Webber was responsible for that. Reporters called him regularly now for comment on the swiftly changing office equipment field. Howie, with an old man's vanity, loved seeing his name in the *Wall Street Journal,* loved speaking to influential business groups, loved seeing articles with his by-line on the business pages. For a backyard tinkerer he'd come a long way. If the situation had been one bit different, he would have fired them both on the spot. But he didn't. He needed them. Kirk for money; Carlys for ego.

Molly also warned him that he was going to have to do something; that the situation was hurting the company. Howie disagreed.

"Let the dumb bastards talk," he said, dismissing her warning. "Talk never meant diddly squat. Ray's just mad because Kirk got him fired."

It had taken Miriam Kuleszchasky a hell of a long time and a hell of a lot of hard knocks to become Miriam Mundees. She had grown up in a grim town in eastern Pennsylvania in which steel was the main product and religion the only diversion. The Poles went to the Catholic church, the Germans went to the Lutheran church, and the blacks went to the Pentecostal church. Miriam's old man— she hated him so much she never called him "father"—was a furnace stoker who drank up his salary every Friday night after work, and when he ran out of money he came home and beat the crap out of her mother, her brother, and her. The minute her brother turned fifteen he got out of that house and out of that town and Miriam had never heard a word from him again. The minute *she* turned fifteen she did the same thing.

Like her brother, she never went back and she tried never to look back. She had few attributes, but she made the most of them. She bleached her blond hair blonder and had her big breasts siliconed bigger with the kiss-off money she extracted from a lover whose name she no longer remembered. Having been frightened to death by her father, she would allow no one to frighten her ever again.

She married twice before she met Howard. The first time her first husband beat her she waited until he fell into a stuporous alcoholic sleep and, packing all her clothes and taking his pride and joy—his beloved white Firebird—left him and Pennsylvania and drove to New York. There she got a clerical job with a real estate broker, had an affair with him, and married him. The day she found him in bed with the receptionist she walked out on him and nailed him pretty good for alimony. Miriam spent the money on a fast-talking real estate developer who, it turned out, developed nothing except his own bank account. Flat broke, Miriam applied for and got a job in the personnel department of SuperWrite. There, she met Howard Mundees, who hadn't had a blow job since high school. The rest was almost easy.

By 1974 Miriam Mundees had what she had always wanted: respectability, money, even social position of a sort. All she wanted was more. Every year Miriam outdid herself for the annual year-end SuperWrite party. Now that Kirk Arnold was in the process of turning SuperWrite around, Miriam pulled out all the stops. This year, the champagne was vintage, the flowers were real, the music was live, and the caterer so exclusive his phone number was unlisted.

Despite her greatly improved status, Miriam still longed to be accepted as part of an elite social circle; the last thing she wanted was a scandal that would remind people of her own past. She had been thrilled when, for a change, that snotty Princeton boy, Kirk Arnold, had accepted one of her invitations. The last thing she expected, though, was that he would have the nerve to bring his girlfriend to her party. There was dead silence as Kirk and Carlys entered the lavishly decorated room. Dead silence—broken, after only a few seconds, by the whispers that rippled through the crowd.

"Jesus Christ!" Miriam whispered to Howie. "He has some nerve bringing her here!"

"Nothing like sleeping with the boss to fill out a wardrobe," Helen Wallenberg said to her boss as she noticed Carlys's elegant black velvet dress.

"It's one thing to have a little something on the side," said Ralph Peretta, the head of manufacturing, to Peter Santangelo from marketing as they both pretended not to stare. "It's something else to rub people's noses in it."

"This time they've gone too far," said Alan Fierstein from accounting to one of the bookkeepers as they glanced from Kirk and Carlys to Ray Mundees, who was taking it all in.

Ray, who usually rigidly controlled his drinking, was on his third Scotch. It was early in the evening, yet his fair skin already showed the traces of scarlet blotches and broken veins. Ray had always liked Bonnie Arnold. He remembered her from last year's party. While other women competed with fancy gowns and hairdos, Bonnie Arnold didn't. Her hair was natural, she wore hardly any makeup, and her clothes were simple and unpretentious. Ray found something soft and touching about Bonnie Arnold. Bonnie Arnold, he thought, was what a woman ought to be. Not one of those aggressive types, like Carlys Webber, who pushed themselves where they weren't wanted. He helped himself to another Scotch and walked over to Kirk.

"What the hell do you think you're doing bringing your girlfriend here?" Ray asked loudly. "Exposing poor Bonnie to public humiliation?"

"Ray, 'poor Bonnie' is thrilled not to be here," Kirk said, but Ray wasn't listening to him; he was listening to the voice in his own head.

"I don't like you," Ray went on, finally standing up to Kirk. "I never liked you—or your fancy ideas. Ten million dollars! For a goddamn word processor that no one even understands! I don't like the way you look or the way you dress or the way you think you're better than everyone who isn't as smart as you are. And, above all, I don't like what you're doing to your wife."

With that Ray threw his drink into Kirk's face and, putting his glass down on a nearby end table, took a wild swing at him. Kirk, shocked at the sudden assault, pushed at Ray and knocked him off-balance.

"Ray! Kirk!" Carlys screamed, inserting herself between them. "Stop!"

"Let me at him!" Ray said, pulling away from Carlys. "I've had it with that bastard!"

He took a step back, poised to take another swing at Kirk Arnold. Miriam, who had seen the fracas from across the room, was there instantly.

"Ray's drunk!" Miriam exclaimed, appalled at her stepson's behavior. It was bad enough for Kirk Arnold to bring his girlfriend; it was worse for Howie's drunken son to take a swing at him and turn her party into a shambles.

"Get him out of here!" she ordered Howie, who took Ray by the arm and propelled him into the kitchen. Miriam turned to her guests and explained, with a laugh, that they hadn't seen what they'd imagined they'd seen. What had *really* happened, Miriam said, was that Kirk Arnold had slipped on the freshly waxed floor and knocked Ray's drink right out of his hand! No one was hurt; no one's feelings were even hurt.

"Just a silly accident!" she said with a too-bright smile, and turned back to Kirk and Carlys.

"Are you all right?" Carlys asked Kirk. She knew, even if he didn't, that they were wading into disaster.

"No damage done. Just a little wet," he said, wiping his face with a handkerchief.

"I want you to leave!" Miriam told Kirk in a nasty whisper, almost hysterical. "Just get out! It's your fault! You and that little whore."

"What?" demanded Kirk in a voice like a rifle shot. The entire room got quiet and every pair of eyes focused on Kirk and Carlys and Miriam. "What did you say?"

"You heard me," said Miriam, wrapped in her fury, oblivious to the attention. "Get out of here and take your little whore with you!"

"Miriam," Kirk said slowly and deliberately so that the whole room could hear. "From what I hear you used to screw Howie on the floor of his office while he was still married to his first wife. Who the hell are you to talk?"

With that he took Carlys by the arm and swept her out of the room.

"We'll have our own party," he told Carlys as they left the Mundees's building and he helped her into the waiting limousine, "and it's going to be a hell of a lot better than theirs!" He took her to the Four Seasons for a champagne dinner, to Studio 54 to celebrity-watch, and to the Empire Diner for a four A.M. breakfast. He took her back to her apartment and kissed her gently.

"There!" he said. "That'll give them something to talk about!" His words were meant to be humorous but his voice was surprisingly husky, and Carlys was moved in a way that she wouldn't have been had he made an ordinary pass.

In one evening she had seen both sides of Kirk Arnold—the best and the worst. The courage, the loyalty, the strength. The recklessness, the bluntness, the unthinking arrogance. Carlys, still thinking him perfect, chose to focus only on his best side.

While Kirk and Carlys felt giddily rebellious, Miriam and Raymond stayed until after the party was over and told

Howie what he already knew: that the Kirk Arnold—Carlys Webber "situation" was poisoning the company. It was interfering with productivity and, if it continued, would certainly be reflected in profits. Miriam thought both Kirk and Carlys should be fired; Raymond was slightly more self-interested.

"Fire her," he said, his pale eyes malicious. "Keep him. He's where the money is. Anyway, it's always the woman's fault when these things get out of hand," he added with a nasty glance at Miriam.

"I know, I know," said Howie impatiently. He had been pushed into a corner and he lashed out. "She's going, that's it!"

The first call he made was to a small moving service owned by a former New York Jet defensive lineman. The second was to his secretary, telling her to open the eleventh-floor offices at six A.M. for the movers. The last call he made that evening was to Molly.

"I'm firing her," he told his sister and before she could comment he added, "I'm telling you, Molly. Not asking you."

The next morning the buzzer of Carlys's apartment sounded at eight A.M. She was dressed for work, expecting no one.

"Delivery!"

Curiously, Carlys opened the door to a man the size and shape of a refrigerator. He had small eyes and a great wiry black beard. He hefted two heavy cartons into Carlys's apartment and handed her an envelope.

"Sign," the human Kelvinator ordered, thrusting a receipt on a clipboard in front of Carlys with a stub of a pencil.

Carlys signed.

Her hands suddenly and unexpectedly shaking, Carlys opened the carton nearest her. On top were the makeup kit she kept in her bottom desk drawer, her folding umbrella and plastic rainboots, the navy cardigan she kept for summer days when the air conditioning was too cold, a copy of *The War Between the Tates,* her battery radio, heated curlers, and two pairs of panty hose still in their unopened cellophane envelopes.

She ripped open the second carton. Folded on top was

her red plastic raincoat. She didn't bother to unpack the rest and by the time she opened the envelope, she already knew what it contained: a termination slip.

She felt literally weak in the knees, filled with humiliation and embarrassment. Deprived of will and energy, she sank into the armchair nearest the foyer, prepared for the tears she knew would come. The tears came, hot and bitter, but then they passed. What came next was anger and, with anger, energy and determination.

I didn't do anything wrong and I'm not going to let them do this to me, she said to herself as she slipped on her coat and got into a taxi.

"The SuperWrite building," she told the driver grimly. "Madison and Forty-eighth."

People stared as Carlys went straight to the penthouse floor.

"You can't go up there!" Howie's secretary said. She got up and stood between Carlys and the door to Howard's office.

Carlys ignored her and, brushing past the startled woman, knocked on Howard Mundees's door at the same instant she opened it. Howard sat behind his desk; Kirk stood at the desk in front of him. Molly and Miriam occupied the sofa. All turned in surprise as Carlys entered the office.

"The nerve!" said Miriam, who had come into the office to enjoy the kill.

"Carlys!" Howie said. His gray eyes darted around, looking everywhere in the room except at her.

"I believe this meeting is about me," Carlys said grimly. Whatever fear she had felt was gone, replaced by righteous fury. She approached Howie's desk and stood over it like an avenging angel. Her open personnel folder was on his desk.

"I'm glad you came," Kirk said, going to stand beside her. Kirk prided himself on never getting angry, but this morning he was livid.

"You're obviously the only one," Carlys replied, glaring at Howie, daring him to look directly at her. "I'd like to know what the hell you think you're doing having my belongings packed up and sent to me?"

His eyes met Carlys's for a moment, then slid away

again. "Carlys, I think it would be better for everyone if you didn't work here anymore."

"It wouldn't be better for me," Carlys said flatly.

"You're a troublemaker," said Miriam, hating in Carlys everything she despised in herself, the ambition, the rejected past, the constant anxious striving. "We don't want people like you."

"Why not?" demanded Carlys, turning toward Miriam for the first time. At a quarter to nine in the morning, Miriam reeked of My Sin and wore a sweater so tight that the bulges of her breasts over the cups of her bra were clearly visible. "Give me one good reason."

"You and Kirk," said Howie finally, taking the bull by the horns. "That's enough of a reason! All SuperWrite's employees do now is talk; they don't work anymore."

"As I was saying," Kirk interjected coldly. "If she goes, I go." He was playing with a sharp metal letter opener, jabbing it at Howie and then back toward himself. It looked almost like a dagger as its blade flashed in his hand.

"The hell with them both," said Miriam, addressing Howie. "We can get along without either of them."

"Shut up, Miriam!" snapped Molly, speaking for the first time. She had come in from Locust Valley, knowing that she'd have to save Howie from himself. Firing Carlys Webber was stupid for about a dozen reasons, not one of which had occurred to Howie or his peanut-brained, big-titted wife or his idiot son. No wonder the goddamn company had almost gone under.

"Howie, for Christ's sake, use your brain! SuperWrite needs Kirk and it needs Carlys." Molly turned to Carlys. "Of course, we didn't plan to abandon you," she said, knowing better than to smile.

"Then what *were* you planning?" Carlys asked, meeting Molly's sharp blue eyes head on. "Because if I don't like it, I'm going to see a lawyer."

"That won't be necessary," said Molly, whose already high respect for Carlys rose even higher at her threat of legal action. She admired worthwhile adversaries. She would have done the same thing in Carlys's place. She knew what it was like to be a woman in a man's world. "I happen to know how much Joshua Hynes wants the SuperWrite account. And I happen to think that you've been invaluable to the company."

Molly, the master manipulator, went into action. Two weeks later the *Times* ran an item that Barron & Hynes had won the now-hot SuperWrite account and that Carlys Webber had been hired as an account executive to supervise that account. SuperWrite, the business press reported, negotiated a new and expensive contract with Kirk Arnold, who was officially named president of the company, the first nonfamily member to hold that position.

There were those, of course, who continued to say that Carlys became the first woman account executive at Barron & Hynes because of her relationship with Kirk Arnold. No one, though, ever denied that she did a brilliant job.

C H A P T E R   10

There were striking parallels—unnoticed by Kirk and unknown to Carlys—between Kirk Arnold's courtship of his first wife and his courtship of his second wife. Both courtships followed periods of profound personal loss. His courtship of Bonnie followed the tragic death of his father; his courtship of Carlys followed the shock of his divorce from Bonnie.

The day that Carlys left SuperWrite Kirk called her four times. The next day, half a dozen times. At first, still conscious of the blaze of gossip that had surrounded them, they were careful to keep their conversations completely businesslike. They discussed marketing strategy for the Alphatec, Kirk kept Carlys informed about manufacturing progress and problems, and she submitted releases and information sheets to him for review. The excitement between them did not diminish and now, with no eyes on them, they allowed their hands to linger on each other as they handed papers back and forth, and their eyes to meet in unguarded moments. They often worked late and fell into the habit of having dinner together at the Chalet Suisse, with their papers and briefcases on the table. They no longer cared so much who saw them, and it was Kirk who broke the impasse when he began to talk about his marriage.

Just as Bonnie had helped Kirk over the loss of his father, Carlys helped him over the loss of his wife. She helped him emotionally; she helped him practically. He blamed himself for the divorce.

"It was my fault. I was selfish," he said, confiding in her, needing to talk to someone. "I didn't pay enough attention to Bonnie. I was too preoccupied with business."

"From what you say, though," Carlys pointed out, "Bonnie was preoccupied with the children during the early years of your marriage and with her own career in the later years. It sounds as if she was as much to blame as you were."

Kirk thought over what she said.

"Maybe I wasn't so bad," he said, beginning to feel better about himself. He listed the ways in which he had been a good husband: "I always put her first. I always gave her everything. I was always there when she really needed me."

Carlys was flattered that Kirk confided in her. Michelle warned her not to let herself get carried away.

"Divorced men!" exclaimed Michelle, who'd been through her share. "They use you as a free psychiatrist and when they've recovered from the guilt, they go ahead and marry someone else. Just make sure he isn't using you."

In the beginning Carlys told herself that Kirk was one more in a long line of men, starting with her father, who had used her. Kirk, at forty-one, had never lived alone. He'd gone from his parents' house to Princeton to Bonnie. He lived in luxury in the SuperWrite apartment at the Carlyle but he had never bought socks or underwear, had never taken shoes to the shoemaker, had never, as far as Carlys could tell, bought a quart of milk or written a check. She stocked the refrigerator for him, showed him how to organize his laundry, kept his personal checkbook for him, and saw to it that the credit cards he carried were up-to-date.

"You're a fool," Norma said. Michelle had seen Carlys as a free psychiatrist; Norma said that Kirk was using her as a free housekeeper and secretary. "Men don't fall in love with women who buy them socks," she advised.

Carlys nodded. "I know you're right," she said."But he needs me."

Being needed was, she admitted, the one sure way to her heart.

Because Carlys did not know all there was to know about Kirk she accepted him at face value. She didn't know—because he didn't tell her—that the losses in his life had been even more devastating than her own. She didn't know—because he didn't know—that life had made Kirk Arnold into a man who was prepared to be hurt. He was more like Carlys than she ever imagined. The difference between them was that he hid his scars better than she did. He had had more practice; he had more to hide—not only from other people, but from himself as well. What she *did* know was that there were surprising parallels in their lives. Kirk had lost his father when he was twenty; she had lost her mother when she was fifteen. Kirk was an only child; so was she.

"I always wanted a brother or a sister," she said, remembering her envy of classmates who had brothers and sisters. "I even thought fighting would be fun."

Kirk nodded."I know what you mean." There were tears in his eyes and Carlys thought they reflected a yearning as intense as her own. She put her hand on his and thought that she would do anything, give anything, to make him happy. Behind the success, behind the glamour, he hurt just the way she did.

Even as her fantasies about him became more loving, more erotic, she told herself that Norma and Michelle were right. He was using her as a free psychiatrist, as an emotional dumping ground. She was good enough to act as an unpaid housekeeper, period. She was the interim woman, the woman a man saw as a convenience, the woman a man kept around until he met someone else and fell in love. She was dreaming of *him* and *he* was thinking only of himself. She had no chance with him, none at all, and she was not only asking but almost pleading to be hurt. Nothing had changed. Kirk was just another Winn in a different guise. He was using her to get over his divorce and she was a fool.

But although it was Carlys who thought about love, it was Kirk who first spoke about it. They were at the Chalet Suisse. He'd just asked for the check. It was late, the restaurant was almost empty, espresso cups stood on the table.

"This summer Bonnie asked me if I was in love with you," he said suddenly. "I told her I wasn't."

"Of course not," said Carlys, speaking too quickly. "We're just business associates."

"No we're not," he said, overriding her. "I think Bonnie was right. I think I am in love with you."

Carlys felt her heart jump into her throat. Love? Had he mentioned *love?* Her heart lodged in her throat, stopping her breath and her thoughts, and she couldn't speak. He interpreted her silence as another denial.

"Does that bother you?" His voice was soft, barely audible. He was afraid he was making a fool of himself. He had never touched her and he was telling her that he loved her. He waited for her to tell him he was being ridiculous.

"No," she said, almost breaking into tears. "It doesn't bother me." Tentatively, not sure of what would happen next, she smiled at him.

He reached across the table and took her hand. It was the first time he had deliberately touched her.

"I'm glad," he said simply, and with those words a bridge was crossed.

"I didn't realize how much I wanted to make love to you," he said later in Carlys's apartment as he held her in his arms.

"And I. . . ." whispered Carlys. She had waited so long to touch him and be touched by him, to hold him and be held by him that her skin seemed to come alive under his hands. She touched his hand gently, caressing it, thinking that this must be a dream, that it couldn't really be happening. Not with him. Not to her.

"It's going to be like this for us always," he said as he touched her face gently, memorizing the texture of her skin with his fingertips and then with his lips. "Isn't it?"

"Always," breathed Carlys, believing and yet not believing his words, having been too often lied to by men whom she wanted to love. She lost herself in the moment and refused to think about the future. She didn't want to be hurt again. She didn't want to be Cinderella. She didn't want the clock to strike midnight and find that, cruelly, the magic was over.

In February, on St. Valentine's Day, Carlys received three dozen long-stemmed classic, exquisite, romantic red roses from Ronaldo Maia, the exclusive Upper East Side florist. Three pounds of champagne truffles came from Teuscher on East Sixty-first Street, via the chocolate geniuses of Zurich, along with the biggest bottle of Joy Kirk could find. As he waited for the salesgirl to write up the sale, he realized he had never sent Bonnie a Valentine's Day gift. In the early years, he hadn't had the money; in later years when he did have the money they'd been married too long for romantic gestures.

"The most interesting thing happened! Flowers and candy and perfume arrived on my doorstep today," Carlys teased when, after a full day's work, they were together. "Who do you think could have sent them?"

"I don't know," he said, taking her into his arms. "But they'd better be *my* flowers, *my* candy, and *my* perfume. If not, you're in plenty of trouble."

Enraptured by the attention, flattered by the extravagance of his gifts, and still feeling a little like an impostor, Carlys received his offerings with a too-long-denied pleasure in sheer material luxury. Later she would learn that Kirk, who could barely express his feelings with words, relied on gifts. Eventually she would long for words.

On the first Saturday morning of March, at eight-thirty, Kirk appeared at Carlys's apartment. She was in her robe, drinking coffee.

"Do you have a bathing suit?" he asked apropos of apparently nothing. His face glowed with the cold; snowflakes clung to his dark topcoat.

"A bathing suit?" she asked, giggling at his outlandish question. "What do I need a bathing suit for? It's twenty-eight degrees out. It's snowing and sleeting and worse is forecast!"

"Some of the time," he said with a smile, "we're going to have to be on beaches with other people around."

"Beaches? This time of year?"

"Sure," he said. "In St. Kitts. I think we deserve some time to ourselves."

He waited while she packed and he carried her suitcase down to his waiting limousine. It was a nasty day with a mixture of freezing rain and snow pelting the city. The chauffeur held an umbrella over Carlys's head as she made her way from the door of her building to the car. As she settled into the backseat she felt sorry for the people on the street coping with packages, umbrellas that twisted wrong-way-out, and mounds of slush left from the previous week's snowstorm. She knew, suddenly, what it was like to be someone who rode in a limousine and, to her amazement, she didn't feel guilty about it. She adored it. She had, she told herself, earned it and if she didn't deserve it, who did?

*The Golden Lemon is private, personal, and very luxuri-*ous. It is one of those rare places that sophisticated travelers know about and prefer to keep to themselves. The owner, Arthur Leaman, had bought an abandoned sugar mill that stood on a velvet-soft beach of black volcanic sand and converted the stone structure into an inn with a handful of rooms—all different, all uniquely charming, furnished with fine antiques and bright fabrics and irresistible art and accessories. Arthur knew as much about food as he did about comfort and beauty, and the graciously served meals featured local specialties—callaloo soup and christophene soufflés and lightly sautéed fish fresh from the nearby sea. As beautiful as the setting, as delicious as the food, as ravishing as the warm, indigo sea, it formed only a shimmering backdrop to the drama that was going on between Kirk and Carlys. Their week in St. Kitts was what changed a tentative romance into a blazing passion and a wounded husband into an intense and ardent lover.

"I want you," he told Carlys over and over, making love to her in the lazy, tropical afternoons. "I have to have you and I'm not ever going to let you go."

"I love you," he told her, holding her and kissing her and stroking her on a private, sun-drenched beach in the freshness of the morning. "I love you. I adore you. There's never been a woman like you."

"I'm going to die," he said, meshing his body, his rhythms, his passion with hers in the blazingly clear star-studded tropical midnights, "if I can't be in you and on you and with you. I need you to live."

As a husband, Kirk had forgotten about sex, about its thrilling sensations and voluptuous possibilities. He had forgotten (or had he ever known?) about the pleasure of licking an erect nipple with a champagne-filmed tongue. He rediscovered the tastes of a beloved woman, of her mouth and her skin and hair. He was an adventurer in the further horizons of sensual pleasure, a man in his early forties with the sexual appetite of a boy in his twenties. He looked back on his marriage now and wondered about sex. Where had it gone? Had he ever done the things with Bonnie that he did with Carlys? Had he ever felt about Bonnie the way he felt about Carlys? If he had, he couldn't remember.

In St. Kitts Carlys began to think that she was wrong about feeling like a Cinderella inhabiting a private fairy tale. She began to think that she was wrong to feel like an impostor. She began to believe that he loved her.

In April, on a day when summer seemed a possibility instead of just another promise that would never be kept, Kirk took her to City Island, where they ate steamers in a waterfront restaurant. When Carlys's lobster arrived, each bright orange-red claw held a diamond earring. Carlys, who had never owned anything so extraordinarily valuable or wildly beautiful, was overwhelmed. Her hands shook so much that Kirk had to fasten the earrings to her ears as she leaned across the table toward him. When he had finished, he handed her the compact from her handbag and she looked at herself in its mirror, barely believing what she saw. Sudden tears pricked at her eyes and she had a brief memory of herself at the Ultima counter in Bloomingdale's. Knowing that people were staring, but not caring, Carlys kept glancing at her reflection, unable to say a word. Her throat was full, choking back her voice.

"You're welcome," said Kirk with the perfect timing of a stand-up comic. Another thing he had forgotten during his marriage was the incredible pleasure of making someone else almost unbearably happy.

In May, on Decoration Day, Kirk took Carlys for a walk in Central Park, a walk reminiscent of a walk he'd once taken with Bonnie Willsey along Lakeside Drive. Except then he had been a young man in pain; now he was a mature man in love. The Japanese cherry and dogwood trees were in bloom, making splashes of pink and white against the clean blue sky. Carlys and Kirk walked along, absorbed in each other. For once, even the ghetto blasters seemed to be playing Mozart.

"I know now," Kirk told her, "that I wasn't the best of husbands. I also know that Bonnie wasn't always the best of wives. I was bitter but I'm not anymore. I'm sad—but I'm determined not to make the same mistakes twice."

He paused, turned, and looked at her, holding her eyes with his.

"Is there going to be a twice?" she asked softly. Her heart stopped, and so did time itself as she waited for his answer.

"If you want there to be."

"We're getting married!" Carlys told Norma later, almost beside herself with happiness. "I can't believe it! But I *do* believe it! He proposed. He really did! Oh, Norma, I'm so happy. Can you believe it? Me? Getting married?"

"Married?" Norma asked wryly. "In this liberated day and age? How unchic!"

Carlys gave her the finger and Norma grinned.

"Carlys, I'm so happy for you!" she exclaimed, hugging her friend. "He's divine! You'll be the happiest couple in the world!"

"I know," Carlys said, almost weepy with joy. "We really had to struggle to find each other. And I know that we'll be happy every single day for the rest of our lives. We both deserve it. We've both lived and learned. We're not a couple of starry-eyed kids anymore."

Norma was thrilled for Carlys. At the same time she thought of her own stagnant life and knew that she would never find a White Knight of her own. She hugged and kissed Carlys and felt so jealous that she thought she would die.

"I'm getting married," Carlys told Winn. She had asked him to meet her for a drink. They sat in the Brasserie, more or less empty at five-thirty, its spare, cool design reflecting Carlys's own feelings toward her former lover.

"No kidding?" he said flippantly. Then he swallowed hard.

"No kidding," she replied.

"For real?" he asked, running his hands through his hair. He tried for insouciance again but his eyes blinked rapidly, betraying him. He had been thinking of proposing to her one of these days as soon as he was sure he was ready for marriage. He toyed with his glass of white wine.

"For real," Carlys replied and, in a way, she felt sorry for him. There was a moment of awkward silence while they looked at each other, unsure of what to say or do next. Finally Winn got up.

"So, good luck," he said hoarsely, not meeting her eyes. He paid the bill and got up to go. "I'll call you sometime."

As he got to the door Carlys noticed him stop and look at himself for a moment in the glass door's reflection before he stepped out onto Fifty-third Street. She realized then how often he looked at himself. She wondered why she had never noticed it before and sat on alone at the table finishing her glass of wine. She realized that Winn had been on the verge of tears and she felt strangely wistful at the ending of a sad part of her life.

As Carlys had known he would, her father approved of Kirk. For once Jacob Webber could find nothing to criticize.

"He's outstanding," her father had said when he'd met Kirk. "Outstanding."

"Outstanding" had been, for as long as Carlys could remember, her father's highest accolade—rarely, very rarely, bestowed.

Carlys began to dream about her wedding, dreams that had nothing to do with a young bride's visions of long white gowns and misty veils and orange blossoms. Carlys was thirty years old and Kirk had been married before. Theirs was a time of living together and open marriage, single mothers, executive women, and men who were getting in touch with their nurturing feelings. A long white gown and orange blossoms seemed ludicrous but the possibilities that remained were delicious. Should she wear a cream Chanel suit? Or a sophisticated Jean Muir jersey dress? Should they be married in her apartment or at the

Carlyle, where Kirk kept a suite, or in some romantic room hired for the occasion? Should they serve vintage champagne and wedding cake at a small reception or have an elegant, private dinner?

Carlys was giddy with the possibilities and she planned her wedding with the certainty that was growing in her day by lovely day. She finally began to accept the fact that it wasn't a dream. It was all real. It was happening to her, with him.

Carlys and Kirk were married by a New York State Supreme Court justice in an elegant private room at the St. Regis in June 1975, four years after they'd first met. At forty-one, Kirk Arnold was a distinguished and romantic bridegroom, unable to keep his eyes or his hands from his new wife. Carlys, in the cream-colored Chanel suit with which she'd resolved her delicious indecision, was a bride who radiated a joy so intense that it seemed to burn from within her. Jacob Webber gave his daughter away and Kirk's mother, Elyssa, and her second husband flew in from Palm Springs where they were living. Geoff and Lucy, Kirk's children, sent wires of congratulations. Norma was Carlys's only attendant. The wedding was discreet, joyous, and loving. The storms were behind Kirk and Carlys; their future seemed clear and untroubled.

The next day they left in the SuperWrite jet for a passionate and romantic brief honeymoon in Nova Scotia. When they returned Carlys sold her apartment and, with Kirk's advice, invested the large profit in IBM stock. She moved into the luxurious SuperWrite apartment at the Carlyle in which Kirk had been living since his divorce.

"A very fancy address for newlyweds," Carlys said, impressed by the paneled rooms and French furniture and silk curtains.

"But only temporary," promised Kirk, thinking how intimidated Bonnie would have been at the fashionable East Side address and how she would have expressed her intimidation by criticizing everyone and everything and refusing to have sex with him. This marriage, he knew, would be different, happier, better. This second marriage was the *right* marriage. "One day soon we'll get a place of our own. Even fancier."

"Meanwhile," said Carlys, smiling. "I'll just have to suffer."

She wondered how many brides had set up housekeeping at the Carlyle. She had always dreamt of falling madly in love. She had never even imagined that money, success, and glamour would come along as part of the package. In the beginning she thought that it all belonged to Kirk. Later she would realize that she, too, had earned money, had achieved success, was, in others' eyes, glamorous. She was, still, in the early months of her marriage, a woman who defined herself in terms of the past. She had come a long way, but her inner image still hadn't completely caught up with external reality.

C H A P T E R   11

For Carlys, being married made all the difference. Never mind the Me-decade propaganda. Never mind doing-your-own-thing and finding-your-own-space and being-your-own-person. Never mind the newly extolled joys of being single, the suddenly unfashionable images of marriage, and the way saying Ms. was supposed to make all women equal. Never mind women's lib and the search for the perfect orgasm, never mind alternate life-styles, sexual freedom, and getting-divorced-and-living-happily-ever-after. Now that Carlys was a Mrs. she was somebody. She noticed the difference in the way other people treated her right away. She noticed the difference in herself a little more slowly.

"I always wondered why someone as nice as you wasn't married," Tom Steinberg said on Carlys's first day back in the office. Carlys opened her eyes in surprise. Tom had never said one word about her being nice, single, married, or the Virgin Mary. "I'm happy for you, Carlys. Now you can settle down," Tom went on. "Virginia is thrilled for you, too. She wants to know if you and Kirk can come to dinner. We're having some people in a week from Saturday."

"Virginia?" Carlys raised her eyebrows.

Tom nodded, oblivious.

Carlys had worked for Tom for more than five years. In that time she had never once been invited to the Steinbergs' Central Park West apartment. Although she met Virginia Steinberg twice a year, once at the Christmas party and once at the Fourth of July picnic, Virginia never remembered who Carlys was and Carlys had to reintroduce herself semiannually. The count stood at ten. Virginia, who had streaked hair and wore Elsa Peretti by day and David Webb by night, went to gym class, the hairdresser, and Bendel's and assuaged her guilt with volunteer work at Mount Sinai. Virginia wanted to be Françoise de la Renta, but she had neither the talent, the taste, nor the right husband. Instead she did the best she could with what she had, which was plenty of money and plenty of ambition. Carlys realized that, single, she had been invisible; now that she was married, she had suddenly become desirable.

"Carlys!" Virginia Steinberg hugged and kissed Carlys, enveloping her in a cloud of Norell, greeting her as if they'd been best friends from boarding school. "How divine of you to come! And Kirk! It's wonderful to see you again!"

"Nice to see you, Virginia," Kirk said wryly and winked at Carlys. On the way over to the Steinbergs' he'd told Carlys that the last time he'd been to their apartment had been when he'd been at Barron & Hynes and still married to Bonnie. Bonnie, as usual, had hated all of the business entertaining connected with Kirk's career. That evening Bonnie, who rarely drank, had had two martinis, and during the appetizer she had left the dinner table, wandered into Virginia and Tom's bedroom, and thrown up on Virginia's Porthault-draped bed. Virginia had had a tantrum, and banished the Arnolds from her dinner table. Now, four years later, Virginia seemed oblivious to the fact that she had never noticed Carlys's existence before and that Kirk Arnold, who hadn't been in her house for four years, was now there with a new wife.

"You two are my favorite people!" trilled Virginia, introducing Kirk and Carlys to her other guests, a judicious mix of social climbers, captains of industry, and Barron &

Hynes's current and would-be clients. Virginia's dinner parties were strictly business and the fact was that she was very good at giving them. She was too insecure not to be.

"You know, Carlys, this is going to be very good for your career. Being married, I mean," Tom told her over coffee and chocolate truffles. For someone who had once hated and feared Kirk, Tom had swooned over him all evening. Kirk's power seemed to have rubbed off on Carlys, and Tom, who had always patronized her slightly, now buttered her up, too. "You'll really be able to take your job seriously from now on."

"I've *always* taken my job seriously," she said, annoyed.

"But now you'll be able to take it even *more* seriously," Tom insisted, aware that David Daye, an economist for a small but excellent venture capital firm, was impressed to meet Kirk, whose career he had followed for several years. Tom noticed that David and Carlys had spent quite a bit of time in intense conversation. Tom had been trying to get David Daye to bring his account to Barron & Hynes for three years. Perhaps, he thought, introducing him to Kirk and Carlys would do the trick. "Being married will be wonderful for your career. Wonderful! And to think," he mused, congratulating himself, "that *I* found you!"

Carlys had never given any thought to what effect marriage might have on her career. She had thought that her career depended on how hard and how effectively she worked.

"Not necessarily," Kirk told her on the way home. "A career often depends more on your contacts than on what you know."

He was right and Carlys realized it as soon as he pointed it out. The irony was that she had had to get married in order to be able to meet the people who might like her. Single, she'd been a hard worker who stayed more or less invisible in the office; married, she could circulate. Married, her light was no longer hidden.

After a Monday morning planning-committee meeting Peter Salzany walked back to her office with her. What he said only confirmed that a married Carlys was simply perceived as more businesslike and more serious than a single Carlys.

"You'll be able to give a whole lot more to your job now, won't you?" he asked. Peter, who was small and wiry, considered himself in the white-hot center of everything new and everything now. He had been the first in the office to be Rolfed, the first to roller skate to work, the first to wear a Walkman at meetings, and the first to sport yellow-tinted Porsche-Carrera wraparound glasses. He was proud of the fact that he read other people's mail (How else would I know what's going on at the office? he said blandly) and he had a predilection for telling malicious, unflattering stories about the clients to whom he owed his very handsome living.

"I've always given a lot to my job," Carlys said. She managed more or less to ignore Tom, but there was something about Peter's blithe arrogance that brought out the sadist in her. "And I intend to continue."

"I don't mean to be insulting," Peter said, earnestly tagging along with her. He was shorter than she, and she wasn't tall. She also noticed that Peter actually liked being put down. It made him anxious to please. "I just thought that now you won't have to go out all the time. Your life will be more stable. You'll have evenings and weekends. . . ."

As Peter rambled on, explaining himself, Carlys wondered what kind of wild image he had had of her. Single, she had been a loser, a wallflower, involved in masochistic affairs or lurching from one awful blind date to the next. Married, she could go out every night of the week and party all weekend; single, she had taken a full briefcase home night after night, happy to have something to do. Peter, obviously, thought all single women were flamboyant *Cosmo* girls, darting from man to man, party to party, singles' bar to singles' bar. Well, perception and sensitivity were hardly Peter's strengths. Still, the unfairness of the stereotype, the grotesque difference between the reality and his fantasy were upsetting. Marriage, Carlys realized, *did* make a difference. More of a difference than she had ever imagined.

Joshua Hynes, the president of Barron & Hynes, thin, bald, and extraordinarily able, also complimented Carlys on her marriage in a way that made her realize that being married totally changed people's opinion of her.

"You've always been a hard worker," he had said in his gravelly, froggy voice, after wishing her every happiness and telling her what a lucky man Kirk was to get her. "But now you'll really be able to concentrate, Carlys. I want you to make the agency pitch to Ada Hutchinson. She inherited Yankee Air from her husband and she needs some savvy PR. She's a tough old bird, but now that you're married she'll take you seriously."

Joshua had never trusted Carlys to make the first presentation to a potential new client. He did now because, he made it perfectly clear, she was married and therefore reliable and trustworthy. If it weren't so pathetic, Carlys thought, it would be ridiculous. She was the same person she'd been two weeks ago—but not according to the people around her.

Serious . . . stable . . . hardworking . . . reliable. That was the way her co-workers saw Carlys now that she was married; although Carlys had seen herself that way all along. Nevertheless, the fact of her marriage had obviously caused an unanticipated transformation.

Men who had power over her now took her seriously. It felt good to be accepted as an equal, to have the slight, almost imperceptible edge of sexual tension taken out of business situations. But it wasn't the change in image that Carlys loved, it was the man she married whom she loved. Kirk Arnold. The man she had loved even before she had dared to admit it to herself.

Just as their courtship, following the crisis at SuperWrite and Kirk's divorce, had been somewhat sober and restrained, marriage seemed to take the lid off their emotions and they ran to each other every evening in ecstasy.

"I finally got out of that taxi at Seventy-first Street. It was *creeping* and I just had to get to you sooner," Carlys said, throwing herself into Kirk's arms. She was slightly out of breath from running the few blocks, her cheeks flushed, her hair windblown.

"You're heart is pounding," he said, touching her breast. "It's that jogging you're not used to."

"It's that love I can't get enough of," she answered and dragged him into the bedroom.

"You've turned me into a madman," he told her when they'd been married two months. "A sex maniac. I'm a public embarrassment."

"We're a public embarrassment," Carlys said. Their happiness was ecstatic, their expression of it almost indecent. They couldn't keep their hands off each other. Their friends teased them about it, and they were also slightly uncomfortable about it. Carlys and Kirk held hands at dinner parties, each maneuvering a fork with only one hand. At one party, while coffee was being served in someone's living room, Kirk got up while the host was pontificating about Carter's Middle-East policy and crossed the room. He went over to Carlys and embraced her, kissing her intensely, temporarily bringing all conversation to a dead halt.

Another time, at a high-profile cocktail party, when Carlys excused herself to go to the bathroom Kirk followed her, and locking the door, they made fast, hot love standing up in the elegant pink marble powder room.

"Pretty soon we won't be invited anywhere," Carlys told him the evening of a party when they'd found themselves on a pile of fur coats kissing passionately until, without even saying good-bye to their hosts, they snuck out the service exit and went home, fleeing to the privacy of their own bedroom.

"We'll be social outcasts," he said and then leered at her, a comic seducer. "All the more time to ravish you, my dear."

Carlys had read somewhere that sex supposedly died after marriage.

"Did you know," she asked Kirk on their six-month wedding anniversary, "that married sex is supposed to be boring?"

"Where did you hear *that?*" he asked.

"That's what all the magazines say," said Carlys. "That's why they're always writing articles about how to put the excitement back into your marriage."

"If there's any more excitement in this marriage," he said, reaching for her, "I'm going to have a heart attack."

They giggled, the two of them sexually intoxicated, sharing their marvelous secret.

Kirk brought Carlys flowers so often that she jokingly called him "the florist's best friend." He wasn't exactly Tiffany's worst enemy either. There were gold bean Elsa Peretti earrings, coral beads threaded with crimson silk, and exquisite stationery monogrammed with Carlys's new initials.

One autumn evening during their first year of marriage Carlys arrived home to find that Kirk had filled the suite with hundreds of white helium balloons. They hovered near the ceiling, each tied with a gold ribbon streamer, and each saying "I love you" in gold paint.

"It's incredible!" Carlys exclaimed.

"I wanted white doves, too," he said, "but they weren't house trained so I decided we'd have to do without them."

They giggled and fell into each other's arms.

On Christmas morning Carlys awoke to a shower of pale yellow rose petals and, under the Christmas tree, a dark mink polo coat.

"I don't know what to say," she said, overcome with emotion. "I don't know how to thank you."

"*I* know," he said, and they made love on the soft fur.

Just as marriage brought out the lover in Kirk, it brought out in Carlys a beautiful and sensuous woman. Men everywhere, who had once failed to notice that Carlys existed, who forgot her name and threw the piece of paper with her telephone number on it away, now reacted to her presence on the street, in a room, at a party. "Hey, beautiful!" a construction worker would yell, and while other women might be offended, Carlys wasn't. She always smiled and waved back.

Tom Steinberg, in his inept way, commented on the difference: "You know, Carlys, I never thought so before, but you're awfully good looking." Carlys took his words as he intended them—as a compliment.

A researcher who worked for Lansing Coons kept inviting her to lunch. She kept turning him down, but did it in a way that didn't discourage him. Because she had gone so long without attention, attention was something of which she couldn't quite get enough.

Peter, who was married and who bragged about his affairs, told her that now that she was married they ought to have an affair.

"I prefer married women," he told her, blinking his eyes rapidly behind the too-big Porsche glasses that made him look like a near-sighted, lecherous beetle. "That way both have a lot to lose. The risk adds to the excitement, don't you think?"

"I suppose so," Carlys said, slightly stunned. "I never thought about it."

"Well, think about it," he directed. "You and me, Carlys," he suggested, spelling it out. "We wouldn't be bad. We might be good together. Very good."

Peter did not let the subject drop. Over and over he tried to sell Carlys on the idea of a sexy, inconsequential, pleasant, no-strings affair.

"Your husband wouldn't have to know. Nor would my wife. You really ought to think it over, Carlys," he proposed. "The fact is, I find that having an affair now and then really adds a little spice to marriage. Especially after you've been married a few years and the sex gets a little routine."

Even though Carlys considered Peter outrageous—and even verging on ridiculous—she also thought that he was, in his hysterical, Now!-crazed way, both interesting and magnetic. She would, of course, never consider having an affair with him, but still, his persistence was flattering.

Just as men began reacting to Carlys differently, so did everyone else. Her father no longer treated her as a combination secretary-cook-maid.

"You've grown up," he told her one Sunday evening when she and Kirk took him out to dinner. Jacob Webber, who had refused to eat in a restaurant with Carlys when she'd been single, now looked forward to the twice-a-month Sunday dinners with his daughter and his son-in-law. Carlys no longer dreaded the time she spent with her father; she began to appreciate him: his integrity, his shrewdness about people, the way he really did want the best for her.

"I love you, Dad," she told him, meaning it, as she kissed him good night. And because her father, although conservative, was very good with investments, Carlys began to give him money to put aside for her and Kirk. Jacob, with something to occupy his sharp mind, now seemed younger, less crabby, less obsessed with the minutiae of his daily life. Now that she was married her father openly appreciated her, and Carlys responded. Little by little she began to stop thinking of herself as a wallflower and an impostor.

Her relationships with Kirk's children also changed the way in which Carlys saw herself. Carlys had read so much about the horrors of stepchildren that she feared meeting

Geoff and Lucy. She decided ahead of time that she would not try to play mommy and that she would not try to win them away from Bonnie. The result was that instead of reacting to her with hostility, Geoff and Lucy seemed to see her as an ally.

Lucy admired Carlys and, because she did, wanted to be as successful as Carlys was. Lucy put away her *I Ching* and love beads and proceeded to get the best marks she'd ever gotten.

"Carlys inspired me," Lucy told her father.

"You had more influence on her in a year than Bonnie and I did in eighteen," Kirk told her happily.

"Not really," said Carlys, but she did see herself flatteringly reflected through the eyes of the younger woman.

Geoff was suspicious of Carlys at first, but when he realized that she wasn't going to try to replace his mother he began to relax with her and confide in her. He told her that it had been difficult for him, growing up with such a dynamic, and often distant, father. Carlys listened without judging and Geoff learned that she wouldn't betray his confidences.

"I can tell you things I can't tell my parents," Geoff told her, and gradually, as Carlys explained the stresses and tensions Kirk had faced in the years that Geoff was growing up, Geoff began to resent his father less and the distance between Kirk and his son began to diminish.

"I never realized it before, but Geoff's a terrific kid," Kirk told Carlys when Geoff got appointed to a committee that set up craft programs in hospitals and schools. Geoff took after Bonnie's side of the family more than Kirk's and for years Kirk had thought of Geoff as "soft." Now he saw Geoff's kindness and impressive manual skills through Carlys's eyes. "He's good at all sorts of things I'm not. I would never have seen it without you."

"You were terrific today," Tom told Carlys after she'd made the third and final presentation to Yankee Air. "You used to be sort of tentative. Today, you went in there and *sold* them!"

What she had done, and she knew it, was to go in there and sell herself. It made all the difference in the world. It also made all the difference in her relationship with Howie and SuperWrite. Because Carlys no longer worked at SuperWrite but at SuperWrite's agency, she found she had the power of the agency and its resources—its research and media departments, its copy and promotional departments— behind her, giving her an authority with Howie that she had never had when she had been a mere employee. On the other hand, being married to the architect of SuperWrite's renaissance gave her complete access to the company.

Carlys and Kirk spent a lot of their time talking about SuperWrite, its plans, its problems, its prospects. On a Saturday afternoon walk along Second Avenue, they passed one of the new video game arcades. Attracted by the noise, the bustle, the crowd, they had elbowed their way in, struck by the fascination young people showed toward the games.

"If schools had word processors, I'll bet kids would be just as interested in their classes as they are in those games," Carlys told Kirk that night as they got ready for bed.

"I'm sure you're right," he said. "I'll bet the school system would be delighted to have some Alphatecs. Who do we know on the school board?"

"No one that I can think of," Carlys said. "But I do know Patti Harris. She worked in Ed Koch's office. I'll call her. She'll tell me who to talk to."

The announcement of the donation of a dozen Alphatec word processors to a Harlem public school for gifted children, and the arrangement for the school system to buy additional Alphatecs at advantageous prices, made the first page of the Metro section of *The New York Times*, and Carlys and Kirk shared a private thrill that their bedtime conversation ended up in the newspapers. The knowledge that what they discussed interested and influenced other people added an extra element of excitement to their marriage.

"Mrs. Kirk Arnold," Carlys said on their first anniversary. "I can still hardly believe it. Sometimes I think I'm going to wake up and find that it's all just been a beautiful dream."

"It's no dream," he told her, and gave her a ruby and diamond ring for their anniversary.

"Do you think we'll ever get tired of each other?" she asked him later. She sat with his head in her lap and she stroked his face, tracing his lips and nose and the scar that bisected his eyebrow, aware of the contour of his bones and the shape of his skull. Physically, he was fascinating to her. She could never get enough of touching him and tasting him and smelling him.

"Does the sun ever get tired of rising?" he replied, smiling up at her and pulling her down to him, kissing her again, as though he had never kissed her before.

The first year of their marriage was a honeymoon. Carlys was wildly, ecstatically happy. She thought that she was the luckiest woman who had ever lived and that Kirk was the most wonderful man in the entire world. She breathed and ate and slept and woke for him. She lived for him and, if she had had to, she would have died for him. She did everything she could to make herself worthy of him. She spent more money on herself and dressed better than she ever had; she spent more time on exercise and massage and makeup and hair and looked better than she had ever looked; she rested enough and slept enough and ate sensibly. She worked hard and succeeded—for him. The result was that in doing everything for Kirk, Carlys felt better than she ever had—better about herself, her life, and her future.

Little by little she began to think that she wasn't an impostor after all. She began to become convinced that the Carlys that other people saw and admired *was* the real Carlys. Now and then she wondered about Bonnie. How, she asked herself, could a woman who was lucky enough to be married to Kirk Arnold even *think* about having an affair?

C H A P T E R 12

In the second year of their marriage Carlys and Kirk bought an apartment at 11 East Seventy-ninth Street between Madison and Fifth. Single, with only herself to think of, Carlys had always been reluctant to spend money on her surroundings, even when she owned her own apartment. Married, motivated by the wish to make a husband proud and happy, she discovered that she had a talent for making a comfortable and pleasant home. She threw herself into Saturday auctions at Doyle and Parke Bernet, she haunted Bloomie's fifth floor and Conran's, she subscribed to *Architectural Digest, House & Garden,* and *House Beautiful.* Dreaming of a beautiful life for her husband and herself she came home every night carrying a tote bag bulging with swatches and samples and paint chips.

"The demented decorator is home again!" she called out as she let herself into the apartment and began taping the yellow-and-cream Laura Ashley print, which she'd picked up on the way home from the office, to the foyer wall. "Yellow," she mused. "What do you think of yellow?"

"I like it. It's cheerful," Kirk said, coming in from the little den they used more than any other room in the apartment.

"You don't think I'm a little crazy, do you?" she asked. The Laura Ashley was the sixth possibility lined up on the wall.

"I think you're terrific," he said, remembering that Bonnie had considered spending time and money on pretty wallpaper and nice furniture almost sinful.

The apartment had four rooms. A living room, a dining room, and two bedrooms, one of which they used as a den. One day, the broker had pointed out, it might be a nursery. Carlys did not know how she felt about having a baby. Her own childhood had not been happy, and she had never felt particularly maternal. Still, the idea of having a baby with Kirk made her think that, someday, she might change her mind.

"I'd love to have your baby," she told Kirk when they talked about it. "But it would change things so. It wouldn't be just you and me anymore."

Kirk, who had already had children, was even less enthusiastic about the idea than Carlys, although he said he would leave the decision about having children up to her. They decided to wait. Later, they both agreed, would be soon enough. Carlys had her career, Kirk had his, and in the meantime they had each other.

"We'll be happy no matter what," Kirk said and Carlys agreed.

Of *that* there was no doubt.

* * *

That apartment at 11 East Seventy-ninth was the first place Carlys had ever really thought of as home. Her parents' apartment had had the sad air of a sickroom. Her Yorkville apartment had a depressing atmosphere that reeked of "next year." Even her pleasant co-op on Seventy-fifth Street was more Lord & Taylor than Carlys Webber.

The week they moved in Carlys spent hour after hour unpacking crates and cartons, some of them going back to the time Kirk had sold the Armonk house and put his belongings into storage. In one of them Carlys found a gun, a small but lethal-looking .32, wrapped in a blue-and-white-striped towel.

"A gun?" she asked, surprised, gingerly picking it up and showing it to Kirk.

"A lot of people in the country have them," he said, suddenly guarded. He had forgotten all about it. He had forgotten that his mother had given it to him. He wished he had gotten rid of it a long time ago. The sight of it brought back violent memories and brutal impulses he preferred to forget. "There was a rash of burglaries where we lived."

"I guess Armonk is no different from anywhere else these days," said Carlys, accepting his explanation, recalling that Joshua had told her that he kept a gun in his night table at his Connecticut home. She also knew that many people—including her own father—kept guns in Manhattan apartments. Doormen and police locks and alarms and window gates sometimes weren't enough. "What should we do with it?"

"Give it to me," he said, extending his hand and taking it from her. "I'll put it away in the top of the closet. Who knows? One day we may be happy we have it."

He put the gun on the top shelf of his closet, shoved it way back, out of sight, and closed the door. He knew that he would never be happy to have it. Never.

The second year of Kirk and Carlys's marriage was a continuation of the happiness of their first and, for a while, Carlys was plagued by a recurring anxiety that her unbelievable happiness would be snatched away from her. She was afraid that Kirk would get sick. She was terrified that he'd die. She feared that he'd be in a terrible accident. She worried that he'd fall in love with someone else. She imagined that he'd announce one morning at breakfast that he wanted a divorce. She was concerned that he'd get tired of her. Every time he left for work she worried that he wouldn't come home. Every time he returned from buying a newspaper she felt that the sun had come out again. But another year passed and none of the disasters she had feared ever happened, and on their second anniversary Kirk gave her a set of monogrammed, handmade Queen Anne silver and took her away for a romantic weekend in Bucks County.

"I don't know how you put up with me," he said. It was his way of apologizing for his preoccupation with work. Twelve-hour days were normal for Kirk, Saturdays barely tolerable, and by Sunday he was restless, anxious to get back to the office. Work was his addiction; but fortunately, as SuperWrite's public relations representative, Carlys knew a great deal about the ins and outs of his office life. "Bonnie always said I ought to be married to my job."

"I'm not Bonnie," Carlys reminded him, feeling momentarily superior to Bonnie, proud that she could discuss Kirk's work with him on his own terms and on a level he respected. Gradually she began to trust her own happiness.

She began to think that perhaps she had been wrong in thinking that loneliness and unhappiness were her destiny. She began to think that perhaps she *was* entitled to happiness, that the years of unhappiness had merely been a payment in advance.

All through her teens and twenties Carlys had been on the outside, forlornly looking in. When she had been a teenager all she had wanted was a boyfriend, someone to go to the movies with on Saturday night, someone to dance with her at the parties she was never invited to, someone to hold hands with in the hallways between classes. None of the boys had ever looked at her, though. She was too shy, too drab, too awkward, too obviously needy. For the first three years of high school she had not had a single date. It wasn't until her senior year that a boy asked her out.

Johnny Rubenstein was plump and pimply, as much of a loser in his way as she was in hers. Johnny came from a rich family, and, although his parents gave elaborate parties as a way of buying friends for Johnny, their strategy didn't work and Johnny, like Carlys, ate lunch alone, walked home from school alone, was picked last on all the teams, and sat home alone on Saturday nights. But like Carlys, Johnny got straight A's. He wrote poetry and, in his junior year, sold a short story to the *Saturday Evening Post*. Johnny invited Carlys to go to the movies with him and they held hands, sweatily, through *Advise and Consent*. The next week Johnny invited Carlys out a second time and took her to see *My Fair Lady*, Carlys's first Broadway play. When he awkwardly attempted to kiss her good night, Carlys surprised him—and herself—by returning the kiss, openmouthed.

The two losers discovered each other and began to spend all their time together, ignoring the other kids, and, with their straight A's, feeling for once in both their lives superior, a league of two. They declared their love for each other and began exploring each other's bodies, always stopping just short of actual intercourse. Carlys was afraid of getting pregnant; Johnny was afraid of getting her pregnant. Johnny was the first human being who had ever paid attention to Carlys, and in the end she rejected him cruelly.

"I bet she pops his pimples and thinks it's sex," Carlys overheard Toni Freyman say one day in the ladies' room. Toni, who was blond and popular, wore cashmere sweaters and was the only girl in the class with a Gucci bookbag. She and her best friend, Alice Holmes, were sneaking a cigarette near the open window. They hadn't seen Carlys come in.

"Do you think they come together?" Alice Holmes replied and they broke into giggles. Alice was bulky and muscular, had a braying laugh, and parents in the Social Register.

"Probably not," said Toni. "I bet Carlys is frigid." The two best friends collapsed into more giggles and Carlys, realizing that it was *she* they were talking about, fled.

The overheard remarks so demolished Carlys that, from that moment on, she refused to speak to Johnny, refused to see him, and refused to tell him what he had done to deserve her harsh rejection. He wrote her a letter, a long one she could tell from the thick envelope, which she returned to him, unopened. She went through the rest of her senior year dateless, lowering her eyes every time she passed Toni or Alice in the halls. Eventually she was bitterly ashamed of the way she had treated Johnny but was too humiliated by her own embarrassment to know how to apologize to him.

Carlys's shyness and social ineptitude continued through college. In her sophomore year she lost her virginity to a pre-law student named Alan Eichner with whom she shared a course in government. After class, one bright winter afternoon, she went back to the apartment Alan shared with three other pre-law students. He took her into his tiny, rumpled bedroom and shut the door. With the noise of a stereo and popping beer cans in the background, he kneaded her breasts and, pulling up her skirt and removing her panties, pantingly entered her and came immediately.

"A virgin?" he'd asked as he pulled out. "No kidding."

Carlys rearranged her clothing, slipped on her panties, and walked back home alone down West End Avenue, looking at herself in shop windows, trying to see whether she looked different and whether there were any external signs that she'd "done it." Except for the hurt and shamed look in her eyes, there weren't.

Although Alan continued to borrow her homework, he never invited her out again, nor did he ever invite her back to his apartment. Once the course was over that spring, Carlys never saw him again. Understandably, Carlys's first experience with sex was an extreme disappointment. She couldn't understand what there was to like about it. The songs, the books, the whispers that indicated ecstasy had to be mistaken. It couldn't be sex they were referring to, could it? Her subsequent experiences, hurried, impersonal, embarrassing, demeaning, only confirmed her initial reaction.

The first time Carlys got a glimpse that sex might be the thrilling experience she'd read about came when, briefly, she worked for an importer of oriental rugs. The owner was a kind and fatherly Armenian man and his son, Alex, who was being groomed to take over the business, was a gentle and handsome olive-skinned young man, just three years older than Carlys. Perhaps it was the difference in their cultures, perhaps it was because Alex Vartanian saw in Carlys what Kirk and George would one day see, but Alex developed a big crush on Carlys. He brought flowers for her desk and samples of his mother's delicious Armenian cooking for her to taste. He invited her to the opening party for an exhibit of fine antique rugs at a Madison Avenue dealer and afterward, took her to dinner at the Ararat Restaurant on East Thirty-sixth Street. He took her home, kissed her good night, and asked if he might take her out again.

On their fourth date he invited her back to his apartment and made delicious, thick Greek-style coffee that he served to her in tiny cups. Very gently he began to kiss her, tenderly running his tongue across her lips and, when they parted, exploring her mouth. Arousing her carefully, paying more attention to her pleasure than to his own, he asked her if he pleased her, and told her that her green eyes were the most beautiful he'd ever seen and that her hair was the texture of silk.

"I never thought I'd meet anyone like you," he told her as he held her in his arms, allowing her body to become accustomed to his touch. "Knowing you has made me very happy." Complimenting her, calling her by name, looking into her eyes, his hands gradually worked their way down her body, and by the time he could no longer wait, she couldn't either.

Carlys and Alex began to see each other almost every night and just as Carlys was beginning to feel the first stirrings of real sexual pleasure, Alex told her, almost tearfully, that as much as his father liked her, he didn't think Alex should continue to see her.

"There's this girl . . . she's Armenian, too. I've known her since we were children. We're going to announce our engagement this spring," he said, not quite able to look straight at Carlys. "I'm afraid my father is right. I *want* to see you. You know how I feel about you. It's just better if we stop now before we get any more involved."

Better for whom? Carlys wondered silently, but accepted his rejection meekly. A month later she told Alex that she had decided to quit her job.

"I hope that what happened between us didn't make you want to leave," Alex said. Carlys had been very good at her job, and they were going to miss her.

"Oh, no," said Carlys, who had denied the pain she felt at Alex's practical acceptance of his father's wishes to such an extent that she didn't even know if the breakup had or hadn't entered into her decision. "I just thought I'd try to find something a little more creative."

The years that followed were sexless. They were the years of blind dates that never worked out, of occasional encounters with men who seemed promising but in the end, for one reason or another, never fulfilled that promise, and of the frustrating relationship with Winn Rosier. Whatever intimations Carlys had had of her own desirability, whatever inklings she might have had about her own sensuality, were prematurely cut off. Without being consciously aware of it, she had buried her erotic energies. The world of pleasure, flaunted throughout the seventies, was an untasted world for Carlys. Her only pleasures were the pleasures of achievement, and when she met Kirk *he* became her world. For years, he would be all the world she thought she needed.

The timing of Carlys's sexual awakening coincided with that of a revolution in sexual attitudes, the full 180-degree shift from nice girls don't to nice girls do. No one who lived through the seventies was untouched by sexual propaganda, and Carlys, perhaps even more than most people, with her years of rejection and sexual starvation still vividly painful, wanted to do it all, feel it all, experience it all.

C H A P T E R 13

*C*arlys began to entertain for the first time and thus discovered career synergism; specifically, that two careers have four times the influence of one. She discovered that it was more beneficial to a woman's career to have dinner with the boss and his wife than it supposedly ever had been to sleep with the boss.

Wives, Carlys learned, mattered. Wives, Carlys learned, had a lot of influence. Husbands turned to their wives as sounding boards, relied on their advice, and trusted their instincts.

Carlys learned that it made good sense to pay more attention to the women and less to the men. For one thing, the women stopped fearing her as a sexual threat; for another, they began to tell their husbands how much they liked Carlys, which did her career no harm at all.

As Kirk's wife, Carlys realized she was extremely important to him. She was touched by the obvious way he wanted to please her, wanted her to be proud of him, wanted her to think that everything he did was right. Most of the time she did, but whenever she disagreed with him she felt free to say so.

In the early years of their marriage Kirk went on a buying spree for SuperWrite. He bought, for less than they were worth, two companies in trouble—a nationwide dealer in office supplies from paperclips to computers and a manufacturer of module filing systems—turned them around, and added their assets and profits to SuperWrite.

"I told Howie he ought to kiss my feet for making him look so good," said Kirk after a forty-five percent rise in SuperWrite's earnings in 1979. Kirk was upset because Howie had given an interview to *Newsweek,* bragging about his corporate strategy. "The old egotist takes credit for everything! Every time I come up with a new acquisition, Howie kicks and screams that I'm spending too much of the company's money. Then, when it turns a profit, he says it was his idea in the first place."

"I know he's annoying," said Carlys, aware of how difficult the paranoid and devious Howie could be, "but I don't think you ought to wave a red flag. Let him have his old man's ego. You know—and everyone in the business knows—who really turned SuperWrite around."

"You're right," Kirk said. Still, he couldn't resist reminding Howie that it was he, Kirk, who had been the real force behind SuperWrite's new success. Kirk seemed to forget that Howie was the owner of the company and that he was only an employee. Carlys warned him that he was playing with fire.

"Be careful with Howie," she said, remembering her own experience. "He's unpredictable."

"I'll be careful," Kirk promised, but he was still a young man impatient with an old man, and Kirk, who was many things, was not a good actor.

*   *   *

In the fourth year of their marriage the wheel came full circle, and the first attempt to heal the social breach with the Mundees family came from Miriam.

"I had lunch with Howie today," Kirk told Carlys as they shared coffee after dinner on their terrace one unseasonably balmy April evening.

"And did he fire you again?" Howie threatened to fire Kirk every time they had the slightest disagreement. Kirk regularly told Howie to take his job and shove it and Howie inevitably backed down. Kirk passed it off as a joke; Carlys thought Kirk should watch his step.

Kirk shook his head.

"Not today," he said. "Howie had something else on his mind. Miriam is giving a Fourth of July party at their Westport place. She wants to know if we'll come." Carlys had been very aware that although the Mundeeses considered her good enough to handle SuperWrite's public relations problems, they had never invited her to any of the family's business-cum-social events since that ill-fated Christmas party.

"You mean I'm finally out of purdah?" Carlys asked, thinking that Miriam was as much of a coward as Howie was. She didn't even have the courage to invite her directly.

"Howie *did* say you'd have to wear your scarlet letter," Kirk replied.

Kirk seemed to think that the invitation was further proof of his solid footing with SuperWrite and the Mundeeses. Carlys, however, wasn't so convinced. At the party Howie, whose idea of an outfit for a Fourth of July party was one of his ill-fitting suits and a pair of sandals with light green socks, introduced Kirk as "someone who works for me." Carlys was infuriated and told Kirk as much as they drove back to the city after the party.

"Now you know why he gives me such a pain in the ass," Kirk said.

"Just be careful," warned Carlys.

*Later that summer Kirk began to talk about a new acquisi-*tion he had in mind. Carlys had never heard him so excited about anything.

"The company's in Detroit," he said, telling her about

Dearborn Paper and Printing. "It prints manuals and brochures, mainly for the auto industry." He went on to describe the company—an excellent firm whose earnings had recently slid. Only a temporary slip, Kirk insisted. "It's a fantastic opportunity!" he said, almost on fire. "We've got to get it! We've just *got* to!"

"We?" asked Carlys, assuming he meant SuperWrite. She had never heard him as intense about *anything* as he was about Dearborn Paper and Printing. Then she said something that had been on her mind ever since the Fourth of July party. "What if you bought it for yourself?" she asked. "Suppose you began making yourself rich instead of Howie?"

"It's a good thought," Kirk said, looking increasingly tired and worn out from the combined stresses of a long and demanding work week and the frustrations of dealing with Howie, who refused to give Kirk any credit or even the slightest appreciation. "I'm sure getting sick and tired of Howie."

He was concerned about conflicts of interest, but he promised to look into it and Carlys was delighted.

"Good!" she said. "It's time you made a declaration of independence." The sooner Kirk was away from SuperWrite and the treacherous Howie, the better she'd feel.

The decade that had begun with Vietnam and the Watergate scandals ended with the taking of American hostages in Iran and the Russian invasion of Afghanistan. To Carlys the images that would most evocatively summon that period were portraits of rage and destruction: the television pictures of the burning of the American flag outside the American embassy in Tehran while mobs shouted "Death to America!"; the ominous scenes of Kabul in the snow, Soviet tanks advancing down silent white streets. The shattering events that took place in the outside world seemed a grim and appropriate background to the events that would forever change their relationship, transforming it from a long-running love affair into an emotional minefield.

But it didn't start that way. On their fifth anniversary Kirk took Carlys to see the New York Drama Critics' Circle Award winner—*The Elephant Man*—and, afterward, to a festive champagne dinner at the Four Seasons. Through the pasta and the veal and the dessert, though, Kirk talked obsessively about his latest battle with Howie: Howie wanted SuperWrite to make a personal computer; Kirk refused.

"Talk about wasting the company's money! I told him the market was already saturated," he told Carlys, strain and impatience obvious on his face and in his voice. "I told him that SuperWrite doesn't know zilch about personal computers. I told him to get off the pot and make the deal for Dearborn Paper and Printing while he still can."

"So why doesn't he?"

"He's cheap and stubborn," said Kirk. "He's screaming that they're asking too much. Christ! So what? It'll be worth it!"

"So what about buying Dearborn for yourself?" Carlys asked, reminding him of his promise, impressed by his determination. For Kirk to overpay—and admit it—was unheard of. Kirk was famous for his ability to spot under-valued and underpriced companies.

Kirk shrugged, embarrassed. "I just didn't get around to it," he admitted.

"The least you should do," Carlys said, "is renegotiate your employment contract. You're doing so much for Howie and I don't trust him." Carlys still worked with Howie frequently, and she knew that he had taken to announcing that he wrote all his own speeches. It was Carlys, of course, who wrote them, but Howie's weasely credit-grabbing was typical. Carlys was endlessly wary of him.

"You're absolutely right," said Kirk. "I'll call my lawyer first thing Monday."

Except that between a labor crisis at the St. Louis plant and the tense negotiations for Dearborn Paper and Printing, Kirk never got around to it. Besides, just when the deal for Dearborn appeared to be lost Howie changed his mind.

"It's a winner," he told Kirk, his hatchet face as sour as if he'd just bitten into an unripe pomegranate. "The deal with Dearborn is the best one I've ever come up with. I told them we were going ahead."

"It's nice of you to inform me," said Kirk sarcastically. *He* had handled all the difficult and tedious negotiations, flying back and forth to Detroit like a yo-yo on a string while Howie sat on his ass in New York and *kvetched* and second-guessed. Kirk didn't even bother to remind Howie of exactly *whose* deal it had been and who had done all the work.

Kirk got on the plane for Detroit, the papers all ready. Only the finishing touches to the deal of a lifetime were required. The agreements were made, the compromises made, the deal practically signed, sealed, and delivered. After almost ten months of work only the mechanics were left. All Kirk had to do was get the sellers' signatures, countersign the papers, and make out the down-payment check and Dearborn Paper and Printing would become a division of SuperWrite. Impossible as Howie was, Kirk thought as the plane headed west, he wasn't crazy. In the end he always went along with Kirk's recommendations. Howie damn well knew whom to listen to and who was responsible for SuperWrite's phoenixlike rise from the ashes. Kirk had never said so, but he thought Carlys's worries about Howie were ridiculous. Howie would never fire him; Howie couldn't afford to.

"Mr. Arnold!" said the receptionist at Dearborn's Woodward Avenue main office. Sally Thompson was black and particularly beautiful. She wore her hair in an intricately braided style and the brightly colored beads on the end of each braid clicked as she moved. She seemed stunned to see Kirk. She had gotten to know—and like—him during the dozens of trips he had made to Detroit while he was negotiating the buyout of the company. "What are you doing here?"

"Making the deal," Kirk said, not quite understanding. Sally, who doubled at the switchboard, always knew everything that was happening at the company. "Haven't you heard? We're buying Dearborn. Howie finally made up his mind yesterday."

She looked confused, and then embarrassed.

"Sally? What's the matter?" Kirk asked.

"It's already been made."

"What?" It was Kirk who was confused now.

"This morning. Howie flew out," Sally said. "The papers were signed, the checks exchanged. It's all been done."

"But I have the papers here," Kirk said, momentarily confused, indicating his attaché case. The look on Sally's face alarmed him and suddenly he began to realize what was happening. He almost lashed out at her. "What's going on here?"

"You don't know?" she asked, now obviously as upset as he was.

"For Christ's sake! What the hell's going on?" The scar that ran through his eyebrow seemed ghost-white.

"Howie said you resigned," said Sally finally. "He said SuperWrite's hired a new president."

Kirk left without a word, slamming the door so hard that its thick glass cracked.

Kirk got on the next plane back to New York and went straight to the SuperWrite building. As he entered the lobby a uniformed guard approached him.

"Mr. Arnold?" he said politely. His voice was soft but he was built like a linebacker, all beef and no shit.

"Yes?"

"I've been asked to stop you from entering the building." Quietly but firmly the guard took Kirk by the arm and escorted him from the building in which he'd worked for seven years.

Carlys was already home when Kirk arrived. She got up to greet him the way she always did when she was the one who got home first.

"I'm out," he said, white-faced, his temples throbbing, as he brushed roughly past her, almost knocking her over. He headed into the kitchen and, stunned, Carlys followed him.

"Out?" Her heart stopped and then began to pound. Her mouth went dry and she swallowed, choking back a sick lump of panic.

"Out!" he repeated furiously, getting out ice and a glass, retrieving the Scotch from the cupboard. He turned to her with a look of black rage that she had never seen on him, or on anyone. "Fired!" he snarled and poured a large drink. Carlys waited in suspended silence, afraid to speak, while he slugged down the Scotch.

"That son of a bitch!" he said, pouring a second drink, his hands shaking uncontrollably. The Scotch spilled over the rim of the glass and ran down his hand and onto the floor. Its fumes filled the kitchen with their rich, heady aroma, a smell that Carlys would forever after associate with catastrophe, a smell that forever after would make her sick to her stomach. "That dirty son of a bitch! I'd like to kill him!"

Kirk was turning red with rage. His skin seemed almost to burn, and suddenly Kirk, who was always in control, completely lost his temper. He took the glass he was holding and threw it against the stainless steel panel of the dishwasher, the glass smashing to pieces.

"Kirk!" Carlys screamed as he took a second glass from the cupboard and hurled it at the refrigerator.

"Stop!" He did not seem to hear her. Methodically he took every single glass in the cupboard and smashed it to pieces while Carlys stood by and watched in horror, afraid for the first time of the man she had married. When he had smashed every glass they owned, Kirk, who never even got high, got drunk. Kirk who prided himself on never getting angry, was murderously enraged. During the next four hours, over Scotch drunk straight from the bottle, Kirk finally calmed down enough to tell Carlys what had happened. Over the next four months, over more Scotch than Carlys had ever seen anyone drink, she found out the man she had married was a man who lived with bitter secrets.

C H A P T E R 14

When Carlys got up the next morning, Kirk was still in a deep, leaden sleep. She cleaned up the kitchen, left a pot of black coffee and some blueberry muffins for him, got out his employment contract from the files in the den, and took it to the office with her. It dated back to 1973. Although she and Kirk had talked about renegotiating it, that was something else he had obviously never gotten around to doing. Once in her office Carlys shut the door and pored over its clauses and fine print, furious at how much Kirk had done for SuperWrite and how shabbily he had been treated. She could understand the rage and frustration that had made him smash all the glassware. She even wondered if she would have done the same thing in his place.

It seemed strange, almost against the laws of nature, to find Kirk at home when she returned from work that evening. He was still in pajamas and a robe, sitting in the living room, a can of beer on the coffee table in front of him. He was pale and red-eyed and hung over and he did not look up as Carlys entered the room. She remembered his rage of the night before and she felt suddenly afraid.

"How do you feel?" Carlys asked warily. Wariness was a brand-new feeling in their marriage.

"Great," he said sarcastically. Anger was easy for him. Hurt wasn't; neither was regret nor apology. He wished he weren't that way, but he couldn't help it. He wanted to apologize for smashing up the kitchen and leaving the mess for her to clean up, but he couldn't. The words weren't there for him.

"I have good news and bad news," she said, sitting down and sounding purposely businesslike. She was determined to get past Kirk's anger. She was determined to be constructive. He went to the kitchen and got another beer as she spoke.

"The bad news is that according to your contract with SuperWrite, Howie has the right to fire you," Carlys said, deciding not to comment about the night before. He had had so much to drink that she wondered if he even remembered it. "The good news is that, if he does, he also has the obligation to pay you a percentage of increased business due to your efforts. I called Judith and she asked you to come in. She wants to talk to you but she said you definitely have a case."

"*You* talked to Judith?" he snarled, slamming the beer can down on the table.

"Yes," said Carlys, taken aback by his tone. She was on *his* side. She was trying to help him. Why was he taking his anger out on her? "I wanted to find out if I was interpreting it correctly."

"Who the hell asked you!" Kirk snapped. "Just stay the fuck out of my business!"

He did not speak to her for the next two days except to order her to buy some goddamn glasses.

*   *   *

"I spoke to Judith," he said three evenings later. On the way home from Judith's office he had stopped at a florist's and bought Carlys a pot of beautiful and fragrant forced paperwhites. His unspoken but accepted apology, they stood on the coffee table next to his drink. "We're going to sue."

Carlys nodded. "Good," she said, sure that Kirk was in the right, sure that he would win. She was naive then. She had never been involved in a lawsuit. She did not know how long lawsuits took or how emotionally devastating they were. As it dragged on and on, a constant reminder of Howie's brutal behavior, she would even begin to wonder whether it was worth it.

It was Carlys who, as SuperWrite's public relations representative, had the sensitive and painful job of handling the announcement of Kirk's departure from SuperWrite.

"Officially, I've said that you've resigned to consider other offers," Carlys told him. "Unofficially, I've made sure that people know exactly what those other offers are and just how lucrative they are so no one can conclude that the announcement is just face-saving."

Kirk gave Carlys a curt nod, his eyes not meeting hers. He appreciated what Carlys was doing for him, yet he still could not bring himself to thank her. His world had fallen apart around him and he had no room for anything but rage and bitterness.

Sure he had other offers, good offers, but so what? Because of the five-year, no-compete clause in his contract, Judith refused to let Kirk accept any of them. She did not want to risk weakening his case.

"You'll just have to turn them down, Kirk," Judith said firmly when Terrell Industries, a manufacturer of the keyboards used in typewriters, word processors, and computers, offered Kirk its presidency. "You have to be like Caesar's wife. Above suspicion."

Not working was driving the workaholic Kirk crazy, but although he threatened to take the job at Terrell no matter how it affected the lawsuit, he allowed Carlys to talk him into obeying Judith.

When a Boston software developer made an offer Judith took the same position. "You'll have to turn them down,

Kirk," she advised reluctantly. "Howie's beginning to make settlement noises. Let's not rock the boat now."

Kirk continued to sit around the house in pajamas and a robe, a drink on the coffee table in front of him, obsessed with thoughts of murder and suicide, and haunted by memories of his father, who had died at the age of forty-eight, only three years older than Kirk himself was right now.

The killer, the absolute killer, was that while Kirk's career was at its depths, Carlys's was rising to new heights. In the years since her marriage Carlys had honed and perfected the techniques she had learned and created working with Lansing and Sergio and Howie Mundees, with David Daye and Ada Hutchinson. In a celebrity-crazed time, Carlys's talent was almost invaluable: She took businessmen and women and turned them into stars.

She had David Daye photographed in running clothes on a cinder track and suggested a headline to the ad agency: "Twentieth Century for the long run." The ad got attention and once she got David attention, Carlys's job was by-the-book PR: She got him an interview with the *Times*'s personal investor columnist, a write-up in *Forbes*, and a guest shot on "Wall Street Week." David Daye's experience and expertise did the rest. If you wanted to make money, people began to say, David Daye was the man to listen to and Twentieth Century the company to invest with.

Outsiders thought David Daye was the star; insiders began to say that Carlys was the star.

Ada Hutchinson was a different story. At sixty-four Ada was not your basic blue-haired widow. She had been one of the first women in the country to obtain a pilot's license. She had met her husband barnstorming in the forties and worked with him on building up Yankee Air. She was tall, close to six feet, had a lean, weatherbeaten face, and her talk was salty and no-nonsense. Her flight record—and Yankee Air's record—was one hundred percent perfect and so was the rock-ribbed Yankee honesty that Ada projected. Ada was, Carlys thought, the perfect image of the rugged pioneer. That image, Carlys also realized, was both a plus and a minus.

The plus was that Ada was a woman you'd want at the controls. The minus was that her blunt talk put off the financial people she needed to stroke to keep money flowing into the company now that her husband was dead and she was faced with running the company alone. What Carlys decided to do was use Ada's strength and conceal her weakness. She kept Ada away from bankers, investment capital honchos, and financial analysts. Instead, she sent Ada around the country and had her meet with the owners of other regional airlines, people who shared the same problems and people who, as often as not, shared the same barnstorming background.

"Those fellows and I speak the same lingo," Ada told Carlys in what was, for Ada, a flowery compliment.

Eventually Ada Hutchinson became known outside the New England area and Yankee Air began to get feelers about merger. With the guidance of her accountants and lawyers, Ada merged her route-rich and cash-poor Yankee Air with a cash-fat and route-lean air transport service headquartered near Winston-Salem. It was Carlys's notion to feature Ada in a pilot's jumpsuit in all the new company's advertising. Eventually, Ada became so well known that a comic-strip character was said to have been modeled after her.

Once again, outsiders noticed Ada, insiders noticed Carlys.

Just as every hostess wanted the Kissingers for dinner, every client wanted Carlys for his or her account. The good job she had done for Ada Hutchinson did not go unnoticed in the airline industry, and when Mid-Atlantic Air wanted a public relations company to help in its quest for new routes, its president, Irv Weston, came to Barron & Hynes. When Georgia Betts, who ran a successful but regional cosmetics business in Texas, wanted national recognition, she came to Barron & Hynes. Both Irv and Georgia insisted that Carlys be assigned to their accounts as a condition of coming to Barron & Hynes. Joshua got the message: Barron & Hynes was getting solid, corporate accounts because of Carlys.

"That's two big accounts we've gotten in the last two months because of you," Joshua Hynes told Carlys in December 1981. "Barron & Hynes has never had a woman vice-president and I think it's about time we did."

Vice-president! Carlys kept repeating the words over and over to herself. Vice-president! Vice-president! She remembered her beaten-down years at the phone company, she remembered all the crap she had taken from Tom, she remembered all the shit jobs she had done that no one else wanted to do—and it had finally paid off! She was so proud of herself she had to force herself not to shout out the news to strangers in the streets.

The only problem was that she couldn't tell Kirk. Not when he was still unemployed, not while she was supporting them, an uncomfortable fact they couldn't even discuss without a terrible fight. Carlys had been stunned to find out several months after he'd been fired that Kirk had never saved any money. Carlys had always assumed that they were fairly well-to-do. After all, they owned a co-op on the Upper East Side, bought their meat from Lobel's, their fish from Rosedale, and their vegetables from Mr. Rowe. Like hundreds of other up-scale New Yorkers, they shopped Madison Avenue and SoHo on Saturdays, used Bloomie's delicacies department like the grocery store around the corner, and had every credit card known to man. Carlys wore designer clothes, owned a mink coat, and their bottle-green Jaguar was parked in the building's garage at a monthly fee that was more than Carlys had once paid in rent on her Yorkville apartment.

Carlys had always assumed that Kirk had handled his personal finances as shrewdly as he had handled Super-Write's finances. She had been appalled to discover that, between them, they had five thousand dollars in the bank—most of it her savings—and sixty thousand dollars in stock, which her father had bought for her. Kirk, an excellent businessman, owned no stocks, no bonds, had no money market fund, did not even own any insurance. Between his divorce and his lavish spending habits, he had no cushion to fall back on. Ever since Kirk had been fired, they had been living on her money and Kirk had resented every moment of it.

"A fucking kept man," he said whenever they used Carlys's American Express card instead of his, whenever bills came in and she paid them out of the account she'd kept from the days she'd been a single, working girl living on a tight budget.

Carlys had always disapproved of the open-handed way in which Kirk had spent money, but she had never said much because it was, after all, his money. Now they fought about money almost constantly because, even though Kirk wasn't earning any, and even though he bitterly resented her supporting them, he also refused to change his habits. He still wanted to eat out every night; he still ordered his custom-made clothes and custom-made shoes.

"Kirk, you have to cut down!" said Carlys, opening another Dunhill bill, this one for a navy blazer with gold buttons. "We can't afford this."

"I can afford any goddamn thing I want," he said. "What do you want me to do? Live like a pauper?"

"No, of course not," she said, trying not to let the battle escalate. "Just cut down temporarily."

"Cut down?" he repeated sarcastically, pouring another drink. "It's nickels and dimes, Carlys. That's all you can think about. Nickels and dimes."

Once again Carlys backed off. Fighting about money was not making things any better. She was grateful for the increase in salary that came along with her promotion. Carlys suppressed the pride she felt. How could she be up when he was down? By the time Carlys got home she had put on a straight face and a sober expression. She placed her key in the door and hoped that Kirk would at least be civil.

Carlys had married for better or for worse, and the months right after Kirk was fired were the worst of their marriage. The man who had always been a pleasure to live with became a nightmare. Carlys never knew what kind of mood he would be in when she walked in the door at night. She never knew if he'd be drunk or sober, if he'd be vicious or drowning in self-pity. He was irascible, irrational, and short-tempered. He screamed if a shirt came back from the laundry with a button missing. He fired their longtime cleaning woman because she had mistakenly put his socks into his shirt drawer. He railed at SuperWrite, Howie, and Molly. When he got drunk enough, he threatened to murder Howie.

"I'd like to kill that son of a bitch!" he said, his anger unleashed by the alcohol. Carlys cringed, remembering the terrifying way he'd smashed up the glasses and wondering, if given the right moment and the right set of circumstances, what Kirk might be capable of.

Besides getting even with Howie and SuperWrite, Kirk was obsessed with trying to get Dearborn Paper and Printing as part of the lawsuit settlement. "Dearborn's mine! I found it! It's mine!" he said, vowing to get Dearborn for himself if it was the last thing he did. Dearborn Paper and Printing became like the Holy Grail to him, and Carlys refrained from reminding him that she had once urged him to buy it for himself instead of for SuperWrite and Howie. She realized now, of course, that one of the reasons he hadn't was that he didn't have the money, something she hadn't known at the time.

Kirk spent hours going over the Examinations Before Trial transcripts, making notes for his lawyers. He alternated between being sexually demanding and sexually indifferent. His moods veered wildly between arrogance and self-hatred, between hyperconfidence and total despair.

He said he wished he were dead and began to talk about suicide.

"I never told you this," he told Carlys in one of his self-pitying moods, "but I got fired once before." He told her about Joe Metzer and how he had totaled his car. "The cop told me I was lucky to walk away. I wasn't lucky," he said bitterly. "I wish I'd killed myself. Then I wouldn't have to go through this."

Carlys, appalled, did not know what to say. Kirk had always seen himself as a winner; now he saw himself as a loser and kept saying he wished he were dead. He did not know how to handle his rage. Neither did Carlys. She just hung on. She just kept telling herself that Kirk was overreacting; she just kept telling herself it was temporary.

"I'm not going to make forty-eight," Kirk announced on New Year's Eve, as 1981 beckoned. He had refused to go out, had refused even to allow Carlys to invite other people in. They had ordered up Chinese food and Kirk, pushing it aside, started getting drunk again. He had almost stopped eating; he was gaunt and his face was deeply lined. "My father didn't make forty-eight and I won't either."

Carlys tried to tell him that his father's life—and early death—had nothing to do with him. Nothing she said made the slightest bit of difference, and as the clock struck midnight, Kirk suddenly got up and went to his closet. He came back into the living room with the gun and, in front of Carlys, put it to his temple.

"Kirk!" she screamed, jumping up and hurling herself at him as he pulled the trigger.

The fireworks exploding in nearby Central Park almost drowned out the click of the empty chamber and Carlys almost fainted in relief.

"Kirk!" she said. "Don't ever do that again."

He merely smiled and hid the gun, tormenting her by refusing to tell her where it was.

Carlys remembered that Tom had once told her that Kirk had spent time in a mental institution. She hadn't believed it then, and she still doubted it, but now she had to know for certain. She told herself that men as competent, as successful, as intelligent as Kirk did not spend time in mental institutions. Yet Kirk's irrational rages and erratic behavior upset her more and more, and she finally called Geoff.

"Geoff, I don't mean to upset you, but I'm worried about your father. He's been very depressed since he left SuperWrite, so depressed that sometimes I can't reach him," Carlys said and paused. Then gathering her courage, she plunged on. "I once heard that he spent some time in a mental hospital. . . ."

"Covington?" said Geoff immediately, obviously knowing exactly what Carlys was talking about. "It wasn't Dad. It was Uncle Scott. He had a nervous breakdown."

"Uncle Scott?" repeated Carlys, wondering who Geoff was talking about. "Who's Uncle Scott?"

"Dad's brother," Geoff continued, answering automatically, puzzled at the question but not realizing the depths of Carlys's shock. "Not that it helped."

"Brother? Didn't help?" Carlys asked, her thoughts racing, her emotions jammed into a knot of pain and fear. "What brother? What didn't help? Covington?"

It was Geoff's turn to pause, unsure about how to continue. When he spoke, he seemed to change the subject. "Carlys, do you know how Granddad died?"

"A heart attack," she said. Kirk had told her all about it.

His father had had a heart attack just as her father had. Except that *his* father's had been fatal. Heart problems ran in the family. It was the reason Kirk was so careful about his health, didn't smoke, watched his cholesterol and his weight.

"It was no heart attack," said Geoff. "Granddad shot himself," Geoff paused again, this time for a long, agonizing moment. "Just like Scott."

Stunned, Carlys could not speak.

"Didn't you know? Didn't Dad tell you?" Geoff asked, shocked, realizing from Carlys's silence that she hadn't known.

The was silence on her end of the line continued. She still hadn't answered. She couldn't. Uncle Scott? Kirk had a brother? He had told her that, like her, he was an only child. The enormity of his lie took her breath away.

"Carlys?"

"Yes?" she said finally, barely able to get the word out. All that went through her mind now were Kirk's suicide threats. Oh, God, she prayed silently, please don't let him do it. Please!

"It's something the family never talks about," Geoff said. He sounded relieved that he had finally spoken about it. He also sounded scared, and his voice seemed to come from a great distance.

"I understand," said Carlys, still absolutely stunned at Kirk's incredible lies, at the thought that his talk about murder and suicide might not be just talk, and at the realization that the man she had married had bitter secrets he had never shared with her. She became enraged at the thought of all the lies he had told her about such crucial facts of his life and at the same time felt compassion for the amount of pain he must have suffered. She both loved and resented him so fiercely that she felt temporarily numb, and all she could do was wonder if there were other secrets in his past too terrible to speak of.

CHAPTER 15

Carlys hung on for dear life. She kept telling herself that this was all temporary. She told herself that people who talked about suicide never did it. That Kirk's threats were the result of Scotch and vodka. That like father, like son, was a meaningless old wives' tale. That Scott's nervous breakdown had nothing to do with Kirk. That marriages went through crises and came out stronger than ever. If only the damn lawsuit would be settled. If only Kirk could go back to work again. If only everything could be the way it used to.

Carlys was beginning to learn that, in real life, success didn't conform to the fantasies she'd had when she'd been struggling with bosses like Bob Ryan and boyfriends like Winn Rosier. Success presented an entirely different set of problems and complexities—and a different set of opportunities. As Kirk seemed headed for some kind of crash landing, it was once again Lansing Coons who would have a major effect on Carlys's life.

"E-Z Tech!" Lansing said in the spring of 1981. He spoke confidentially, as if he were sharing the secret of creation with her. "Remember that name."

"Why?" asked Carlys, with a sudden vision of the man who had said "Plastics!" to Dustin Hoffman in *The Graduate*. "What's so special about Easy Tech?"

"It's in English, and even a moron could understand it," Lansing said, drawing even closer to her desk. "Seriously, Carlys, *you* could understand it."

"Thanks, Lansing."

He went on to tell her that a man named Marion Kramer, a local Charleston English teacher, had translated the instruction books that came with computers into easy-to-understand English.

"All the kids' parents were buying computers for them

and no one could understand the manuals that came with them," Lansing said. "Marion ran them off on the school's photocopier and gave them away. Gave them away!" Almost a year later he was still horrified at the mere thought of someone giving away something that could be sold.

"I set him up with a local printer and he began selling the booklets at five bucks a pop through local newspaper ads. That was last year. This year he can't handle the business," Lansing said, the frown lines across his forehead deepening as he became more intense. "For one thing he needs capital. For another he needs a professional manager. He needs a quarter of a million dollars and that's where you come in, Carlys. It's the opportunity of a lifetime. He's selling fifty-thousand-dollar shares and I'm giving *you* the opportunity to buy one of them."

"Lansing, if this is such a terrific deal, why don't *you* give Marion Kramer the money he needs?" Carlys asked. "After all, a quarter of a million is pocket change for you."

"Of course you're right about that," Lansing said, rocking back on his crepe-soled shoes. He loved to brag about how rich he was. "But how can I? Between my books, columns, lecture tours, television appearances, and handling my own portfolio, I just don't have the time to invest in something when I can't be personally involved."

"Easy Tech?" Carlys asked, writing on her pad. He read it upside down.

"E-Z Tech," he corrected. "The name was my idea. Marion hates it. He says it's illiterate. I told him he had to think of the marketplace. We had a big fight about it. Of course I won. I was right."

"E-Z Tech," Carlys repeated and made a note of it. Unlike Lansing's usual can't-miss, once-in-a-lifetime propositions, something about E-Z Tech caught her attention. It nagged at the back of her mind all day long and that night, at two in the morning, she sat up in bed bolt upright.

"Kirk?" she asked softly.

"Yes?" he replied from somewhere in a deep sleep.

"Are you awake?" She reached out and touched him.

"I am now."

"Maybe this is a crazy idea," she said, wondering even as she spoke where on earth they'd get a quarter of a million dollars. Even if she sold all her stock, they'd still need two hundred thousand dollars. "I heard of a company in trouble today that might be perfect for you. The only difference between E-Z Tech and all the other companies you've ever been involved with is that the problem isn't failure but success. *And* it doesn't violate your no-compete agreement with SuperWrite."

Kirk went to Charleston to talk to Marion Kramer as Ju-dith Rosen continued to talk to SuperWrite's lawyers. He made his deal with Marion, who wanted to go back to schoolteaching, at the same time that Judith made her deal with Howie.

"The timing is perfect," Kirk said, his bitter disappoint-ment at not being allowed to take Dearborn Paper and Printing in settlement apparently tempered by the conclu-sion of the lawsuit. "Marion wants to sell and I want to buy. The settlement is just enough to make the purchase—if you're still willing to sell your stock and lend me the money." For once he seemed tentative, unsure of her response.

"Of course," she said, and risked a smile. She was rewarded with a kiss. She thought for a minute that, once again, everything would be the way it always had been.

"And now," swore Kirk, causing her fantasy to col-lapse, "I'm going to make Howie sorry he was born. I'm going to make E-Z Tech so goddamn successful that I'm going to buy SuperWrite with pocket change and fire the son of a bitch!"

Carlys raised her eyebrows but said nothing. She wished Kirk would forget about Howie and SuperWrite. It was time for him to put the past behind him and get on with the rest of his life. She was sure that, as he got involved with E-Z Tech, he would.

Now that he was back at work Kirk seemed, magically, to be once again the man she had married. The Scotch disap-peared and so did the rage. The demons that haunted him departed. The wild talk about suicide stopped. Once again, Carlys had both a marriage and a husband.

Except that the marriage had changed and so had the husband. And, so, finally, would the wife.

* * *

Carlys's marriage had begun as a love affair, it had weath-ered a major crisis, and now it was settling down into a routine—a routine in which Carlys came second to Kirk's obsession with his work; a routine in which her successes, however impressive, were less important than his; a routine in which her needs were subordinated to his. Carlys was no longer a sweetheart, a mistress, a lover. She was, she realized, a wife. Someone to be depended on, someone to be taken for granted, someone to be loved—when her husband remembered. Carlys tried not to resent it. She told herself that that was what marriage was like: the romance faded, the excitement dissipated, and habit set in. In the beginning she didn't realize that she had replaced Bonnie, and that she felt just what Bonnie had felt. She didn't real-ize that she and Bonnie shared not only a husband but a destiny. In the beginning, like Bonnie, she had only wanted someone to talk to.

In the spring of 1982, on the Boston-New York shuttle, Carlys sat next to a man named George Kouras—a dark-haired, amber-eyed, sensitive-featured man who was more than handsome, a man who could only be called beautiful, the kind of man who had once never looked at her. She sat back in her seat and when the stewardess came by, Carlys ordered coffee and wondered if she'd have the courage to speak to him. She thought she might. It was one of the big differences between being married and secure, and single and desperate.

George noticed Carlys because, even though he and Jade were living together now, he always noticed women. Women were rare on the Boston-New York shuttle—attractive women even rarer. She took the seat next to him and he noticed that, as she crossed her legs, a glimpse of lace-trimmed burgundy slip flashed under her well-cut blue suit. He noticed her expensive leather briefcase, the scent of a discreet and alluring perfume, and her gold wedding ring. George usually wasn't attracted to married women, but as the Fasten Seatbelts sign flashed on, he began to think of what he was going to say to her.

PART TWO

The Single Woman

"Married? Me? Never again! Once was enough!"
—JADE MULLEN, 1977

CHAPTER 1

*J*ade and George. George and Jade. Theirs was a very modern romance. The first time they met, she was married and so was he. The second time they met, she was divorced and so was he.

The complications were inevitable. In the very beginning, though, it was as simple as any male-female relationship could have been in the nervous seventies. They hadn't seen each other for several years. They remembered an unusual rapport and that they were attracted to one another—very, very attracted.

It was the early spring of 1977 at a loft-warming party on lower Fifth Avenue. The loft belonged to Titian Fellowes, the last surviving member of a once-proud, now run-down Savannah, Georgia, family. Titian, albino pale and gazelle thin, had turned his interest in hilarious decadence into a successful career in fashion photography. Jade had styled some of his most eye-catching pictures and George had designed his newly renovated loft-cum-studio. People were drinking Perrier, white wine, or kir,; Brie was on its way out and *chèvre* was on its way in; EST was hot, jogging was in and so was talking to your plants. On the stereo, Mary MacGregor was singing "Torn Between Two Lovers." Jade was turning on every man in the room and George was watching, just waiting for an opening.

Right from the very beginning George loved the way she looked: her hair the color of wet sand; her unique gold-flecked bronze eyes; her generous mouth unashamedly painted American-flag red. That evening she wore two ruffled high-necked Kenzo blouses, one over the other—one bright red, one electric blue—tucked into black sweatpants and belted with a hand-tooled, jewel-studded cowboy belt.

In a loft full of striking fashion models, mucho macho photographers, tanned and groomed-to-the-toenails Seventh Avenue cloakies, manicured fashion editors, and with-it designers, Jade was the woman who turned the most heads, the woman every man looked at—including George. He had noticed her the moment he walked in and had remembered her instantly. He was almost shocked at the way she had changed from drab to dazzling, from ordinary to extraordinary, from low key to high voltage. She was irresistible, and George was a man who did not know the meaning of the word resist.

"Jade Hartley!" he said, touching her hair for just a moment. He could smell her perfume, hear the slight crackle of her taffeta blouses as she moved, see the glow in her hair and eyes. Although he had met her in New York, he knew she lived in Fort Wayne, Indiana. "What are you doing here?"

"Jade Mullen," she corrected him, smiling back at him, thinking that if any man deserved to be called beautiful, it was George Kouras. He had thick dark hair; perfect, even features; pearl-white teeth; flawless olive skin; and intelligent, expressive amber eyes. Yet what attracted her to him most of all was the warm and unusually sensitive, even almost feminine quality that George possessed. It was a quality that Jade had always appreciated in men, something completely different from the All-American killer she had once married.

"Mullen?" he asked, surprised, raising his eyebrows slightly. He assumed she was divorced but he wasn't sure. Perhaps she had simply gone back to using her maiden name the way some women were doing now. "What happened to Barry?"

"We're divorced," said Jade. Her tone of voice was final; the hurt in her eyes wasn't.

"I'm sorry," he said, his eyes warm. He was sorry about her pain. He wasn't sorry about her divorce. "I am, too," he added with a wry smile. "Divorced."

It was her turn to say she was sorry although she was hardly surprised. After all, she'd known George when he was married. She remembered the way his partner Rollie

Leland, who was happily married, had envied George's track record with women. She remembered the jokes about George's little black book and trail of broken hearts. She assumed his wife had found out and left him. Jade was on the wife's side; she would have done the same thing. In fact she *had* done the same thing.

"Did you meet someone else?" Jade asked, imagining that he had. From what had apparently been a cast of thousands, one had obviously taken him away from his wife.

George shook his head. "*I* didn't. Ina did."

"Oh," said Jade, shocked and suddenly embarrassed. *That* was a twist!

There was an awkward moment of silence, and then George invited her to leave the party and have dinner with him.

"I'd love to," she said, leaving with him and, in the process, breaking half a dozen hearts.

George took Jade to the Pantheon, where everyone from the *Times* eats the shoulder of lamb and the porgy and the homemade yogurt and only the tourists order moussaka. They talked about the movies they'd loved: *Network* and *Carwash*. The movies they'd liked: *Black Sunday* and *Fun with Dick and Jane*. The movies they'd hated: *King Kong* and *The Other Side of Midnight*. They talked about Joe D'Urso's latest work (Jade knew a great deal about George's business, which was interior design) and Bendel's sensational windows (George knew a great deal about Jade's business, which was fashion). George told her about Rollie's sudden death four months after they'd moved their offices to an expensive brownstone and how, between the divorce and Rollie's death, he'd been emotionally and financially demolished. Jade told him that her divorce, too, had left her devastated—financially and emotionally—and how her only interest was in getting her life back on a sane and solid track.

On the surface they talked trade, gossip, and frivolity. But underneath an entire drama was taking place. They were wildly attracted to one another both physically and emotionally—and each reacted to it differently. Jade shied away from the attraction, even refused to admit it to herself. She hated love. Love was the worst thing that had ever happened to her. George, on the other hand, gave in to the attraction, even wallowed in it. He loved love. Love made him feel like a man.

"So tell me what happened with you and Barry?" George finally asked as the tiny cups of Greek coffee arrived.

"No way," said Jade, withdrawing instantly. Although she said it nicely she also meant it and George sensed it. "It happened a long time ago and I never think about it anymore."

"I see," said George, letting it drop although he was dying of curiosity. A long time ago? She had said it was only a year ago. And she never thought about it anymore? George didn't believe that one either. "I guess I don't blame you," he said out loud, not wanting to push her.

He wondered if she'd ask him about his divorce, but she didn't. She talked about how she wanted to give up free-lancing, about how she wanted a job—a real, grown-up, nine-to-five job. Making money was Number One on her list, she told George. She had been one of the few women in the history of the world to walk out of a marriage to a rich man dead broke.

"I found out," she said bitterly, "that when it comes down to love or money, rich people always choose money."

She did not say that some rich people even chose money over life itself. She was still too shattered to even get the words out.

As he paid the bill, George wondered if she was involved with someone, and by the time he got out of the taxi with her in front of her building, he wondered if she was living with someone.

"Aren't you going to ask me to come up?" he asked as he walked her to the building. She was living in the Deauville, just off First Avenue on Sixty-sixth Street, right in the middle of singles' territory.

"Nope," she said. She smiled and aimed a kiss some-where in the direction of his left cheek. "I've got a seven o'clock call tomorrow. We're going out to Jones Beach for a shoot." The last thing she needed was to invite him up. The last thing she needed was to get involved again.

She disappeared into the lobby, leaving him alone on the sidewalk. But the way she'd said no made George feel that, more than anything, she wished she could have said yes.

Jade, who wasn't rich and who wasn't pretty, had something that men couldn't resist. She had had it for as long as she could remember. The only time she'd lost it was when she'd been married.

"I didn't sleep last night," George told her the next morning on the phone. He called at six o'clock, a moment before her alarm went off. "I was thinking."

"About what?" Jade asked, giggling and flipping off the Sony. No matter what was happening in her life she always woke up in a wonderful mood. Even in the middle of a disaster, Jade woke up happy.

"About you," he said. His voice was like his eyes—expressive and intense and enveloping. George, unlike Barry, was a warm man who was not afraid of emotion. "Let's have dinner tonight."

"I'd love to but I can't," she said, meaning it, the way she always meant everything she told a man. She couldn't have dinner that night. She had a date with Dan Daryam, a television news director who had introduced her to Japanese food and Swiss graphics. She had known Dan for almost four months and he had just begun to talk about their living together. Dan was energetic and dynamic. Jade enjoyed his company and liked him in bed, but she didn't love him and she didn't want to live with him. She didn't want to live with anyone.

"Then tomorrow?" George persisted.

She couldn't have dinner the next night because she was going out with Martin Schultz, an industrial psychologist whose specialty was behavior in organizations. Martin had helped her understand Herb and Barry Hartley's hitherto mysterious behavior. She'd only known Martin for two weeks, and even though he was a little pompous Jade liked him, too—mostly because he kept her from focusing too much on Dan.

"What about the weekend?" George asked.

That weekend she was going to Bucks County with Dan. "Monday?"

On Monday night there was going to be a celebrity tennis players' fashion show for which Jade had done the styling, choosing the props and accessories. She would be attending with Peter Hailes, a tournament organizer who, on their first date, had taken Jade all the way to Montauk for lobsters.

"So when?" George asked, getting annoyed with her prom queen routine.

"Tuesday?" He could hear her shuffling the pages in her date book.

"Tuesday," George confirmed, resigned to waiting, knowing that she would be worth it.

It never occurred to him that Jade was playing hard to get. Jade, he could tell, didn't have to play hard to get. She *was* hard to get and George was a man who, when it came to women, couldn't resist a challenge.

C H A P T E R   2

1976
MANHATTAN

*W*hen Dorothy Mullen had gotten divorced in 1957 people were shocked; when Jade filed for divorce in 1976 no one noticed. By then, almost one out of every two American marriages ended in divorce. Divorce, like a driver's license or graduation, like a first job or first romance, had become a rite of passage. For many people, getting married and living happily ever after had been replaced by getting divorced and living happily ever after.

Nineteen seventy-six had been a year of transition, a year of looking forward and looking backward. It was the bicentennial year, the first post-Vietnam year, the year Gerald Ford, the first nonelected president, sat in the White House. The good news was that the Dow hit one thousand and the bad news was that unemployment and inflation figures were creeping up. Howard Hughes died and a born-again Christian from Georgia named Jimmy Carter won the Democratic party's nomination for president.

It was also a year of transition for Jade, a schizophrenic

year. There was crazy-Jade, happy-Jade. "Happily ever after" did not happen immediately for her. Instead, right after her divorce she returned to New York and moved into an ugly high-rise building pretentiously called the Deauville on First Avenue and Sixty-sixth Street. She shared a box-like two-bedroom apartment with three roommates whom she barely knew. Their names and faces—and boyfriends—changed from month to month—and the anonymity suited Jade just fine. In New York, where no one paid the slightest attention, she went temporarily crazy—sexually crazy, financially crazy, emotionally crazy.

Jade did things that scared her; she picked up strangers, told them her life story, and realized the next morning that, for all she knew, she could have picked up a killer and ended up dead. She drank to obliterate her pain and woke up with such vicious hangovers that she couldn't get out of bed. Early one afternoon, in a white wine haze, she took all the clothes that she had owned when she'd been married and burned them in her bathtub, setting an enormous fire that had ended with the fire department hacking their way through her front door. Later she realized that she could have burned the building down, killing not only herself but dozens of others as well. She felt wild, out of control, filled with a rage that sometimes exploded, other times imploded. She abused salesgirls and doormen; she abused herself with alcohol and grass and sleeping pills. Sometimes she lashed out in her pain; other times she directed it inward, descending into depressions that kept her a prisoner in her apartment for weeks at a time. It was a period when she didn't recognize herself. She was another person—a person she despised.

Jade, who had never slept with anyone except Barry, began to sleep with every man who asked, and plenty did. She felt like a slut and told herself that it served Barry right. Her favorite song was "Fifty Ways to Leave Your Lover," and she told every man she met that she was going to work her way through all fifty and then start at the beginning again. She thought it made her sound tough and in control when in fact she felt particularly vulnerable. Jade, who had never drunk more than two mai tais a year, now kept a jug of Gallo Chablis in her refrigerator. When she got high enough, she either went down to one of the singles' bars that lined First Avenue to find a man or telephoned Barry and poured out her rage. She was a sloppy, blowsy female drunk, and she told herself that she was larger than life and more sensitive than most. Jade, who had always been lavish with money, now became a miser, walking everywhere to save the bus fare and taking the remnants of dinners home to eat for breakfast the next day. She counted pennies and wasted dollars and told herself that she didn't care if she ended up on Skid Row. When she looked back, what she would remember most about the first days of being single again were cold nachos for breakfast.

For a while she didn't care what happened to her and felt as though no one else did either. She hid in the big city, away from her mother and her friends from home, and told herself, with a proud defiance, that if she was going down she was going to go down in flames. What saved her was that the city was expensive and she was out of money. If she was going to go down in flames, she realized, she'd need money—money for white wine and grass and the margaritas she liked to order in First Avenue bars.

Out of a regular job for the first time in her life, Jade began to work as a free-lance photographer's stylist. It was Jade who scouted down the accessories and props and backgrounds for fashion shots. The unpredictable schedule was perfect for this unpredictable time in her life, and being involved with fashion put her back in touch with the business she loved most. Consulting the listings in the *Madison Avenue Handbook,* Jade began to get assignments, small ones at first, styling for mail-order catalogs, and then, gradually, more lucrative ones for prestigious fashion and cosmetic accounts.

It was as a stylist that Jade began to discover Manhattan and its riches. She haunted the Mott Street Chinese pharmacies for exotic medicine bottles in gorgeous colors and shapes; the Amsterdam Avenue bodegas for white, seven-day Puerto Rican church candles in handsome glass cylinders; Casa Moneo on Fourteenth Street for rough Mexican terracotta pottery; a warehouse on the Bowery that had floors and floors of architectural columns and pediments salvaged from buildings about to be demolished. She found a kosher chicken slaughterhouse on Essex Street, a cluttered Arabic grocery store on Third Avenue in the Thirties, a shop on East Twenty-eighth Street that sold nothing but canes and umbrellas, a restaurant in the West Forties that looked like an Italian palazzo—all perfect backgrounds for fashion shots.

Always a passionate shopper, Jade knew where to find the perfect pair of sandals that would turn a twenty-dollar pair of pants and a ten-dollar T-shirt into an outfit that looked as if it summered in Southampton. Always the possessor of an original eye, she used a hundred-and-fifty-dollar printed Porthault towel as a hip wrap on an ordinary white man's shirt and presented it as a beach look. Always off-beat and on-target, she styled a series of white cottons against a field of red tulips as an insert in a white sale mailing and moved a line of dresses, pants, and blouses that had been headed for the markdown racks. By the time she ran into George at Titian Fellowes's loft, Jade was one of the top stylists in the city and her crazy-time was coming to an end.

MARCH 1977
JONES BEACH—MANHATTAN

The bathing suit shoot at Jones Beach was ordinary—for a fashion shoot. The March weather, although sunny, was so cold that the model's blue skin and erect nipples would have to be retouched out. One of the models was pregnant and hysterical because her boyfriend didn't want to marry her; the other was so luded out that she had to be propped up for the shots. The makeup artist was in the midst of a *crise* with his new lover and the hair stylist had a cold that verged on double pneumonia. The bathing suits were boring—cut too low on the thigh and too high on the bosom, a problem Jade dealt with by having the models lean slightly into the camera to hide the unflattering tops, and wear extremely high heeled shoes to lengthen the leg line.

"You're the best," said Titian on the drive back to the city, everyone frozen and exhausted. "You can make dreck look like diamonds."

"Some talent!" Jade laughed, even though she knew she was good at what she did. "The problem with free-lance," she told him as they drove through the toll booth of the

Triboro Bridge, "is that the time between jobs goes too slowly, and the time on the job goes too quickly. I wouldn't mind a regular nine-to-five job. Not to mention a regular nine-to-five salary."

Jade was tired of financial crises; she was tired of her crazy life. She was over the worst of her post-divorce crash and she wanted to take control of her own life again. One of the things she wanted most was to make money—money that would really be hers, money no one could ever take away from her.

"Lordy," Titian sighed, adding a flick of purple shadow to the interesting hollows beneath his eyes. "How bourgeois!"

"Well, it takes all kinds," said Jade, laughing, because, outrageous as he was, Titian was kind and sensitive and she liked him. He was one of the people who had put up with her during the worst of her crazy-time. "Seriously, though, if you hear of anything would you let me know?"

Jade looked forward to stability—financial and emotional—the way other people looked forward to excitement and adventure. The jug of Chablis disappeared from Jade's refrigerator, the casual men disappeared from her bed, and Jade was just beginning to feel good about herself again. She was learning, as many women were learning at that time, that the right work could be more dependable, more exciting, more rewarding than any man had ever been and Jade told everyone she ran into that she was looking for a job.

"Goddammit!" said the Missouri mule trainer's voice on Jade's answering machine on Sunday evening when she got back from Bucks County with Dan, leaving him with a kiss and another halfhearted promise to think about moving into his big Central Park West co-op with him. "How dare you set foot in this city and not call me *instantly?"*

That voice could belong to only one person: Mary Lou Tyler, Jade's former boss and nemesis, the top fashion buyer for Savin's Department Store. The message concluded with an order for Jade to call Mary Lou at Savin's sooner than instantly. There was also a message from Marty inviting her to a screening of Stephen King's thriller *Carrie* and a reminder from George about Tuesday. Underneath the door was a handwritten note from Peter asking if she'd like to go to a party for John McEnroe.

Jade got into bed feeling good about the future, the way she had when she had been at Cornell, the most popular girl in her class. The married Jade had been a good little girl drowning in a good little life. The recently divorced Jade had been a scary stranger steering crazily toward self-destruction. *This,* now, was the real Jade.

"Mary Lou! How did you track me down?" Jade returned Mary Lou's call first thing Monday morning.

"How do you think? You told everyone and his brother you want a job," said Mary Lou. "I heard it through the grapevine." Jade could hear papers rustling as Mary Lou went through memos, mail, confirmations, orders, invitations. Nothing, obviously, had changed. Mary Lou was a one-woman torpedo. She rattled windows and people and, once upon a time, she had rattled Jade. "So how the hell are you?"

"Fine," said Jade. "Now."

"And the kid?" Mary Lou asked. "You never even told me whether it was a boy or a girl."

"Don't you remember? I had a miscarriage," Jade said.

There was a moment's silence on the other end of the phone. Even the rustling of papers stopped for a moment. "I'm sorry," said Mary Lou, embarrassed. "I didn't remember. I guess I blocked it out. I don't know what to say. . . ."

"I'm over it now," said Jade, supposing that she was. The miscarriage was quite firmly relegated to the past where it belonged. But not the abortion. Not the abortion that had killed both her baby and her marriage.

"When did you get back to the city?" Mary Lou wanted to know. "And why the hell didn't you call me?"

Jade told Mary Lou about her divorce and that she returned to the city in 1976. "I didn't call you because I didn't call anyone. I had a post-divorce nervous breakdown and I had to get over it by myself," she said. "I wasn't fit for human companionship."

"Oh," said Mary Lou, who remembered her own divorce and understood perfectly. "One of those. So meet me for lunch,'' Mary Lou said. "La Grenouille. A week from Friday. One o'clock.''

Jade hung up, wondering what Mary Lou had in mind. Mary Lou always had *something* in mind. Meanwhile there was Tuesday and George Kouras.

On their first date they talked about themselves; on their second date they talked about each other; on their third date they talked about their divorces.

"Barry and his father never got along. Not from day one. I was always in the middle. Barry complained to me about his father. His father complained to me about Barry. I felt like a punching bag,'' Jade said. As she spoke of her ex-husband and ex-father-in-law there was still bitterness in her voice. "When we got divorced, though, they turned into best friends and ganged up on me. *That's* when I found out that blood is thicker than water. *That's* when I found out that when it comes to love and money, money matters and love doesn't.''

"It must have been terrific,'' George said, sensing, even though Jade had never gone into any of the details ("too sordid,'' she had said) that her experience must have been harrowing.

"It was wonderful,'' she said sardonically. "Now let's change the subject.''

Jade didn't like talking about her divorce; George, it seemed, couldn't *stop* talking about his. It was Ina-this and Ina-that. It was Ina and Ina's rich family and Ina's shocking announcement that she had fallen in love with someone else. And when it wasn't Ina, it was his son, Bobby. He adored Bobby. Bobby was the light of his life, the best thing that had ever happened to him; the cutest, brightest, nicest, most adorable two-year-old on the face of the earth.

"She's marrying him!'' he told Jade in appalled disbelief. For a change, he was talking about Ina and her lover. He and Jade sat at a table for two against the wall in the Grand Ticino, the light-hearted laughter and conversation from other tables a counterpoint to the intensity in George's recital. "He's a loser. Why would a woman leave her husband for a broken-down ex-first baseman who can't even keep a job?''

George went on and on and when he finally stopped Jade

shrugged—not unkindly, but uncomfortably. The last thing she needed was to attempt to psychoanalyze George's marriage, divorce, his ex-wife, *or* his ex-wife's lover.

"I don't know," she said finally, as he looked at her intently, waiting for an answer. "I guess you'd have to ask a psychiatrist."

"She blind-sided me," George continued compulsively, not wanting to admit that he *had* seen a psychiatrist, and that it hadn't helped. He was obsessed with Ina. He had always been the one to leave the relationship. No one had ever left him—until Ina did and took Bobby with her. He wanted to kill her. He wanted at least to get even with her—to make her hurt the way he hurt. "I thought we were happy."

"Happy?" Jade couldn't help showing her incredulity. "But you were running around with other women."

"None of them meant anything," he said, not denying it. "And anyway, I only began seeing other women after the marriage had already fallen apart."

Jade shrugged again. She didn't know whether she believed him or not. Starting with her father and ending with her husband, Jade had had a lot of practice in not believing what men told her. She was uncomfortable, and George sensed it.

"I don't know why I'm talking about it now," he said, shaking his head, knowing that one thing a man should never do is talk to one woman about another. He took her hand. "It happened almost a year ago," he said ruefully, not wanting to turn her off. "I guess I sound like a neurotic mess."

"We all do when we talk about our marriages," she said, glad that he was obviously winding down. She smiled sympathetically and remembered the men she had bored with the story of her own marriage and divorce. "Just call us the walking wounded."

"I don't know why you put up with me," George said after they'd seen each other three times. When he hadn't talked obsessively about Ina, he'd spoken about Bobby and Ina's custody of Bobby and the fact that they had moved to Denver where Ina's boyfriend lived so that George rarely saw Bobby. He *hated* the idea of Ina's future husband, the

broken-down ex-first baseman, bringing up *his* son. "Ina did it to punish me," he said. "She moved Bobby halfway across the country to punish me. It was her way of getting back at me."

"I'm sorry," Jade said uncomfortably. She had heard so many sad and bitter stories of men and their ex-wives, of fathers separated from their children, of men who couldn't cope with the wreckages of their marriages and their families since she'd come back to New York that she felt half the male population of the city were emotional basket cases. George, apparently, was just one more. "You must miss him."

George nodded. "I'm crazy about Bobby. He's the best thing that ever happened to me," he said. "But he's almost a stranger now. And I'm a divorce-bore."

"That's for sure," Jade said, breaking the mood with a dazzling smile. "I get the feeling you think I'm a free psychiatrist."

"But there must be *something* about me that you like," George said, not letting the edge in her voice put him off.

"I guess so," she admitted; she did, after all, keep seeing him. "But what?"

He knew what the something was. It was a combination of chemistry, an almost magical sense of rapport, the feeling that they'd known each other forever and that even if they hadn't seen each other for fifty years, they could pick up again in the middle of a sentence. All that—*and* an incredible sexual electricity that sizzled between them like an August lightning storm that made the night skies white. He knew it, but he didn't intend to spell it out for her. He planned to let her find out for herself. He would give her plenty of time, and plenty of rope. One thing George never did was crowd a woman.

"If you're not careful," George said to Jade in the middle of April, "I'm going to fall madly in love with you." They were having dinner at Parioli Romanissimo, and he reached across the table, took her hand, kissed each finger one by one, caressed her with his eyes, and seduced her with his voice. He wasn't giving up, and she still wasn't giving in.

"Don't," she warned, instinctively pulling back. "I don't trust men who fall madly in love." That was something else she had learned from her marriage—to beware of men who loved too much. They ended up strangling you. She pulled her hand away and when George took her home, they sat as far from each other as they could in the back of the big cab.

"I have to go to Boston Friday on a job," George said suddenly, as the cab pulled up in front of Jade's building. "How would you like to meet me? We could go to Nantucket for the weekend."

"Nantucket? For the weekend?" She thought he was outrageous. He was pushing too hard, coming on too strong.

"Why not?" he asked nonchalantly, defusing her outrage with humor. Falling in love with her, he thought, was like falling in love with a porcupine. He had to keep watching out for the bristles. "I didn't invite you to downtown Hoboken."

"I have a lunch date," she said coldly. "With Mary Lou."

"So leave after your lunch date," he said, not giving up, porcupine or no porcupine.

"Absolutely not!" she exclaimed, furious that he'd pushed her into a corner. She was exhausted from holding them both off—herself and him. She was on an emotional highwire, scared, exhilarated, afraid to fall, too terrified to take the next step. "What makes you think I'd want to spend the weekend with you? I've never even really kissed you!"

"I can take care of that," he said and, right there in the back of Pascal Gomez's taxi, he did. Now that whole books were being written about the joys of sex it seemed as though a lot of men had forgotten how to kiss. Not George Kouras.

Jade finally pulled away, breathless and dizzy, and getting out of the taxi, she fled into the safety of her own apartment. She had just begun to get herself together, to get her life on an even keel. The last thing she wanted to do was to go to bed with George. The last thing she wanted to do was to go to Nantucket with George. The last thing she wanted was to be anything more than friends with George. George was not like Dan or Marty or even Peter. George would not be easy to handle. Her feelings for George would not be easy to handle. George, she knew, was a womanizer, just like her father. George was also still hung up on his ex-wife and desperate to get Bobby back. Becoming involved with George, she knew, would create nothing but complications, and the last thing she wanted was complications. She had already just barely survived too many complications.

C H A P T E R   3

Mary Lou Tyler was like a diamond. Pear-shaped. She had nonexistent shoulders, low-slung breasts, and as they said back home in Missouri where Mary Lou came from, an ass like a fifty-dollar horse. Her mop of hennaed hair was permed in a Little Orphan Annie frizz, eyeglasses swung from a ribbon around her neck, and a smear of raspberry lipstick and black eyeliner passed for makeup. She dressed in an assertively indifferent, I-don't-give-a-damn-about-fashion way that Jade knew many old-time buyers affected. Mary Lou spoke rapid-fire New Yorkese with a deep southern accent sprinkled liberally with Yiddishisms. In the YSLed and Blassed, perfumed and hand-kissing hothouse atmosphere of La Grenouille at lunch, Mary Lou was something else.

"You look wonderful!" Mary Lou said as she greeted Jade, taking in her Perry Ellis sweater, Rykiel skirt, and armload of wide ivory bangles. Broke or not, Jade always wore the best clothes. She bought showroom samples, army-navy surplus, and East Village oddments and put them together with an individual flare that spelled Style. "What did you do to yourself?"

"Mainly," said Jade, slipping onto the banquette next to Mary Lou, happier than she thought she would be to see her former boss again, "I got divorced."

"Good girl!" said Mary Lou practically slapping Jade on

the back. Marriage, Mary Lou had thought ever since her own divorce, did not bring out the best in a woman. She told the waiter to bring them the special striped bass, Mary Lou's salute to calorie-counting, and then turned to Jade. "So. I hear you want a job."

Jade nodded.

"Have I got a job for you!" Mary Lou announced and then, in the maddening way she had of getting to the point the long way around, went back to 1976, a year Jade remembered well.

Just as 1976 had been a transitional time for Jade, it had been a transitional time for fashion. The maxi-skirt disaster of the early seventies and the two-year recession that had begun in 1973 had turned fashion to the right. The Calvin Klein–Halston brand of tailored American classics, the classic crepe de chine shirts and good wool skirts, reigned—conservative clothes for a conservative mood. Practically no one had heard of Perry Ellis; Norma Kamali was working out of a modest shop on the second floor of a brownstone on Madison Avenue in the sixties making avant-garde-looking clothes that only a tiny coterie of fans appreciated; designer jeans were still in the future and so were sweats as fashion, Zoran's minimalist separates, and the Japanese invasion. There was almost nothing between the Calvin-Halston safe-and-secure clothes and Claude Montana's space-Fascist leather jackets. The only real look was the "Annie Hall look," a schizzy amalgam of bits and pieces rescued from the attic and borrowed from a boyfriend's closet, which seemed to reflect the times perfectly.

"Fashion was in limbo," Mary Lou said over the poached striped bass, "and in the midst of limbo I discovered opportunity. Do you remember Steve Hirsch?" Jade nodded again. Steve was the son of Ira Hirsch, president of Rainy Dayz, a raincoat manufacturer that had been one of Jade's larger resources when she'd been a buyer. Steve Hirsch was your basic, assembly-line-model, plump and sweaty Jewish prince who knew how to walk but, thank God, didn't have to. Steve was no cartoon, though; he was a very gifted designer. When Jade visited Ira's showroom, Steve, who knew that Jade wanted to be an illustrator, used to show her his own sketches. He always vowed he'd never waste his talent on the jungle called Seventh Avenue. He wanted to be an Artist, and pronounced it so that Jade could almost hear the capital *A*. An ambition, he told Jade with both pride and fear, that would both shock and displease his very businesslike father.

"Now he's Stefan Hitchcock."

"So?" Jade shrugged slightly, unconsciously imitating Mary Lou. (Jade, who had a style all her own, still thought that Mary Lou had written the book.) Stefan Hitchcock? The name meant nothing to her.

Steve had been gay and he had been straight, but he had always been successful.

When he worked for his father at Rainy Dayz, Steve had designed a low-priced line of nylon ciré rainwear in Crayola colors that his father had manufactured. The coats had retailed for under twenty dollars and the line, called Rain Drops, had been a great success, but Steve did not intend to be trapped in the raincoat business. As he kept telling anyone who would listen, he considered himself an Artist. The commercial success of the raincoats was strictly a fluke.

The first Monday in April 1975 was the pits. The sixteen-month November 1973–March 1975 slump had been the worst since the 1929–1933 depression. Nothing was selling, no one was buying. Retailers always complained about business, but this time they had something to complain about. Nevertheless, the newly minted Stefan Hitchcock showed up in Mary Lou's office on April Fool's Day, a sample in a plastic garment bag over his arm.

"I wonder if you'd be interested in this," he said and began to unzip the garment bag.

What Steve pulled out was an evening dress that made Mary Lou remember why she had become a buyer. Made of heavy white satin, it had long sleeves and slightly padded shoulders. Cut on the bias, it clung slinkily, like a lover's hands, to the lines of the body, showing bosom, waist, and hips. Diagonally across the front, reaching from the left shoulder to the top of the right hip, was an art nouveau-ish, larger-than-life peacock feather worked in sequins of blue, fuschia, orchid, emerald, gold, and black. The dress was very thirties, very Cole Porter, very silver-fox-and-white-satin—it was the kind of dress Carole Lombard had worn to perfection.

"Fan-fucking-tastic!" Mary Lou had exclaimed. "Could you make three?"

Steve could, would, and did.

"The dresses retailed for eleven hundred dollars each," Mary Lou told Jade as she continued to relate her story. "On the *morning* that the first ad appeared in *The New York Times* we sold all three! Customers were calling from Chicago and Dallas. Women were dying for that dress!"

"Incredible!" exclaimed Jade. Eleven-hundred-dollar dresses, she knew, did not fly out of stores in one morning every day in the week.

"It gets better," said Mary Lou. "The 'feather dress' showed up on the front page of *Women's Wear Daily* on a real estate tycoon's daughter. Suddenly *everyone* wanted a Stefan Hitchcock original. Steve's next dress was black hammered satin with beaded silver inserts running down each side of the dress from armhole to hemline. It was the most flattering dress I ever laid eyes on," continued Mary Lou. "It made *me* look thin! I ordered three and sold them all." Feeling virtuous over the striped bass, Mary Lou contributed to advancing ass-spread by ordering an apple tart drowned in *crème fraîche*.

"Steve," Mary Lou continued, "was on the map."

"But I don't understand," said Jade. "Why haven't I heard of him? If he's as talented as you say, why isn't he successful?"

"He *is* successful," Mary Lou said. "So successful he's almost bankrupt."

When Steve had been selling three dresses here and three dresses there, he had been able to handle his business with one assistant and a few pieceworkers. Now that Mary Lou had ordered eight and was backing them up with a window, other stores began to pay attention. Orders had come in from stores all over the country. Steve suddenly had to buy dozens of yards of fabric and trimmings in quantity, had to adhere to promised delivery dates, had to establish and control a cash flow. He was a designer suddenly faced with the need to run a business. What he didn't know was that he had made the classic mistake of doing everything backward. He should have known better, but Steve considered himself an Artist and had never paid any attention to the financial end of his father's business. He'd already put his life savings of fifteen thousand dollars into his business and it wasn't nearly enough. He owed fabric and trimming houses, his contract workers refused to pick up needle and thread until he paid their back wages, and the trucker he owed was promising to break his knees unless he paid up.

"I made a commitment for a corner window and a Sunday *Times* ad and now he tells me he can't deliver the goods!" Mary Lou fumed. Mary Lou wasn't used to being put into a corner and she didn't intend to get into deep shit over Stefan Hitchcock. "I'd like to kill him!"

"Why doesn't he borrow from his father?" asked Jade.

Mary Lou rolled her eyes. "He wants to make it on his own," she said, obviously mimicking Steve. "He doesn't want to run to daddy."

Jade nodded. For once she didn't agree with Mary Lou. She wished Barry had been more like that.

"Why are you telling me all this?" Jade suddenly asked.

"Because you can bail him out. Him—and me!" Mary Lou replied.

"And what's in it for me?" asked Jade.

"A job," said Mary Lou nonchalantly.

"A job!" Jade exclaimed. "Some job! You just said he can't pay his bills. How is he going to pay me?"

"With the money he'll make when we sell out the god-damn dresses you're going to make sure the little *pisher* delivers," said Mary Lou, polishing off the last of the special chocolate truffles that Giselle Masson always kept for her. "Seriously, Jade. Steve has it all—except a partner. I think you'd be the right partner."

Jade left La Grenouille and went over to the Forty-second Street library. She spent the afternoon poring over back issues of *Women's Wear Daily* and the *Times*. She found the photo of the real estate tycoon's daughter in the feather dress. She found an Antonio sketch of the black dress with silver beaded inserts in an article about the opening of a Diana Vreeland show at the Metropolitan. She checked out *Vogue* and found one mention of Stefan Hitchcock in

Vogue's Eye View pages. Mary Lou was right: Steve had it all. Whether or not she wanted to help pick up the pieces was another matter, but she made an appointment to meet him. After all, she had nothing to lose.

All biz is show biz, especially the fashion biz. There's Seventh Avenue, where the stars and the big-ticket productions reign, where Bill Blass and Ralph Lauren and Calvin Klein have their showrooms. There's Off-Seventh Avenue in the West Thirties, where the second tier of designers have lofts and showrooms. Off-off-Seventh as in SoHo and Tribeca were where new and avant-garde designers show. And then there was Stefan Hitchcock's workroom in a former printer's shop on Nineteenth Street between Fifth and Sixth avenues, precisely in the middle of nowhere.

The next day, first thing in the morning, Jade stood on the sidewalk and pushed the buzzer and waited for the responding buzz.

There was none. She waited a moment, then buzzed again. Still there was no answer. She was about to give up when she heard a window open.

"Jade Mullen?" a voice called from an open window. Jade looked up. It was Steve. "Come on up. You'll have to walk. The elevator doesn't work."

Cautiously, Jade made her way up four flights in the pitch-dark.

"That goddamn Con Ed!" Steve exclaimed as he opened the door for her. She blinked, slightly blinded by the bright daylight that poured into the showroom. Slim and compact, in khaki slacks, a navy Lacoste shirt, and Topsiders, Steve was totally changed from the plump and sweaty son-of-the-boss and scourge-of-the-gay-bars Jade remembered from the old days. Steve was in the middle of a major overhaul on himself, but right now he was so upset that he didn't focus on Jade. "They shut off the goddamn power!"

"The idea is to pay the bill," said Jade, looking around the workroom, the sewing machines silent, the electric clock on the wall stopped, piles of half-cut garments abandoned in heaps.

"For Christ's sake, I know that!" Steve said, as if it were Jade's fault. "If I had the money, I would!"

"You're in a lot of trouble, Steve," she said, annoyed. "A tantrum isn't going to help."

"A tantrum makes me feel better."

"It doesn't make *me* feel better," said Jade. "Mary Lou sent me over to bail you out."

"And will you?" he asked belligerently.

"Maybe."

The first thing Jade did was take two hundred dollars out of her own checking account over to the Con Ed payment center and have the electricity turned on that same afternoon.

"You're incredible!" Steve said, and instantly calmed down.

Mary Lou had said Jade was fantastic. Steve had been dubious, but since he was desperate he figured he'd give her a chance. He remembered her from when she'd been Mary Lou's assistant, hard-working but sort of mousy. Even in the midst of his hysteria over the turned-off power, he had been bowled over when he'd seen her standing on the sidewalk. She was wearing a turquoise linen jacket, the sleeves rolled up a few turns, over an olive jumpsuit thrust into red cowboy boots. A pair of red-framed glasses were stuck up into her hair, and Steve thought she was the best-looking thing he had ever seen. Like everyone else, Steve never noticed the things about Jade that she didn't want noticed. "You're just incredible!"

"So are you," said Jade sarcastically. She had gone over to Con Ed in a moment of high resolve. Now that she was back in the workroom she was wondering what she was getting herself into. Steve was a prima donna who considered himself an Artist. His business, so-called, was a mess. For one thing, she told herself right up front she was not giving up free-lance styling for Steve Hirsch. Steve seemed to read her mind.

"Actually, I'm a big success," he said seriously, suddenly businesslike. He gestured to a bulletin board with press clippings and a wicker basket containing orders. "I have orders for a dozen of the beaded dresses. They wholesale for six hundred dollars. That's over seven thousand dollars."

"That's over seven thousand dollars *if* you deliver," said Jade, just as seriously. "Mary Lou's committed to an ad and a window. She went crazy when you said you couldn't deliver. Steve, designers don't miss windows and stay in business. Not ever.''

"So what am I supposed to do?" Steve said, suddenly belligerent again. He fiddled with the Star of David he still wore despite his current preppy incarnation. "I don't have any money. Some of the stores still owe me from my last shipment. How can I get the dresses made?"

"Sew them yourself if you have to," said Jade.

Steve looked at her as if she were insane but that is, in the end, almost exactly what happened. The bodies of the dresses had already been cut and stitched. What remained to be done was the intricate hand beading that was becoming the Stefan Hitchcock trademark. Jade and Steve and two Colombian women, whose wages were paid with money that Jade persuaded Mary Lou to advance, sat up for two weeks until four in the morning beading dresses.

"I'm going blind," Steve complained.

"It's that," Jade said. "Or going broke."

Steve kept stitching.

"You used your own money?" George said incredulously when she told him. Jade always did the most extraordinary things in the most extraordinary way. She had the energy of an Amazon and the resourcefulness of a one-man band. He couldn't remember ever spending one boring moment in her company.

"Why not? Steve's broke but his father owns half of Florida," said Jade. "Anyway, Steve is talented. He's going to be a big success."

"And you're going to help him?"

Jade nodded.

"Yes," she said. "I think Steve and I can make a lot of money together."

"And does Steve?"

"He says he's not sure if he's interested in money or not," said Jade.

"Rich kids!" exclaimed George, remembering Ina's cavalier attitudes toward money. Then he changed the subject. "Are you free for the weekend?"

"Yes I am but no I won't," she said with her most dazzling smile. She knew what he'd ask next.

"You mean you still won't go to Nantucket with me?"

"That's right."

"I won't give up," he promised.

"And I won't change my mind," *she* promised.

The tension crackled back and forth between them. Jade was aware of feeling unusually keyed up, while George was aware of feeling patiently impatient. Foreplay, he knew, never killed anyone, but *this* was getting ridiculous.

C H A P T E R 4

Ever since George could remember, what he had loved most was love. In the fifties, when other boys talked about cars, George talked about girls. In the sixties, when other boys talked about politics, George talked about love. Other boys wanted to get laid; George wanted to fall in love. He loved the way loving made him feel. As a lover he was a genius; as a lover he was an artist. Being a lover brought out the best in him.

He sent Jade flowers: white lilacs from Madderlake, the Madison Avenue florist, who he thought did the best flowers in the city; and truffles, champagne truffles, only the very best, from Teuscher. He sent her a handsome, one-of-a-kind antique Japanese lacquer trunk from a gallery of Japanese folk art in SoHo to hold the glossy French and English and Italian fashion magazines she bought compulsively.

"I want you to fall in love with me," he said, putting her off balance with the direct approach. His voice was seductive, his amber eyes caressed her. Amber eyes? she had once asked him. I thought all Greeks had brown eyes. Not northern Greeks, George had replied. Not the Greeks from Thessaloniki where his family was from. Where the best-looking girls in Greece were from—and the best-looking men.

"I told you," she said firmly, "I'm not going to fall in love again. Not with you. Not with anyone."

"We'll be different," he promised her. "We'll be good together, Jade. Very good."

She didn't believe it. Ever since her divorce Jade didn't believe she'd be good with anyone. She wanted to control herself, to hold herself in. She wanted a calm and orderly life, a sane and stable life. She didn't want to let go, to fall in love again. She knew all about love. Love meant hurt and disappointment and the most bitter betrayal. If she fell in love again she'd be vulnerable again, and she just didn't want to risk it. That was why she liked Dan, who wasn't threatening, and Marty, who wasn't aggressive. That was why she liked Peter, who traveled so much with the Pro tour that he wasn't around enough to become threatening. That was why she shied away from George. George didn't fool around with tentative approaches and half-articulated emotions. He was crazy about her, he was madly in love with her, he was dying for her—and he made no secret about it.

When the direct approach didn't work George backed off. He knew that patience always paid off—patience, he knew, was everything; so, too, was persistence. But George couldn't stay away from her, didn't even try to stay away from her, never considered staying away from her. He wanted to fall madly in love with her. She was everything Ina wasn't—creative, independent, unspoiled. Jade, he knew, wouldn't smother him. Jade would make him forget all about Ina.

"I can't stay away from you," he'd say, caressing her hair, unable to resist the way she looked, the way she talked, the way she crossed a room or brushed her hair or put on her coat. "I'm an addicted man. Addicted to you."

He tried to kiss her but Jade moved away. She wasn't ready to believe what he said, wasn't ready to believe protestations of love and passion, wasn't ready to be seduced by words and promises. She had been brutally betrayed; her capacity for trust had been destroyed. The only relationships that interested her were safe ones, ones she controlled.

"I want you," he told her. He was gentle with her; he was careful and tender. "I want to kiss you. I want to make love to you. I want to love you."

"No," she said, moving away both physically and emotionally, putting a fence around her body and her feelings. Her heart had been broken and she did not want to risk the little bit of herself that was left whole. "No, George, I don't want you to."

"What are you afraid of?" he asked, his warm eyes tender and compassionate. He was feeling the chemistry, the incredible attraction and rapport between them. He knew she was, too.

"Nothing," she said evasively.

He knew she was lying even if she didn't.

"You're afraid of two things," he said gently. "For one thing, you're afraid of me."

She shrugged, a sudden sardonic shrug that saw everything, questioned everything, trusted nothing. He was right. She *was* afraid of him. "And the second?" she asked.

"Yourself," he said, taking her hand. "You don't trust me. You don't trust yourself."

"No," she said abruptly, almost harshly, pulling away. He had come too close. She didn't want him to be that close. She didn't want *anyone* to be that close. "Let's not. Let's leave things the way they are."

But George didn't want to leave things the way they were. He wanted to change things. To make things better. To make them happier.

"I'm a lover," he told her, trying to persuade her, his lips on her face. "Not a destroyer. We'll be happy. More than happy. Ecstatic."

"I'm happy the way I am," she said, moving away.

"I'm not Barry," he said, getting to the heart of her refusal to give herself to him.

"I know you're not!" she said impatiently.

"Then don't confuse us," he said.

"I don't!"

"I think you do," he insisted. "I think you're afraid every man is like your ex-husband. But I'm not Barry, Jade. I'm not going to hurt you. I'm not going to betray you."

He didn't give up, her rejections only spurred him on, her pain only made him more anxious to comfort her with love. He gave her gifts and attention, strawberries in season and raspberries out of season. He deluged her with perfume and flowers and attention. He called her in the morning so he would be the first person that day to speak to her, and whispered tender good nights so that he would also be the last. He took her to movies and openings, brought her umbrellas when it rained, and wrapped her in his coat when it was cold. He did everything right, and the only thing he did wrong was to constantly talk about Ina: Ina and her rich father; Ina and her lover; Ina and the way she'd left him; Ina and the way she'd taken Bobby away from him.

"I think you're still in love with Ina," Jade told him, giving herself the best reason of all to resist him.

"No," he said, rejecting the very idea. "It's *you* I love."

When he didn't talk about Ina, he talked about Bobby: How Bobby already showed amazing musical talent. How Bobby seemed to be a natural athlete. How Bobby had walked at eight months and spoken entire sentences at sixteen months.

Jade wasn't sure if Ina was her competition or Bobby. She wasn't sure if George even knew.

He tried not to mention Ina and he kept up his pursuit. The gifts continued and so did the phone calls and the flowers and the love notes. She thanked him, she responded to him, she smiled at him—she did everything but open herself to him. She had staggered away from her marriage in barely one piece. She had vowed that she would never get involved again. She had thought that never included George, but never ended four months after she'd run into him at Titian Fellowes's loft, when she saw him with another woman and thought she'd die of jealousy.

If he had planned it, it couldn't have been more perfect. Maybe, a little voice whispered inside him, he *had* planned it. After all, he knew Jade well enough by now to know her favorite places. Le Relais was one of them. When he made the dinner reservation for two it crossed his mind that he might see her there. As a matter of fact, he planned on seeing her there. It was no accident that George's date was an actress, a very, very pretty actress. Or that he chose the seat facing the entrance. It was also no accident that he saw Jade the instant she walked in with her own date, who happened to be Martin Schultz.

"Hi, Jade," he had said pleasantly as she and Martin passed his table. He introduced her to Lisa Knight.

"Hello, George," Jade had said coolly and walked on, barely acknowledging Lisa's existence. She did not even introduce Martin.

"Your friend is jealous," Lisa said.

"Just nearsighted," George had answered, trying to make an excuse for Jade.

"No one's *that* nearsighted," Lisa said and wondered what was going on between George and Jade Mullen.

"Who was that?" Martin asked when he and Jade sat down at their own table.

"I can't remember his name," Jade fibbed, and began to look at the menu. "That's why I couldn't introduce you."

Martin knew she was lying and wondered why. Lying wasn't the least bit like her.

George called Jade the next day at home and then at Stefan Hitchcock's loft. She didn't come to the phone or return the messages he left on her machine. He called again the day after that, and again she mysteriously wasn't available and did not return his calls. She continued to refuse to speak to him and, by doing so, played right into his hands. George the lover understood all about women's rejections and he knew just how to handle them.

Four days after the chance encounter at Le Relais George showed up at Stefan Hitchcock's loft in the middle of the afternoon, carrying an armful of white freesia. Steve was sorting through fabric samples; Jade was on the telephone. Jade was *always* on the telephone.

"Later," he said, interrupting her in midsentence, taking the phone from her hand, and hanging it up.

"That was Ultimo's!" she said, grabbing for it, furious. "What's the matter with you!"

"It's what's the matter with you," he retorted. He was angry and he was out of patience. The relationship was at a turning point. It was time to take control and George, always the lover, knew exactly what to do and how to do it. "You're jealous because you saw me with someone else and you can't stand it!"

"I'm *not* jealous!" she flared, denying his words, denying her feelings. The one thing she could not tolerate, would not tolerate, was a man like her father, a man who used one woman to punish another, a man whose attitude was: Why make one woman happy when you can make two women miserable? "I don't own you! I don't care who you go out with!"

"That's right," said George, knowing he had her now. "You don't care so much that you couldn't even say hello to her. And you don't care so much that you won't even talk to me on the phone."

"God! You're conceited." She turned to Steve for support. He fiddled with his tortoiseshell glasses, avoided her eyes, studied the laces of his Topsiders and shrugged. Steve's own love life, vacillating from left to right, from radical to conservative, from gay to straight was stalled right now in muddled bisexuality. He was even more confused than Jade. He was the last one to give aid and advice.

"No, I'm not," said George, refusing to be put on the defensive. "I'm just a realist. Jade, when are you going to stop running away from me?"

"I'm *not* running," she said, backing away from him.

"Steve, you're going to have to survive without her for a few days," he said and, without waiting for an answer, took her by the arm, led her through the loft into the now-working elevator, out onto Fifteenth Street, and into a taxi.

"La Guardia," George told the driver. "The Marine Air Terminal."

"Where are we going? What are you doing! Driver, stop this car this instant!"

The driver glanced back, confused.

"Keep on, driver," George said firmly, handing him a ten-dollar bill.

"We're going to Nantucket," George said. "That's where we're going. As to what I'm doing, I'm just trying to talk to you and since you refuse to talk to me on the phone, I'm going to talk to you in person."

"Nantucket! But the Bendel's buyer is coming in this afternoon!" He had tricked her, and used her own feelings against her. She hated him. She was afraid of him. She wanted to get away from him.

"Steve can handle it," he said, firmly holding her so that she couldn't move.

"But I don't have any clothes!"

"Jade," he said, kissing her so she couldn't speak and crushing the fragrant freesia between them so that she was dizzy from the scent and dizzy from his kiss. "You're not going to need any."

He took her to the Jared Coffin house where, in a four-poster bed, he made love to her for the first time, quickly and hungrily, deliberately satisfying himself first, leaving her slightly up in the air, wanting more. Then, a bit later, when it suited him, he made love to her slowly and carefully, playing her body and her feelings like the master of love he was, exploring every curve and every crevice of her body with his fingers and tongue and finding every place on her arms and legs, on her throat and on her face that pushed her over the edge and out of control.

"Jade, Jade," he kept whispering, saying her name over and over. "Jade, Jade. I wanted you so. Jade, oh, Jade."

She had forgotten about sexual intoxication. Or had she ever known about it? She wasn't sure. With Barry, she had been too young. With the other men, she had been too angry. Now, all she wanted was for the feeling to go on forever. He had finally won, and she knew that all along she had wanted him to win.

"It wasn't so bad, was it?" he asked, teasingly, three days later as they flew back to Manhattan. Three days in which they had barely left the bed, in which they couldn't keep their hands off each other, and had barely slept or eaten, existing merely on each other's taste and touch. Three days in which he didn't think of Ina or even mention her name, and three days in which Jade forgot Barry, forgot her anger.

"I don't know," she said, shrugging indifferently and matching his tone. "I sort of thought you'd be the sexy type."

He threw one of the airline's small pillows at her and she threw it right back at him catching him on the side of the head.

"Wait until I get you home," he threatened.

"Just because you kidnapped me for a few days doesn't mean you own me," she said, suddenly serious, suddenly withdrawing, raising a theme she would return to over and over again.

"I never said anything about owning you," he said seriously, instantly responding to the warning in her voice. "All I'm interested in is loving you. I'm never going to hurt you."

"That's what they all say," replied Jade.

Underneath the teasing and the badinage was something else, something neither wished to admit nor explore. What neither of them understood was that both were hurt and that each had a different prescription for the pain. George thought it was love that would make him whole again; Jade believed in independence.

C H A P T E R 5

The first thing Jade had done for Stefan Hitchcock was to get the lights turned back on. The second thing she had done was to get his first important order delivered. The third thing was to turn down the best offer Steve had had so far.

Buddy Meister was a legend among retailers. He was the president of Marks & Company, a carriage-trade specialty store located on the site where De Pinna's once stood. He was the seventh of thirteen children, "lucky seventh" he always said, from a poor family in Bridgeport, Connecticut. Buddy had started his career at the age of twelve sweeping up and making deliveries for a local drugstore. He progressed to the stockroom of the local Woolworth's and, from there, to its hat and scarf department, ending up, at the age of sixteen, as an assistant floor manager. He left Bridgeport, never to return, upon his graduation from high school. He worked his way through Boston University, couldn't figure out a way to evade the draft, and went into the army. While other boys were getting shot at, Buddy was making the first real money of his life. He was a consistent winner at the eternal poker games, but more to the point, he got himself assigned to the receiving department of the PX where he proceeded on a classic theory: one for Uncle Sam, one for Buddy Meister. He emerged from the army with thirty-five thousand dollars in cash and went immediately to New York to look for a way to get rich.

What he found was a knitted hat company that had been one of Woolworth's vendors. The company was on its way under. It wasn't that the hats didn't sell; just that collecting the receivables was a problem. Buddy convinced the boss that the job was made for him. The legend is that in six weeks Buddy collected money that had been due for as long as two and a half years. The legend is that the hat company never had a moment's union problem, that there was never a problem with yarn deliveries, that the hot styles showed up at the company Buddy Meister worked for *before* they were even shown in Paris and along Seventh Avenue, that when the owner retired he sold the company to Buddy for exactly thirty-five thousand dollars. The legend is that Buddy Meister never left for work without a gun in his pocket. Buddy never bothered to deny the legends. "They make me sound glamorous," he would say with a wink.

By the time Steve Hirsch had become Stefan Hitchcock, Buddy was an important force in retailing, a prominent figure in New York philanthrophy, a recipient of various awards for his contributions to orphanages, educational funds, hospitals, and cultural groups. His tailor was Caraceni of Milan, his shirtmaker was Turnbull & Asser of London, and his shoemaker was Lobb of Paris. He never said who made his guns. No one ever dared ask, although in his spacious, elegant office overlooking Fifty-second Street an entire wall was given over to a display of valuable, handtooled weapons from Smith & Wesson, Remington, and Purdey. Buddy, at sixty, looked much the way he had at forty: he was on the short side, muscular but trim, and had dark skin pitted from a bad case of adolescent acne. Buddy Meister was very much the picture of the tough guy. Yeah, Buddy admitted, with his steely smile, a real tough guy—with a heart of hot fudge. He liked to complain that he was a soft touch.

* * *

Buddy, who heard everything first, was among the first to hear that Stefan Hitchcock's brand-new enterprise was already in deep trouble. Buddy had known Ira Hirsch from the days when Ira was struggling along with the raincoats and Buddy was collecting receivables. Buddy saw a way to help out the son of an old friend while making a few pesos for himself. He offered to back Steve—if he'd sell his clothes under the Marks & Company label. Steve was tempted to go along with Buddy's offer.

"That way they'll have all the financial worries," Steve told Jade, seeing a way out of the anxiety that was giving him rashes, hives, and sleepless nights.

"That way they'll also have all the profits," Jade said and told Steve to turn Buddy down.

"No one turns Buddy Meister down," Steve said. On a certain level, Steve was always looking for a rescuer— whether it was Jade or Mary Lou or Buddy Meister.

"If you're afraid to," Jade said winningly, "I'm not."

"Are you sure you know what you're doing?" Buddy asked Jade. He had a gravelly voice that went with the legend. Jade sat in Buddy Meister's grand office facing the wall of guns. There were dozens of them. It was like having a meeting in an arsenal.

"Sure I'm sure," said Jade with her trademark smile. "Why should Steve sell his clothes under your label?"

"Easy," said Buddy. "For the prestige. For the Fifth Avenue aura. For the upscale ambiance."

"But Steve can get all those things without Marks & Company," Jade pointed out. "After all, Steve already sells to Savin's and Bendel's has just given him a nice order."

"So? Why be a *pisher* at Savin's and Bendel's when he could be a star at Marks & Company?" Buddy wanted to know.

"A star?" Jade asked, zinging him. "Or a house designer?"

Buddy looked at her a moment, frankly assessing her. "Who's got the ambition?" he asked suddenly. "You or Steve?"

"Both of us," Jade said, although it wasn't strictly the

truth. At the moment it was she who had more ambition. Steve still had not resolved his conflict between being an Artist and a businessman. Part of him wanted to differentiate himself completely from his father, while part of him wanted to be *like* his father. All Steve knew at this point was what he didn't want—to be lost in his powerful father's shadow. Because he was so candid about it, and because he was so directly the opposite of Barry, Jade had much more patience with him than she might ordinarily have had.

Buddy looked at her another long moment. "You *shtupping* him?" he asked.

Jade got up instantly and, looking straight into Buddy Meister's flinty gray eyes, gestured toward the wall of guns, smiled a thousand watts' worth, and asked, "You shoot many people?"

Situations that Carlys handled with direct hostility Jade handled with a sassy charm. Both were effective, but people were afraid of Carlys. They *liked* Jade. Even tough guys like Buddy Meister.

Buddy was taken aback, shocked into silence for a moment. Then he laughed, a short, hard snort.

"You're not bad," he said, warming up to her in that instant. "You know," he added, shaking his head, "no one's ever mentioned those guns. Not once in all the years they've been there. You're the first."

"And the first, Mr. Meister," said Jade, who contrasted her firm words with her dazzling smile, "to tell you no. Go find another talented designer you can buy for next to nothing."

Buddy was about to say something, but Jade was out of his office before he could open his mouth.

"Jesus Christ!" Steve said, turning a pale shade of anxious when Jade told him what she'd done. "No one turns down Buddy Meister to his face."

"I just did," said Jade blandly. Steve's moods went up and down like an elevator gone haywire. Right now he was scared and furious. It was one of the days when he wondered, frequently and out loud, what an artist as sensitive as he was doing in a jungle like the garment business. He was in his paranoid mood, thinking that everyone—including Jade—was out to get him.

"And you're sure, absolutely positive, that it was the right thing to do?" he asked. Steve was a world-champion second-guesser. He also, basically, wanted Jade to do *everything*. That way, when things went wrong—and they did because this was the garment business—there was someone to take the blame.

"I hope so," Jade said sounding more casual than she felt. "Because the next thing I do is going to upset you even more."

"What's that?" Steve asked, worried. He showed his anxiety by chewing on the cuticle of his right index finger. In photographs, he always made a point of hiding that finger to conceal its ravaged condition and, by extension, *his* ravaged condition.

What she was going to do was get rid of all the deadwood and marginal accounts. She knew that the mere thought of it would drive Steve crazy. It was going to deprive him of his security blanket, and she wasn't reckless enough to announce her intentions.

"Never mind," said Jade. She glanced at her watch. "It's time for your shrink. You'd better get uptown."

"Where did you learn all this?" Steve asked Jade three months later when she had secured a bank loan with which to design and show a first full-fledged collection, hired a bookkeeper, sent sketches announcing the first collection to all the important buying offices, and convinced Steve to drop the overaged preppy look for classic English tailoring. She had shaped up his business and she had shaped *him* up—and had done it in a charming, confident, but unbossy way that made him both madly in love with her and slightly scared of her.

"I learned about the fashion industry while I worked for Mary Lou and Savin's," Jade replied, recalling Mary Lou's crash course in retailing, fashion, style, price points, and, most of all, what Mary Lou called "moving the merch."

"I learned about sound business practice from my husband and father-in-law," Jade added, recalling the way Herb and Barry knew *everything* that went on at Hartley's. "*Ex*-husband," she amended immediately, aware of her slip, "and *ex*-father-in-law."

Jade kept trying to put Barry and Herb firmly into the

past, but they kept popping up in the present. She kept trying to tell herself that she could get over seven years of marriage in one.

George saw Nantucket as a turning point. Jade told him it was just a weekend. All summer long George was after Jade to spend all her time with him—evenings and weekends. All summer long Jade tried to keep George from taking over her life. She continued to see Dan even though when she was with him she thought of George. She continued to see Marty and Peter even though when she was with them she thought of George—something she barely admitted to herself and something she certainly did not admit to George. It was Jade who invented the Four-Day Rule.

Jade spent the four-day Labor Day weekend on Fire Island with Peter. When she got back there were four messages—one for each day—on her machine from George telling her how much he missed her. She called him back that same evening even though it was almost midnight.

"I missed you," she was appalled to hear herself admit. The weekend had been fun—tennis and swimming and a clambake—but all along Jade had been thinking about George, wishing she were with him, wondering if he was spending as much time in Denver thinking about her as she was in Fire Island thinking about him.

"What did you say?" he asked in humorous shock. His own weekend had been like a roller coaster ride. He had flown to Denver to see Bobby and his heart was broken when Ina told him that Bobby was visiting a friend in Vail. He had accused Ina of sending Bobby away so that he couldn't see him, and he and Ina had spent the rest of the weekend fighting—over money, over the past, over George's women, over Ina's boyfriend. Most of all they fought over Bobby. George wanted to see more of Bobby and Ina wanted to keep Bobby to herself. The one real weapon she had over her ex-husband was her child and she used it viciously, tormenting George by promising that he could see Bobby and then never keeping the promises. They had ended up falling into bed together and talking about a reconciliation. George wanted his wife and child back; he also wanted Jade. He got back to New York confused and agitated, wishing that life were simple.

"You heard me," she said and quickly changed the subject. She was afraid of having emotional conversations with George, of admitting too much about the way she was beginning to feel. "How was Denver?"

"Bobby was in Vail and Ina was a pain in the ass. All we did was fight," he said, sloughing off the weekend. "I thought I heard you say you missed me."

"I didn't see you for four days," she admitted. She gathered that his weekend had been a disaster, and she was glad. "I guess that's what did it."

"So four days away made you realize how much you like me?" he pressed.

"Yes," she said, but when he asked her to save every night that week for him she refused. "I'll tell you what," she said, wanting to see him but not wanting to let him get too close. "Why don't we see each other every four days? That seems to be the perfect amount."

"Perfect for you," he said, annoyed, thinking that this was kid stuff and he wasn't a kid anymore. "Not for me." Still, he agreed. It was the first commitment he'd been able to wrest from her and he wanted to get Ina out from under his skin.

They spent the fall seeing each other according to Jade's Four-Day Rule. Jade metered out her time and her emotions like a miser. She wanted George and she wanted her independence. She kept trying to find a way to have both as she frantically juggled free-lance assignments and her increasing involvement with Steve's rapidly growing business.

In late October George went to see the Broadway show *Annie* with a potential client who was in town from Chicago. Jade sat three rows in front of him, and he spent the entire show thinking about how boring his client was and how much he wanted to be with Jade. It had been three days since he'd seen her and when Andrea McCardle sang "Tomorrow!" George kept thinking about the following day when, according to the Four-Day Rule, he'd be able to see Jade again. At the intermission he waited until the client went to the men's room and Jade's date went to the bar. She stood by the open theater doors, enjoying the cool evening air.

"Jade?" he said, touching her shoulders. The song had given him an idea.

She jumped in surprise.

"I'll meet you at one o'clock," he said, caressing her arm, aware of her perfume.

"I have a date," she said, taking her eyes from his.

"Get rid of him," George said. "Nice girls do, you know. Get rid of their dates," he added.

She smiled again and shook her head. "Not this nice girl. Besides," she reminded him, "don't forget the Four-Day Rule."

"I haven't," he said. He stood close to her, his eyes intense, devouring her with them. "I said one. One A.M. That's tomorrow. Four days. . . ."

They agreed to meet at the Carlyle to listen to Bobby Short.

From that evening on, the Four-Day Rule was forgotten.

"I guess the Four-Day Rule was sort of a dumb idea,"Jade admitted on Thanksgiving. They had spent almost every evening and every weekend together since their chance meeting at *Annie;* they had had their turkey at Mary Lou's yearly "orphan's party." Since the day after Thanksgiving was a big retailing day, the first official day of Christmas shopping, Jade and Steve worked that Friday and Jade didn't want to make the long trip upstate to Auburn for the one day. And since George's family was in the restaurant business in Tarpon Springs, Florida, his own family worked on the holiday. Ina and Bobby, he said, were spending the holiday at her parents' Vail home. *He,* of course, was not invited. Jade and George, "Thanksgiving orphans," were invited to Mary Lou's traditional party. Now, filled with turkey and cranberry sauce, they were snuggled together in Jade's bed under her red-and-white quilt.

"I was afraid I'd feel trapped," she said, referring to the Four-Day Rule. "That's what made me think of it."

"I know what you were afraid of," he said. "That I'd be as possessive as Barry. But I'm not, am I?"

"No," she said, shaking her head. "You're not."

"I just want to love you," he said. "I never wanted to own you."

He said it as if he meant it and Jade began to trust him. She began to tell him about her past, about her marriage, about her divorce. She told him what went on at the office, about the difficulties in dealing with the talented but insecure Steve.

"Sometimes I feel like his mommy," Jade said.

"You sure don't look like his mommy!" George said. He still thought that, with no close comparison, Jade dressed with more wit and imagination than any woman he had ever seen.

They spent Christmas apart. Jade went home to Auburn and did not even consider inviting George to meet her family. To do so would have smacked too much of a more serious involvement than she wished to admit—even to herself. George took Bobby to Anguilla, the about-to-be chic island near St. Maarten. He did not tell Jade that Ina had also come along. George and Bobby stayed at the luxuriously private Cinnamon Reef. Ina stayed at the livelier Cul de Sac. Every day they would meet at a different one of the island's spectacular, deserted beaches.

"I've been thinking about our conversation on Labor Day," Ina told him as they walked along the powdery white beach at Rendezvous Bay. "I think Allen and I are breaking up."

"You *think?*" George asked with a sudden, righteous feeling of triumph. "Or are you sure?"

"It depends," Ina said, carefully, veering toward the crystal water, getting her feet wet both literally and figuratively.

"Depends on what?"

"On whether or not I'd be welcome back in New York."

George, who wanted his wife back—on *his* terms—and Bobby back on *any* terms, reminded Ina that she still had the key to his apartment.

George spent New Year's Eve with Jade, and in the second week of January, Ina and Bobby appeared in Manhattan. They stayed with Ina's parents in their brownstone on East Seventy-second Street. Ina held out the possibility of a reconciliation and George was torn between his ex-wife and the child he adored and the new woman in his life. He didn't know how to handle his conflicting feelings or the conflicting demands on his time; then he remembered the Four-Day Rule.

"You were right about the Four-Day Rule," George told Jade at the end of January.

Jade blinked. George had hated the Four-Day Rule.

"What do you mean?" she asked, suddenly wary.

"I think we're seeing too much of each other," he said, using her words as he held her in his arms. They had just made love. It was always the moment at which they felt closest to each other. "I'm not sure I can handle it."

"But you were the one who wanted us to spend all our time together," Jade reminded him, wondering what he really had in mind.

"I know. I'm sorry," he said, torn at the unspoken choice he was making and knowing that it made him sound as if he didn't know what he thought or felt. "The thing is that Ina and Bobby are back. We're going to give it another try," he said, feeling that he owed her an explanation.

Jade was quiet a moment, collecting her feelings, glad that she had been cautious, glad that she had held back.

"I wish you luck," she said, thinking that if he hadn't broken it off, she would have. He had been getting too intense lately, moving in too close. "I mean it."

He looked at her and knew that she wasn't lying. He had sensed that she had been on the verge of bolting for freedom.

They parted with regrets but no bitterness. This was the late 1970s. No one came into a relationship a virgin anymore. Everyone brought along baggage: ex-wives and ex-husbands; ex-lovers and children. Nothing was simple anymore, and although Jade missed George, she had other interests and diversions. She buried herself in her work and comforted herself with the admiration of other men, glad that she had learned from her marriage, glad that she hadn't gotten more involved, glad that she had resisted George. Breaking up a romance that she had kept at arm's length didn't hurt nearly as much as a divorce. Then again, nothing did. Nothing ever could.

CHAPTER 6

*W*hen Jade Mullen was twelve she and her best friend, Heidi Diehl, vowed that they would never get married. Jade was going to grow up and become the editor of *Vogue;* Heidi was going to grow up and make a million dollars. Heidi's parents had divorced when Heidi was three; she had never met her father from whom, once a year on her birthday, she received a check for ten dollars. Jade's parents had divorced when she was nine. Jade's father left Jade's mother for his girlfriend and made sure that everyone in Auburn, including Jade, knew about it. Jade's father frequently failed to send the support check, and Jade's mother frequently hauled him into court. There were times when Jade saw more of her mother's lawyer than she saw of her father. There were times when Jade saw more of her father's girlfriends than she saw of her father. Arnold Mullen was a man who had good intentions but no follow-through. He promised to take her ice skating—and he never showed up. He promised to come to her piano recital—and he arrived after she had played. He promised to buy her a charm bracelet for Christmas—and gave her bunny slippers instead. He broke her heart a thousand ways and Jade grew up learning from him that promises were made to be broken.

Jade also grew up in the middle: between her older sister and her younger brother, who fought constantly and looked to Jade as a mediator; between her mother and her father, who did whatever they could to hurt each other and used Jade as their messenger; between her father and his girlfriends, who were always in tears over Arnold's latest infidelity.

Between love and money, Arnold Mullen could never get his act together.

"Tell your father I'm taking him to court again if he doesn't give you that check today," Dorothy Mullen told

Jade as she sent her over to her father's house eight blocks away to collect the overdue support check.

"Tell your mother that if she were as pretty as Sandie I'd never have left," Arnold Mullen told Jade as he scribbled a check, always for less than he owed, as the pretty Sandie or sexy Annette or sweet Carol waited patiently in the bedroom.

Arnold Mullen entertained a parade of girlfriends, and he always made sure Jade knew about them so that she could tell her mother. Dorothy Mullen never forgave Arnold for his betrayal and brought Jade up never to trust a man. "They're all alike," Dorothy Mullen said over and over. "You can't trust them. You can't believe a word they say."

Jade saw the tears of hurt and anger in her mother's eyes whenever her mother spoke of Jade's father; she saw her father's cruel desire to punish her mother whenever she heard him talk of how every other woman was more desirable than she was. Marriage, from what Jade saw of it as a child, meant unhappiness. When she and Heidi made their vow they were twelve and they were serious. Heidi broke her vow when she was eighteen and discovered she was pregnant two weeks before she was due to graduate from high school.

Jade broke her vow when she was twenty, for two reasons. The first was that she desperately wanted children. The second was Barry Hartley.

Jade adored babies; she loved to hold them, to play with them, to diaper them, and to take them out in their carriages. She spent her entire teenage years known as the best, most reliable baby-sitter in Auburn. Jade wanted to rewrite her own unhappy childhood with children of her own. All the things Jade had missed she longed to give to her own children as a way of making up for the unhappy, insecure childhood she had had. What she couldn't resolve was the conflict between her desire for children and her wish never to marry.

"Some people have children and don't get married," advised Heidi who, even at twelve, liked to say outrageous things.

"I'd never do that!" exclaimed Jade, shocked. "My

mother brought us up without a father. It was terrible! I'd never do that to my children!"

Heidi, despite her outrageous opinions, married right out of high school. By the time she was twenty, she already had two babies. Heidi adored her husband, her husband adored her—and they both doted on their children. Seeing how happy Heidi was, "Aunt" Jade, more than anything, wanted babies of her own.

The solution to her dilemma came when she met Barry Hartley.

Barry was in Jade's class at Cornell—the class of sixty-eight, the last college class for a while that would be more interested in rock and roll than in revolution. Jade was an art major. She wanted to be a fashion illustrator like Antonio, who was her idol. Barry was an economics major. He lived for the day he would join the company that had been in his family for two generations.

Barry was six-foot-two, blond, and very athletic. He always skied the killer slopes. He played aggressive tennis and had such a powerful serve that his nickname was Ace. He swam the freestyle and the breaststroke and anchored the eight-hundred-meter freestyle relay. Barry had blue eyes and even features and sported a year-round tan. Everyone, including Jade, thought he was extremely handsome. Most people also thought he looked sensitive—a few wondered if he didn't seem weak. What Jade really liked about Barry was that he seemed nice, protective, gentle, and loyal—the opposite of her father—a lovely lover who would be a wonderful father. When she first met Barry, though, she was the most popular girl in her class and marriage was the furthest thing from her mind.

"I'm going to marry you," was the first thing Barry ever said to her. They had met at a post-game party in their sophomore year. Cornell had beaten Columbia and, even though it wasn't the Big Ten and no one on either team would win the Heisman Trophy, the mood on campus was electric with excitement and celebration. The fraternity house on Cayuga Avenue was noisy and comfortable. Cold beer flowed from kegs, the air was thick with cigarette smoke, and young men and women, away from home for the first time, enjoyed the still-new taste of delicious free-

dom away from parents' eyes. The girls wore plaid kilts fastened with safety pins and cashmere sweaters and the boys wore khakis and shetland sweaters over J. Press shirts. On the stereo, the Beatles were singing "Love Me Do."

"How do you know that?" she teased, knowing that he had noticed the fraternity pin on her sweater. Boys were always saying outrageous things like that to Jade. She was cute and friendly and easy to talk to. In her freshman year she had been voted best dressed and most popular in her class. Being away from home, away from the rancorous divisions between sister and brother, mother and father, father and girlfriends, Jade had blossomed. She was already putting together a portfolio of fashion sketches and looked forward to the day when she'd take New York's fashion world by storm.

"I always know things like that," he said earnestly. Barry had transferred to Cornell that year from the University of Michigan because his father felt an eastern education would be more helpful later on in business. "The minute you walked into the room, I knew you were the one for me."

"I have bad news for you," she said with her cheerful smile. "I'm not getting married. Not ever."

"Everyone gets married," he said, his blue eyes sober.

She shook her head. "*I'm* not. My father left my mother for his secretary. She never got over it. She still talks about my dad. I think if he decided to come back—which he won't—she'd let him. I'm never going to let a man do to me what my father did to her. Therefore," she concluded, an Aristotelian of emotion, "I'm not going to get married."

"I'm going to make you change your mind," Barry said. He didn't leave her side, even when other boys came over to ask Jade to dance. "I'm famous for getting what I want."

"Good luck!" Jade said, never taking him seriously for a moment.

Barry took her back to her dorm that night, thought about kissing her, decided not to, and was amazed when she kissed him.

"I thought you weren't going to get married!" he exclaimed, delighted.

"I'm not," she said. "What does kissing have to do with getting married?"

In the next days and weeks Barry made a point of looking for Jade, of finding out when her classes were. He walked her to and from her classes, and when she got home from a date with another boy, Barry was waiting for her. He took her to lunch and dinner and bought her coffee in the afternoon; he took her books back to the library, helped her with her homework, lent her his skis, and put his VW at her disposal.

He did not give up his pursuit over the summer vacation. He returned home to the Midwest and Jade went home to nearby Auburn. All summer long he wrote to her and telephoned her and that September, the week that college began again, Barry took her to the area around Hammondtown where New York State wine is made. It was a lovely, crisp fall afternoon. The leaves were just beginning to change, the sun shone on the Finger Lakes, sparkling like jewels below the steep hillsides planted with grapes. There they sampled wine all afternoon, going from vineyard to vineyard until they ended up slightly tipsy at a drive-in and gorged themselves on hamburgers and french fries.

"You're different," he told her when the food had sobered them up. "Most of the girls are too silly or too serious. Either they're out for a good time and nothing else or they want a proposal on the second date. You seem much more mature."

"My mother always said I was very mature for my age," Jade said. It was a familiar compliment, a double-edged compliment, part praise, part a reminder that, unlike other children, Jade had never really been free to be a child.

"That's what I like about you," Barry said. He had a strong face, a strong smile, a strong sense of himself. The more Jade knew him, the more she realized that all men weren't alike, that there were some men on whom a woman could depend. Barry Hartley was one of them.

When he took her back to the dorm that night, he kissed her and said, "You're my girl, aren't you?"

"How could I not be?" Jade asked. By then she had returned the fraternity pin she'd been wearing the afternoon she met Barry. By then the conflict between her vow never to marry and her intense desire for children was diminished. Meeting Barry, knowing Barry, was what made the difference.

*   *   *

She hadn't been able to resist him—he had made sure of that. Other boys brought flowers, Barry brought bouquets. Other boys wanted to see her Saturday night, Barry wanted to see her Saturday night—and Sunday night, Monday night, Tuesday night, Wednesday night, Thursday night, Friday night, and Saturday night, again. Other boys had been interested. Barry was fascinated. Other boys had been attentive. Barry was there twenty-four hours a day. Other boys had courted her. Barry had pursued her. Other boys said they loved her, Barry made her *feel* that he loved her. There was nothing Barry wouldn't do for her or be for her.

"I love you," Barry told her for the hundredth time almost a year after they'd first met.

"I love you," she told him now that she felt safe with him, now that she felt secure with him, now that she felt that he'd never do to her what her father had done to her mother. Barry never looked at another girl. He was interested only in Jade and he made sure that she knew it and that she felt it.

They started going steady during their sophomore year, got pinned during their junior year, got engaged during their senior year, and two days after they graduated from Cornell they went to the city hall in nearby Auburn, where Jade had grown up, and got married. After the ceremony the bride and bridegroom went out to lunch with Barry's parents and Dorothy Mullen. Herb Hartley, gruff and patriarchal, had a bit too much to drink and, sitting down next to her, put his arm around Jade.

"When am I going to have a grandson?" he asked, hugging her affectionately.

Jade blushed.

"Oh, Herb!" said Doris Hartley, also blushing, even though she was used to her husband's bluntness. Then she looked at Jade and said in a very nice, no-nonsense way, "You don't have to answer him if you don't want to."

Still blushing, Jade looked shyly at her new husband. "As soon as we can," Jade said, wanting to please her new father-in-law and thinking how nice Doris Hartley was. The Hartleys seemed so happily married. Jade interpreted it as a good portent for her and Barry. Like father, she told herself, like son.

Dorothy Mullen wept and said that her tears were tears of joy.

Jade's father did not attend the wedding although Jade had invited him and he had absolutely promised to come. Jade was shattered. He had told her that he wouldn't miss his best girl's wedding for anything. And although she should have known better, she had believed him and looked forward to having both her mother and her father there. Jade sobbed in the ladies' room after the ceremony and her mother consoled her.

"It's better that he didn't," Dorothy said, knowing that she and Arnold could not be in the same room without getting into a battle. "We wouldn't have meant to, but we probably would have had another fight and ruined your wedding day."

But it *was* ruined, Jade thought unhappily. She loved her mother for comforting her, and she tried to hate her father but she couldn't. No matter what he did, she would always give him another chance.

That summer they moved to New York. To Jade it was like going to paradise; to Barry it was a stopover on the way back to Fort Wayne. Barry was going to Columbia for a degree in business administration, and although he came from a rich family, Herb Hartley did not spoil his son with a big allowance. Herb Hartley wanted a hard-working heir, not a playboy. Jade had to work to help support them. Her dream was to work in the art department at *Vogue*. She dropped off her resumé and portfolio at *Vogue* and every other fashion magazine in the city. No one seemed interested in her except the art director of *Style*, who advised her to take the course he was teaching at Parsons and then, maybe, he'd be able to hire her.

Meanwhile, Jade needed a job—and a salary—and all she cared about was that it had something to do with fashion. She got a job at Savin's huge Forty-second Street department store selling sportswear. She spent lunch hours trying to sell her fashion sketches. She wanted to build a free-lance business, since working free-lance would be ideal when the first baby came.

Barry got a job working part-time at the Hallmark galleries at Fifth and Fifty-sixth to help out with the finances.

They pooled their salaries and found a studio apartment in Morningside Heights. Their rent bought them a view of a brick wall and a corner on the cockroach market. Jade bought Raid the way Elizabeth Taylor bought diamonds.

"Our first slum," Jade called it and laughed. Every night when they went to sleep they had to move the dining table to open the hide-a-bed.

"We're not going to live like this forever," Barry said, hating the apartment, hating the city, "and that's a promise. You're my wife. You deserve the best."

"I *have* the best," she said, thrilled to be breathing the exciting air of New York, willing to overlook what she saw as its temporary discomforts. "I have you."

Barry was exactly the kind of husband Jade wanted, the precise opposite of her here-today, gone-tomorrow father. He cared about her and showed that he cared in a thousand ways both big and small. He liked to help her with the dishes after dinner, drying while she washed, telling her what had happened during the day. Every month on the twenty-first, the day on which they'd gotten married, he brought her a present: a cake with "I love you" spelled out in frosting; a bunch of flowers; a bottle of toilet water; a handful of paperbacks he knew she'd like; a glossy, expensive, foreign fashion magazine like *Queen* or *Donna*. Whenever he could he drove down from Columbia to give her a lift home from Savin's.

"We're married," he explained when she told him he didn't have to, that she could just as easily take the subway. "We're in this together."

Everything he said and did, the intensity of the attention he focused on her, made Jade feel as if, finally, the sun had come out. She felt totally loved.

The girls at work teased her: "You'll know the honeymoon's over when he lets you go home on the subway alone."

Except that for Jade and Barry the honeymoon was never over. Until the day they left Manhattan, Barry picked her up at work almost every day. The sight of his VW parked at the Forty-third Street employees' entrance became a symbol of the permanence of their marriage and the permanence of their affection.

* * *

Late one afternoon at the height of the Christmas selling season Jade's boss, Effie Gordon, the sportswear buyer, called her into her office.

"Did you know that you outsell everyone else on the floor?" Effie Gordon was a brisk, no-nonsense monument to energy and efficiency from the top of her wash-and-wear mouse-brown hair to the tips of her sturdy, cuban-heeled, made-for-walking, lace-up oxfords. She also had the warmest brown eyes and softest, dimpled smile.

Jade shook her head. "No, I didn't," she said. "I never kept track."

Jade still imagined her drawings on the cover of *Women's Wear Daily,* in *Vogue,* in department store ads in the Sunday *Times.* She spent her lunch hours schlepping her portfolio around to the art directors of all the fashion magazines, to the ad agencies who specialized in apparel, to the art departments of the big department stores, to Seventh Avenue manufacturers and designers. To anyone, in short, who might buy fashion illustrations. So far she had gotten two jobs and earned eighty dollars. She had known that breaking in would be hard; she hadn't anticipated that it would be quite *this* hard.

"Well, you do. You move the merchandise, Jade, and you make me look good. I appreciate it," Effie said, as she put her immersion heater onto a mug of water. "Have you ever thought of retailing as a career?" Effie asked.

Jade shook her head again. Since she met Barry she hadn't given any particular thought to any career. Just a few nice little free-lance jobs here and there to earn some extra money.

"I'm bringing this up," Effie said, adding a packet of Sanka to the now-boiling water, "because the executive training program starts in January. If you're interested, I'll recommend you."

"Should I?" she asked Barry that evening. Working at Savin's was exciting and she was intrigued and tempted by Effie's suggestion even though it didn't fit in with the image Jade had begun to paint of herself since her marriage. She had begun to see herself as the vague, dreamy type because Barry kept telling her how artistic she was. She had a

vision of living in a charming, slightly rickety Victorian-style house. She would do her fashion sketches at an easel that would be permanently set up in a corner of a big, airy kitchen that smelled of cinnamon and freshly baked apple pies. Barry would support them and she would earn extra money from her illustrations—extra money that would buy cute clothes and not-too-expensive American antiques. The main thing, of course, was that there would be babies who would grow into children who would bang the screen door that led to a big, shady porch. The thought of herself as an executive seemed outrageous, yet oddly compelling, in the winter of 1969 when all the talk suddenly seemed to be about women and their rights and talents and abilities. Jade definitely didn't see herself as a bra-burning women's libber, but she didn't quite see herself as a dull-as-dishwater housewife either. Being artistic was one way to define herself that didn't fall into either category.

"It sounds good," he said, proud that Effie had singled Jade out. "You'll be in line for a good job, and who says you have to spend your life at it? You can work until we have our first baby and then you'll quit."

That night, as they did every night, they made love. Barry just couldn't seem to get enough of her. And, Jade reminded herself, vice versa. Executive or no executive, buyer or no buyer, she adored her husband and looked forward to a baby and the real beginning of her life.

When she graduated from the executive training program, Jade was assigned to the "Forward Fashion" department where she would work for Mary Lou Tyler.

"Mary Lou Tyler!" the other new graduates said, rolling their eyes. "Poor Jade!"

"No one can work for Mary Lou Tyler more than two weeks!" Effie warned. "She goes through assistants like Kleenex!"

"Don't worry about her. You're not going to work there forever and we're not going to live like this forever either," Barry said that night at dinner when Jade told him that everyone was terrified of Mary Lou Tyler. They were eating chicken, rice, and salad. "This is just until we go

home and I can support us. Then we'll have steak and roast beef and you won't have to work."

"I can't wait!" Jade said, tasting what seemed like the three hundredth chicken recipe she'd tried. "We eat so much chicken I think I'm going to grow wings and a beak!"

"Better not!" he said. "Because then how could I kiss you?"

When they made love that night Jade wondered why she wasn't pregnant yet. They'd been married over a year. Shouldn't she have conceived by now?

CHAPTER 7

"*This department looks like shit*" was the first thing Mary Lou Tyler ever said to Jade. She was sitting in her cluttered, airless office going through a pile of confirmations. She did not look up at Jade as she spoke. In fact, two weeks would pass before she even bothered to ask Jade what her name was. The turnover was so fast that Mary Lou never bothered to call her assistants anything but "You." It saved her the trouble of learning a string of names she'd never use again. "I want you to line up every sweater, T-shirt, blouse, dress, jacket, and pants in this department size by size, color by color."

The department occupied the prime selling area right in front of the fifth-floor elevators. The job would take Jade most of the morning, which did not seem to enter into Mary Lou's plans.

"When you're through with that," Mary Lou continued, still checking orders, "go over to Plum Pudding on West Thirty-eighth," Mary Lou gestured to four huge cardboard cartons of blouses, "and tell Hy Fishback to eat them. They were delivered with black buttons and I *told* him I wanted red heart-shaped buttons."

"When you're done with that gonif," Mary Lou continued full blast, still not even glancing up at the new body personnel had sent down, "stop at Elgin Long's. I'll meet you there. His velvets walked for holiday and I want him to cut the same styles in linen for spring. He's supposedly such a hotshot designer," Mary Lou snorted. "Ha! You know what *Vogue* said a month ago? 'A dazzling new talent,'" she quoted. Jade nodded, not that Mary Lou noticed. She remembered seeing the luscious four-page spread of Elgin Long's Elegant Edwardians.

"*Vogue* should know that that *fagelah*'s buyers design for him," Mary Lou continued, sifting through orders, drinking tea, puffing away at a cigarette, and checking a layout for an ad all at the same time, never once looking up at her new assistant. "When we're done with Elgin—by the way, he's a very nice guy and that's why everyone tries to help him so don't take me wrong—we have an appointment at Rainy Dayz to look at raincoats. The boss's son, God help us, is introducing a new line called Rain Drops."

Mary Lou rolled her eyes, fielded a phone call, and then, without coming up for air, continued with Jade.

"Now get out of here and start straightening up the department. I'll see you at Elgin Long's at two. Oh, and by the way, when you have a minute, run over to Doubleday's and return these books." Mary Lou gestured to a shopping bag on the floor by her desk.

Mary Lou spoke so fast that Jade could not keep up. By noon she was walking on her knees, by three she could not remember the names of people she had met that day; she could not remember the names of resources, their addresses, or what styles Mary Lou had ordered; she could not remember what she had had for lunch or even what her own name was; and by the time she had helped Mary Lou close out the registers at nine—Monday and Thursday were late nights at Savin's and the buyers were responsible for closing out the registers—Jade was so tired that she wept in the car on the way home.

"*Let's make a dinner date,*" Jade said to Barry over the phone two months after she'd started with Mary Lou. Or, to be more accurate, two months after Mary Lou had started with her. After two weeks Mary Lou had asked her what her name was. For the next month Mary Lou called her Jane, Judy, Julie, Joan, and Joanne. After six weeks she finally got it right.

Although Mary Lou was inconsiderate, crude, rude, demanding, and otherwise impossible, Jade found herself in awe of her. Mary Lou Tyler had forgotten more about fashion than most other people had ever learned and she didn't mind passing her knowledge along to whoever was around. "Whoever" happened to be Jade, who got, gratis, a one-student course in the past and present of fashion. She learned about Norman Norell and Charles James, could spot the difference between a designer original and a knock-off at fifty paces, and knew the work of every hot, new "youthquake" designer coming out of London. She kept up with op and pop and mini and maxi and micro. She learned to tell the difference between what was new and good and merely new and gimmicky, between style and mere fashion, between a fad and a look. She had also found that the tears on the way home weren't due just to fatigue.

"Just the two of us. Tonight," she asked Barry. "Can you?"

"Sure," he said, always happy to have an excuse not to work on his thesis. "What's the occasion?"

She left work early and stopped at Lobel's butcher shop on Madison Avenue, which sold meat like Tiffany's—by the carat—for some baby lamb chops; at Empire for the best, smallest string beans; and at the Eighty-sixth Street florist for a big bunch of white daisies. She went over to Dumas for some Napoleons, which Barry loved but for diet's sake rarely ate, and indulged in a six-dollar bottle of red wine, which the dealer assured her was up to the quality of the rest of the dinner. She took time for a bath and a change of clothes, arranged the flowers, and set the table. Barry arrived with a bouquet of red and white carnations.

"You're still the best date I ever had," he said, handing them to her and kissing her. "So what's up?"

"You'll find out," she said mysteriously, opening the wine. "Go wash up and get comfortable," she ordered, and when he had, she put the platter with the chops surrounded by watercress on the table. "Medium rare. Just the way you like them."

"Ummm," he said, taking his first bite. "Delicious."

"From Lobel's," she confessed.

"What'd you do? Sell your soul?"

"No," she said, leering at him. "Just my sable coat."

He laughed; he was in a good mood. Jade's timing had been perfect.

"I started a new chapter today," he told her, talking about his thesis. He rarely spoke about his courses, said they were pretty dull, but tonight he seemed expansive. "Dumont television . . . how a company that was first in the market ended up bust." Barry's specialty was finance and the handling and manipulation of money came as naturally to him as accessorizing an outfit came to Jade.

"That's wonderful," Jade said, knowing how hard Barry found writing the thesis, glad he was making progress. "I started a new chapter today, too."

"No kidding! Did Mary Lou declare a national holiday and give you a coffee break?"

"I'm pregnant," she said, finally allowing herself to bubble over. "I've missed my period for two months in a row. I think I'd better find a doctor. You're going to be a daddy."

She waited for him to hug her, to kiss her, to twirl her around the room in a dance of celebration. Instead, he looked at her for a moment, silently.

"Are you sure?" he asked.

"Aren't you happy?" she wanted to know, crushed. The disappointed expression on her face pierced him.

"Of course I'm happy! It's wonderful!" he said suddenly, taking her into his arms and dancing her around the room. Jade realized that his first reaction had just been his usual caution.

Dorothy Mullen was delighted.

"I'm so happy for you!" she told Jade, meaning it. She remembered how unhappy she'd been when she'd learned she was pregnant the first time. She wasn't married. She'd allowed Arnold Mullen to talk her into sleeping with him and she wasn't sure what he would do when she told him. What he did was insist the baby wasn't his. Eventually, though, his parents and Dorothy's parents had talked some sense into him. She would have been better off, she realized later after Arnold had walked out on her, if she had just had the abortion her mother had wanted her to have. She was too young to have a baby, and Arnold was too immature to be a father. She was so happy things were different for Jade. "I know how much you wanted a baby."

Herb Hartley was nothing short of ecstatic.

"Good!" his voice boomed on the telephone. "Another generation of Hartleys! You'd better make sure it's a boy. We need heirs."

"I'll do no such thing!" Jade said, imbued with the spirit of feminism that was in the air. "Haven't you ever heard of heiresses?"

Barry, who knew how intimidating his father could be, was delighted at the way Jade handled him.

"A kid!" said Mary Lou. Jade, terrified of Mary Lou, had waited until the last possible moment to tell her. It was the beginning of her fifth month and she was just beginning to show. "In August? Jesus Christ! That's when the fall merchandise starts coming in."

"Mary Lou, it's nature and there's just not one single thing I can do about it," Jade said.

"I *know* that!" Mary Lou said, exasperated. "I suppose the next thing you're going to tell me is that you're quitting and going back to the Midwest with your husband to become a hausfrau."

"Well, yes, as a matter of fact, I was," Jade admitted.

"What a waste," muttered Mary Lou searching through the blizzard of notes she scribbled to herself and coming up with the one she wanted. "You could have a fantastic career."

"Maybe one day I'll have both," Jade said, not wanting to hurt Mary Lou who, she knew, had devoted her entire life to her career.

"If you're smart, you will," Mary Lou said, and then returned to business. "Now call Steve Hirsch and find out about the new shipment. Those coats have sold out again!"

As Jade left the tiny buying office Mary Lou called after her. "Jade?"

"Yes?" Jade turned back.

"Take it a little easy now!" Mary Lou said kindly in one of her split-second changes of mood. "I don't want you to hurt yourself, you hear?"

"Okay, Mary Lou," said Jade with a smile. "Thanks."

"And Jade?"

"Yes?"

"I'm happy for you. I really am." For once Mary Lou did not look like the fire-breathing tiger of Seventh Avenue; instead she looked more like a woman who might once have wanted a baby of her own.

That evening, as usual, Barry was waiting for her outside Savin's employees' entrance. The VW was parked across Forty-third Street, and as Jade and Barry crossed, a beat-up Mercury ran the red light on Fifth Avenue and roared along Forty-third, coming out of nowhere.

"Jade!" Barry screamed. With his athlete's fine-tuned reactions he saw the car a split-second before she did and pushed her out of its path, smashing her to the sidewalk, literally saving her life. Unaware of his own injuries, he helped Jade up.

"Are you all right?"

"Yes," she said, feeling numb. It had all happened so blindingly fast that it still hadn't really registered.

"Are you sure?" he asked, helping her up.

She nodded again and then she screamed.

"Barry!" she screamed again as a bolt of pain shot through her and she felt her insides ripping open. "Something's wrong!"

She looked down and saw blood pouring down her legs, drenching her skirt and gluing it to her.

"The baby!" she screamed as another agonizingly sharp spasm of pain ripped through her.

"Barry?" she asked weakly when the pain let her speak again. She tried to reach out for him, but before she could, she was pulled under by a tidal wave of pain. She never heard his reply.

Jade knew nothing more until she woke the next afternoon. She was in Mount Sinai Hospital. She didn't have to say a word, didn't need to ask the question. She knew.

"The baby?" she asked to the nurse.

"You'll have another," the nurse said comfortingly. Jade knew she was trying to be nice but it didn't stop the tears.

"Where's Barry?" she asked when she could finally speak. She needed Barry, she had to see him. He was the only one who could comfort her, the only one who could make her feel better. "Where's my husband?"

The nurse paused a moment.

"He's dead! Oh, my God, he's dead!" Jade screamed.

"No!" said the nurse, trying to calm her. "He's not dead. He's alive. He's in the orthopedic ward," she said. "He's broken his leg and his kneecap is shattered but he's alive. He'll be fine."

Jade never went back to Savin's. She never even went back to Morningside Heights. The day she got out of the hospital Barry, in a hip-to-toe cast, helped her onto a plane and they flew back to Fort Wayne.

C H A P T E R   8

In the midwest, Hartley's was a name synonymous with tradition and quality. For seventy years Hartley's had manufactured paper products for parties and celebrations: paper plates and napkins, paper tablecloths, paper hats, and noisemakers. Hartley's had been there as long as most people could remember, to help celebrate birthdays and anniversaries, Christmas and New Year's, Valentine's Day and the Fourth of July. Hartley's was a one-man operation, and Herb Hartley was the one man. From the moment Barry had been born Herb had looked forward to the time his son would join him in the family business and now that time had come.

Until she went to live in Fort Wayne, Jade had not realized that Barry came from such a prominent family. The name Hartley seemed to be part of the Fort Wayne landscape. On the way from the airport to the house, they passed the big red-brick factory where the Hartley products were made. Jade saw a fleet of delivery trucks with the name Hartley painted on the sides in orange on white; a brand-new school auditorium donated, according to the plaque outside, by the Hartley family; and an eye and ear clinic, also built thanks to donations from the Hartleys.

"You never told me that the Hartleys are such a prominent family," Jade said, both impressed and surprised.

"We aren't," said Barry, taking her hand and squeezing it. "We're just local people who try to help out if we can."

Jade learned that the Hartleys made a point of downplaying whatever wealth they had. Barry's parents lived in a comfortable but plain wood shingle house in a nice but hardly ritzy neighborhood, and, although Herb Hartley drove a Cadillac, it was five years old and in need of washing. Doris Hartley was a housewife who did all her own housework and whose primary entertainment was church on Sunday and a Bible study class that met every Thursday evening. Barry's parents welcomed Jade almost as if she had been their own child. Doris Hartley installed her in a big, airy bedroom and proceeded to wait on her hand and foot, and Herb Hartley seemed to fall in love with her.

"You have to get your strength back," Doris Hartley said, bringing her bowls of homemade soup and slices of thickly buttered homemade bread. "You've had a terrible experience and you need time to get over it."

Herb Hartley brought her flowers and magazines and had a brand-new television set installed in the room just for her. "You take all the time you need to get well," Herb said in his gruff, affectionate way. "You're young. You've got plenty of time ahead of you."

Jade gradually gained weight but, although she soon felt rested and the doctor pronounced her physically healthy, the gray sense of depression that had begun the moment she'd regained consciousness in Mount Sinai did not seem to lift.

"What you need is a trip," Herb suggested in his positive way. Herb liked to say that he was a doctor without the license; he said he always knew what to prescribe for other people's problems. "How about if I send you and Barry to Bermuda for a week? That ought to fix you up."

Bermuda was blue and sunny and beautiful, but it was a mistake. Although Jade swam in the clear turquoise water, Barry couldn't because of his cast. He seemed perpetually angry. Not at Jade, but at the world.

"Shit!" he kept saying. "I used to anchor the freestyle and now I'm a pansy who can't even get wet."

"It's just temporary," Jade said. "Your leg will heal and then you'll be fine."

"No, it won't," said Barry, his square jaw seeming squarer, set in anger and frustration.

"But the doctors said it will," Jade said, understanding how he felt and trying to make him feel better.

"The doctors are wrong," Barry insisted. "I'm an athlete. I know my body. That leg is never going to be right again."

Although they drank rum punches at sunset and shopped for dutyfree cashmere sweaters in Hamilton, every time Jade saw a young couple with children, unbidden tears came to her eyes. She wanted children so badly. Why had she failed when every other woman in the world seemed to have succeeded? Why had she left the hospital with empty arms when every other woman left with a baby? Why, when she knew how to make a baby happy, was she the one whose baby was dead?

"You'll feel different when you get pregnant again," Barry promised.

"Do you think so?" she asked anxiously, wanting to be reassured. She felt that Barry knew everything. She always believed what he said.

"Of course," he said positively. "I'm sure of it"

"You always make me feel better," she said, relieved.

"I hope so," he said, smiling affectionately. "I love you."

Still, when Jade got back to Fort Wayne, the depression returned. She couldn't get over the accident. She kept blaming herself. She kept thinking that the loss of her baby had been her own fault. If she hadn't stopped in the advertising department to look at the sketches for the Sunday ad she'd have left work ten minutes earlier and the accident would never have happened. If she'd stopped at the perfume counter and tried the Dioressence that smelled so good on Effie's niece she'd have left five minutes later and she'd still be pregnant, her baby would still be safe inside her.

Even though time was passing, time that should have eased her depression, she didn't feel any better. She felt sad and mournful, as if the life and vitality were invisibly bleeding out of her. Jade couldn't understand why she still didn't feel like her old self. She had lost her baby, yes, and it was terrible, but so had other women. Other women recovered. Other women picked up their lives, put the past behind them, and looked forward to the future.

But not Jade. She didn't seem to be getting any better, and yet she had every reason to go on with her life, to look forward to another pregnancy, one that would have a normal, happy ending. She had a husband who was madly in love with her. She had more money than she'd ever had. She lived in a beautiful house and had adoring in-laws. She was still young and healthy and her doctor had assured her that she had suffered no serious permanent damage during the miscarriage. She'd be able to have other babies, other children. Still, something was wrong and, eventually, Jade thought she understood why.

"You know how much I like your parents," Jade whispered to Barry one evening before they went to sleep. They were using the bedroom that had been Barry's when he was growing up, sleeping in the twin beds that were still decorated with the Cornhuskers football decals Barry had applied when he'd been in high school. Perhaps it was the proximity to his parents' room, perhaps it was sleeping with mementos of childhood all around, but the room seemed to have a dampening effect on their sex life. Jade could barely remember the last time they'd made love. Ever since the accident, even after his cast had come off, Barry was hardly ever in the mood and neither, she realized, was she. "I'm not sure living with them is the best idea in the world, though. Maybe we should have a place of our own."

"Of course we should," said Barry, agreeing immediately. "I don't know why I didn't think of it myself."

More than anything, Barry wanted to make Jade happy. There was something magical about her—he'd seen it the moment he'd first laid eyes on her at Cornell. She brimmed with energy and vitality and an enormous, unquenchable sense of life that made him feel alive. He absolutely adored her and seeing her sad and unhappy made him determined to see her smile again.

"I'll talk to Dad about it," he said, coming into her bed and snuggling up to her, loving her warmth and the way she smelled and thinking he'd die if anything or anyone ever took her away from him.

It turned out that there was a piece of property not five miles away that Herb had owned for years.

"I'm giving it to you kids," said Herb, his eyes twinkling as he generously signed over the deed. "I'll lend you the money to build a house on it. I know a local builder. I'll make sure you get the right deal." And then he winked at Jade. "And you'll see that I get the right deal, too, won't you?"

"I'll try," said Jade, grinning, not knowing what he had in mind. She was thrilled at the idea of having a place of their own to live in. "What right deal did you have in mind?"

"Oh," said Herb craftily, letting her in on the joke. "Seven pounds, eight ounces. You think you could manage that?"

"I think so," said Jade confidently. She liked the way Herb teased her and she enjoyed teasing him right back.

At the time, she *did* think so.

Three months later, Jade and Barry had moved into a pleasant three-bedroom house. Jade loved her brand-new house and indulged her artist's eye as she furnished it with plain pine furniture that she discovered in the rural areas around Fort Wayne. She spent hours on the big back lawn stripping the furniture and scrubbing it down to its lovely pale color and handsome rustic lines.

"It looks damn nice!" Herb said admiringly. Herb had good taste and he was very aware of always getting the most value for his money. He was very impressed with the way Jade had furnished the house so attractively on almost nothing.

"That's some girl you married!" he told Barry. "You'd better be careful or I'm going to get jealous of you."

Doris gave Jade the family recipes and Jade learned to make all of Barry's favorite dishes.

"I'd never say this to Mom," Barry said, finishing off a delicious vinegared pot roast, "but I think you're even a better cook than she is."

Jade smiled and wondered how it could be that although everyone loved her and appreciated her so much she still felt sad and depressed. Almost a year had gone by and still she wasn't pregnant. Everyone told her not to worry, and she tried not to—after all, there was still plenty of time, and love was supposed to be the answer to everything, wasn't it?

Jade asked herself why love suddenly seemed suffocating. Barry's love seemed almost like too much love. He enveloped her in love and attention and she almost never had a minute alone except for the hours that Barry was at work. Barry had gone through a series of painful knee operations that left him with a limp, and the limp seemed to have changed him. Just as Jade mourned the lost of her unborn baby, Barry seemed to mourn the loss of his strength and mobility. He wanted to spend all his time with Jade, every evening and every weekend. He no longer went to the pool or the tennis courts on Saturdays and Sundays; he gave his skis to the thrift shop and abandoned his golf clubs in the garage. Now that they were living in their own house, Barry's sex drive seemed to have returned. He made love to her every night and he told her it wasn't enough.

"I just want to be with you and in you," he told Jade. "You're all that matters to me."

She wondered for the first time ever how her father had felt during his marriage. Could he have felt suffocated? Could her mother have asked for more attention than he felt comfortable giving? Could he have needed more time to himself than she was able to give? Jade didn't know. All she knew for certain was that the empty bedrooms seemed to accuse her.

"I can hardly believe it," Jade told Barry after they'd been in Fort Wayne almost a year, "but I think I miss Mary Lou." She felt guilty that she'd left the city without saying good-bye to Mary Lou. Of course she'd been very weak after the miscarriage and in no condition even to pick up a telephone. The more time that passed the guiltier she felt toward Mary Lou. Still, she never got around to phoning her old boss or writing her. It was just one more thing— like not getting pregnant again right away—to feel guilty about.

"Come on, Jade!" said Barry, helping Jade unload the dishwasher. He was one of those one-in-a-million husbands who actually seemed to like helping around the house. Jade felt guilty, but she resented it. She wished he'd at least leave her alone in the kitchen. "No one could miss Mary Lou."

"I'm serious. I really think I miss her," she insisted, thinking nostalgically of Mary Lou's energy, the continual excitement of new shipments coming in, the new lines, the new looks. Jade felt tired all the time, as if she'd left her energy on Forty-third Street along with the blood and the fear and the pain. "I even think I miss the impossible customers. The ones that tried to return the coffee-stained dresses, swearing they'd never worn them."

"Maybe you're just lonely," said Barry, worried by her sadness. He wanted her sparkle back. He tried to think of how to help her. "After all, I'm at work all day and you're here alone. Maybe you should go to Bible study with my mother. That way you'd meet some of the women here. They're nice. You'd like them."

They were nice, and Jade did like them. The problem was that most of them were wrapped up in their children and being with them and listening to their talk of formulas and toilet training and terrible twos just made Jade feel worse. She'd have given anything for the two A.M. feedings and temper tantrums other women complained about.

"I wish I'd get pregnant," she kept telling Barry. The wish was becoming the focus of her existence, all she could think about and talk about.

"You worry about it too much," he said, trying not to feel annoyed at her constant talk about getting pregnant. Wasn't he enough for her? It was a warm November Saturday afternoon and they were outside, planting daffodils for the spring. Jade thought he was probably right, but she didn't know how to stop thinking about it. She had nothing else to think about.

Perhaps it was the limited mobility his accident had left him with, but Barry seemed to have gotten older and more settled. He was very attached to his routine. He liked to leave for work at exactly eight-fifteen and he returned promptly at six-thirty, when he expected Jade to have dinner ready and waiting for him. He adored her; he kept telling her she was the most wonderful wife in the world. He also wanted her to fit into the life of Fort Wayne. He didn't like her to wear the minis she'd brought with her from New York or the pale lipstick and emphatic eye makeup that was fashionable there. Some of his friends told him that she looked weird. Others teased him about being married to a teenybopper.

"People just stare at you," he told her, trying not to hurt her feelings, and she realized that the way she looked embarrassed him in conservative Fort Wayne. "You're my wife. I want them to respect you."

Jade wanted to be a good wife because she was lucky enough to have such a loving husband, a husband who had literally saved her life. Barry, as she'd sensed from the beginning, was the opposite of her father. He loved her and wasn't afraid to show it. She loved him and she wanted to show it, too. She began to dress conservatively and she toned down her makeup. She began to fit in and she told herself she was happy because she made Barry happy. She even began to look forward to trips to the supermarket, telling herself that she didn't miss Saks or Design Research or Bonniers. The only thing she was conscious of missing besides the baby she longed for was work. It was too boring and too lonely to be home alone all day. Waiting for Barry to come home, no matter how much she loved him— and she *did* love him—just wasn't enough.

"I wish I could get a job," she said forlornly. "But there are no department stores in Fort Wayne."

"Why don't you go to work for Hartley's?" he asked suddenly, surprising her.

She looked at him in amazement. "Are you serious?"

"Why not?" Barry said. "My father's crazy about you. He'd love the idea."

The next day she spoke to her father-in-law.

"I always went for the idea of a family business," he boomed at Jade. Herb Hartley was small, rotund, and bald. His Santa Claus looks and folksy manner hid a keen intelligence and an enormous competitiveness. "I always wanted Doris to get involved but she wasn't interested."

"What job could I have?" Jade asked.

"Poke around," Herb suggested expansively. "Whatever needs doing, do."

* * *

"I'm going to take an executive training course, for one," she told her father-in-law a week later after poking around and thinking it over. "I'm going to base it on the course at Savin's. That way I'll find out about the business and find out where I might fit in."

Jade assigned herself to one week in every department: shipping, receivables, design, promotion, advertising, sales, distribution, and customer relations.

"Design is what I really love," she told Herb when she'd spent some time in every one of Hartley's departments. "After all, my background is in art. I'd like to start out in the design department."

"It'd be a waste," Herb said flatly, leaving no room for argument. "I've been watching you. That's a good idea you had, spending time in every department. It's a smart idea. All our management people ought to spend time in every department. It would give them an overview of the company."

"Thank you," Jade said. "But it's not my idea. I just adapted the Savin's executive training program."

"That's what I want you to do here," Herb said, bulldozing on. "I want you to establish a training program. Hartley's is getting bigger every year. We need to train more people and do a better job of it."

"My father thinks you hung the moon and painted the stars," Barry said proudly eight weeks later when the first group had graduated from the program Jade had initiated.

Jade smiled, but the smile covered her newly troubled feelings. Working at Hartley's had changed the way Jade saw her husband—and her father-in-law had been the reason. Herb Hartley bullied Barry, second-guessing him, criticizing him in front of other employees, and dismissing his opinions almost contemptuously. Herb's behavior disgusted Jade and she began to feel fiercely protective toward Barry.

"We ought to have three lines of Valentine's Day cards," Barry told her. "Red and white, red and pink, and pink and white. Last year we found that people bought multiples if multiples were available. We ought to give them as much choice as possible this year. I think it would show up in sales."

"It sounds like an excellent idea," said Jade, who had

seen the marketing reports and the sales break downs. "Tell your father."

"You tell him," Barry said, deferring to her, as he had begun to do lately. "He listens to you when it comes to merchandising."

"That's a damn good idea!" Herb had boomed when Jade had suggested the multiple-packaged Valentine's Day items.

"It's not my idea," Jade had been careful to point out. "It was Barry's."

"That's nice of you to say, but Barry never had an idea in his life!" Herb said, speaking to Jade as if they shared a secret about Barry. Herb, oblivious to anyone's feelings except his own, was blind to Jade's anger and discomfort. He barged on ahead, paying her a compliment she didn't want: "What I like is that you're damned loyal to him and I really go for that!"

Jade tried to buttress Barry's ego.

"You're an excellent businessman," she told him when he found a way to prepackage sets of plates, napkins, and cutlery *and* keep the prices competitive.

"I know I am," Barry said. "Now if only the old man could see it."

"He will," Jade said. "You just have to let your father know what you did."

"I already did."

"And?" Jade asked, thinking that one day Herb would *have* to see and acknowledge Barry's abilities.

"He said anyone could have done it." Barry's voice was full of bitterness. "I told him to go to hell."

"Barry! He's your father!" Jade said.

"I don't care. He's a bully and I'm not going to put up with it anymore."

Except that he did put up with it and when Jade mentioned it, Barry said that one day he'd inherit the company, and that his father's bullying was a small price to pay.

It was the first time Jade had ever heard Barry speak about inheriting the company one day. It was almost as if he were waiting around for his father to die. Jade thought it was awfully creepy, and she shuddered at the idea.

*   *   *

As Jade rose higher and higher in her father-in-law's eyes, Barry became more and more attached to her. He drove her to work in the morning, he came into her office to have lunch with her, and drove her home after work. The constant attention that had seemed loving when she'd been a bride working at Savin's now began to seem oppressive. One day when Jade left the hairdresser Barry was waiting outside in his car.

"I'll drive you back to the office," he offered, opening the car door for her.

"I want to walk," Jade said, annoyed. She turned her back on him and walked away. She knew she was hurting him and she felt guilty about it, but she had to have some time alone—even if it was just for the short walk back to the office.

"I can't stand it when you reject me," Barry said that evening. His eyes were hurt and his faced looked sad. "It's bad enough that my old man treats me like dirt. I can't stand when you do it. You know how much you mean to me."

"I'm sorry. I really am," Jade said, immediately going to him and taking him into her arms. Between his limp and his father's abuse, Barry felt constantly diminished and Jade ached for him. "But sometimes I need to be by myself. Can't you understand?"

"Of course," he said tenderly. "But I need you. Can't you understand my feelings, too?"

Jade did understand, and they made up in bed.

She began to think it would be better if they moved away from Fort Wayne and made a life of their own, away from Hartley and the Hartleys. When she mentioned it to Barry, he reacted with rage.

"Never!" he said, turning white at her suggestion. "Never! Hartley's is going to be mine one day. It's my heritage. I'll *never* walk away."

Because she loved him, because she was loyal, because she had married him for better or for worse, Jade stayed.

CHAPTER 9

ust when Jade thought she would suffocate, her father-in-law opened the doors. "It's time Hartley's went national," Herb told Jade in 1972, the year of the Nixon landslide, the thawing of relations with Red China, progress in the ceasefire talks in Vietnam, and a "third-rate" burglary of Democratic headquarters in the Watergate complex. It was also the year of the Concert for Bangladesh, the year *of Jonathan Livingston Seagull,* the year Marlon Brando was *The Godfather,* and the year Bobby Fischer won the world chess championship—all of zero interest to Herb Hartley. Population trends and the economic news, though, *did* interest Herb. "The birthrate has flattened out, the economy is stagnating, and sales are going to fall unless Hartley's expands its markets."

Herb had graphs and charts to support his theory, and a survey he'd commissioned had concluded that expansion into new markets was the next logical step for the medium-sized company.

"I want to open up the East Coast, starting in New York," he told Jade, looking at her over his half-glasses. "You lived there. You know it. The hows and whos are up to you."

"New York?" Barry said when she told him about her conversation with his father. "That means you're going to be away. What am I going to do without you?"

Jade hid the fact that she was dying to go to Manhattan. She couldn't wait to get back to New York, to see Effie and Mary Lou, to hit the stores and boutiques, to see what was new and fresh and exciting. Instead, on the morning of the day she left, she mentioned something to Barry that she'd been thinking about ever since she'd read an article on Joe Namath's post-football career.

"His knee was shattered, too," Jade said at breakfast. "But now he seems fine. He underwent a lot of physical therapy. I wonder if it would help you?"

At the time of his surgery, Barry's own doctor had suggested therapy, but Barry, angry and depressed, had refused to do the exercises. Now that a few years had passed he felt differently.

"That's a good idea," he told Jade, wanting to please her as much as anything else. "I think I'll make an appointment with Dr. Nadries. He'll probably be able to recommend someone."

In April 1972 Jade spent a week in New York with real estate agents. She had never spoken to a real estate agent in her life, much less rented commercial space, but doing something new had never fazed Jade. Ever since she'd been a little girl her mother had looked to her as the strong one, the reliable one, the one who could take care of things. Mary Lou, in her turn, had recognized that quality in Jade. Herb Hartley was just the newest person in her life to look upon Jade as the one who could do anything and everything. It never occurred to Jade that she couldn't do whatever she set her mind to, just as it never occurred to her that her confidence, capability, and independent point of view were the positive by-products of her unhappy childhood.

Everything in the city was up-tempo; everything was expensive, exclusive, and exciting. Jade felt as if she were coming to life again after a long sleep. As always in New York there was change everywhere.

Le Drugstore on Third Avenue in the East Sixties was the hot new place to buy cosmetics, records, T-shirts, and have a hamburger and a glass of wine. Le Pavillon, long a landmark on East Fifty-seventh Street, had closed, and although Jade had never been able to afford to go there, she missed just knowing that Henri Soulé was there, guarding standards of luxury and excellence. SoHo hadn't even existed when Jade had left the city a few years before, but the zoning changes passed in 1970 had transformed an area of run-down factories into a thriving artists' community. Leo Castelli, Andre Emmerich, and the Sonnabend galleries had opened there; interesting out-of-the-mainstream boutiques had sprung up selling clothes and housewares and gourmet foods. Serious cooks made the pilgrimage to Dean & DeLuca, clothes hounds checked out Tales of Hoffman, and high-tech design freaks cruised Turpan & Sanders. On Saturdays the residents stayed in their lofts and the tourists flooded in, coming to look and buy.

There was change, too, at Savin's.

"Since you left I've had a parade of what's-her-name's," Mary Lou growled from behind her paper-strewn desk as the telephone blasted away, unanswered. Her ass was bigger than ever, her voice deeper, and her temper shorter. She had brushed aside Jade's apologies about not saying good-bye, the continually ringing telephone not giving her the time to hear Jade's teary attempt to tell her about the miscarriage. "If you ever leave the Midwest or wherever it is you disappeared to, your job is still here. You understand that?"

"Yes, Mary Lou," said Jade, much less meekly now that she had learned to contend with Herb Hartley. "I understand."

"Good! If you ever come back, you're to call me first thing."

"Okay, Mary Lou," said Jade, with a smile, never dreaming that she'd come back. Never dreaming that when she did, she'd be so depressed that she'd hide for six months. "Only I'm happy where I am."

"Yeah," said Mary Lou, looking sourly at Jade's demure pastel shirtwaist dress and remembering her stylish Mary Quant minis. "So is Nixon every morning when he picks up the *Washington Post.*"

By the end of the week Jade had settled on a location—at Fifth Avenue and Fifty-third Street. Two weeks later she flew back to New York to sign the lease. Now that she had space for the shop she needed someone to design the interior. The real estate broker suggested two experienced designers. One did work so sophisticated that it would have overwhelmed the basically homey Hartley line. The other was a tired hack whose banal work reminded Jade of all the worst features of every store she'd ever been in. The only store designer Mary Lou knew was currently in Smithers recovering from Valium addiction, and of the two that Effie recommended, one was in Dallas on a shopping mall project and the other had retired to a farm in Bucks County.

Always resourceful, Jade went to Gordon's in the St. Regis and bought every home furnishings and interior design magazine on the market. She walked back to the Regency, where she was staying, ordered a chicken salad sandwich from room service for dinner, and spent the entire evening looking through the magazine, making notes of the names of the designers whose work appealed to her. The next morning, the Manhattan phone book on her lap and her list on the table next to her, she began to make calls. She found out, and she wasn't the least bit surprised, that many of the people whose work she'd liked were so busy that they had waiting lists months and sometimes years long; in the meantime, Jade set up appointments to interview those who were available.

There were designers she rejected, and designers who rejected her. Some were eliminated because they were too expensive; and some she just didn't like (personal chemistry was a factor she always took into account in business because, after all, she'd have to work with them). Others, once Jade saw their complete portfolios, she didn't like as much on second glance as she had at first. And then there were those who weren't interested in her because they were too busy, because the budget was too small, or because no one had ever heard of Hartley's.

She spent three solid days interviewing designers and getting nowhere. Late in the afternoon of the third day, leaving the East Sixty-fifth Street office of the last one, she felt, suddenly, horribly depressed. She was accomplishing nothing, and taking too much time to do it. The last designer she'd interviewed had been a male person who wore pancake makeup and eyeliner. He was hostile in the extreme, commenting snottily on the brochure of the Hartley line that Jade had shown him.

"Pleasant prints for peasants," he had snipped, handing it gingerly back to her with two extended fingers as if he feared contamination.

As Jade explained what she had in mind he sighed heavily and took a crystal perfume atomizer from the gilt Louis Sixteenth table he used as a desk and sprayed himself with tuberose perfume. Jade couldn't wait to escape but once she did, revived by the wholesome (compared to tuberose) bus-exhaust-scented air of nearby Madison Avenue, she realized that she was back at square one.

She had a space; what she needed was someone to make the space into a store that people would want to shop in, browse in, buy in. As she walked down Madison, she decided she'd go into every famous New York department store and take note of which departments particularly impressed her. Then, back at the Regency, she'd call their executive offices and try to find out who had been responsible for the design. Madison Avenue was, Jade noticed, an obstacle course. She side-stepped wooden construction barriers, dumpsters loaded with ripped-out woodwork, and old pipes and plaster; she detoured around staked-off new cement sidewalk, ducked electricians wielding electric drills and plasterers in their white and powdery work clothes.

Then she found the shop she'd been looking for in her dreams.

Paco Rioja's shop was obviously brand-new. The letter man was still stenciling the name on the window; a huge green ficus, sent as an opening gift, stood in the large plate-glass window with three beautiful handbags. The front door was held open by a wedge of wood and a delivery boy brought in cartons of merchandise. Jade stopped and peeked in, holding her hand to the window to shut out the reflection and the glare. The interior was warmly paneled, the tile floor was covered by a richly faded oriental rug, and the center display table looked like something Jade imagined had once stood in an English aristocrat's country castle.

"Come in!" a voice with a light Spanish accent welcomed, noticing Jade staring inside. "Not everything is out yet but come in and look around."

"I'm Paco," he said with a big smile that showed the whitest teeth Jade had ever seen. "This," he said, gesturing to the tall and remarkably handsome man who had just come into the selling area from a back room, "is George Kouras. The architect."

"Designer," George corrected, smiling at Jade. Even at a glance he seemed warm and intelligent and humorous. She returned the smile, aware of the instant attraction. No one had looked at her like that since college. No one in Fort Wayne *ever* looked at her like that. Everyone in Fort Wayne knew she was a Hartley.

"Designer," Paco said, chastened. "I hope you want to buy a handbag."

He began to open the cartons for Jade, showing her the different styles. Some were made of bits and pieces of suede, lizard, and snakeskin in the most fabulous colors patched and stitched together; others were made of the most sumptuous calfskin, the softest pigskin; still others were of natural-colored hemp, of knitted string, or lacquered basketry. As George supervised, Jade chose one: a pouch of ruby and emerald lizard patchwork on a background of bottle-green suede.

While Paco wrote up the bill and phoned American Express for an okay, Jade spoke to George.

"I wasn't really looking for a handbag," she told him, acting businesslike and ignoring the fact that he looked like a real-life Warren Beatty—bedroom eyes, soft, sensitive mouth, and all. "I've just rented space here in the city for a retail shop and I need someone to design it for me. I really like what you've done here. . . ."

Everyone in New York had told Jade that the Midwest was a negative; George saw it as a plus.

"Most New Yorkers come from someplace else," he pointed out, saying that although he considered himself a real New Yorker he came from Tarpon Springs. "And most people are nostalgic about it. Let's go for the heart."

"An Indiana farmhouse on Fifth Avenue," Jade said, picking up on his energy and enthusiasm. "White muslin and bleached pine and cotton rag rugs. Imagine," she continued, her eyes sparkling, her voice coming to life, "the first warm day of spring, the windows open and clean, starched curtains blowing in the prairie air."

George smiled and nodded, seeing what she saw, the way he always did and always would.

*The Hartley shop on Fifth and Fifty-third was a twentieth-*century evocation of a nineteenth-century Indiana farmhouse. Wainscoted and whitewashed, the interior George designed was open and plains state plain—natural woods, unbleached muslins, raw plank floors, simple yellow-and-white checked fabric—in a romantic, appealing way. Entering Hartley's was like leaving the city for the country, an instant journey to a past most Americans—wherever they were from—shared in an unconscious dream. People were attracted to the different look as if to a magnet and, from the day it opened, sales in the New York Hartley's outperformed expectations.

Herb Hartley was beside himself with pride. As far as he was concerned Jade was perfect. Well, almost perfect. If she had a son *then* she'd be perfect, but when he asked Barry when they were having children, Barry said that it looked as if Jade couldn't have any. She had been trying to get pregnant ever since the miscarriage and had been unable to conceive. Herb was very disappointed. When Jade had first become pregnant he had written a will leaving Hartley's to his grandchild because he wanted the store to stay in the family for another generation. Now he rewrote the will making Jade and Barry the beneficiaries. "Don't tell Jade what I said," Barry had told his father. "Talking about it upsets her too much."

When Herb came to New York to inspect the store he was impressed by what he saw. "Who thought of this anyway?" he asked Jade and George.

"She did," George said.

"He did," Jade said, at the same instant. They looked at each other and laughed. In the five months since they'd met, they'd learned to talk in shorthand, to read each other's minds and moods, to anticipate each other's ups and downs. During those five months they'd spent more time with each other than they had with their mates.

"There's only one thing wrong with us," George told Jade as the job came to an end.

"Which is?"

"Timing," he said. "We're both married."

"I notice," Jade said cheekily, flirting with him the way she often did, "that marriage doesn't stop you." George's little black book was a source of much laughter and many jokes in the Kouras-Leland office. Jade knew that if she gave George the slightest opening he'd take it. She made sure never to step over the invisible line between flirtation and invitation with him, and George, sensitive to women and responsive to them, never did anything to upset her.

George had the grace to flush.

"Well," he shrugged, "boys will be boys. Anyway, with you I'd be different."

"No you wouldn't," she said. "Tigers never change their stripes."

"This one would," he said seriously. "For you."

The dialogue was getting a little too intense, a little too close for comfort, and, by unspoken agreement, they both dropped it and never referred to it again. Sometimes, they both realized in silent concord, fantasies are best left to the dreamers who weave them.

"We could move to New York," Jade suggested to Barry when the store had been opened and a manager hired. She was homesick for the city she had come to love and think of as home. She was feeling increasingly trapped between father and son. It wasn't marriage she blamed, it was being in the middle. She had always feared that marriage would mean what it meant to her mother: having to share a man with other women. It had never occurred to her that there could be another rival for a husband's attention: his father. As time went on Barry seemed increasingly obsessed with his father, with winning his attention and his approval. Although Barry went to Jade for comfort, as time went on he seemed more and more to look to his father for love.

Barry shook his head at her suggestion. "Hartley's headquarters is here," he said adamantly. "And we're not leaving."

All the things Jade loved about the city Barry hated. He was intimidated by its energy and speed and the confidence of its people. Jade thrived on them. All the things that suffocated Jade in Fort Wayne Barry loved. He knew everyone and everyone knew him; he was a big shot in Fort Wayne and he and Jade couldn't go out to dinner without running into half a dozen people they knew. Jade felt she had no privacy; Barry felt like a local celebrity.

"Our future is here," he said. "We'd be crazy to leave. Anyway, Dad wants to open a shop in California. Either Los Angeles or San Francisco. He says the choice is up to you."

In the next three years Hartley's New York success was repeated in Beverly Hills, Dallas, and Chicago. Herb Hartley gave Jade all the credit.

"Hartley's is in the big time," Herb told her in front of Barry. "And it's thanks to you."

Jade saw the look of anger cross Barry's face. The truth was that the success of the new Hartley's lines and branches was due to both Jade *and* Barry. Jade was the creative one, Barry was the one who brilliantly handled all the finances. It was because of Barry that Hartley's earnings had gone up in each quarter since he'd moved back to Fort Wayne. Herb, who was basically a merchandiser, could understand Jade's talents; he couldn't really understand Barry's. He thought finance was something any halfway competent accountant could do.

"Hartley's is in the big time," Barry told his father, "and it's thanks to *me!* Profits are up. Our line of credit is up. Gross sales are up. Without me you'd still be selling Halloween napkins in the Midwest. Period!"

"Halloween napkins are what paid all your bills, young man!" Herb reminded him. "And don't you ever forget it!"

With that Barry stormed out.

"Always was temperamental," Herb told Jade, once again dismissing Barry and his contributions.

An hour later Barry returned carrying a suitcase. He barged past Herb's secretary and into his father's office. Herb was behind his desk discussing Fourth of July display units with Jade and the marketing manager. Barry approached his father's desk, hefted the suitcase, and, without a word, unsnapped its locks and opened it. A cascade of thousand-dollar bills fell onto Herb's desk, some fluttering to the floor around it. Jade gasped and stared at Barry. His face was white with anger and determination.

"Count it, Dad!" Barry ordered, as, speechless, Herb began to pick up the bills that had fluttered down and settled on his sleeves and fallen into his lap. "Three hundred sixty-six thousand dollars. That's how much more Hartley's earned this quarter over last quarter. Because of me!"

Barry then turned on his heel and, shaking with rage and triumph, left the office.

"Jesus Christ!" said Herb, shocked, turning to Jade. "What the hell's the matter with him?"

"He wants your attention," Jade said quietly as the

embarrassed merchandise manager began scooping up the bills.

"He's got it, for Christ's sake!" Herb exploded. "*And* he's going to inherit the goddamn company when I croak. What the hell else does he want?"

"Love," said Jade quietly. "He wants to know that you love him."

Herb glared at her, his face red with anger. "Over my dead body."

C H A P T E R 10

By the seventh year of her marriage Jade found herself where she'd sworn never to be: in the middle of a triangle. A love triangle but not a lovers' triangle. Her rival was not another woman, but another man—her husband's father. Father and son competed desperately; it seemed almost as though they were trying to destroy each other. Physical therapy had improved Barry's knee to the point that Barry and Herb played tennis every Sunday morning. Herb directed all his shots toward Barry's left side, the side on which he still limped.

"That son of a bitch!" Barry complained to Jade. "He knows I can't go to my left!"

Jade remembered seeing Barry and his father play tennis at Cornell before they'd gotten married. Barry had smashed service ace after service ace past his father. The older man hadn't had a chance. Jade had noticed it at the time and she remembered telling Barry that he ought to go a little easy.

"Your father's thirty years older than you are," Jade had said. "Give him a break."

"No way," Barry had said. "When I play, I play to win."

Now that the tables had turned, Jade remembered the incident and told herself she should have realized then that father and son had probably always been bitter rivals and fierce competitors. She should have realized—and warned Barry—that going into business together would inevitably lead to disaster. But she hadn't realized it, and if she had, Barry would probably never have listened to her, anyway. Beating Herb, taking over for Herb, meant much too much to him.

Herb continually denied Barry any attention or affection or recognition. Barry, in turn, looked to Jade more and more to make up for the love he missed from his father. Both turned to her with complaints about the other while Doris, telling both father and son they were perfect, refused to admit that there was any problem. Jade felt she was being torn in two. In an attempt to resolve the increasingly tense situation, Jade tried to leave her job, but each time she suggested quitting Herb and Barry both refused to hear of it.

"You're more of a Hartley than he is," Herb told Jade in Barry's presence. "You've done more for Hartley's than he has."

"I don't want you to quit," Barry said. "Then it will be just me and him." He meant his father. "This way you can be a buffer between us."

Jade's heart went out to her husband. She understood the terrible position he was in and she felt infinitely sorry and infinitely helpless as she watched the timeless battle that was being waged between an older man and the youthful son whose vigor was a daily reminder of the father's own fading powers. She was on Barry's side because she was his wife, but she also understood how Herb must feel. Still, there was nothing she could do to change either of them and she told herself, as she had a thousand times, that the minute she got pregnant she'd quit work and stay at home. A baby would be the solution for everyone. Herb would have the grandchild he yearned for; Barry would finally have the love of a family of his own. Once she had a baby her marriage would improve and so would Barry's relationship with his father. A baby would solve everything.

But having a baby, which seemed natural for every other woman in the world, was very difficult for Jade. Four times since her miscarriage she had thought she was pregnant; all four times she had been mistaken.

"You worry about it too much," Barry always said tenderly, holding her, reassuring her. "Try to relax."

Jade's doctor, using medical terminology, told her the same thing. He could find nothing physically wrong with her, he said, although she *was* a bit torn up from the miscarriage. Still, it was nothing to worry about.

"Tension and stress," he concluded, "very often interfere with ovulation."

Tension and stress, Jade told herself, were the story of her life. Still, she insisted on fertility tests. They indicated that she functioned normally. When she asked Barry to undergo the tests he refused.

"There's nothing wrong with me," he said adamantly.

"But we've been married seven years,"Jade replied, wanting to know if something was wrong. If it was, they might be able to do something about it. "Seven years is a long time to wait."

"No it's not," he said calmly. "We're still young. We have plenty of time. Anyway, aren't I enough for you? We're happy, just the two of us, aren't we?"

"Of course," Jade said, going into his arms. Barry considered the subject closed.

Jade was convinced that she'd never conceive when, in May 1975, she skipped her period. She remembered the four false alarms and did nothing, but when she skipped her period again in June, she went to the doctor.

"I refuse to get my hopes up," she told him, but when he told her that the test had come back positive, she broke into tears.

"We're going to have a baby!" Jade told Barry the minute he came home that night. She had gone straight home from the doctor and waited for her husband, hugging her delicious secret to herself, not wanting to see anyone or talk to anyone before she told him. She was half-crying, half-laughing, bubbling over with her long-denied happiness. "I went to the doctor today. The test came back positive!"

She threw her arms around him.

"You're sure?" he asked quietly, as if he were afraid to believe it.

"I'm sure!" she said. She was also sure that she was the happiest person in the whole world.

*   *   *

"Jade, don't have it," Barry said later that night. They were in bed, the lights were off, his arms were around her.

"Not have it?" Stunned, she repeated his words, not sure she'd heard what she thought she'd heard, thinking she must have misunderstood. "What do you mean, 'don't have it'?"

"It isn't the right time," Barry said, stroking her back lovingly. "The house isn't big enough. We'd need another bedroom at least."

"Another bedroom?" Jade asked incredulously. "Are you kidding! We already have two empty bedrooms!"

"I need one of them for a study," Barry said calmly, still holding her. "And anyway we don't have enough money. We can't afford a baby."

"We have plenty of money!" Jade exclaimed, outraged. They were talking about money! Why on earth were they talking about money? After seven years she was finally pregnant and Barry was saying they couldn't afford a baby? It was crazy. "We have your salary and mine and we've always saved money."

"But you won't work once the baby comes. Our income will be cut almost in half," he said.

"We'll still have your salary," Jade said, positive that he couldn't mean what he was saying. He was rich. They were rich. The Hartleys were rich. What was he talking about? "You earn almost fifty thousand dollars a year."

"That's not nearly enough to bring up a child," Barry said patiently.

"Millions of people do it on much less!" Jade said. "My mother did it on a fourth of that and she had three children!"

"We're not millions of people," he said. "And we're not your mother. We're Hartleys."

"Hartleys?" Jade exploded. "You make it sound like we're the king and queen of England!"

"We have a position to think of," Barry said reasonably. It was the first time Jade got a glimpse of Barry's profound sense of being special, of being different, of being better than anyone else.

"Barry," Jade said, moving away from him. She turned on the lights and faced him, looking into his eyes. Their color was blue, the deep, dark blue of a fjord, cold and bottomless. "What are you trying to tell me?"

"I want you to get rid of it," he said, not flinching from her gaze, his eyes calm and serious. "I don't want to share you, Jade," he said. "I have to share you with my father. I don't have to share you with a baby. I *can't* share you. I need you too much. I love you too much. Please, Jade. Get rid of it."

Jade did not sleep that night and the next day, still barely believing their conversation of the night before, she asked him if he really meant what he had said. Yes, he said, of course he did.

"How can you?" Jade asked, shocked beyond belief, thinking that her husband was more of a stranger than she had ever imagined. A stranger? she asked herself. A killer. "How can you think of killing our baby?"

"It's not a baby," Barry said. He loved Jade. Jade was real. The baby wasn't. "It's just a bunch of cells. Besides, if you really want, maybe we'll have another. Later."

"But Barry, I want *this* baby!" She wept, clutching her belly, protecting her unborn child from its father.

A week passed; a week in which she had begged, pleaded, and cajoled. She wanted her baby. Barry was her husband; he had to want it, too. He *had* to! But he had a thousand arguments about why he didn't.

"Children can ruin a marriage. Look at my cousin, Sarah," he said, thinking of the way Sarah was totally hung up on her kid. "The minute she had her baby she never looked at her husband again. All she could think about was the kid. No wonder Eric's having affairs."

"And look at that couple we saw this weekend at McDonald's," he said, thinking of another depressing example. "The mother was totally obsessed with those two kids. She and her husband never said one word to each other the whole time. All he did was pay the bill. I don't want us to end up like that. Not even talking to each other."

"And what about Tommy Briers?" Barry asked, pointing out how children had screwed up Tommy's life. Tommy Briers was a childhood friend of Barry's. When Jade had first come to Fort Wayne she and Barry used to go out with Tommy and his wife, Suzanne. "The minute Suzanne had their first kid they never went anywhere, they never did anything. Now they have two more. She's getting fat and he's drinking too much. I don't want to be like them. I want us to have an interesting life."

An interesting life? Jade asked herself bitterly. In Fort Wayne?

When Barry saw how determined Jade was to have their baby he changed his tactics. Barry became especially loving. He brought her flowers and took her out to dinner. He told her, over and over, how much he loved and needed her, how he couldn't live without her, how she had been the best thing that had ever happened to him, how she was his entire life and how his first thoughts in the morning and his last thoughts in the evening were of her.

"I don't want this baby," he insisted. "Not now. You know how tough things are for me right now. I need you, Jade. I need *all* your attention, all your help. Can't you understand that? I don't want to share you with anyone else!"

"But it's not just 'anyone else'!" Jade said, appalled. "It's our child."

"Not yet," Barry said adamantly. "You're all I have, Jade! You're all that matters to me! I need you! I love you."

Nothing Jade said made the slightest difference to Barry. He was desperate, panicky, torn between his father who shattered him and an unborn baby he feared would take his wife from him. Jade, again, was in the middle. This time between her husband and the baby she had wanted for as long as she could remember.

By the time Jade was nine weeks pregnant she had lost twelve pounds. Barry had not changed his mind, nor would he. She felt cornered, threatened.

"I'm going to tell your father," she said finally. "I'm going to tell him that I'm pregnant and that you want me to get rid of it."

Barry turned white.

"Jade, please!" he begged, taking her hand. "Don't do that! How can you go to my father? You know how he treats me! How can you go to him when I'm the one who loves you?"

Later Jade would tell herself that she'd been a fool not to

go to Herb. At the time, though, she was still loyal, still on Barry's side.

Jade did the only thing she thought she could do.

"I've got to get away," she finally told Barry. Her nerves were in shreds. She had painful shingles down both sides of her torso. Just putting on clothes was agony. How could she defy the husband she loved? Could she really bring up a child whose father already resented it? Did she want her child and Barry to echo the destructive relationship Barry and his father shared? Jade had to get away. She had to get some perspective. "I've got to think things out for myself."

"I'll go with you," he said reaching for her. He was still trying to persuade her to change her mind with love and attention and kindness. "I'll take you anywhere you want to go. Just tell me."

"No," she said pulling back from him. "I have to be by myself. I have to think."

"You don't love me!" he said, looking shattered.

"I do!" she said tearfully. "That's the problem."

Jade went home to Auburn, only Auburn wasn't home anymore. It was a small and pleasant upstate town and Jade had become a halfhearted midwesterner who thought of New York City as home. She told her mother everything.

"Mom," Jade asked, dry-eyed, beyond tears, unable to think straight, unable to feel anything except pain. "What would you do?"

"I once *was* you," Dorothy said quietly. She had Jade's hair, now heavily streaked with gray. She seemed, as she had seemed for as long as Jade could remember, perpetually tired. "The only difference was that I wasn't married. I got pregnant. Your father didn't want the baby; he didn't want the responsibility. Our parents insisted we get married. Three babies later your father did what he wanted to do in the first place: He left me."

"But you had us," said Jade. She knew half of her mother's story, had heard the small-town whispers and rumors. For the first time she was hearing her mother's story from her mother's point of view. "Didn't we matter?"

Dorothy nodded. "Of course," she said.

"And you loved us, didn't you?"

"Yes, I did," said Dorothy. "But I paid a terribly high price and you did, too."

"Too high?" asked Jade, remembering her unhappy childhood.

Dorothy was quiet for a moment.

"Too high," she said finally, swallowing hard and turning away. The price had been her youth, her energy, her hope. Dorothy Mullen was a pretty woman who had gone through life pathetically in love with a man who rejected her, and her children had suffered from her bitterness and unrequited love.

"Where would you live?" Heidi Diehl wanted to know after Jade confided that having the baby would probably mean the end of the marriage. Heidi had forgotten her dreams of making a million dollars. The moment she had graduated from high school she had married an engineer who ran the heating and electrical plants at the big state prison in Auburn. She had two children, and her dreams now centered around getting a secretarial job because, between inflation and with another baby on the way, her husband's salary just didn't stretch far enough. "Would you come back to Auburn?"

"I don't know," Jade admitted. She didn't know what she'd do or where she'd go or how she'd live. She did know, though, that if she went ahead and had the baby it would almost certainly be the end of the marriage, sooner or later. Barry had already written the script. Babies ruined marriages. Babies came between husbands and wives. Babies subtracted love, they didn't add to love. All that was left was to live it out to its inevitable unhappy ending. "I'd need a job."

"All your experience is in retailing," Heidi pointed out in her sensible way. "Could you find that kind of job here in Auburn?"

"I don't know," said Jade, knowing that she couldn't. No matter what she did she would lose either her marriage or her baby. She had to choose and she couldn't. She was in emotional agony and she saw no possible solution.

"And what if you lived in New York?" Heidi asked. "Who'd take care of your baby while you were at work?"

"You're awfully practical."

"Babies make you practical," Heidi said, and Jade knew that she was right.

Barry had been calling every day, pointing out that time was passing quickly, begging Jade to have the abortion, pressing her to make her decision. He wanted her to get rid of her baby and he didn't care what he said or what he did as long as she did what he wanted.

"I love you," he began the way he always did. "If you loved me, you'd have the operation. Can't you understand that? Can't you think of me?"

"Barry!" she said, shocked. "I always think of you."

Barry didn't care. He didn't hear her, didn't want to hear her. Relentlessly, driven by his own fear of losing her, he continued.

"Just remember, Jade, I saved your life," he reminded her. "I'm a cripple because of you. My leg hurts me with every single step I take. I limp around a tennis court and I'm too gimpy to ski. I'm half a man because of you, Jade. You're alive because I put you first. The least you can do is the same for me."

Shattered, Jade hung up. She remembered how she'd once thought that having an unfaithful husband was the worst thing that could ever happen to a woman. Now she realized how naive she'd been.

The family planning clinic in Auburn was just a few steps north of the light on Main Street. The counselor's name was Catherine Harrold, whose cousin had been in Jade's class in high school. Catherine was only a bit older than Jade. She had blond hair and light-blue eyes, a round face, and glasses with pale blue rims that tended to drain the color from her eyes, giving them a deceptively watery and colorless look.

"Call me Catherine," she said, offering Jade a chair. The clinic had once been the county's agricultural center. Books on crop conditions and livestock diseases still lined the bookcases. "How old are you, Jade?"

"Twenty-seven."

"And is this your first pregnancy?"

"No. I had a miscarriage several years ago."

Catherine asked for details about the miscarriage, making notes on a yellow legal pad. "And have you had any problems with this pregnancy?" she asked. "Any spotting? Any cramps? Anything unusual?"

"No." Jade felt the wetness on her cheek. At first she didn't realize it was tears.

"And how many weeks pregnant are you?"

"Just twelve weeks today."

Catherine looked up from the mimeographed form she was filling out with Jade's replies. "Twelve weeks is the usual cut-off point for the procedure."

"Yes," said Jade. She had waited until the last possible moment to make her decision. "I know."

"You're married?" Catherine glanced at Jade's left hand.

"Yes."

"Does your husband know you're here?"

"It was his idea." Jade swallowed. Her voice was calm and steady; her hands lay still in her lap, neatly folded; only the quiet tears that streamed silently down her face gave any sign of what she was feeling.

"I see," said Catherine. "And what's your idea?"

"It's my idea, too," she said, blinking. Now that she'd made up her mind she didn't want them to turn her down. After all she'd gone through, she just wanted to get it over with.

"You're sure?" Catherine asked, looking straight into Jade's eyes.

"I'm sure." She swallowed again, hard, but involuntarily she withdrew her eyes from Catherine's gaze.

"I have two children," Catherine said, suddenly becoming personal for the first time. "I didn't have the third one. It was a hard decision. What I want you to know is that I know how you feel. I've been there myself."

"Why didn't you?" Jade asked, relieved at not having to talk about herself even if it was only for a moment. "Have the third one?"

"Because I'd been pregnant three times in a little over two years. I was only twenty. We didn't think we could take care of a third one."

"Do you ever regret your decision?"

It was Catherine Harrold's turn to shift her gaze.

"Sometimes."

*　　*　　*

"I want to do it," Jade said, decisively, when the interview was over. "I definitely want to do it. I want to make an appointment," she said. "As soon as possible."

The doctor examined her. Catherine told her that the clinic had the most modern vacuum apparatus. The procedure—the word put a chill through Jade—would take less than fifteen minutes.

"Will it hurt?" Jade wanted to know. "I mean, physically?" She already knew how it felt emotionally.

"A little," Catherine said softly. "You'll forget the pain as soon as it's over."

Dorothy Mullen drove Jade to the clinic and waited in the waiting room with Heidi. The operating room was just like a gynecologist's office with a leather examining table and metal stirrups set at each side of one end. Jade kept her blouse on and removed only her skirt and panties. The doctor, who was young and gentle and bearded, held her left knee reassuringly while Catherine stood behind her and held her hand.

"Just breathe in. Take a great big breath," Catherine prompted. "It will relax you. In and out."

Jade tried to obey, but it was hard to breathe. Silent tears ran from her eyes, pooling in her ears and hairline. Catherine kept wiping them away with a piece of Kleenex.

"Breathe, Jade, breathe. In. Out," Catherine said softly. "All the way in. All the way out."

Gradually Jade began to breathe, exaggerating the breaths, concentrating on them, not on what was going to happen to her. She was aware of the doctor removing his hand from her knee and she heard the slight rustle of his sleeve as he moved to pick something up from the tray of instruments that stood to his right.

"The next thing you're going to feel is the speculum," Catherine said gently. "It'll feel real cold. . . ."

CHAPTER 11

*J*ade was absolutely positive it had been a boy. She didn't know why, but she named him Herb.

Everyone agreed that she had done the right thing.

"Bringing up children without a husband is the hardest job in the world," her mother assured her. "I don't know how anyone does it. I don't know how I did it. I'm glad you're not going to have to do it."

"This way you aren't stuck," Heidi said, comforting her. "You're only twenty-seven. You're still young. You still have choices. You still have your freedom."

And now that she had done what he wanted, Barry acted as if he had never said the things he'd said, as if the things that had happened had never happened. He was a genius at stepping over the past as if it had never been.

Herb Hartley behaved as if Jade had been away on vacation. They had told him the truth, or at least part of the truth: that Jade had gone home for a visit with her family.

"Have a good time?" he boomed. "You look good. Roses in your cheeks!"

"I've lost ten pounds," Jade said quietly. The "roses" was blusher. "I'm as pale as a ghost."

"You look good to me!" he said.

Jade looked at him in disbelief. Barry, more than anyone she had ever met, had an ability to ignore reality and dismiss his own emotions. Now, in dealing with Herb, she realized where he had learned it. Herb saw only what he wanted to see, heard only what he wanted to hear.

"Your going away made me realize just how important to Hartley's you really are!" he said. He reached into his top-right desk drawer and pulled out a plain manila envelope and handed it to her. "A few years ago I wrote a will leaving everything to you and Barry. You're like a daughter to me, Jade, and I figure you might as well get some of the loot now. You've earned it."

Jade looked at him and opened the envelope. Inside was a certificate for one thousand shares of Hartley's stock made out in her name.

"Thank you," she said, touched by the surprise gift. Involuntarily, tears sprang to her eyes as she thought of her dead baby. The stock seemed a pathetic and bitter consolation prize. Still, she knew how possessive Herb was about everything he considered to belong to the Hartleys. The stock, she realized, was Herb's way of saying that he considered her a real Hartley. From him, this was the greatest compliment of all. She managed a smile. She managed to thank him again. "It's very nice of you."

"Don't thank me!" he said, stopping her, embarrassed as always by tender emotions. "You've earned it. I want you to have it. Barry wants you to have it. That way," he boomed, enjoying his own sense of humor, "you can tell us all to go to hell if you feel like it."

Jade smiled wanly, kissed her father-in-law on the cheek, and put the envelope into her bag. When she got home she put it, still in its manila envelope, in the bottom of her jewelry box.

Although Barry acted as if everything were the same and Herb seemed to feel that giving her the stock made things even better than ever, Jade didn't feel the same way. She was weepy and depressed. Even though everyone told her over and over that she'd done the right thing, she didn't feel as if she'd done the right thing. She felt empty and lonely and she knew that what she'd done couldn't be undone. She'd made one of those mistakes in life that couldn't be apologized for, or corrected. She'd given in to blackmail and it had been a mistake. She'd made her decision and, now that it was too late, she regretted it more and more.

Barry didn't see it that way at all.

"See? It was nothing," he said. Now that she'd done what he wanted, he was more tender and loving than ever. "You did the right thing. In a few weeks you'll forget all about it. Who knows? Maybe one day we'll want to have others."

She didn't bother to say anything, but she knew she

wouldn't forget about it. As for having others, the doctor in
Auburn had told Jade not to have sex for at least six weeks
after the operation and not to get pregnant for at least six
months. Jade followed his instructions, but she did not
seem to recover normally. Two months after the operation,
she was still bleeding.

At first Dr. Nadries, her own doctor back in Fort Wayne,
wasn't concerned.

"Different people heal differently," he told her casually,
dismissing her concern, leaning forward in his big leather
chair and buzzing his nurse for the next patient as he spoke
to her. "Just take it easy, and remember no sex until
you've stopped bleeding for three weeks."

But another month went by and she was still bleeding.

"You're still torn up internally. You *were* three months
gone," Dr. Nadries told her. He sounded annoyed with
her, as if her body's refusal to heal was her fault, as if she
were being stubborn on purpose, to give him a hard time.
"That's just at the borderline. You'll have to be a little
patient."

He did, though, tell her that all the bleeding had led to a
slight anemia, which was probably why she was feeling so
listless and weepy. He advised her to take iron tablets and
eat a lot of red meat and spinach. Red meat and spinach
didn't really seem to help very much and neither did the
iron tablets, and Barry began to get impatient.

"You're my wife," he told her as 1975 turned into 1976.
He loved her; he wanted to make love to her. He seemed
annoyed that she was thin and exhausted, hardly able to
drag herself through the day. The sexual passion that had
once seemed so flattering to Jade now seemed selfish.
"You're my wife. I want to make love to you. How long is
this going to go on?"

"I don't know," said Jade miserably and made another
appointment with Dr. Nadries. She sensed that there was
something wrong with her. She wanted to find out what it
was.

*"Jade, you look lousy. Thin as a rail and white as a
sheet,"* Herb Hartley told her one day at lunch in the
employee cafeteria. Even Herb had finally noticed. She
had spent the morning at Dr. Nadries's and she felt terri-

ble, empty and forlorn, lost and aimless. She wasn't even thirty and she felt her life was over. Everywhere she looked she saw women with children. The elementary school she passed every day on the way to work was a knife in her heart. She heard the laughter and shouts of children and the sound was like a scream in a nightmare. She had been right. There *was* something wrong with her and that morning Dr. Nadries had told her what it was.

"You ought to fatten up," Herb was saying, playing doctor, giving her one of his unsolicited prescriptions. "Put some meat on your bones. No wonder you can't have children."

Jade looked at him in shock.

"Can't have children? Said who?" Jade asked, stunned. "Who said I can't?"

"Barry," replied Herb, obliviously stepping into a mine field. He dug into a slice of applesauce cake with gusto.

"Barry? *Barry* said I can't have children?" Jade's voice rose. People turned and stared. She didn't care. "When?"

"A few years ago," Herb said nonchalantly, adding whipped cream to the cake. "That's why I changed my will."

Jade stared at him. "Did Barry tell you why I went home?"

"Sure," Herb said, spooning up another big mouthful. "To visit your mother."

"And did he tell you I had an abortion?" Jade asked. The spicy, cinnamon smell of the applesauce cake was making her sick. Nauseated, disgusted, she stood up, looming over her father-in-law, almost shouting at him. "An abortion because *he* wanted me to? *Did* he? Did he tell you that I aborted our child? Your grandson, Herb! And did he tell you that I named our little boy Herb? After you!"

Herb's expression was one of confusion, followed by immediate, stunned shock. He looked up at Jade, turning white, and his body began to shake violently, almost as if he were having a seizure. The forkful of cake fell from his hand. The rich white cream spattered Herb's blue suit as the fork clattered back onto the dish with a sound that seemed like a rifle shot, but no louder than the cry that came from Herb's mouth.

Without waiting for him to recover Jade threw down her

napkin and stood up, looking around the cafeteria for Barry. He wasn't there; nor was he in his office. She threw on a coat, got into her car, and went to the red-brick factory where Barry often worked. He wasn't there either. She checked the restaurants he frequented and, finally, drove home. His car was in the garage. A yellow Honda Jade had never seen before was in the driveway. Jade let herself into the house through the back door. She walked through the laundry room and into the kitchen.

A girl Jade didn't know was sitting at the kitchen counter calmly drinking coffee. She was short and stocky and, under Jade's yellow pique housecoat, she was nude. She looked up as Jade stood in the doorway.

"I guess you're the wife," she said, with a friendly smile, as if they were at a cosy kaffeeklatsch. "Barry went out to get lunch. He'll be back in a minute."

Jade looked at the girl, at the coffee tin, the coffee cup, the robe, and the oak kitchen chair in which she sat. *Her* coffee, *her* coffee cup, *her* robe, *her* oak chair, which *she* had bid on and bought at a country auction and which *she* had personally stripped and stained. She felt the anger burn and sizzle in her. She suddenly knew how her mother had felt, and while it was terrible, it wasn't nearly as terrible as killing her own baby.

"Get out!" Jade ordered, grabbing the coffee cup out of her hand. "Take off my robe and get out of here!"

She grasped the girl by the elbow and propelled her roughly toward the bedroom. Half her clothes were thrown on a small, upholstered chair and the other half were strewn on the carpet. The bed—the bed she shared with Barry—was rumpled and the air seemed to reek with sex.

"I didn't want to come here," the girl babbled as she picked up her things and got dressed, not bothering to tuck in her blouse or tie her shoelaces. Jade stood over her, hurrying her. "I told Barry we could go to my place. But he said it was all right."

"It's *not* all right," Jade said, throwing the girl's sweater at her and pushing her toward the front door. She opened it and shoved the girl out.

"Out!" said Jade shaking with rage. "Get out!"

"I really didn't mean to upset you. I mean, I *like* women.

I'm a feminist," the girl said, tripping over her shoelaces and almost falling, as Jade slammed the door on her. "I have a subscription to *Ms. . . .*"

Jade washed the coffee cup, then she ripped the sheets off the bed, put on fresh ones, and threw the soiled ones into the trash along with the yellow housecoat. She had to stop several times and sit down to regain her strength. When Barry returned with a McDonald's bag she was sitting on the bed, shivering, wrapped in the red-and-white quilt she had once loved. The smell of hamburgers nauseated her and she swallowed the bile that rose to the back of her throat.

"What are you doing home?" he asked, looking pale and not meeting her eyes.

"I could ask you the same question," Jade said calmly, clutching the quilt around her, the quilt that seemed to hold the stale, animal smell of strangers' sex.

"I guess Debby was still here," he said tentatively, swallowing so hard Jade could see his Adam's apple bob.

"Yes, Barry, I met your girlfriend," she said in a superficially reasonable tone of voice. She was aware of the weight of the quilt on her body, giving her warmth, giving her strength.

"She's not my girlfriend," he said, finally glancing at her and then glancing away in his shame. He put the bag of hamburgers down on the bureau.

"Then who is she?"

"Just somebody. Nobody," he said, sounding miserable. "It's nothing. It was just sex. I'm going crazy without sex."

"It's not nothing!" Jade said, her tone no longer reasonable but rising in anger and betrayal. "She's not nobody! She's a person. She was wearing my bathrobe. She was sitting in my kitchen, drinking my coffee out of my mug. She was screwing my husband in my bed!"

"Jade?" Barry said, reaching out for her. There were tears in his eyes.

"I abort *our* son at *your* request and you tell me you can't live without sex?" Jade began to quiver, from rage, from fever. She was flushed and sweaty. "And you tell *him* I can't have children? How could you?"

"When I told him I thought it was true," Barry said, his voice filled with shame. "You were having so much trouble getting pregnant."

"And what did he mean when he told me he changed the will?"

"The first time you were pregnant my father made a will leaving everything to our children," Barry explained, sitting down on the end of the bed. "He wanted Hartley's to stay in the family for at least two more generations. When he asked me a few years ago why we didn't have children I told him we couldn't. And he changed his will again, leaving everything to you and me."

"And if I had had the child, he might have changed his will back?" Jade asked, suddenly beginning to understand.

"Jade, this way we'll get everything!" Barry exclaimed, his voice strong again. "The stock he gave you was just a down payment. We're going to be rich, Jade!"

Jade gasped. Everything was finally clear. Now she understood the *real* reason Barry put up with his father's abuse. The *real* reason he had wanted her to have the abortion.

"You mean all of this was about money?" she asked, the odor of the hamburgers revoltingly greasy. Once again the bile rose, leaving a sick, bitter taste in her mouth.

"No," he said. "It was just what I told you. I didn't want to share you."

"Then why didn't you tell me about the will?" Jade was furious. Barry said he loved her, yet how could he not talk to her about something that was obviously so crucially important to him—important enough for him to want her to abort their child.

Barry was silent. He didn't really know why.

"Barry, I can't live like this," Jade said, her anger suddenly gone. Barry was right. The girl didn't matter, but their marriage did. She had even killed their baby in order to save their marriage. She wasn't going to give up so easily. Barry had given her a choice; now she was going to give him one. She knew the marriage couldn't survive as long as she felt suffocated, and as long as she felt that Barry was just waiting around for Herb to die.

"Either we move somewhere else and start a life of our

own or I'm leaving," she said softly. "You have to choose, Barry. It's me or Hartley's."

She looked at him for an answer and he sat there silently staring into space. She couldn't believe that he wouldn't choose to go somewhere else with her and begin again. After all the things he'd said about how much he loved her, about how much he needed her, and how he couldn't even share her with a baby. She waited for him to tell her that he didn't even have to think about it, that he would choose her. That together they would leave Fort Wayne, and Herb, and Hartley's.

The moment stretched on, and still he didn't speak. He didn't even turn to look at her. He continued to look out into space and Jade realized what the answer was.

"Hartley's?" she asked softly.

He nodded.

Jade stared at him for a moment and realized that it *was* the money. She tried to swallow the bile that rose a third time into the back of her throat but couldn't, and she fled into the bathroom where she finally vomited, and kept vomiting until her stomach was empty.

Barry stood at the door watching her heaving back. He wanted to touch her, to comfort her, but he knew she would refuse him.

Pale and shaking, Jade rinsed her mouth and went back into the bedroom. She took her suitcase down from the top of the closet and began to throw her clothes into it. Barry watched, not quite knowing what to say or do.

"Can't we talk about this?" he asked finally, and took her hands in an affectionate gesture. Jade had the sense that it was the first time in years that he'd touched her without wanting sex.

"I've spent years talking. I wanted us to leave here. I wanted us to have a life of our own. I wanted us to have a family," she said, withdrawing her hands from his. There were tears in her eyes and her lips were quivering, but she wasn't crying. "You never listened to me or to what *I* wanted."

"I'll be different," he said, not denying her words. "I'll change."

"I doubt it. Money means too much to you," she said, putting the jewelry box into her suitcase and closing the suitcase with a snap. She walked toward the kitchen and Barry followed her. She unplugged the nine-inch black-and-white portable television set she'd won in a raffle three years before, wrapped the cord around the handle, and picked it up.

"Where are you going?" He spoke as if they were discussing what to have for dinner. He was superficially calm now, as though none of this were really happening.

"To a motel," she said, making the decision on the spur of the moment. She hadn't thought about where she was going, just that she had to get away.

"Do you have enough money?" he asked.

"Yes," she said, experiencing an unexpected moment of tenderness. They had been married for almost eight years. She had loved him once. He had been, once, a long, long time ago, it seemed, worth loving. "Thanks for asking."

As she walked out of the house she had once thought of as hers for the last time, she turned back.

"Barry?"

"Yes?"

"You were right," she said.

"Right?" He didn't understand.

"I *can't* have children," she said. "Dr. Nadries told me this morning. It was the abortion. I never should have had it. It ruined me inside."

"Jade, I didn't know. . . ." he said, and it was his turn for tears. He *did* love her. She was the best thing that had ever happened to him. He reached out for her but, blinded by her own tears, she didn't see him. She turned away again, and this time she did not turn back. It was over, she thought, all over.

But it wasn't. Not the last, bitter betrayals.

Edwin Hall was gray and plump and businesslike. His office was across from the courthouse, a neutral, beige office for a neutral, beige man. He had been happily married for thirty-two years. Happily, that is, if the definition of happiness included three affairs that he broke off when his wife threatened to leave him. It didn't look good for a divorce lawyer to be divorced, or so Edwin Hall believed.

"I want a divorce," Jade said, and told him the story of her marriage, ending with the abortion and the adultery.

"Is there any property involved?" Edwin Hall wanted to know, getting down to dollars and cents. The emotions of divorce were always the same and Edwin Hall was bored with them after thirty years of practice. Only the money and the property differed. Only the money and the property made it interesting.

"No," said Jade. "My husband owns the house. I don't want it."

"Any money?" he asked. "Any savings accounts? Insurance? Investments?"

"No," said Jade, not even thinking of the stock. The stock was hers, it had been given to her, she had earned it. Her name was on it. All she wanted was her divorce and her freedom. Asking for money or property had never crossed her mind. "All I want is my freedom."

"And what does your husband think of this divorce?"

"He's not going to fight," Jade said.

"So you want it and he's not going to fight and there's not going to be any arguing over money," he summed up and shrugged casually. "Then there shouldn't be any big problems," Edwin Hall said, relieved. A fight with the Hartleys was something for which he had no stomach. They were a rich and powerful local family. Edwin Hall, like anyone else in Fort Wayne with half a brain, didn't want to be on Herb Hartley's wrong side.

Barry made a stab at a reconciliation. He asked Jade to meet him in his office.

"This is a marriage, not some shack-up arrangement you can walk out of anytime you feel like it," he said, sounding sad and pompous and confident all at the same time. He suddenly got up and walked over to the sofa where she sat. Jade noticed how badly he limped. She had gotten so used to it over the years that she hadn't noticed for a while. "We're married and we're staying married."

"I gave you a choice. You chose Hartley's," Jade said.

"There's never been a divorce in the family. Never," Barry said, thinking of how his father would react, of what his father would say; thinking, too, that he loved and needed Jade and desperately wanted her to stay. "My father would kill me."

"He managed to survive when I told him I killed his

grandchild," Jade said cruelly. If Barry had said anything about her, about them, she *might* have reconsidered. Instead, all he could talk about was his father.

"You told him?" Barry asked, turning pale. "You *told* him?"

"Don't worry," said Jade, knowing what he was thinking. "He won't change his will again. You'll still inherit the company. After all, Barry, thanks to you, there's no one else to leave it to."

"They want the stock back," Edwin Hall said a week later. "They," it was clear, meant the Hartleys.

"It's mine," Jade said firmly. "I earned it. Herb said so when he gave it to me."

Edwin Hall shrugged. "Your husband is making it a condition of the divorce."

"I'm not asking for a dime," Jade said. She was outraged. She had no money. Barry had cleaned out their joint account—an account into which she had deposited her savings during all the years of their marriage—the morning after she'd moved out. "No alimony. No settlement. Nothing. All I want is to keep what's mine. What I earned. After all," Jade pointed out, "I supported Barry for the first two years we were married. I think I deserve something."

"Let me talk to them," Edwin Hall said.

"About the stock," Edwin Hall said three days later. Sun shone through the windows of his office, turning his graying hair white. "They won't even talk about it. They consider it nonnegotiable," he said. "Their position is that the company is a family company and that after the divorce you'll no longer be family."

"I won't return it. It's my property," Jade said, refusing to give back what was hers, ready to fight the Hartleys if that was what they wanted. Since she had left Barry she had not heard one word from her father-in-law who had supposedly loved her as much as he would have loved a child of his own. Nor had she heard a word from Doris Hartley, who had told her that she was the daughter she had always wished she'd had. "They gave it to me and I'm keeping it. Just tell them that."

*   *   *

Another week went by. Jade had been living in a modest motel, but even that had caused the balance in her small checking account to fall below a hundred and fifty dollars. Barry had called twice since she'd left—once to beg her to come back, the second time to ask her how much the once-a-week cleaning woman got paid. Edwin Hall opened a file on his desk and looked at some Xeroxed sheets in it.

"You had an abortion during your marriage?" he asked, looking up.

"Yes, I told you all about it," Jade said. She had a sick feeling in the pit of her stomach. "Where did you get the records?" she asked, recognizing the forms Catherine Harrold had filled out.

"Your father-in-law gave them to me," Edwin Hall said. "If you don't return the stock, things will get nasty," he said. "Very nasty. I understand the abortion was your idea."

"The abortion was Barry's idea!" Jade exploded.

"That's not what Barry told his father. He told Herb that *you* wanted the abortion and Herb believes him," said Edwin Hall.

Jade was no longer in the middle, she realized. She was bitterly aware that Barry and his father were finally united—against her. She—and her marriage—were the victims of Barry's weakness and greed. The relationships upon which she had depended, the ones she had thought would last all her life, turned out to be transient and superficial, as insubstantial as bubbles. Edwin Hall slipped the papers across the desk and pointed out Jade's signature. "Your signature is here," he said, and she couldn't deny it.

"But it was Barry's idea," Jade said. "It was *Barry* who insisted on the abortion."

"Do you have any proof?" Edwin Hall wanted to know. "Anything in writing?"

"Writing?" she asked bitterly. She looked across the desk and realized that Edwin Hall probably believed Herb and Barry. "Sure, I had Barry sign a confession. Doesn't every wife?"

She remembered the leather examining table, the bearded doctor, and the whooshing sound of the aspirator. The memory of pain and loss triggered other memories. She thought of a son who wanted to "kill" his father on the tennis court. She thought of her first apartment, the cock-roaches and Raid, of the endless chicken dinners, of the illustrations she occasionally sold. She remembered the one-hundred-forty-dollar-a-week salary from Savin's. "I earned about six thousand dollars a year when we were first married," Jade said. "I used it to help support Barry when he was getting his master's. I think I'm due at least twelve thousand dollars."

"You'd have to sue," Edwin Hall said. "It would be expensive."

"How much?" Jade asked, wondering whose side Edwin Hall was on.

"I'd require a retainer of fifteen hundred dollars."

Jade looked at him and she burst into tears. She didn't have the energy for a fight. It had all been drained out of her on the leather operating table.

Later, when she had calmed down, she called Edwin Hall and told him that she'd leave the stock at his office in the morning. All she wanted was her freedom; she didn't care what it cost. She left Fort Wayne the next day after eight years of marriage with nothing but her clothes and a black-and-white television set she'd won in a raffle.

Jade began to bleed on the flight back to New York. By the time the plane landed she was hemorrhaging. She went from the Port Authority Bus Terminal to the nearest emergency room and spent her first night back in the city she loved at Bellevue.

A month later, spending money she had earned on her first styling job, she consulted a private gynecologist who had been recommended by one of her temporary stewardess roommates. He confirmed what Dr. Nadries had said.

"You're all torn up inside," he told her in his office. "I don't know if it was the abortion or the miscarriage, but you're not going to be able to conceive."

"Never?" she asked tearily.

"So devote yourself to a career," he said. "That's all you women are interested in nowadays anyway."

C H A P T E R   12

*F*or Carlys, *getting married made all the difference;* for Jade, getting divorced made all the difference. Married, she had tried to be the person her husband wanted her to be. Single, she could be who she wanted to be. Married, she had been alone and lonely; single, she could do what she wanted with whomever she wanted. Married, she had felt unattractive; single, she felt desirable. Married, no one had ever noticed her; single, everyone did. Married, she never went anywhere; single, she never stayed home unless she wanted to. Married, she'd felt trapped; single, she felt free.

Free to dress the way she wanted to dress. She combined cheap and expensive, old and new, safe and outrageous. It was Jade who first combined a smashing yellow Armani jacket with a black jogging outfit and red cowboy boots. It was Jade who thought of wearing a sexy, low-cut gold lamé tank with a man-tailored tuxedo to the Red Parrot. It was Jade who decided to layer a black turtleneck sweater under a turquoise silk poet's shirt, tuck them both into a pair of khaki Army-Navy-store pants, and tie the whole outfit together with a Navaho concha belt.

Free to experiment with makeup, she discarded the subdued peach lipstick and tentative rosy blusher Barry had insisted she wear when she was married. Now she wore the brightest red lipstick and blusher with khaki eyeshadow and charcoal gray eyeliner. Her gold-flecked bronze eyes looked bigger and deeper in color and her wet-sand-color hair, blond rinsed, now seemed shot with golden highlights. She replaced her pretty Diorissimo with Piguet's disturbing Fracas and her conservative tortoiseshell eyeglasses with oversized bright red frames.

Free to decorate a new apartment in Chelsea exactly the way she wanted. Jade had alwys loved to do things with her hands and she had stripped down the floors and painted them white, leaving them bare except for made-in-Hong-Kong straw matting. She left the big windows uncurtained except for Japanese rice paper shades, slipcovered her odds-and-ends of furniture in yellow-and-white-striped cotton canvas, and called her apartment a tribute to the United Nations and decorating-on-the-cheap. Shopping at Conran's, Azuma, and Jensen-Lewis, she created an apartment that was sunny and serene and very inexpensive. *The New York Times* wanted to photograph it but Jade refused.

"It's my home," she explained to the editor who called. "I want to keep it private."

Home, she realized, meant a lot to her. It meant safety, comfort, pleasure, a place to read quietly, a place to entertain her friends, a retreat, an escape, and a shelter. And home, she realized, did not have to mean a husband—not anymore. Not in the late 1970s.

Jade, who had once thought that love meant marriage, now felt that love was better without marriage. She felt free to date the men who interested her and to turn down the ones who didn't, free to sleep with men who attracted her and free to say no to the ones who didn't. Free to have several affairs at once if that was how she felt, and free to commit herself to one man when someone special came along. Free to make the first move when that seemed the right thing to do and free to wait when waiting seemed appropriate. Free to bring a man flowers and champagne and free to accept them in return.

"The difference between being married and being single," Jade told Mary Lou over brunch at Mary Lou's one Sunday, "is that when I was married life was predictable. Now that I'm single it's an adventure. I've either just met a new man, or am about to meet a new man, or wonder *if* I'll meet a new man. When I was married we used to spend Friday nights with Barry's parents and Saturday nights at The Pines restaurant where all the other young married couples in Fort Wayne went. I don't know why *anyone* gets married."

Mary Lou's own marriage had lasted six years. She had supported her young husband through the rigors of medical school. The same year in which he set up a practice of his own he divorced her, announcing to her that he had outgrown her. For the past fifteen years Mary Lou had been having an affair with a married sportswear manufacturer. Every time Irwin Witkin began to talk about leaving his wife, Mary Lou found a reason to leave the country. She saw things the same way Jade did.

"I don't know what I'd do if Irwin ever left his wife," she said. "As his girlfriend I get dinners in fancy restaurants, fur coats, jewelry, and trips to the Caribbean. What does his wife get? His pot-smoking children, a housekeeping budget, and listening to him *kvetch* about his bad back. Irwin *needs* a wife. Thank God it's Shirley and not me!" Mary Lou rolled her eyes at the mere thought and reached for the Häagen-Dazs chocolate-chocolate chip ice cream. After all, she'd only had water-packed tuna and celery sticks for lunch. She had to keep her strength up, didn't she?

Being single, Jade discovered, meant having a great social life. When she was married she had lived like a hermit. Now that she was single she enjoyed the kind of hectic, high-profile social life that only the rich or those in fashion enjoy. If she wanted to, Jade could go out every night of the week: there were openings and dinners; discos and nightclubs; and parties of endless variety: parties at galleries and museums, at private houses and public places; parties for jewellers, artists, sculptors, visiting royalty, the rich Italians and the titled French, for corporate bigwigs, department store executives, and visitors with clout from Washington. The only time Jade had no plans was when she didn't feel like having plans.

She met men, married and not, attractive and not, appealing and not; men who offered invitations and jobs, travel and adventure. Unlike the brief, wild period of sexual experimentation in which she had indulged during the crazy-time after her divorce, Jade was now very particular about the men in her life.

Men, yes; love, yes; marriage, *no*.

There were nice men, interesting men such as Dan Daryam and Martin Schultz and Peter Hailes who had become part of her life. There was Stefan Hitchcock, who asked her out and at least *said* he understood why she wouldn't accept, and there was Gordon Sirota—a tall, bald, handsome photographers' rep with whom she went jogging, who took her bike riding through the deserted, winding streets of Wall Street on crisp autumn weekends. Gordon had been divorced for four years, enough time to recover from his marriage, enough time to want to get married again. Gordon asked her to marry him.

"I adore you," she told him. "But I don't want to marry you. I don't want to marry anyone."

As for George Kouras, almost two years had gone by since she'd last seen him and she never thought about him. Well, almost never.

Besides, in the meantime, Jade's career had become her passion. It was a safe passion, a consuming passion, a highly rewarding passion.

Stefan Hitchcock's first official collection, designed by him and edited and accessorized by Jade, was a big success. "Grown-up clothes" *Women's Wear Daily* dubbed them in a rave review. There were crepe smokings à la Chanel; a series of "movie star" dresses of crepe and satin and *cloque* inspired by Harlow, Dietrich, Crawford, and Colbert; evening pajamas in emerald, ruby, and sapphire slipper satin; and for a fabulous conclusion to the show, there were evening wraps in jet, white, and canary maribou. Their appeal was immediate and obvious and both the press and the buyers responded—the press with coverage and the buyers with orders.

"*Vogue* said I was an artist!" Steve exulted after the show. Now that the world recognized him, Steve had dropped the capital *A*. The models, the hair stylist, the makeup artist, and the assistants had left. Jade and Steve were alone in the loft sharing some Dom Pérignon and smoked salmon. "An artist! Isn't that terrific?"

"It sure is!" said Jade, just as thrilled as he was. She and Steve had become so close that nowadays they practically shared the same nervous system. "A *successful* artist! Buddy Meister left a thirty-thousand-dollar order and I know that Mary Lou is going to come through big, too."

"Jade?" asked Steve, turning to her. "Do you know

who we remind me of? You're like George Bernard Shaw and I'm like Sam Goldwyn."

"We are?" Jade didn't know what he was talking about.

"Yes," said Steve. "You think about money and I think about art."

Jade giggled, partly from the Dom Pérignon, partly from their success, and partly from exhaustion.

"I also think," she said, when she had stopped, "that it's time we legalized our relationship."

Since it was the late 1970s, Steve was perfectly aware that Jade wasn't talking about marriage. She was talking about an employment contract, stock ownership, and a division of the profits.

The making of a top designer doesn't just happen; someone makes it happen and, in the years between 1977 and 1979, Jade was the person who helped make it happen for Stefan Hitchcock. The actual clothes—their designs and fabrics, their execution and pricing—are the beginning of a designer's career, but only the beginning. There are delivery dates to keep; quality standards to adhere to; relationships with the top stores and buyers to maintain; well-mounted shows to present several times a year; the need to staff and furnish a showroom; the necessity of setting up the all-important back rooms where the actual designing, cutting, sewing, and inspecting of the finished garments are conducted.

Of all these necessary elements, Steve had started out with none. It was Jade who created the organization that made Stefan Hitchcock the designer into Stefan Hitchcock the corporation. It was Jade who hired a showroom director who had run Ralph Lauren's showroom and a sales director brought over from Anne Klein. Mary Lou had recommended the showroom director, and the sales manager was someone Jade had worked with when she had been a buyer.

"Now we need someone to run the shipping department," she said, fretting because she had been interviewing and hadn't found anyone she could trust. Shrinkage was a serious problem in the garment business, and the shipping department was a highly vulnerable point. It had to be run by someone completely honest.

"What about Sid Zilkha?" asked Steve. "He ran the

Rainy Dayz shipping department for twenty-five years. He's retired and he told me that he hates every minute of it."

Stefan Hitchcock, who as Steve Hirsch had sworn he'd never be in the rag trade, was now in it up to his eyebrows. The surprising thing was that he loved it—most of the time. He kept talking to his analyst about it. He kept thinking there was something wrong with him. His ambition had once been to bury himself in Art. It bothered him lately that the business side of Stefan Hitchcock didn't upset him nearly as much as it once had.

Once the mechanics of design, production, showing, and shipping are in place, there is the crucial factor of exposure, and exposure means the fashion press. The ones who count, the ones who can make or break a line, are John Fairchild and Michael Coady of *Women's Wear Daily*, Carrie Donovan and Bernadine Morris of the *Times*, Grace Mirabella of *Vogue*, and Nonnie Moore of *Harper's Bazaar*. The right attention in the press ensures acceptance by store buyers and recognition by customers. Coco Chanel was one of the first fashion designers to understand the power of the press; Christian Dior was another. People hated his New Look when it was first shown at the end of World War II. They objected to its lavishness after years of suffering and deprivation; moreover, they thought the nipped-in waists and full skirts downright ugly. Only the press, which Dior had assiduously cultivated, liked it—and the press put it over. The New Look became the Only Look of its era.

"We need someone to handle public relations," Jade said. "For fashion, Michelle Delande is the best. She used to be the vice-president for public relations at Savin's when I worked there. Now she specializes in fashion accounts for a company called Barron & Hynes. They're expensive but excellent."

Steve's second collection showed that he was taking a new direction. The lavishly beaded evening wear for which he had first become known was, of course, represented. But for the first time, there was also a line of day wear, and it looked like no one else's. The shapes were soft and slouchy, loose but always revealing of the body inside.

"Classy but sexy," said Mary Lou.

The colors were clear, bold, and fresh and the combinations were original. Yellow and violet. Orange and pink. Red and khaki. Turquoise and cream.

"Early Renoir," said Buddy.

"Late Warhol," said *Harper's Bazaar*.

"Jade Mullen," said Steve. "Right now."

The line was ready-to-wear that was easy to wear and everyone who knew Jade said that, most of all, the clothes looked as if they had been taken from her closet.

"Not fantasy clothes," Steve told *Women's Wear* in an interview. "But real clothes inspired by a real woman."

It was a line Steve had first uttered in a session with his analyst when he discovered, to his surprise, that his fantasies no longer revolved around the unreachable goddesses of the movies of his youth, but were about the very contemporary woman who worked next to him every day.

As Steve's business grew he outgrew his loft on Fifteenth Street.

"Five-fifty is Seventh Avenue's best building," Jade said when they discussed the move. "Oscar de la Renta is there and so are Bill Blass, Ralph Lauren. . . ."

"It's funny," said Steve, suddenly in a pensive mood. "You know my father's dream was always to be in Five-Fifty. He never made it. He'll be thrilled."

In the same week that Steve signed the lease for half of a floor at 550 Seventh Avenue, at Jade's insistence he also signed a new contract with Jade.

"If I learned only one thing from my marriage," Jade told Martin Schultz, "it's not to work hard to help make someone else get rich without taking care of myself, too."

The contract guaranteed Jade five years of employment at seventy-five thousand dollars a year with bonuses and overrides. It was negotiated with Judith Rosen, the same lawyer who handled Carlys's negotiations with Tom Steinberg. So far, unknowingly sharing the same lawyer was the closest the two women had ever come, except for the time they had passed in the hall at Barron & Hynes and nodded politely to each other, instantly registering each other's clothes, hair, makeup, confidence, and guarded eyes, successful Manhattan women acknowledging each other's success.

Jade was becoming accustomed to having money and the comforts that money could buy, yet now and then, despite all her protestations about the joys of independence, she did think about love. Half of her yearned for dry champagne and wet kisses, red roses and white satin sheets, for that electric buzz and out-of-control high, for that heart-pounding, thrilling and giddy, dangerous and dizzying feeling that only romance can give. The other half of her mocked those feelings and bitterly derided that adolescent buzz, knew its traps and disillusion, its broken promises and bitter ending, having already paid its deadly price. She wondered if she'd ever fall in love again. She hoped she would. She didn't, at thirty, want to believe that romance was dead. She prayed she wouldn't. She prayed that she had finally learned her lesson, that she had finally grown up.

In Manhattan, a city of working men and working women, no one has time to cook at home. Eating in has become ordering up, and gourmet take-out the new growth industry. Most dining takes place in public, and restaurants have become the arenas for the advancement of careers and romances, for wheeling and dealing, for making up and breaking up, moving up and trading up. The cuisine might or might not be nouvelle, but the passions and ambitions definitely aren't.

There's the Regency for financial and political power at breakfast and the Four Seasons for media and publishing power at lunch. The Quilted Giraffe, so chic it's closed on Saturday nights, is for local, national, and international power, all categories, at dinner. The Carlyle is for celebrities at breakfast, the Russian Tea Room ("Slightly to the left of Carnegie Hall") is for celebrities at lunch, and Elaine's is for celebrities at dinner. Le Cirque is for social climbing and consolidation, the Odeon sizzles with with-it style from Punk to New Wave and beyond, and the River Café, particularly the waterside tables, is for romance.

One evening in the spring of 1979 George Kouras and his partner, Will Goldberg, took two of the draftsmen who worked for them out for a working dinner at the classic and low-key but definitely always good and always "in" Gino's, across the street from Bloomie's, where it had been even before the neighborhood was nicknamed Drydock Country. Kouras-Goldberg had survived its early struggles. It was now considered one of the better small design firms in the city. Kouras-Goldberg had won the job of designing the office space, ticket counters, and lounges for a small but profitable New England airline called Yankee Air.

"My wife is going to kill me," Will said, ordering the linguine with clam sauce and a rugola salad. "I haven't been home before midnight for the last two weeks."

"That's what you get for being married!" George teased. It was a running joke. George's reconciliation with Ina had not worked. Love, they had learned the hard way, was definitely not better the second time around. Defiantly single now, George liked to poke fun at Will, the married man, with his obligations and commitments.

"At least I don't have to worry about getting sued for palimony," Will retaliated. The Lee Marvin case that spring, a first even for California, was making headlines, a constant reminder of the new look in man-woman relationships.

"No one's safe anywhere anymore," George joked and then got down to business. He'd reviewed the blueprints and wiring diagrams for the ticket counters and noticed a problem. "We haven't allowed enough space for electric wiring under the counters," he said. "Yankee Air is computerized. The electricians are going to need more under-counter clearance. They're going to have to run in a separate dedicated line for each one of the computer terminals."

As George spoke he sensed the slight excitement that ripples through a room when someone special enters and he looked up. It was Jade and he forgot all his wise-guy resolutions about not confusing a tickle in the groin for a lurch of the heart.

She drew eyes like a magnet draws steel. She was the one who sparkled, the one whose colorful clothing—tonight a shoot-the-moon ruffled chrome yellow silk taffeta blouse, black flannel pants, and sexy, highheeled Maud Frizon sandals—was so right for her. She was with a man, a fortyish, well-dressed, well-groomed, and very attractive man. George immediately wondered who he was and what Jade's relationship with him was.

As he took part in the design talk at his own table George kept glancing over at Jade. She was totally absorbed in her conversation, and didn't notice him. All the old feelings came back as if they'd never left. He remembered the way she'd looked at Titian's loft, and the way she'd left him, stranded on the sidewalk, with a kiss and confusion. He remembered the scent of freesias as he'd crushed her to him, and the taste of her mouth as he'd kissed her for the first time in the back of Pascal Gomez's taxi. He remembered the first time he had told her he loved her. He remembered that the script had had an unhappy ending, and how much he had regretted it later. He let his veal get cold and let the talk of specs and installation and materials float around him while he felt the same *ping* go through him that he had the first time he'd ever seen her, the day Paco Rioja opened his shop on Madison Avenue years ago, when he was married and so was she.

What was it about her? The way she laughed? The way she held her head tilted slightly to the side? The intense expression on her face when she listened to someone else talk? The way—original and totally unique—she dressed and made up and did her hair? George didn't analyze it, couldn't analyze it, didn't even think about analyzing it. He almost got up in the middle of a sentence and walked over to her, but he didn't.

The next day, though, he did something he'd been thinking about doing for a long time. He called her. He had a good reason, since he had heard that Steve had signed the lease on a new showroom. He wanted Kouras-Goldberg to get the job, and, of course, Kouras-Goldberg got the job.

"Kouras-Goldberg is the best in the city," Steve said.

Jade could only agree.

C H A P T E R   13

The showroom put George and Jade back at the beginning—working together, seeing the best in each other, becoming comfortable with each other again, rediscovering that working together was one of the sexiest things a man and a woman can do together. They had the same rapport they'd had right from the very beginning when George had designed the New York Hartley shop. That design had been voted one of the ten best commercial designs of its year. It had led to the first commissions George had gotten that hadn't depended on his father-in-law. The quality of his work on the Hartley's shop, he knew, owed everything to his collaboration with Jade. The magic they had created together when they had worked on Hartley's still crackled. They could finish each other's sentences, knew each other's likes and dislikes, could take a good idea and make it great. Steve's showroom would be a combination of all the best things about each of them: modern, lucid, romantic, charming, comfortable, and witty.

"I was a mess, wasn't I?" George asked one evening at seven. The showroom was under construction. The electricians and tilemen and mirror men had gone home for the day. Sawhorses and sawdust and electric drills, now silent, stood around the deserted area, and George and Jade, reviewing the partially made installations, shared coffee from a Styrofoam container.

Jade nodded, remembering them both. He had been too intense, too anxious to replace one woman with another. She had been too wary, too shell-shocked to be able to see that all men weren't like Barry.

"I wasn't in such great shape myself," she admitted. She wore jeans and leg warmers and a bulky hand-knit scarlet sweater and, at the end of a long, tiring day, looked the way a thousand other women looked only in their dreams.

George smiled and decided to take the leap.

"Would you like to have dinner?" he asked. "The Pantheon isn't too far away."

She accepted. "Back to the beginning?"

He nodded.

"This time I'll try not to screw it up," he said and took her hand.

For both of them it was the second time around. Jade was almost thirty-one; George, thirty-six. They were too old for first love and too young to have given up. They had happy memories of each other, unhappy memories of each other, and they both had regrets. Both had, at one time or another, drunk to "never again!"

"I was still too bitter about Barry," Jade said, referring to their earlier romance and admitting her extreme wariness. "I just didn't know it."

"And I still had unfinished business with Ina," George admitted. "I didn't know it then either, but I know it now."

They were far enough past their divorces to think about trying again. Jade was no longer bitter; George was no longer trying to get even. There were no third parties—past or present.

"It's a fresh start," George said the first time he made love to her the second time around.

"Our timing was lousy," Jade said, thinking that no man had ever understood her the way George did, thinking that no man—or woman—she had ever known was more fun or made her feel better than George did. He always told her that she brought out the best in him. She always replied that he brought out the best in her. "We were out of synch."

"That was then," he said, kissing her, feeling himself falling for her all over again, thinking that the fit was perfect, that Jade and only Jade could make his heart go *ping*. "This is now."

"You were right about having to be free," George told her a month after they began seeing each other again. Work on the showroom was almost finished, and even though there was no longer a business reason to spend so much time together there was now a compelling personal reason. "When Ina and I reconciled I realized just how possessive she was. She didn't want a husband. She was a rich girl who wanted another possession."

"You're safe with me," Jade teased, aware that, this time, George did not talk about Ina obsessively. He talked about her as if she were definitely part of the past. She sensed that his unfinished business with his ex-wife had now, finally, been finished. "I'm not rich and the only possessions I'm interested in are the ones I can wear."

"That's for sure!" said George. Jade, he thought, had more clothes than Nancy Reagan, Cher, and Jackie Onassis put together. What he liked was that she bought them for herself. Unlike with Ina, there was no shock every month when the Saks and Bergdorf bills came in. Unlike Ina, Jade never ran to Daddy.

This time around George and Jade were careful to talk about the present, about how they felt now, about what they wanted now. This time around they avoided the past, its traps and snares and disappointments.

"I'm happy now," Jade said. She felt better than she ever had—better about herself, about the world, and about her place in it. Steve was happy to give her credit—both verbal and financial—for her huge contributions to his success. Buddy Meister had offered her a job as fashion director of Marks & Company. Mary Lou had given her a blank check—which she had turned down—to oversee the reorganization of the fashion floors at Savin's. Her professional talents were being amply rewarded and, at last, her personal life seemed to be on track. She realized that she had been fooling herself with Dan and Martin and Peter. She used to say that being "in like" was better than being "in love." She wondered now whom she thought she'd been fooling. "I'm happier than I've ever been. I don't want anything to change. All I want is more of the same," Jade told George.

"Ditto," George replied.

This time, the second time around, they both knew exactly what had gone wrong the first time—with each other, with other people. They were determined not to make the same mistakes twice. The old rules no longer applied and they made new rules as they went along.

Love and marriage, they told each other, were holdovers from another century and they smiled and drank to "never again!"

As 1979 turned into 1980 they were seeing each other at least once a week in the city and almost every weekend in the country at George's house on the top of a mini-mountain in Sullivan County. He would pick her up at 550 Seventh Avenue late on Friday afternoon and they'd stay over until Monday morning. George had a simple, sleek house of wood and glass set high on a hill in the woods, accessible only by an unmarked dirt driveway. There was a combination living room–dining area, an open kitchen, a big fieldstone fireplace, a master bedroom, and a guestroom.

"Bobby uses it when he visits," he told Jade. One of George's bitterest regrets was still how little he saw the son he adored.

"It's a beautiful room," Jade said. The room had bunk beds and a windowed tree house, complete with telescope, that could be reached both from inside the room and from the outside. There was a huge armoire filled with toys and a television set with an attachment for video games. A big walk-in closet held tennis rackets, skis, riding clothes, and bikes. One wall was windowed, and Jade admired the views of meadows and foothills and open sky and wondered when she would meet Bobby. She wondered if Bobby could become the child she'd been denied. "He's a lucky boy."

"Almost as lucky as I am," he said and reached for her.

Sex, which had been intensely passionate from the very beginning, had stayed passionate the second time around.

"One day, maybe, I'll get enough of you," he told her, his body on hers, his hands in her hair, on her throat, on her breasts.

But from Jade's point of view that was the perfect thing about George. He loved her enough, but never too much.

They made a point of never doing boring things when they were together. They had both learned the hard way that the details of daily life were what helped kill the romance in marriage. They never paid bills or sorted laundry when they were together; they never went grocery shopping or cleaned house. Their time together was special time, and they made a point of keeping it that way.

Jade had never seen George pale and cranky with the flu; George had never seen Jade red-nosed and unmadeup, suffering the ravages of a cold. George never complained to Jade about how hard it was to keep talented people at the office; Jade never complained to George about Steve's creative ups and downs. George never told Jade that his monthly payments to Ina prevented him from keeping any of the money he made; Jade never told George that her periods had never returned to normal after her abortion.

"Romance is what I love," George said bringing her

freesias in early spring and bronze chrysanthemums to match her eyes in the fall. "Not reality. Spare me reality."

"Love is what I love," said Jade, "not strings that break and promises that can't be kept."

Although George spent many of the nights he was in New York with Jade in her apartment, she never gave him her keys and, although she spent most weekends with him, he never gave her his. They both valued their privacy.

"You've never seen my apartment when it was a mess," Jade told him. "You've never seen *me* when I'm a mess. And I want to keep it that way."

"It's perfect," George said. "You're perfect. I never want a thing to change."

Jade felt the same way. George was always there for her; but he didn't always have to be. There was a definite distinction, and it made all the difference in the world between routine and excitement; between familiarity and adventure; between not-knowing-each-other-well-enough and knowing-each-other-too-well.

They did everything they could to keep the status between them exactly quo.

What they couldn't do anything about was the way they felt about each other and the way they fit into each other's lives.

Because Kouras-Goldberg designed so many boutiques and showrooms, George knew almost as much about retailing as Jade. He knew store presidents from the time they'd been buyers; he knew designers from the time they'd been assistants schlepping sketches around Seventh Avenue; he remembered Halston when he designed hats at Bergdorf's, and Bendel's when it had been a dowager's store and Geraldine Stutz was hired to breathe life back into it. He remembered when Oscar de la Renta had been the house designer at Elizabeth Arden; he knew where bodies were buried; who'd been up and who'd been down; what "designer" lines were really designed by assistants and free lancers; whose work was better than their publicity, and vice versa.

"You almost know more about my business than I do," Jade said over lamb and okra at the Balkan Armenian, a restaurant, like all the restaurants George took her to, that was easy, up-beat, and casual, a restaurant that suited the relationship they wanted with each other. High in quality but low in demands.

"Only because I'm older and have been around a little longer," he said.

And although Jade wasn't a designer she had an art background and a trained and sensitive eye. George was impressed when she told him that the *Times* had wanted to photograph her apartment but that she turned them down.

"I never knew anyone who turned the *Times* down," he said admiringly. "You're one of a kind."

He loved everything about her, he told himself, the way she looked, the way she talked, her sense of humor, and her sense of perspective. He loved the way she brought out the best in him, the way she made him feel secure but never bored, loved but never suffocated. It was wonderful, he told himself, to love everything about someone but not feel responsible for her.

They felt one way, behaved another. Both wounded emotionally, they refused to trust their emotions. They played it for fun and games and convinced themselves they could get away with it. They added up all the pluses and couldn't think of any minuses.

George traveled constantly on business: He was designing a boutique in Chicago's Water Tower and a designer department in Houston's Neiman-Marcus. He was usually out of town two or three days a week. They saw it as a plus.

"Isn't it wonderful?" Jade asked. "We'll never get bored with each other."

"Every time I see you, it's as exciting as the first time," George agreed.

Jade was just as busy as George, working as hard as he did. Stefan Hitchcock had now become a name. Women who bought his two-thousand-dollar originals and women who could afford only a scarf wanted the Stefan Hitchcock look—a look that was a combination of Steve's yearning for a never-never land of croquet lawns and Stutz Bearcats and Bailey's Beach, and Jade's up-to-the-minute 1980s I-want-to-be-me longing for independence and individuality.

"What I'd love," mused Jade, "are stand-alone boutiques where a woman could buy everything from Stefan

Hitchcock sunglasses to Stefan Hitchcock beaded evening sweaters." What she meant was that she wanted a Stefan Hitchcock boutique where she could spend five dollars or five thousand. What she wanted, she had discovered, was usually what millions of other women wanted.

"Stand-alone boutiques?" snorted Mary Lou, for once disagreeing with Jade. "Forget it! You'll lose all your store accounts."

"Why not?" said Ira Hirsch, who hadn't gotten rich with a closed mind.

"Never!" decreed Buddy Meister, a retailing traditionalist. The wall of guns had been joined by a fifteen-inch scale model of a rocket launcher that stood on his desk as a paperweight. He liked to pick it up and run his hands over it for comfort the way old Greek men used their worry beads. "You can't sell popular-priced merchandise and high-priced merchandise in the same area. No way!"

Jade and Steve listened to everyone's opinion and then decided to go ahead. A separate company was established called Hitchcock Unlimited and Jade was named its president. Jade owned half the stock and Steve owned the other half, which was worth nothing except the new company's debts. Jade's first job was to find the locations for the first three stand-alone shops and, by mid-1980, she was traveling even more than George.

"I'll never take *you* for granted," George said, trying to hide his disappointment when she told him that she wouldn't be able to go to the opening of the Water Tower boutique. She had to go to Georgetown. She had found space there and had to sign the lease. George assumed that Kouras-Goldberg would get the job.

"Of course not," Jade told him. "This is 1980! Being taken for granted went out with crinolines and poodle cuts."

Right from the very beginning George had always liked rich girls. Rich girls smelled good, rich girls looked good, rich girls never cared what anyone else thought, and rich girls were terrific in bed. Rich girls never cared about the consequences. Ultimately, though, he had decided that one of the problems with Ina was that her money was really her daddy's money. He thought that a woman like Jade, a woman who had made her own money, would be different—and she was. What he hadn't anticipated was that there would be other problems, different problems. He didn't realize, for example, how hurt he would be when Jade hired a local Washington firm to design the Georgetown boutique.

"Why didn't you ask Will and me to design the Hitchcock Unlimited boutique?" he finally asked in the fall of 1980. The party for the Georgetown opening had been held the week before and, although Jade had invited him, he had refused to go. "You loved what we did at the showroom." Steve's showroom had by now been copied so often that he and Jade joked that they'd have to re-do it just to keep ahead of the copycats.

"That was different," said Jade in an evasive and thorny way that immediately reminded George of the old Jade. The hurt, wary Jade.

"Different?" he asked, stung. "What was different?"

"I thought it might be too complicated," she finally admitted. "Now that people know we're together."

"You mean you're afraid people might think I'm sleeping my way to the top?" he asked, spelling it out.

"Something like that. Don't forget," she said, "I once worked with someone I was married to. It was a disaster. I don't want to take the same chance again."

"We're not married," he pointed out.

"That's true," she said guardedly. "Still, I don't want to take any chances."

George did not call her for a week. Finally she called him.

"You're mad at me," she said.

"Yes," he replied. "And hurt."

"Does that mean you don't want to see me anymore?"

"No," he said. "I miss you."

"I miss you, too."

They met for dinner and everything was just the same as it had always been between them. It was more than just sex, more than just chemistry. They were soulmates, survivors, creators and not destroyers, lovers and not killers.

"I love you," he finally told her that night. They were in bed, entangled with each other physically, entangled with each other, they now realized, emotionally. No matter what they said about freedom and independence and no strings, they just weren't happy without one another.

"I love you," Jade said.

"I swore I'd never fall in love again," George said, holding her, aware of how much she excited him, amazed that he could feel the way he felt.

"Me, too," she said, and they felt strong enough and liberated enough to laugh about how they had once drunk to "never again!"

C H A P T E R 14

$\mathcal{E}$*ven though George and Jade now talked about love* they were relieved to find that love didn't have to be a trap. Love, they found, didn't have to mean old-fashioned strings or promises or legal bonds. Love, they found, could even be liberating. Love, they found, didn't have to mean the end of romance.

"Isn't it wonderful?" George asked her early in 1981. He had just spent a week in Dallas; she had just returned from Chicago. Their suitcases stood in the foyer of Jade's apartment, their airline tickets were on her night table. Being together was more exciting because they knew that the next week they'd be apart. "We never see too much of each other, or too little. But just enough. Every time I see you it's like the first time. I love you, Jade."

"I love you, too," she said, reaching for him, wanting him and wanting him to know it. Barry had always complained that she never initiated sex; George could never make the complaint. "Every time I see you it's better than the last time."

They had, they decided, discovered the secret of perpetually exciting sex. Being lovers who didn't see too much of each other had kept sex fresh and alive. Each time was like the first time—but better.

"Like this?" he asked, doing something almost unbearably exciting to the rim of her ear with his tongue.

"Like that."

"And like this?" he asked, moving to her throat.

"You've never done that before."

He moved further down with his hands and his mouth. "I've never done this either."

"Oh," she breathed. "More. Don't stop."

"Never," he promised. "Never."

Because he never made claims on her, because he never took her for granted, Jade felt completely free with George. She told him things about herself that she had never told anyone: about the intense pain she'd felt as a child when her mother had sent her to get money from her father; about the humiliation she'd felt when her father, who drove a Cadillac, refused to support her and her brother and sister; about the way she and Heidi Diehl had sworn never to marry; about the agony of her abortion that had made it impossible for her ever to conceive. And she felt sexually free—free to be made love to, and free to make love. She did things with George she'd never done before. In the middle of one Tuesday afternoon in May she telephoned him at his office.

"I want you," she said.

"When?" he asked.

"Now."

"Where?"

"My apartment."

"I'll see you there," he said, and they met there twenty minutes later and, beginning with kisses in the elevator, made love all afternoon.

One evening before going to the theater Jade met George in his apartment. They'd had an omelet, and as they stood in his kitchen cleaning up he reached behind her for a dish towel, and as he did she suddenly moved back and his hand brushed her shoulder, naked in the short Zandra Rhodes dress. The touch, the moment, was electric. The dish towel was forgotten as they moved toward each other and into a kiss that ended with a stand-up quickie, hot and demanding and passionate, in the kitchen. They barely made the curtain.

They celebrated their discovery of unattached paradise with an out-of-season weekend in Nantucket in early December. They walked along the picturesque, cobblestoned Main Street; bought mohair throws at Nantucket Looms;

shared hot dogs on deserted Surfside beach; had the perfect native bluefish at Chanticleer; watched the ferry round Brant's point; rode horseback over the holly-thick dunes, and wished it would never end. On Sunday morning, as a light snow drifted down, they made love in the same four-poster bed where George had first conquered her.

"Friends and lovers?" George asked as they held each other, finally realizing that he had found the words to describe the way he felt and the way he wanted to feel.

"Friends and lovers," she answered, thinking she had finally found the ideal way to live—attached but not tied down, loving and being loved but still independent.

For them it was perfect.

Other people didn't always understand.

"When are you two going to get married?" Heidi wanted to know. Heidi Diehl still had her first husband, three children, two dogs, and a cat. She wanted everybody to be as happy as she was.

"Why?" Jade asked. "The only reason to get married is to have children and I can't."

Tears filmed her eyes and Heidi realized that, although she had gotten over everything else, Jade had never gotten over her abortion.

"I'd give it all up," Jade said, meaning her glamorous career, the money she was making, the travel and excitement and success, "if I could stay home with a child of my own."

George agreed with Jade about everything. "I'm for love," he told her. "Without the strings."

As for children, he told Jade that, since they weren't planning to marry, the fact that she was unable to have children made no difference to him. "Besides," he said, wanting to comfort her, "there's Bobby, not to mention fourteen nieces and nephews. I've diapered enough babies to last me the rest of my life. I've decided to dedicate myself to population control from now on!"

All in all they were in complete agreement. What they had was already perfect. How could marriage make it any better?

Their friends thought of them as a couple. So did they. They didn't date others, not because they had tied themselves down with promises but because others didn't interest them. They had a past, a present—and, although they tried to resist the idea, a future. They bought film festival tickets and a ballet series for the fall; they planned a winter vacation in St. Bart's and in the spring they rented a beach house in Bridgehampton for the summer. They even met each other's families and friends: Heidi adored George, and Dorothy Mullen thought that if Jade ever married again, George should be the man she married. Bobby was initially suspicious of Jade, but his suspicion soon passed.

"I knew he liked me when he asked if I could get him a Reggie Jackson warm-up jacket with the number forty-four," said Jade, looking forward to the next time she'd see Bobby, looking forward to their relationship growing. Perhaps George's child could be the child she never had.

Jade loved George's big, exuberant Greek family and their noisy and emotional ups and downs. There were brothers and sisters, wives and husbands, cousins and nieces and nephews, aunts and uncles who all seemed to talk—and laugh and fight and tease and cry and make up—at the same time.

"Greeks aren't WASPs," George told Jade. "They're more like Jews."

"They're wonderful," Jade said after Artemis Kouras's great Easter feast, featuring a whole roast lamb. "I've never been in a room with so many people who liked each other."

Laughing, George told Jade what his mother had asked him. "She wanted to know if we were going to get married," George said. Artemis Kouras was appalled at George's unmarried state—a state she considered unnatural and, even worse, un-Greek.

"And what did you tell her?"

"That we didn't want to ruin a good thing," George said and they both laughed.

But underneath the laughter something else was happening. Underneath the new George was the old George, George-the-lover, George-the-wanter. George the lover wanted Jade all to himself. George the wanter always wanted more. He just couldn't help himself.

"What did you and Buddy Meister talk about at lunch?" George asked in February 1981.

"Why I won't go to work for him," Jade answered with

her wicked giggle and then she did a double take. She was annoyed at having to answer for her whereabouts. She still thought of independence as the perfect balance to love. "How did you know I had lunch with Buddy?"

"There was a photograph in *Women's Wear* of you in front of La Grenouille," George said. "Don't you remember?"

"Oh, I did forget. Anyway, we talked about the usual," Jade said. "We discussed why I won't go to work for him." At lunch Buddy had offered Jade, for the third time, a job as vice-president and fashion director of Marks & Company. For the third time she had turned him down, driving him crazy.

"You're sure?"

"Of course I'm sure!" Jade said with a flash of irritation and they both let it drop, uneasy about anything that seemed like jealousy or possessiveness. They just didn't want to be like other people. They had been there before, and they knew what all the pitfalls were.

Stefan Hitchcock received a Winnie at the Coty Awards. In his acceptance speech, he mentioned Jade Mullen and Mary Lou Tyler as the two people who most helped his career.

"I think Steve's in love with you," George said, trying to sound objective.

"His wife wouldn't be too thrilled to hear that," Jade said, brushing the comment aside. Steve had been married— happily as far as Jade could tell—for almost two years.

"But he's attracted to you," George persisted, unable to keep his cool. "He's said you're his muse. Have you ever noticed the way he looks at you? He looks as if he'd like to devour you."

"Only to get ideas," Jade joked, not wanting to admit that Steve was, in fact, attracted to her and that she responded to his admiration. They had never done anything about it; they never would. The partnership was too important to risk. The attraction was a fantasy, part of the positive creative spark between them.

Once Barry called while George was at Jade's. They had shared a bottle of wine with dinner and Jade was a little high. Or at least that was the reason she gave herself later to explain the fact that she had stayed on the phone with

Barry for almost twenty minutes while George was in bed, fuming, waiting for her.

"Obviously you still care about him," George said when she finally came back to bed.

"Not at all," she said honestly. Barry had called, as he did occasionally, to talk over a business problem. He was remarried, to a Fort Wayne girl, someone Jade didn't know. Probably, Jade thought without rancor, the kind of girl he should have married in the first place. Herb was dead and Barry ran the company now. He had everything he said he wanted, and yet every time she spoke to him Jade thought he sounded sad. Sad and sort of old. "He hurt me too much."

"Some women can't get free of the men who've hurt them the most," George pointed out.

"I'm not one of them," Jade said crisply, but George wasn't completely convinced. Sometimes, and he couldn't help himself, he felt very possessive toward Jade and jealous of every other man in her life.

George began to talk about living together.

"It doesn't make sense to keep two places," he told her in the spring of 1982, the spring of the war in the Falkland Islands, the spring that Detroit was bowing to Japanese imports, the spring of escalating war in El Salvador, of massive antinuclear demonstrations and Pac-Man mania, Koo Stark and Randy Andy, and Claus von Bülow and intimations of murder among the rich and social in Newport. "We'd be happy."

"We're happy now," Jade pointed out, not wanting anything to change. She was happy with things the way they were. Very happy. She had work and romance—everything a woman who couldn't have children could possibly want. Why change it? A lover took nothing for granted; a live-in lover might be too much like a husband.

"We spend most of our time together anyway," he pointed out that summer. He tried to be casual about it, tried not to let her know how important living together had become to him. The were sharing a Bridgehampton house for the third summer in a row. George liked living with Jade. He liked waking up with her, going to sleep with her, cooking with

her, and walking the beach with her. All he wanted was
more. All he ever wanted was more. He couldn't help
himself; *more* had been the story of his life.

"I'd like to share an address with you," he said on a
clear and sunny Labor Day, caressing her, seducing her
with his hands as well as his words as they watched the sun
set over Mecox Bay. "In fact I'd love it."

"Maybe an address," Jade teased, still clinging to her
independence. "But not a closet." Her immense wardrobe
was a private joke.

"Even a closet," he said seriously. "Please, Jade. I
think we were wrong when we said we didn't want to get
involved. What we meant was that we didn't want to be
suffocated. Living together doesn't mean we'd lose our
freedom."

"You've let one bad experience sour you," he told her that
fall, the season of death in Tylenol capsules, the season
that an American dream crashed with the arrest of John
DeLorean, the season that Grace Kelly died in an automobile accident. He shifted his tactics, moving the spotlight
away from his passion to her faults. "You've got to be
willing to let go of the past."

She nodded thoughtfully. "That's true. I don't want to
be a prisoner of the past," she said softly, thinking his
words over.

"I'm not Barry; I'm not going to do the same things
Barry did," George said, sensing that the tide was beginning to turn. "I'm not as dependent as Barry. I'm not
scared of my father, hiding behind my wife. I'm a different
man, Jade. Don't confuse us. Don't make the mistake of
thinking we're alike."

"You know that I don't think you and Barry are the
slightest bit alike!" she said, defending herself. His arguments were beginning to affect her and he sensed it and
moved in for the kill.

That winter, the winter of hope, the winter that Barney
Clark received an artificial heart, the winter that the economy seemed, finally, to recover, she began to waver and he
was not above threats.

"If you won't live with me I can't guarantee what will

happen." His amber eyes were serious. He didn't want to be unfaithful to her. He wanted her to help him be a man.

"What do you mean?" she asked, suddenly alarmed. She had never been happier than she had been with George. She assumed he was as happy as she was. He often *said* he was. "Don't you love me?"

"You know I do," he said tenderly, holding her, kissing her. They'd just made love; their bodies were stretched the length of each other, their arms and legs entwined. "But I'm human, too. How long can I stay faithful to a woman who keeps me at arm's length?"

"Is that what I'm doing to you?" she asked, shocked. It was the first time he'd told her in so many words that he was faithful to her. She had sensed that he was although, because they were careful not to put demands or strings on each other, she had never asked. The one thing that had always bothered her about George was the way he'd been unfaithful to his wife with other women and unfaithful to her with his wife. Now, she knew, she was the one woman in his life and he was telling her that he planned to keep it that way—as long as he knew she loved him as much as he loved her. "Am I really holding you at arm's length?"

"Yes," he said. He adored her independence, but at the same time he wanted her to be his. "I want us to be close, to be everything to each other. You keep saying no. You keep saying everything is perfect. But it isn't perfect for me. Not as long as I want to live with you and you refuse. I'm madly in love and you're as cool as a cucumber."

"Is that what you think?" she asked, shocked by his perception of her as cool. She had always thought of herself as being warm; she had been proud of being as passionate as he was. "That I'm holding you at arm's length?"

"What else can I think when I love you and want to live with you and all you tell me is no?" he asked, pointing out the confusing chasm between her words and her deeds. "What else can I think?"

"You know I love you," she said, trying to reassure him. He didn't answer. "Don't you?" she asked anxiously.

"I know you *say* you do," he answered.

"Then I'll think about it," she said finally, softly relenting. "About living together."

"Don't think about it," he said, kissing her, wanting her

to make up her mind that minute, wanting her to end his doubts about how she felt about him. "Do it, Jade! Just say yes."

As he caressed her and began to excite her all over again she had a sudden, anxious thought: "Suppose I said yes? Would it scare you away? Would you run out the door?"

George laughed. She was just incredible!

"*Nothing* you could do would scare me away! Nothing!" he said passionately. "Say yes," he said, taking his mouth away from hers just far enough to speak. "You'll never regret it. Never. All I want to do is be with you and make you happy."

"Then, yes," she said, terrified and excited, suddenly seized with the giddy childhood feeling she remembered when she just closed her eyes and dove into the dark, cool water of the mill pond near Auburn from the high rocks above. "All right! Definitely! Yes!"

Now that she had taken the plunge, she was amazed not only at how good it felt but at how *right* it seemed. For the first time in her life she realized she was free. Free of the invisible chains that connected her to a father who always disappointed her and to a husband who had been another version of her father: a man who said one thing and did another, a man who made promises that were never kept. She realized she had been too attached to her independence. Only what she had been calling independence was really fear—fear that now belonged firmly to an unhappy past in which her mother's word had been proven correct, a past in which men could not be trusted. The future would be different. George was different. *She* was different!

What was wrong with wanting to live with someone you loved? It wasn't a jail sentence! People who loved each other naturally wanted to be together. Jade felt that she had taken the final step away from all the things that had ever hurt her in her life. In making a commitment she had found her freedom.

"Living together is perfect," she said to George as they began to look for an apartment. "It has all the advantages of romance and none of the disadvantages of marriage."

"Love without strings!" he agreed and kissed her so that she would never get away.

They toasted themselves and each other, secure in their new definitions of love and caring and the possibilities between men and women. To George it was a new beginning. To Jade it was the end of a nightmare.

To Carlys it would be a casual meeting with an attractive stranger.

The Lover

"Love? I'm *always* in love Oh, once I wasn't. I was fifteen. It was the worst ten minutes of my life."

—GEORGE KOURAS

CHAPTER 1

George and Jade. Jade and George. They were the quin-tessential successful, single New Yorkers. Each had found a way to live a maximum life in minimum space. The only thing in either of their apartments that was big enough for two was the bed. Nevertheless, George's apartment was a floor-through and somewhat larger than Jade's, and now that she had finally agreed to live with him he couldn't wait.

"Move in now!" he urged, almost giddy with excitement. She had driven him crazy for so long and now she was his. Finally! "Tonight! Now! This second!"

"Don't you think we should wait until we find an apartment of our own?" Jade asked, giggling, flattered, excited but still a *little* cautious. She was worried about trying to cram two people and two people's belongings into a space for one.

"No way!" said George, his eyes warm and teasing. "It was hard enough to get you to agree to live with me. I'm not going to give you the time to change your mind! We'll live here until we find a place of our own," he said, taking charge. "It'll just be temporary."

It was flattering to be wanted that much, that intensely, and Jade, looking forward to living with him as much as he was looking forward to living with her, let him persuade her to give up her apartment, put her furniture into storage, and move uptown to Sixty-second Street. She found a new cleaner, a new drugstore, a new grocer, and a new bank branch the first afternoon. She couldn't walk to work anymore, and she couldn't find closet space. George's one closet was filled with his clothes; hers were hung on rented racks in the living room and, in the beginning, they laughed about it.

"It's like living in a showroom," Jade said, amused by

277

the vivid colors of her wardrobe against the neutrals with which George had furnished his living room.

"A showroom? Hell, no," said George, as he moved his favorite Eames chair almost into the middle of the room to make space for the clothes rack that was much bigger than he had imagined. "More like Macy's."

"Not Macy's" Jade teasingly cautioned him. "Savin's!"

They laughed about department store chauvinism and because George said the apartment wouldn't be *theirs* until they'd made love in every room, on the first night Jade moved in they made love in the bedroom, the living room, and the tiny kitchen where they had to do it standing up. Now that she'd moved in, and given George what he wanted, he seemed casual about looking for an apartment. He seemed to think it would be easy. He also seemed to take it for granted that Jade would do all the legwork.

"You deal with the brokers," he told her. "Anything you like, I'll like."

Jade fell in love with an apartment on Central Park West in a well-built, beautifully maintained prewar building. There were five rooms off a large foyer. The sunken living room and spacious bedroom had spectacular views of the park. The rest of the rooms were nothing special, but in Manhattan real estate as in life itself nothing was perfect.

"You'll just love it!" Jade said, making an appointment for George to see it. "It's got plenty of light and plenty of space for us both!"

"It's nice," he agreed indifferently after the broker had shown it to him. "But I'm spoiled by living over the store. I'd like to find something closer to the office. It's damn nice to walk down the stairs to work."

"Why didn't you tell me before that you wanted to live close to your office?" Jade asked when they got home. She had spent three weeks looking at dark, gloomy, small, depressing, and otherwise unacceptable apartments before a broker showed her the one on Central Park West.

"I thought you knew," George said.

"I can't read your mind," Jade replied.

Jade couldn't really blame him, but she wished he had told her about his geographical preferences before she'd spent weeks trekking all over the city searching for an apartment. Nevertheless, it was only the first apartment they'd considered and she didn't dwell on it. Her search continued.

In the beginning they found that they had been absolutely right: Living together wasn't at all like being married, it was more like playing house, a romantic adventure. Jade amused herself by thinking up dinners that could be cooked in George's pocket-sized kitchen that didn't even have an oven. George promised that he'd design a storage case for the makeup that didn't begin to fit in his tiny bachelor's medicine chest that held, with no room left over, a tooth-brush and toothpaste, a razor and blades and shaving cream, a box of Band-Aids, a bottle of aspirin, and a jar of Alka-Seltzer.

They lived, together, exactly the way they had when they had lived apart. When they were together, they were intensely romantic. When one of them was out of town, the other was free to pursue unshared interests. Jade would have gone out almost every night of her life—and when George was away, she did. She went to the openings, dinners, or cocktail parties that were inevitably connected with her job. When he was away Jade was free to see the friends George didn't like—friends with whom she enjoyed the ins-and-outs of fashion gossip and clothes talk that bored George into a stupor. She did not see other men. Not from moral or puritanical restraints, but because she was so involved with George that she simply wasn't attracted to anyone else. She just wasn't available.

George, on the other hand, was more of a homebody. When Jade was out of town George enjoyed quiet evenings alone in his apartment with the newspapers, the stereo, and late-night television after an early dinner at Gino's hashing over business problems with Will. He went to the Knicks games and Rangers games she hated and indulged himself in all-male sports talk over a few drinks at P.J.'s Some-times someone suggested picking up a girl, a model or an actress, just for sex, but George never did. He felt good that he wasn't even really tempted. He was, he thought with relief, over that particular itch.

On the nights they were both in the city they enjoyed the luxury of being together in the same place.

"No more taxis!" said George, rolling his eyes in comic relief. He had spent enough on taxis during their affair to buy a medallion. "I was beginning to feel like one of Scull's Angels!"

"And no more getting dressed in the morning and going home to get ready for work!" Jade did not miss the cruddy feeling of putting on last night's clothes in the harsh light of dawn and standing on the street hailing a cab, feeling just a little bit like a hooker.

"I don't know why we waited so long," George said as they cuddled close in bed. Tomorrow he would be in Chicago; she would be in Philadelphia. They probably wouldn't see each other until the weekend. He felt free, he felt safe, he felt he never wanted to let her go.

"We were scared," Jade said, smiling in the dark. "Just plain chicken!"

The next apartment that caught Jade's eye was on Sixty-first Street between Park and Lexington close to George's office. The red-brick building was covered with ivy and the apartment, large and spacious, was the classic real estate broker's fixer-upper. The bathroom was an eyesore in gold-spattered pink tile and the kitchen, with a torn linoleum floor and a refrigerator with a condensor coil on top, had been the last word somewhere back in 1925. What made the apartment special, though, and what attracted Jade's attention, was the beautifully planted terrace and graceful french doors opening out onto it. Jade thought that the apartment had the shady, romantic atmosphere she imagined in apartments in New Orleans's French Quarter.

"It's a little run-down," she warned George when she took him to see it, "but since you said you wanted to renovate anything we bought anyway, I don't think we should let that matter. It has loads of space and it's very romantic. Just think, we can have dinner outside on the terrace in the summer."

"Come on, Jade!" George said the moment he set foot inside. He hated it. It was gloomy and oppressive; he could almost feel the ivy and the branches of the trees strangle him. He stood at the door with his hand on the knob while the agent pointed out the pluses and the minuses. Mostly the pluses.

"It's a dump!" he said when he and Jade were alone, shocked that she would even drag him to such a gloomy cavern. "I can hear the Lexington Avenue buses from here. Not to mention the pushers outside Bloomingdale's whispering 'smoke, toke.' "

Jade could hear no such things. In her mind she saw them sharing a picnic out of a wicker basket in the garden on August nights and she could smell the autumnal scent of wood burning in the fireplaces on crisp fall evenings.

"What do you know about pot pushers outside Bloomingdale's?" she teased. "Besides, just think! I could roll out of bed and be in the Rykiel boutique."

George was in no mood for teasing.

"Jade, forget it!" he said impatiently. He couldn't wait to leave and get home except, he realized with a start, that home wasn't even his anymore. He was beginning to think that Jade had been right about not moving in together until they had a big enough apartment, but he didn't want to admit it. He felt irrationally angry at her and, ashamed of himself, he tried to think of something to say to make it up to her. "That dump's just plain not good enough for you and that's all there is to it!"

Jade thought it was plenty good enough for her but she gave up, not wanting to begin their new arrangement with an argument. The broker turned up two more possibilities. Jade liked them both. George found something fatally wrong with each. One was in a modern building on the Upper East Side on the thirty-second floor. Jade liked the height and the light, rare commodities in Manhattan. George thought the space nondescript. "Banal," he said, refusing even to consider it. The other, a sleek, crisp duplex, appealed to Jade's affinity for the up-to-date. "Milanese moderne," George sneered.

"Trying to find an apartment that suits a designer is like trying to buy a chocolate bar for a diabetic!" Jade complained to Mary Lou. "Impossible!"

Still, she took George's objections at face value and continued to bug brokers who were already beginning to get turned off. Manhattan real estate sold by the carat and brokers did not have to put up with demanding and picky buyers. It took all of Jade's considerable charm to get them to continue to call her when new listings came in.

* * *

After six weeks the novelty of top-of-the-stove cooking wore off and Jade gave up. They ate pasta and omelets, omelets and pasta, and once in a while a sautéed chicken dish. They were perfectly good but, with exactly eleven inches of counter space and a sink so narrow that dinner plates couldn't be stacked, cooking the simplest meal was a nerve-racking three-Valium juggling act. George's bachelor kitchen, Jade concluded, was fine for photographs in glossy interior design magazines and an occasional cup of instant coffee. Period.

Not only George's kitchen, but George's entire apartment was beginning to get on Jade's nerves. She had been right in the first place: It had been a mistake to give up her own apartment so quickly. She missed the window seat where she liked to sit and read and her reasonably sized kitchen in which to bake, stir, and sauté whenever a cooking fit took hold of her. Having to go back and forth from the bedroom to the living room to get dressed wasn't a quaint novelty anymore, and not having a telephone of her own was a considerable inconvenience since she made and received many business calls after normal, nine-to-five hours. She was getting irritable and short-tempered and, she was all too aware, so was George.

"Can't you get this goddamn makeup off the sink?" he demanded, retrieving a mascara wand from the sink for what seemed like the twentieth time. George still hadn't built the shelves for her makeup, and the ledge of the sleek, stainless steel sink was so narrow her makeup was constantly falling in. He hated picking up after her; he hated the clutter she brought into his spare, cleanly designed apartment. Sometimes he even hated her.

"What am I supposed to do with it?" Jade asked, just as annoyed. "Balance it on the end of my nose?"

He did not reply; instead he went downstairs to the office and escaped to his drawing board, leaving her in an apartment that didn't feel like home. That night, for the first time since they'd begun living together, they didn't make love.

Jade kept at it with the brokers. There was a townhouse on Sixty-third Street between Lexington and Third that George called an overpriced railroad flat and a large Park Avenue apartment he thought was too dark. Nothing, he declared over and over, was good enough for Jade. But even though George kept saying that nothing was good enough for Jade and even though he kept telling her how much he loved her and how thrilled he was that she had finally agreed to live with him, he seemed angry and on edge most of the time.

"What's happening to us?" she asked after they'd snapped at each other because she'd left some files on the coffee table. He liked it bare; so did she, but she had no other place to put them. She had a helpless feeling that things were not working, that living together was ruining what had been an almost perfect relationship. "You seem different," she said. "We seem different."

"It's me. It's my fault," he said, willing to take the blame. He had been the one who had insisted that they live together. He had bugged her, pressed her, almost black-mailed her into it with threats of infidelity. Now that they *were* living together he was disappointed. He had looked forward to romance, not to arguments over drawer space, not to feeling choked and suffocated as if an invader had commandeered his very living room. "Everything's getting to me. The office. The clients. Even Will."

"And me?" she asked, refusing to let him put the blame where it didn't really belong. "Am I getting to you?"

He didn't want to lie, so he evaded.

"I love you. It's just living like this—on top of each other. It's getting to me."

"Maybe I should move out," Jade said. Living together was not working out. Maybe she should leave before it got any worse. She didn't want another emotional disaster on her hands. "Maybe we should go back to the way we were. Combined lives, but separate apartments."

"No! Absolutely not!" he said immediately. He wanted her. He adored her. He didn't want her to leave him. It had been too hard and taken too long to find her. He had been too unhappy without her. "We'll find a place soon," he said, touching her, wanting to keep her, not wanting to let her go. "Then everything will be fine."

That night, lovers again, they made love and the next day when George left for Boston he kissed her good-bye as passionately as if they would be parted for eternity.

"As soon as I get back," he told her, "we'll make

finding an apartment the number one, top priority. I'm not going to throw away the best thing that ever happened to me over closet space.''

He wanted Jade; he wanted to make things work with her. He was tired of one-night stands and two-week wonders. He was tired of chasing things—women and jobs and happiness and contentment—that, once won, no longer seemed worth getting. He was almost desperate for an attachment, yet being attached suffocated him. He was a man at war with himself and the solution to his inner battles had always been to find a new woman—a woman he could chase and idealize and who would keep saying no to him. This time, it would be a woman named Carlys Arnold.

CHAPTER 2

C.A.?'' *he said, after she sat down in the aisle seat* next to his. He gestured toward the monogram on her briefcase. ''Coryan Associates?'' Coryan Associates was an industrial design firm that had once offered him a job.

''No,'' Carlys said; she smiled although she was still tied up in the tensions of the day. Yankee Air had had its first accident. A plane dead-heading from Providence to Boston had gone down, landing in severe crosswinds. No one had been hurt, but the investigation afterward had turned up half an ounce of cocaine in the copilot's uniform. The copilot hadn't been at the controls and a blood test showed him to be drug-free. Carlys had seen to it that the news never got out but, understandably, Ada had had a fit and fired the man on the spot. He had called in the pilot's union, which threatened all the publicity Carlys had worked so hard to avoid. She had spent the day caught between Ada's fury, the pilot's anger, and the maddening bureaucracy of the pilots' union. ''The initials are mine. Carlys Arnold.''

She smiled again. He was extraordinarily handsome. Not

distinguished-handsome the way Kirk was, but intensely, magnetically, movie-star-handsome, with dark hair and olive skin and light, almost transparent amber eyes fringed by thick, dark lashes. Not handsome, she suddenly realized, but beautiful.

"Carlys Arnold?" he'd repeated, noticing her remarkable green eyes for the first time and thinking that a man could drown in them. Jade's gold-flecked bronze eyes, on the other hand, were mirrors in which a man could see himself—as he was—the reflection sometimes flattering, sometimes too truthful. "Then maybe we do have a connection anyway. Are you any relation to Kirk Arnold?"

"Only by marriage," she said and smiled again. Her smile was soft and vulnerable and anxious-to-please; Jade's was confident and filled with sexual energy.

George returned the smile, a sensitive, intimate smile, a warm and, although Carlys didn't know it, practiced smile. He told her he knew her husband, had once almost done business with him.

"Really?" she asked, aware that her fatigue was magically beginning to lift.

"We lost the job to Tydings-Owen-Brennecke," George said, telling her that his firm had bid for the job of redesigning SuperWrite's corporate logo when Kirk had first gone to work there and he had started his partnership with Rollie Leland. "Not that I would say a word against T-O-B. After all, I worked there once," he said.

He told her that he was an architectural designer and, over Eastern Airlines's white wine and smoked almonds, proceeded to tell her hilarious and libelous stories about egotistical designers, meddling and second-guessing clients, and the explosive results when the two were mixed.

As Carlys listened she wondered why so many men made such a point of being uncharming. They seemed to think that somehow charm wasn't masculine. Carlys knew different. And she knew that this man knew different, too.

It was raining when the shuttle set down at La Guardia. Not just raining, but pouring. Buckets and torrents of rain lashed down, overwhelming the drainage systems. Water washed and sloshed up to the curb, the storm had cast a dark pall over the sky and, although it was just six o'clock, streetlights had been turned on. There was an ugly mob scene, as shuttle passengers battled for the few taxis that were out in the downpour. Two middle-aged men in expensive suits who used their briefcases as weapons fought over a taxi.

Carlys stood there, wondering how on earth she was going to get home. Kirk, she knew, would have thought ahead. A limo would have been waiting. Ever careful with money, she would never have ordered a limo even though the client would have been billed for it. Standing there, suddenly tired again and anxious to get home, she thought that Kirk was right and that the economizing was really another form of extravagance—extravagance with her own time, temper, and energy.

From twenty feet away George watched Carlys watching, caught her eye, and shook his head in silent amusement at the mayhem. At that, the car he'd ordered that morning drove up and, as he was about to get in, he shouted at her, and gestured her on, "Come on! I'll give you a lift."

Gratefully she ran toward the car and got in, slipping off her wet shoes.

"What luxury," she said, thanking him and leaning back.

"Unaccustomed luxury," he replied as the car jockeyed for space in the exit lane.

"Unaccustomed?"

"I only do it because it drives my client crazy," George said, giving the driver Carlys's East Seventy-ninth Street address. "I usually take a cab like everyone else. But for Ada, I order a limo just because it bugs her."

"Ada? Not Ada Hutchinson?" Carlys asked, suddenly aware of the double coincidence—George had once almost worked with Kirk, now apparently they both worked with Ada. "Skinflint Ada?"

"Skinflint Ada," George laughed. "The one, the only . . . ." It turned out that George was designing the renovations for the Yankee Air office in Cambridge. They had both been in Boston for the same reason: Ada Hutchinson and Yankee Air.

She laughed out loud at the thought of Ada being confronted with a limousine service bill. Ada lent a new dimension to legendary New England thrift. Ada's cheapness was another reason Carlys had given herself for not ordering a car. *This* man, Carlys thought, certainly knew how to handle her! The trip into Manhattan seemed to take no time as they regaled each other with Ada Hutchinson stories.

"Thank you for the lift," Carlys said, realizing she didn't know the name of her rescuer, as the limo stopped in front of her building. "If it weren't for you, I'd still be at the airport."

"George," he filled in for her. "George Kouras. A nice Greek boy from Tarpon Springs. . . ."

"Thanks, George," she said and opened the car door and got out, her mind already filled with wifely thoughts. Would Kirk be home? What kind of mood would he be in? Would he want to have dinner at home? Would he want to go out? All *she* wanted to do was collapse.

By now Carlys had learned all the differences between being married and being single. Had she been single, she would have gone home, eaten some scrambled eggs, taken a hot bath, and gone straight to bed. Since she was married, however, she had to think about Kirk and consider how he might feel. Even so, Carlys would never, not for an instant—even considering the stresses they had been under recently—wish to be single ever again.

"I met someone today you almost did business with," Carlys told Kirk casually as they were getting ready for bed. "George Kouras."

"George Kouras?" Kirk repeated and shrugged indifferently, vaguely remembering him. "If you say so."

"We flew down from Boston together," Carlys continued, although she didn't know why. Kirk obviously wasn't interested. In fact ever since he'd bought E-Z Tech he barely seemed interested in anything much except his rapidly growing business. "He gave me a lift home."

"That was nice of him," said Kirk absently, kissing her cheek and turning off the light. Kirk not only moved fast and thought fast, he wished he could sleep fast. He was always impatient to get sleeping over with so he could wake up early and start the next day with a jump on everyone else. "I was afraid you'd have a hard time getting a taxi in this rain. I keep telling you to use limousines," he said, bringing up an old argument.

"You're right," said Carlys, for the first time considering the possibility. If she were the kind of woman who could flirt with a man like George Kouras, Carlys told herself, she was the kind of woman who probably deserved the luxury of a limousine. The thought was kind of exciting. "Maybe I will."

As she tried to fall asleep Carlys thought about George Kouras. She wondered if he was going to bed alone. Somehow, she doubted it.

Jade was in Palm Springs doing a trunk show, and after he dropped Carlys off, George had dinner with Will. After dinner he walked the few blocks home, watched the eleven o'clock news, and got into bed. He missed Jade and wished she were there. He was in the mood to make love to her. Then his mind turned to Carlys. He wondered if she was making love to her husband tonight. He wondered if she was as restrained in bed as she was in public. Somehow the red lace slip made him doubt it.

He was aware of the beginnings of an erection. Here he was, all turned on, living with an exciting woman who was several thousands of miles away. Alone in his bed George smiled to himself. He was a little old, he told himself, for the cold-shower routine. He made a mental note to tell Jade. He couldn't wait for her to return. She was the only one who really understood his sense of humor.

"What would you think of living in a house?" Jade asked two days later when she'd returned from Palm Springs where, she told George with appalled excitement, one woman, the wife of the owner of an independent Oklahoma oil company, had bought sixty thousand dollars' worth of clothes in an hour and a half. "One of the brokers has a house on East Sixty-fourth Street. We could live on two floors and rent out the others."

"And be a landlord?" George replied, as horrified as if she'd suggested living in a cave. He wished Jade would give him a rest. He wished she'd drop the talk about an apartment for a while. He was sick of the way she kept pressuring him. "All you'd listen to is complaints about the plumbing, the security, the garbage. Forget it!"

"But there are no new listings," Jade said, totally frustrated with the whole apartment search. She hated being squashed into George's two rooms and yet he was impossible when it came to finding a new place. "I called every broker we're listed with."

"Keep trying," he said impatiently, wishing she'd drop the whole subject. "Something will turn up."

Jade was beginning to doubt it but, amazingly, just three days later there was a new listing. The apartment was between First and York avenues on Seventy-seventh Street. George went to look at it.

"Forget it," he told Jade. "Schlock modern construction. We don't want to live there."

"Where *do* you want to live?" asked Jade, annoyed. "Nothing suits you. Nothing's good enough for you. Nothing's built well enough for you. Nothing's convenient enough to your office. I'm beginning to think you don't *want* to find an apartment."

"Of course I do," said George, equally annoyed. "Whose idea was it for us to live together in the first place? I just want it to be the *right* apartment."

Jade, feeling frustrated, withdrew and they spent a monosyllabic evening with Blake, Krystle, and Alexis.

When they got into bed, George stayed on his side and made no attempt to reach over for her. Obviously he was annoyed, but she didn't know why since she was the one who was traipsing all over, doing all the work, trying to find a decent place for them to live. She was glad he stayed over on his side of the bed. She was definitely in no mood to make love to him.

The next day Carlys got a telephone call from George Kouras.

"I was in Cambridge again," he said, aware of the contrast between her warm "hello" and Jade's cool "good morning." "Ada asked me to drop off the releases you sent her last week. She's okayed them with a few changes."

"How does she even know we know each other?" Carlys said.

"I told her we ran into each other on the shuttle and spent the whole time talking about how cheap she is."

"You didn't"

"I most certainly did," said George, enjoying her shock. God, it was nice to talk to a woman who wasn't on his back about something, he thought. "That's when she got the idea of my bringing back the releases. She figures she's saving the price of Overnight Express. Of course I don't plan to let her get away with that. I'll buy you lunch. On Ada."

"Lutèce, no less?" Carlys teased when she met George that Friday. He was even more striking than Carlys remembered. The word definitely *was* beautiful. He was also shorter and stockier; something about him gave Carlys the impression of exciting physical strength. "Ada's going to have a fit."

George smiled. "It'll be good for her," he said, aware of Carlys's perfume, more ladylike, less sophisticated than Jade's. Taking an attractive woman out to lunch made George feel good. He smiled at her. "Now, what would you like to eat? The poached salmon? The filet?" The expensive food demanded an expensive wine, of course, and while the envelope containing the press releases sat on the table proving the legitimacy of the meeting, they began with more Ada Hutchinson stories. By the cheese course, however, Carlys knew that George Kouras ran a successful design business with a partner, that his office was in a townhouse on East Sixty-second Street, that they specialized in the design of commercial spaces—boutiques, showrooms, offices, restaurants—and had jobs in cities across the country.

"It sounds like you travel almost as much as my husband," Carlys said, wanting, although she really didn't quite know why, to remind George that she was married.

"Kirk's gone a lot?" George asked and smiled at her with his transparent amber eyes as she flushed, aware that her words contained an implication and possibly an invitation she hadn't intended. "Don't you get lonely?"

"Oh, no," she said too quickly. "I'm much too busy for that." She glanced at her watch, suddenly anxious. The conversation with its personal undertones was making her nervous. "And speaking of busy, I'd better get back to the office."

They said good-bye on the sidewalk before George went back to Sixty-second Street and Carlys returned to the Olympic Tower offices of Barron & Hynes.

"I hope it was a really expensive lunch," she teased, suddenly reluctant to leave George. She couldn't remember the last time she'd had such a relaxed few hours. Kirk was all business all the time lately. He worked twenty-five hours a day, eight days a week.

"Oh, yes," said George, aware that he had never touched her. Her skin was beautiful. He knew that it would feel like velvet. "Ada could buy Overnight Express for what that lunch cost."

They both laughed, enjoying their childish game.

That evening George made love to Jade even more passionately than usual. She noticed the unusual intensity in his lovemaking.

"What's going on?" she teased. "Have you done something I wouldn't like?"

"Yes," he said, smiling wickedly, knowing that she'd be jealous of Carlys the way he was sometimes jealous of Steve. Then he turned serious. "I know I've been a real pain in the ass lately. I'm sorry."

"I accept your apology," she said, relieved to get it out in the open. "You *have* been a pain. What's the matter? Is it me?"

"No," he said, unaware that he was lying. "It's business. We're overworked and understaffed right now. It's been getting to me."

"*And* the apartment," said Jade. "Living on top of each other like this would drive anyone crazy."

They made up although there hadn't really been any fight or argument that had to be reconciled, just a slight tension. Jade felt that everything was just the way it had always been between them. However, the next morning when he went into the bathroom to shave, George noticed that she had moved his shaving cream to make way for some of her moisturizer. He cursed under his breath and threw the moisturizer into the trash, annoyed at the way her crap was taking over the whole bathroom.

Still, when he came out of the bathroom he was pleasant. After all, he'd just apologized for being so irritable.

That night Jade came home with a lavish dinner from Word of Mouth and an expensive bottle of burgundy.

"Filet, rare, just the way you like it. Potatoes au gratin. Broccoli vinaigrette," she said, putting the food on plates. She had an artist's eye and the way she arranged the food made it even more appetizing. "*And* Vosne Romanee, especially recommended by Sherry's."

"Beautiful!" said George, appreciating her thoughtfulness, the food, and the appealing way she served it. No matter how tempted he could be sometimes by another woman, there was no one like Jade. There never had been and there never would be. "What's the occasion?"

"Us!" she said, pleased at the way he obviously enjoyed her treat. George loved food and had very good taste. It was part of his overall sensuousness, a quality Jade adored in him. It had been nice of him to apologize. It made all the difference in the world.

"To us!" he said, toasting her with the wine, glad he had controlled his irritation that morning. "I was being a real drag."

For dessert, she had bought some *chèvre*, his favorite cheese, and a loaf of David's bread, also his favorite.

"I loved it," he said, when they had finished eating. "Every single morsel. Now, what do I owe you?"

"Nothing," she said, clearing the dishes and washing them in George's tiny sink. "It was a present."

"No way!" he said, reminding her of their agreement to split expenses fifty-fifty down the middle. "We agreed. We're sharing expenses. Fifty-fifty. I want to pay my share."

"Absolutely not!" she said, smiling and handing him the dish towel. "One of the things you're going to have to learn is how to accept gracefully. After all, I like to give presents sometimes, too."

It was a reference to George's generosity, but he was angry. It annoyed him that she had bought such an expensive meal and then refused to let him pay. He wondered how much money she was earning these days. Steven had become very, very successful, and George had a feeling that Jade was making more money than he was. He helped her finish the dishes and put them away, feeling like a henpecked husband.

They made love that night but, for the first time, it was over too soon.

"That's not like you," Jade said affectionately, teasing him.

"For Christ's sake!" George exploded, the angers of the day suddenly coming out. "I'm not a goddamn machine. It happens to every man now and then!"

"I'm not criticizing," Jade said, stunned at the outburst. "Where's your sense of humor?"

"I have some swatches for Ada to look at," George told Carlys on the phone the next afternoon. He'd been thinking of calling her ever since the night before and he finally thought of a perfect excuse. Jade was getting on his nerves. Talking to Carlys, thinking about her, made him feel better. "She said you were flying up tomorrow. Would you mind taking them with you?"

"No," said Carlys, not admitting to herself that she liked having a reason to see George again, particularly since Kirk had told her he'd be away in Charleston most of the week. Carlys was learning that having a successful husband could be a lonely business. Lonely—and no fun. All she did was work and run the house and, when her own day at the office was over, if Kirk was at home, which wasn't all that often, listen to *his* business problems. She couldn't remember the last time they'd laughed, gone to a movie, gone for a walk, or relaxed over the Sunday papers. "Of course not."

"Good. I'll drop them off later. Is five-thirty okay?"

The five-thirty fabric drop turned into a couple of drinks at the Waldorf. George got home in a good mood, his irritation at Jade forgiven and forgotten.

As the weeks passed Carlys and George joked that they ought to go into the messengering business. The little game they played with the crotchety Ada was an amusing shared secret. The messengering continued, so did the lunches, and the relationship that went along with them—a relationship that was a combination of friendship and chemistry, a flirtation that was a first for Carlys and familiar territory for George.

George didn't feel guilty about his lunch and drink dates with Carlys because that's all they were. There was nothing to feel guilty about. Carlys didn't feel guilty either. She gave herself a thousand reasons not to.

Of course it was all right to see George Kouras for lunch. It was casual, it was friendly, it was public. After all, they talked primarily about business. He helped with Ada, he was a gold mine of tips on how to handle her and, above all, how to get checks out of her. And, one day, who knows? George's company might want to hire a public relations firm or, if George's company didn't, perhaps one of his clients might—Ada Hutchinson wasn't George's only rich client. So why shouldn't she have lunch with George Kouras? He was a business contact. It was just a nice plus that she liked him, too.

Besides, Carlys was honest enough to admit to herself, there was something terribly flattering about having a man as handsome, as attractive, as charming as George openly flirting with her. For one thing, it was fun and fun was something she hadn't had very much of for too long. For another, seeing George was like having all the benefits of an affair with none of the risks. One of the things that marriage does to a man, Carlys had learned, was to turn him from a lover into a husband, and Carlys was beginning to consider herself an authority on the subject.

A husband wonders if you've remembered to pick up the dry cleaning. A lover wonders if you liked the flowers he sent. A husband is often tired and sometimes ill-tempered; a lover is never tired and never ill-tempered. A husband can be unshaven; a lover, never. A husband might forget a birthday; a lover, never. A lover will admire your blouse and always say so; a husband might like your dress but never bother to mention it. And so, added to the reasons she gave herself for seeing George was the simple fun and flattery of it all. Carlys's relationship with George was like having a lover—without the guilt—because George was, as he had told her, involved.

"Jade and I are lovers—and best friends" was how he described the relationship. He did not spell out that he and Jade were living together. He didn't consider it necessary.

"*Will and I are having a party on Wednesday for Matthew* Robinson," George told Jade in April. "He's a big builder in Washington who's building a fancy shopping strip near Steve's boutique and we'd like to get the job. It could lead to big things. Matty would be impressed if he could meet you."

"I'd love to," Jade said. "But Steve and I are due in Philadelphia. There's a factory there that sounds good and we've been unhappy with our factory downtown."

"Can't you change the date?" George asked. Matty Robinson could open some important doors. Besides, the fact that Jade had commissioned another designer for Steve's Georgetown boutique still rankled. George wanted Kouras-Goldberg to have an impressive showpiece in the nation's capital. So far they hadn't done a job there.

"Not really," said Jade, regretting it but unable to do anything about it. George knew the problems they'd been having with their old factory and how important it was to find a new one. "We've already changed it twice."

"But I need you," said George, thinking that one of the nice things about having a nonworking wife like Ina was that her time was his time. Ina was always available to do whatever he wanted.

"And I need you, but I can't change the appointment a third time," said Jade. "Maybe next time?"

Next time, thought George, would be too late. Matty was coming to town *this* week. He was accepting bids *this* week. What was the point of having a girlfriend who was a big deal in retailing, he asked himself, if she couldn't help him impress an important client?

"We're having a party at the office on Wednesday," George told Carlys the next day on the phone. If Jade couldn't be in town, maybe Carlys would be. Maybe Matty was looking for PR representation. All the big contractors used PR firms and Barron & Hynes was one of the best. Jade wasn't the *only* person who could impress Matty. "A client from Washington is in town. He's got a huge construction company in Maryland. Why don't you join us? I think you'd like to meet him and I think he might like to meet you."

Instinctively George always knew what to tell a woman to make her feel better, to make her feel secure, to make her feel safe and unthreatened. Carlys, of course, was flattered and accepted his invitation.

Sixty-second Street between Second and Third avenues is one of the most beautiful blocks in the entire city, more European than American, more Henry James than Norman

Mailer, a landmark street of some of the finest townhouses in Manhattan. One of them, painted a soft Venetian ochre, contained the office of Kouras-Goldberg. As George introduced Carlys to Will, to the draftsmen and secretaries who worked for him, to Matty Robinson, who turned out to be black and had a voice like C-3PO, Carlys suddenly realized that George lived in an apartment above the office. She could swear she hadn't known, that he had never mentioned it.

"You have experience in the real estate business?" Matty asked in his plummy voice. White hair stood in distinguished contrast to his ebony skin. "And contacts in Congress?"

"Yes," said Carlys, feeling strangely nervous to be in George's office knowing that his apartment was upstairs just a little distance away. She felt unexpectedly anxious and wanted to leave. She wondered where his girlfriend was and why she wasn't at the party. She wondered if he'd broken up with her. She wondered—and she couldn't help herself although she knew it was incredibly arrogant—if meeting her had had anything to do with it. "In fact, we have a Washington office in the Watergate complex," she told the construction magnate in her business voice.

"Perhaps you have a card?" he asked. He had slow, slightly mechanical gestures to match his mechanical voice, and Carlys handed him her card.

At seven-thirty the party broke up and Carlys headed for the door, her anxiety dissipating in the activity of retrieving her coat.

"Want to have dinner?" she suddenly heard George ask. "Will and I are going around the corner to Gino's."

She was certain she was going to hear herself say no but instead she paused, uncertain, aware that George and Will were waiting for her answer.

"Let me call home," she temporized. She didn't know what she wanted to do. Part of her wanted to go, to see what it would be like, to see what *she* would be like, having dinner with an attractive man who wasn't her husband. The other part of her absolutely did not want to go. Why play with fire? Why ask for trouble? She hoped that Kirk would be home and that the decision would be made for her. She dialed her number from one of the draftsmen's tables.

There was no answer. She dialed a second time, and when there was no answer a second time Carlys accepted her fate.

"I'd love to," she told George and Will, making a point of addressing them both.

They went around the corner to Gino's where they ordered linguine with clam sauce. They laughed about the new sex symbols, and the way Richard Gere and Mel Gibson had replaced Bo and Farrah and Cheryl as pinups. They agreed that they were all hooked on Joan Rivers subbing for Johnny Carson, and when Mike Wallace walked in they discussed the previous Sunday's "Sixty Minutes." Although Carlys had never been in the army, she supposed she felt as if she were on a pass—giddy, irresponsible, totally free.

In what seemed like no time Will glanced at his watch. "I can get the nine-forty-two if I leave now." He wanted to get home; he was also uncomfortable. He liked Carlys but he liked Jade, too, and knew her much better. He wondered what George was doing and why he was doing it. George, he thought, seemed to have a fatal compulsion to find happiness and then screw it up. He had done it with Ina and now it looked as if he was doing it again.

"So leave," George said, teasing. "You don't want to make Judy mad." Judy was Will's wife.

"Do you have to?" Carlys asked, feeling a little panicky. Will was her safety belt. As long as he was there she felt totally secure. "Can't you stay a little longer?"

Will shook his head and got up. "I'll give Judy a little surprise. Who knows? Maybe I'll find her in bed with someone."

Everyone laughed and Will said good night and left.

"He's always in a horrible mood the next day when Judy's mad at him, and Judy's always mad when he gets home too late for dinner," George explained. "I'm the one who has to put up with his lousy mood."

Carlys understood how wives felt when their husbands came home late night after night, but she said nothing. She would never say anything even slightly negative to anyone about Kirk's unpredictable schedule. Particularly to someone like George.

George paid the bill and a moment later he and Carlys

stood alone on Lexington. The street was quiet. On the next block, Bloomingdale's windows were panels of bright light.

"I know what I want," George said softly, taking her hand and raising it to his lips. She could feel his warm breath on her fingers as he spoke. "I want you to come back with me."

"No!" she said sharply, yanking her hand away. "No, it's impossible!"

She spun around and ran up Lexington Avenue wishing it went the other way, wishing she could get into a taxi headed uptown and get away from him faster. She felt panicky as she ran away from him—and from herself, panicky because she had come so close to saying yes instead of no. She was a damn fool for accepting his invitation in the first place. She should have known better. She *had* known better. She had encouraged him and it was her fault that he had come on to her. She just hoped she'd get home first and have time to compose herself before Kirk came home. *Fool!* she told herself as she ran, accusing herself of acting just like a naive high school girl and then running away like a scared rabbit.

George watched her go and made no attempt to follow her. He knew that this wasn't the end. A rejection by a woman was never an end. It was just a different kind of beginning. It was something George had known for as long as he could remember.

When George got home the racks of Jade's clothes in the living room were the first thing he saw and he wondered what he had been thinking about when he had invited Carlys to come back with him. She wasn't one of the casual models or actresses he used to screw when he was married. He had, of course, wanted to make love to her. But why? Why would he want to make love to someone else when he was so deeply in love with Jade? Agitated and disturbed, he got into bed alone with the familiar, almost-forgotten, but now freshly painful feeling of not understanding himself at all.

CHAPTER 3

Later that week Jade found the perfect apartment. Even George could find no objections. Two twenty-two East Sixty-fifth was only a few blocks from Kouras-Goldberg. It had five rooms, huge closets, a wraparound terrace, views to the south, east, and west, and because it was part of an estate, even the price, by Manhattan standards, wasn't too horrendous.

They made an offer and a week later Jade called him at his office.

"We've got it!" she said happily. "The closing's Thursday!"

"Time to celebrate," George said after the closing. He felt like a prisoner who was being led to jail although he was careful to hide his feeling from Jade. He stopped in at Sherry-Lehmann's on the way uptown from the lawyer's office and bought a bottle of champagne, trying to delay the moment when he'd be alone with Jade in their new apartment. He wished he had the nerve to back out right now. Living together was a mistake and it had been his idea. He realized he preferred being the pursuer. He didn't quite understand it, but he liked it better when the woman kept saying no. The fact was that he had been happier when Jade had kept him at arm's length.

"We won't even have to fight about space anymore," said Jade, laughing and excited, as they toured the empty rooms and spacious closets of their new apartment. "There's only one way to make it really ours," she said, smiling at him, repeating what he had said the first night she moved into his apartment, "and that's to make love in every room. Starting right here. Right now."

She opened her arms to him and he kissed her, wishing she had let *him* make the suggestion. Slowly and sensuously he put his tongue into her mouth. He caressed her with his hands, moving down skillfully, arousing her by careful but unfalteringly escalating degrees. He aroused her, but not himself. Carefully, so that she wouldn't notice, he moved his hand down to his penis. He touched himself several times as he kissed and caressed her, but he stayed limp.

"I love you," she said, slightly hoarse, already excited.

"I love you," he replied, feeling suddenly panicky, knowing that she wanted him to make love to her, knowing that right now he couldn't. The more he tried to arouse himself, the more his body defied him. He excused himself and went into the bathroom. He began to rub himself, closing his eyes and remembering all the sexiest moments he had ever had with Jade. He remembered the wild, abandoned way she looked when she came; he remembered the first time he made love to her in Nantucket; he remembered the time they made love standing up in his kitchen. He tried to imagine himself hard and throbbing with desire, about to enter her. But he remained limp, feeling anguished and frustrated. He loathed the idea of his body not doing what he wanted it to do. He loved her and there was nothing he could do to please her. He hated himself and his body, and his shame at his impotence was the most humiliating thing of all.

"George?" Jade asked through the door. "Is something wrong?"

He glanced at himself in the mirror, hating himself.

"I don't think this is the night," he said, opening the door. "I guess it's the champagne."

Jade smiled and touched his hair. "Don't worry," she said. "It's not important. We have the rest of our lives to make love."

"But it *is* important," George said. The way she said they'd have the rest of their lives to make love made him feel even worse. She wanted something he couldn't give and he didn't know what he resented more, *his* failure or *her* demand. He hated himself and, at that moment, he hated her.

Jade reached out and gently touched him, trying to arouse him. "Maybe I can help," she said lovingly.

He knew that she meant well, but her touch felt like an

accusation. He was silent as she stroked him, but when she bent to take him into her mouth, he pulled away.

"Leave me alone!" he almost shouted as he pulled on his clothes and turned his back to her, humiliated, ashamed, resentful. "Just leave me alone!"

They got dressed and went back to George's apartment. He was silent and brooding, and when he got into bed stayed as far away from her as he could. There's something wrong with me, he thought. This has never happened, he said to himself, still panicked over his failure, wondering what had gone wrong. He wondered if he'd ever be able to get it up again. He reached down and touched himself. He was still soft. He took his hand away, unwilling to be reminded of his failure.

Unless it was Jade! he suddenly thought. Unless it was her fault. Unless she was turning him off with her money and her success and her pressure to find a place so that he would be stuck with her permanently. She kept saying she liked her independence, she kept saying she wasn't like other women who wanted to own a man, but he didn't believe her. She was just like all the rest. First they wanted to hang their nightgown in your closet, and the next thing you knew their makeup was cluttering up the bathroom and their fucking clothes were hanging in the goddamn living room. He remembered when men used to be the aggressors, but no more. No wonder he went limp. She should have let *him* suggest it; then everything would have been all right. What he needed was a woman who understood that it was up to the man to make the moves—a woman who appreciated him, who was flattered when he called, who was grateful to him.

He didn't sleep much that night, but in the morning he felt much better. He woke up knowing what he was going to do. He got up before Jade and stopped off in the office downstairs to pick up some blueprints. Going outside, he hailed a cab.

"Eleven East Seventy-ninth Street," he told the driver.

"Mrs. Arnold," he said to the doorman. He had the rolled-up blueprints with him. "Would you please tell her that Mr. Kouras is here."

From the moment George met Carlys on the Boston-

New York shuttle he had known that he wanted to go to bed with her. He didn't know how it would happen; all he knew was that it would happen. What he never dreamt was that it would be her husband who would set it up.

It was a tender March day and, at seven o'clock, Carlys was still in a nightgown and robe. She was in the bathroom putting on her makeup when the house phone rang.

"What is it?" Carlys called to Kirk. She expected no one. No deliveries were planned. The cleaning woman wasn't due until tomorrow. Carlys was in a rush. She checked her watch, worried about getting to the airport in time to make the eight o'clock Boston shuttle. Kirk, already dressed and ready to leave, had answered the house phone on his way to the door.

"George Kouras," Kirk called back. Although he still said he didn't remember meeting George, Carlys had made a point of telling him about their occasional lunches and even about the party to meet the potential new client. She wanted to keep everything above board and Kirk seemed totally uninterested. The way Kirk was these days she could have told him she was having lunch with Adolf Hitler and he wouldn't have blinked. "He's coming up with some blueprints for Ada Hutchinson."

"Shit! Tell him to leave them with the doorman," Carlys said, annoyed and alarmed. What the hell was George doing on her doorstep at the crack of dawn? She shivered as she remembered the touch of his hand on hers, the way she had run away from him, the panicky way she had blurted out "no." She hurried with her makeup and her hand began to shake as she applied her lipstick. She called through the bedroom to Kirk, who was still in the foyer. "I'm not even dressed. I don't want him to come up here."

"It's too late," Kirk said a moment later, coming into the bathroom.

Mr. Oblivious, Carlys thought. Here she was in a nightgown and robe and he was inviting an attractive man into her apartment. Didn't it occur to him that it might be construed as an invitation? She wondered what went through Kirk's mind. Was he so preoccupied with business and so confident of her that nothing went through his mind? Was it only Kirk who could be so tuned out, or were most men that way? "He's already in the elevator," Kirk continued blithely, pecking her on the cheek, a well-trained husband, careful not to disturb her makeup. He picked up his brief-case and left her alone with her fantasies and her wavering resolution.

Carlys opened the front door slightly, not taking off the chain, when the buzzer sounded. She hugged her robe tightly around her.

"You can't come in," she said in greeting.

"So I won't," George said, then shrugged and smiled to show he wasn't insulted. He handed her the rolled-up blue-prints through the crack in the door. "They didn't get back from the copy shop until late last night, Tell Ada they're the finals. She can go ahead and put them out for bids."

"Okay," she said and, taking the blueprints, began to close the door as George turned back toward the elevator.

"Oh, Carlys?" he asked, turning back toward her.

"Yes?" She asked crisply, annoyed and showing it, anxious to get rid of him. She inched the door open again.

"Good morning." He said it pleasantly, with a wink and a humorous smile, and turned again toward the elevator.

Carlys was about to close the door when she found herself removing the chain.

"I'm sorry," she said through the open door, embarrassed. She smiled, asking for forgiveness. "Good morning," she said as pleasantly as he had. "Do you want some coffee? There's some on the stove."

"Don't you have to make the shuttle?" he asked.

She glanced at her watch. "I have ten minutes," she said, letting him in. Ten minutes. That was all. Just ten minutes.

She went into the kitchen and he followed her. She poured two cups of coffee and handed him one. She leaned against the refrigerator, too nervous to sit down, and began to sip her coffee.

"Your hands are shaking," he said gently. Tenderly he reached for her fingers and held them in his hand.

"No, George!" she said, pulling her hand away as if it had been burned. "No!"

He let her hand go and, as he did, he began to feel the excitement.

"I'm sorry," he said. "I'd never do anything you don't want to do."

He stood near her in the small kitchen, leaning against the refrigerator, careful not to touch her. He talked about Ada and the blueprints, standing slightly turned to conceal his hardness, and Carlys began to relax a little.

"More coffee?" she asked.

He nodded and as he held out his cup, his hand grazed her arm slightly. Because she knew it was accidental it did not make her uncomfortable. As she filled his cup with coffee he moved slightly so that his thigh just touched hers. She did not move away and he moved against her just a bit more. With his fingers he touched her hair.

"No!" she said again. "We . . ."

But she didn't move away and George bent over and let his lips touch hers very lightly. Carlys put her coffee down and heard the cup tumble off the saucer and clatter against the stainless-steel counter. George pressed his mouth against hers and she began to respond to him. Her arms were around his neck, and suddenly she couldn't fight him—or herself—any longer. George put his arms around her and pulled her closer to him, feeling her breasts against his chest and his erection hard and full against her body.

"You're beautiful, so beautiful," George whispered as he explored her with his hands and mouth, with his fingers and his tongue, caressing her, exciting her, removing his clothes and her robe, making her lose control as he led her into the living room. They lay on the banquette making hot and frenzied love, clutching and grabbing at each other as if both had been famished for the moment.

She was used to the familiarity of a loving husband's embrace; she had forgotten the hot urgency of a lover's touch. She abandoned herself to his words and his hands, to the texture of his skin and the scent of his hair.

He whispered to her constantly as he made love to her, using her name over and over, personalizing the act, making it theirs alone. Fully hard, fully in command, he brought her to orgasm again and again. First, quickly and piercingly, satisfying his appetite and hers, and then more slowly, holding her eyes with his the entire time, watching her changing expressions and smiling in satisfaction as he saw how helpless she was under him. Then, once again, taking his time, caressing her slowly and carefully, caring for her pleasure and for his own, making sure that she understood how much pleasure she gave him, telling her over and over how beautiful she was and how much she excited him and how much he desired her.

"Ecstasy," he whispered over and over. "Ecstasy. Oh, Carlys, this is ecstasy for me. Tell me it's ecstasy for you, too. Tell me."

"Yes," she said, hardly able to breathe, her eyes closed, her body limp and drained, filmed with sweat and satisfied desire. "Oh, yes. Ecstasy."

And that was his reward. He had made her happy. He had proved, once again, that he had nothing to worry about.

"You missed your eight o'clock flight," he told her a little later when they had showered and dressed.

"I can make the ten o'clock," she said, looking at her watch, "if I leave in ten minutes." Then, embarrassed, she spoke out loud the thought that crossed her mind. "I think you'd better leave ahead of me. The doorman. . . ." she added in half-explanation.

"We don't have to sneak, you know," George said. "After all, your husband told him to let me up."

Carlys avoiding meeting George's eyes. It was one thing for her to realize Kirk's complicity in her adultery, it was another to share that knowledge with her lover. *That* betrayal, even after the act of adultery, was unacceptable.

"Let's go," she said, suddenly wanting to get out of the apartment. She picked up her briefcase and locked the door behind them.

They went down in the elevator together and, as if nothing had happened, said good-bye on the corner of Seventy-ninth Street where Carlys got into a taxi for the airport while George headed down Park suddenly in the mood to walk all the way to his office.

That night, as George lay next to Jade in bed, he thought about Carlys and the memory of their lovemaking excited him. He reached over for Jade and a moment later he was inside her. He pounded her again and again and when it was finally over, he moved away, exhausted with pleasure.

"You see?" she said, when she finally caught her breath. "I told you there was nothing to worry about."

Carlys got home that night at a quarter after eight. Kirk was already home, on the telephone as usual. When he hung up he kissed her hello, a husband-to-wife peck on the cheek.

"Good day?" he asked automatically.

"Nothing special," she said, not knowing whether she was relieved or guilty to see her husband on the banquette where she and George had made love. "And you?"

"The usual. I may have to go to Charleston again later this week. I'll let you know."

She nodded and went into the bedroom and took off the clothes she had worn all day and headed into the bathroom for her third shower that day. She and George had taken a brief shower together and her body burned as it had all day long from the inside out, her knees seeming weak and rubbery, her breasts almost unbearably sensitive. She turned the water to cool, rinsed off, and, in her big white terry robe, went back out into the living room.

"Trastavere or Parma?" Kirk asked, naming two neighborhood restaurants they frequented.

"Can't we just order in?" Carlys asked. The thought of sitting opposite her husband in a public restaurant and making conversation as if nothing had happened was beyond her. She felt she had to get to know him again—in private. She wanted to obliterate that morning from her memory. "I'm exhausted. And, anyway, I'd like to spend one evening alone with my husband."

"You're sure?" he asked. Kirk Arnold would have eaten out every night of his life if he could have. He was a thoroughly urban man, not a man to whom the joys of domesticity mattered.

"I'm sure," she said. "Chinese or deli?" Carlys asked, naming their usual order-up standbys.

"Deli," he said and went back to the financial sheets he'd been studying.

While Carlys was on the phone ordering up the roast beefs-on-rye with mustard for her and Russian dressing for him and two bottles of Heineken's, she realized that there was only one way to erase that morning. As she spoke to the man at the deli she reached out with her leg and began to stroke Kirk's ankle with her bare foot. Then she moved her foot up under his trouser cuff and caressed his bare leg above his sock with her toes.

"Sexy," he said, smiling, as she put down the phone.

"That's nothing!" she said and sat down next to him. Putting her arms around him, she began to kiss his ear, following the contour of its rim with her tongue, just the way George had kissed her.

"Wow!" he said, putting down the financial sheets and turning to her. "What did I do to deserve this?"

"Shhh," she said, not wanting to talk as he parted her terry robe with his hands.

While the sandwiches got soggy and the beer warm, they made love on the sofa in the same place where, earlier, Carlys had made love with George. As she reached her climax Carlys felt that symbolically the act with her husband canceled the earlier act. It would never happen again, of course. She had decided that a long time ago, in the taxi to the airport just a few moments after she had left George on the corner of Park Avenue. Never again, she swore to herself. Never again.

The thing is, she didn't want to be a creep about it. She called George and asked him to meet her for a drink at the St. Regis. She chose the St. Regis on purpose. Sometimes she ran into Kirk there. She'd introduce him to George. It would be public, safe, innocent, the end to something that she had already more or less convinced herself was completely meaningless. Men could screw without getting emotionally involved. So could women. The fact that men and women were more or less alike, had the same feelings, talents, aspirations, frailties, abilities, strengths, and weaknesses was certainly one of the lessons that everyone, including Carlys, had learned in the past decade.

C H A P T E R   4

George was a man who adored women. He adored the way they walked and talked, the infinitely beautiful way their waists curved in and their hips swelled out, the tender shadows their breasts cast, their shiny, silky hair, and their soft velvety skin. His response to women, though, was far more than a physical response. He didn't merely adore women, he also liked them. He preferred them to men; he preferred their company, their sensitivity, their earthiness, their vulnerability, their need to please and their generosity when pleased. He found men one-dimensional and too guarded; women he thought complex and open, yet, ultimately and inevitably, mysterious.

George considered himself a lover and he knew that the first time he made love to a woman was never the best time. There was still too much to learn, too much to know, too much to discover. Love, he knew, needed patience, and so when Carlys telephoned him the first thing Monday morning and asked to see him, he agreed to meet her for a drink at the St. Regis. When she told him she regretted the incident in her apartment that past Friday morning he told her that he understood.

"I just want to tell you," she said, twisting her wedding ring around her finger and avoiding his eyes, "that it can't happen again."

"I understand," he said and, of course, he did. "You're married. You love Kirk. You don't want to hurt him."

Relieved, she nodded.

"Thank you for understanding," she said, beginning to relax. "I felt I owed you an explanation."

She'd hadn't known quite what to expect. She had been

prepared for anything. A scene, a tantrum, an accusation. There was something else she wanted to say, something else she wanted him to know about her.

"I don't want you to think that I'm in the habit of . . . seeing . . . other men."

He let her go on. She expressed her love for her husband, her regard for him, her regret about the "incident," her wish that he not think less of her for it, and her hope that she hadn't hurt him. Part of her was still the old Carlys who wanted everyone to like her, who didn't want to offend. When she had finished he said, once again, simply: "Carlys, I understand. I really do."

He paid the check and took her out to the front of the St. Regis and put her into a taxi.

"Thank you," she said, smiling, her confidence restored, as he closed the door behind her. She could barely believe how easy it had been, how understanding he had been, how sympathetic and compassionate. "Thank you," she repeated, "for understanding."

George watched the taxi disappear into the Fifty-fifth Street traffic and he turned and walked back east and uptown to 222 East Sixty-fifth, where he was going to meet Jade. He knew one other thing about the first time: It was never the last time.

George, the third of six children, had always been different. He was the boy who got along with the boys—and with the girls. He was a good student and a good athlete. He had an innate attraction to art and design in a hardworking community in which art was irrelevant and design a word no one had ever heard of. He was his father's boy—going fishing with his dad and drinking watered ouzo with the spongers who had built a flourishing Greek community in Tarpon Springs on the West Coast of Florida. He was also his mother's boy—he had drawn and executed plans for the renovation of the family living room when he'd been ten, making his mother's house the envy of her friends, and he listened to his mother's sighs and tears over her husband's lively and wandering eye. He was a man's man when he listened to his brothers' plans and plots for getting girls and he was a woman's man when he sympathized with his sisters' problems about boys who were too fresh and "wanted only one thing." He knew all about lonely Saturday nights—from both a boy's and a girl's point of view.

George fit in everywhere, but belonged nowhere. Although no one else was, George was acutely aware of the difference between the way other people saw him—as a likable and easygoing young man—and the way he saw himself—as an outsider, as someone different and, by the conservative, family-oriented, and work-defined standards of Tarpon Springs, as alien, even sinister. The first time he'd ever been made aware that he was different and that there might be something wrong with him was when he was four and his father had taken him to the barber shop on Aristotle Street for his first haircut.

"How do you feel about losing those beautiful black curls?" asked the barber.

George shrugged. He didn't know. A little sad. And, although he didn't understand it, scared, too.

He could still remember, years and years later, the feeling of the electric clippers running over his head, near his scalp. He could still see, years later, the dark, glossy curls lying on the white tile floor of the barbershop. He could still see the pink scalp showing through the dark hair when the barber held up the hand mirror, and he could still feel the prickly stubs of his crew cut when he ran his hand over it. Most vividly of all, he could still remember the vulnerable and exposed way he had felt.

"Nick! What did you do to him!" his mother had exclaimed when his dad brought him home, newly shorn. "What happened to his beautiful curls?" George's hair had been his mother's special pride and joy. It was dark and glossy and grew in lovely thick waves and curls. Despite George's itchy restlessness, she had loved to brush and comb it, making it shiny and beautiful. She loved the way people stopped them on the street when she was with him and complimented her on how beautiful her little boy was. They always said that it was a shame to waste such good looks, such long eyelashes, such soft skin, such beautiful curly hair on a boy.

"I got them cut off," Nick said belligerently, knowing that Artemis would be furious. Just like a woman! "What do you think? You think I'm going to let him grow up to be a fag?"

* * *

The compliments on George's beauty that Artemis had loved so much had embarrassed George for as long as he could remember. He wanted to be tough-looking like the other boys. His heroes were the sullen, brooding James Dean and the unkempt, beatnik Jack Kerouac, the rebel and the artist. He considered his own looks a curse and wished he could get rid of them. He was glad when his father got him that first, ugly haircut and, for years, he purposely had his hair cut too short so that at least his ears would seem to stick out. His first real chance to get rid of his looks came when he was eight and Mike Papagiannis, the son of the owner of the Poseidon Bakery, called him a pansy on the way home from school.

"Some pansy!" George had snarled, dropping his books and taking a swing at his tormentor. "I can beat the crap out of you!"

Mike dropped his own books and retaliated with a swing of his own. Mike outweighed George by twenty-five pounds and George staggered from the impact of the blow, but he didn't give up.

"You creep!" he said, righting himself and coming in for a second swing. He got Mike on the cheek but Mike, grabbing George's shirt with his left hand, began to pummel George, knocking him to the ground. Mike jumped on top of him and began to hit him in the face. George punched back as best he could, but he was outweighed. The painful sting of an open cut on his face brought involuntary and shameful tears to his eyes.

"Crybaby!" snarled Mike, pinning him down. "Just like a girl!"

"Go ahead! Hit me again!" George taunted. He *wanted* to be hit. He *wanted* to be punched. He *wanted* to be tough like the rest of the guys. He wanted to come home bruised and bloody so that everyone could see that he was a real man. "You can't hurt me."

Mike hit him again and, as he felt the blows, George thought that maybe his nose was broken and that maybe, if it were, he wouldn't be so beautiful anymore. He stopped punching. Mike thought he had won an easy battle; George thought maybe people would stop tormenting him by telling him he was so beautiful, and for the next three years

George kept getting into fistfights. Artemis couldn't understand what kind of gangster her beautiful little boy was turning into.

"He's turning into a man," Nick said. "Leave him alone."

George was just as interested in, and just as curious about, sex as all the other boys in his class. Hercules Meletiou, who lived next door, was the first to lose his virginity.

"I went up to Tampa," he bragged to George and the others. "To a real hooker. I got fucked in style. Her name was Terry and she was beautiful. She even let me touch her thing before we did it."

The sublime experience, Herk confided, cost twenty dollars. As soon as he could get another twenty saved he was heading straight for Tampa again. The next time Herk went to Tampa, he didn't go alone. Five of the boys in the neighborhood, George included, went along. They knocked on Terry's door.

"You'll have to take turns," she said, looking at them with weary hazel eyes and seeing a fast hundred bucks. "I'm not taking you all on at once. You," she said, pointing at George, running her hand through her cotton-candy bleached-blond hair. "You come first."

Flushing, George followed her into her pink-lit, pink-walled bedroom. He couldn't wait. He was hard as a rock. He had been for weeks every time he thought about sex—and even a few times when he was thinking about something else. The hard-on would come back involuntarily and remind him. He'd been hard all the way up from Tarpon Springs. He hoped he wouldn't come too fast.

"The twenty?" Terry said, closing the bedroom door, putting out her hand.

George handed her the money and began taking his shirt off.

"Hey!" she said, stopping him. "What do you think this is? A romance or something? Just unzip your pants and take it out."

George obeyed and buttoned up his shirt as Terry took off her robe and got on her bed.

"Okay," she said. "Get on top and stick it in."

George got on top of her. He was dying to put it in, but he wanted some contact with her first, something personal.

He wanted sex to be beautiful and romantic, not cold and impersonal.

"Why me?" he asked, wanting to talk to her, wanting to know her a little. "Why did you pick me first?"

"Easy," she said. "Looks. If I have to screw a bunch of horny kids, I might as well start with a good-looking one. Hell, kid, if I had your looks, I'd be a movie star. I wouldn't be a twenty-buck hooker. You're beautiful, you know. Did anyone ever tell you that?"

"Yes," said George, happy to have some kind of conversation with her, wondering if they might fall in love with each other. Suddenly, though, and with a terrible sense of helpless panic, he felt his erection begin to subside the minute she said the word *beautiful*. "I don't like it when they do."

"Honey," she said, looking wise and worn at twenty-three. "Don't knock it. If I weren't doing this for business, in your case, I'd be doing it for pleasure. You're beautiful. Gorgeous! Now, let's get going."

She pulled him down on her, spread her legs, and realized that his hard-on was gone.

"What's the matter?" she asked. "You got a problem?"

She hustled George out of her room and turned to Herk.

"Okay," she said, "your turn." She looked at Herk a little more closely. "You I remember. At least you can get it up and off. Not like your faggy friend here."

George never got over the private shame and the public embarrassment and even though he compulsively kept going back to Tampa, back to Terry's, and even though he never again failed, he couldn't wipe the devastating humiliation and the terrible doubt from his mind. It stayed with him and preyed on him even though by his senior year in high school he had forgotten all about Terry and was notorious in his class for having seduced every seducible girl in school.

*George went to the University of Miami and worked week*ends as a guide in Marineland. Marineland, like the University of Miami, was a good place to meet girls.

"I majored in design and minored in girls," George used to say and then, depending on whom he was talking to, sometimes added: "Actually, it was the other way around." George was telling the truth; what he left out was the motivation.

*Miami was, above all, a social school. The social grada-*tions were strictly delineated by a fraternity and sorority system that had been unchanged since the twenties. The handsome kids, the rich kids, the desirable kids all belonged to the top fraternities and sororities. They were the kids whose lives were cut out for them—a place in their old man's business, the right clubs, the right addresses, the right marriages, the right children. They were the golden boys and girls; they ran the campus; they drove the expensive convertibles, ran the acceptable drinking parties, and decided who was in and who was out.

George, naively thinking that good looks, good grades, and a top spot on the tennis team would get him everywhere, went out for Sigma Delta, the top fraternity on campus. When the voting was over, he was informed that he hadn't even come close, and he couldn't believe it. For the first time since a twenty-dollar hooker in a rundown section of Tampa, he had wanted something desperately and had failed. He was as privately devastated and as publicly humiliated as he had been outside of Terry's pink bedroom.

"But why?" he asked Sandy Tresnor, who was on the admission committee. Sandy was on the tennis team with George, and Sandy and George had spent a lot of time double-dating. George was sure Sandy was on his side; George was sure Sandy would have voted for him. "Did I do something wrong?"

"It's nothing you *did*," Sandy said. He was blond and suntanned, so tanned that his eyebrows were bleached white. He didn't have the remotest idea that his words were destroying George. "The guys didn't want a Greek whose old man works in a diner."

"But my father owns a restaurant," George said, as sensitive to social status as Sandy was. "And he's the mayor of Tarpon Springs."

"Big deal," said Sandy. "To them, you're just a dirty Greek."

George was dumbstruck. He had never encountered prejudice. Almost everyone in Tarpon Springs was Greek and no one hid it. Being Greek was something to be proud of. Greeks had invented democracy. Thousands of years ago Greeks had created art and architecture and philosophy and mythology and religion that still lived.

"For Christ's sake, Sandy, where do you think Sigma Delta got its goddamn name?" George said, outraged. "From the Greek alphabet!"

Sandy shrugged. "I'm sorry, George. It wasn't me. I voted for you. The other guys didn't go for it."

Crushed, George realized that there was nothing he could do, no way he could change himself to make himself acceptable. He couldn't make himself bland and blond; he couldn't make himself un-Greek. He felt rejected and humiliated, exposed and vulnerable. He wanted to tell Sandy to take his lousy fraternity and his lousy friends and shove them; instead, he left campus, went to Lefty's, the local hang-out, and decided to get good and drunk. Tomorrow he would decide what to do.

He was on his second beer when Sandy and his girlfriend, Lois Duncan, came in.

"Hi, George," Sandy said with a big grin. "Can we sit down?"

George nodded.

"Listen," Sandy said, ordering a brew, "you took that course in American fiction last semester, didn't you?"

George nodded, electrically aware of Lois. She was just as blond as Sandy, just as blue-eyed, just as popular. She drove a white T-bird and had been an attendant to last year's homecoming queen. He remembered her on the float, remembered noticing her breasts under her white strapless gown as she waved to the crowd. Looking at her gave him a hard-on.

"Did you have to write that dumb essay on Fitzgerald and the rich?" Sandy asked. He had a tenor voice and he spoke in a droning, uninflected way. Brains definitely weren't his long suit. His father's money and mother's social position were.

George nodded again, thinking that he'd love to screw Lois. *That* would serve Sandy right. It would make Sandy feel just as betrayed as he felt, just as rejected and humiliated. He wished he could fuck Lois right on the table in front of Sandy.

"Give me a copy, would you?" Sandy droned on in his self-centered way, oblivious to the looks George and Lois exchanged and the way she unconsciously licked her lips. "What with rush week I haven't had time to get around to it. Professor Hales is so senile he won't remember it from last year. I'll just put my name on it. So, how about it?" he asked George unaware that George was pressing his knee against Lois—and that she was returning the pressure.

"How about you write it yourself?" George said, throwing money down on the table for his beer. He turned to Lois. "Do you want to stay here with this creep or do you want to come with me? I know a place on the beach where we can go dancing."

George courted Lois and won her away from Sandy. And then, one by one, the boys who ran Sigma Delta found that their fraternity pins were being returned to them, that they were spending Saturday nights alone, that the girls who, by rights, should have been theirs, suddenly weren't. Women, George learned, were a way to get what he wanted. The boys who ran Sigma Delta had rejected him, had tried to ignore him; now they couldn't.

George with his dark suntan, white teeth, and strong features became notorious as the campus lover. But he was not a heartless seducer, he was a lover who put his body and soul into his seductions. Perhaps because he'd grown up with so many sisters, perhaps because he had an unusually gentle streak and because he was always acutely aware of being an outsider, he not only loved the coeds he slept with, he liked them as well. He liked so many things about them—the way they laughed; the way they cried; their intuitiveness; the way they thought, sat, danced, skipped, and waltzed; the way they stood up for what they wanted; their sudden withdrawals; the mystery about them; the ways in which they were like each other, yet totally individual. And there were so many of them! Small and dainty; tall and strong; blond and brunette and tawny and copperhaired; they smelled different, they tasted different, the ways they touched him were different, and the ways they loved him were different. In the early sixties when

George was in college the sexual revolution had just begun and George was one of the primary beneficiaries of that revolution. Losing himself in sex, he became something of a campus celebrity as a lover.

The yearbook called him Warren, after Warren Beatty. And an autograph from the queen of the orange blossom festival wrote that the George was for another George: George Hamilton. George never denied it.

He had his vengeance—only it wasn't really satisfying. Every conquest simply demanded a new one.

Once out of college, George went to work in the interior design department of a Miami architectural firm, where he had an affair with one of the partners' daughters. From there he went to Washington, D.C., where he did renderings for the Historical Preservation Society and had an affair with the daughter of a senator from an influential western state, and from there, in a move that reflected the rebel in him, he hooked up with a wildly avant-garde husband-and-wife architectural firm who worked out of their Virginia farm designing and building outlandish rainbow-colored houses with pentagonal shapes and oval windows for rich clients. Although hired to do elevations, George found himself picking paint chips from the limited palette in which his employers worked: the ice cream hues of pistachio, robin's egg blue, lemon, and coral. Just at the precise moment when his affair with the wife turned serious, she had a religious revelation that her husband shared and, leaving houses half built, floor plans scuttled, and commissions in midstream, they packed one suitcase between them and moved to an ashram somewhere in the mountains of northern India, where they planned to wear saffron-colored robes and meditate.

George accepted his fate as a gift from God and went to New York where he had always wanted to be anyway and, within a week, found a job at Tydings-Owen-Brennecke, an enormous, very well respected architectural firm that built skyscrapers, shopping malls, office buildings, factories, and plants. Tydings-Owen-Brennecke was the Tiffany of architectural firms, and being hired by T-O-B felt to George like a long-delayed recompense for being rejected by Sigma Delta. He was finally where he wanted to be, where he thought he deserved to be. No one at T-O-B thought of George as a dirty Greek; they thought of him as a personable and talented young designer.

*"Very talented," observed Ezra Tydings, one of the found-*ers, who took George under his wing and assigned him to the elite group of designers who did what at Tydings-Owen-Brennecke were called "partners' jobs." Partners' jobs were commissions from friends and contacts to which the partners of T-O-B paid personal attention, jobs that got the gilt-edged treatment because they were the jobs that ensured and continued the success and reputation of T-O-B.

In the three years George worked at Tydings he was involved in the design of several private planes, a yacht, any number of expensive cooperative apartments and lavish country retreats. George—and his work—were well liked at Tydings. Neither alarmingly avant-garde nor fussily old-fashioned, George's work, like George himself, fit in perfectly at Tydings. It was made clear to him that he had a very good future there.

"If you stay," Ezra Tydings said, "you can look forward to heading up the partners' division. If that doesn't appeal to you we can find something that will."

The only problem was that George was not really tempted to take Tydings up on his offer. Now that he was finally wanted by the people he most longed to be accepted by, he felt compelled to reject them.

"I'm not a company man. I'm a lover and a loner" was how George explained it to his girl-of-the-moment, Ezra Tydings's youngest daughter, Ina.

Still seeing himself as an outsider, as a loner, George wanted to be in business for himself. He wanted, once and for all, to free himself of the need to be accepted by others. When Rollie Leland, a T-O-B graduate with a small but gilt-edged firm of his own, asked George to join him, George accepted and the partnership was born.

"A WASP and a Greek," George said, half humorously but shrewdly indeed, knowing the city and its peculiar amalgam of snobbism combined with liberal prejudices. "No one will be able to resist us." He turned out, of course, to be right.

Although George and Rollie started small, as a two-man shop, they never really had to struggle. The economy of the early seventies was with them and three years later, by 1974, Kouras-Leland had been responsible for many of the expensive showcase boutiques along Madison Avenue's Temptation Alley—the almost-gold-plated blocks between Fifty-seventh and Seventy-ninth.

"Come back," Ezra Tydings told George over lunch in T-O-B's executive dining room. "You're welcome any time." It was the same thing George's girls always told him. George never left broken plates or broken hearts behind him.

"No way," George said and added, with a straight face, "I don't want to work for my father-in-law."

The older man indulged in a quick double take and then got up and embraced George. "I never said anything," he said, beaming. "But I was kind of hoping you and Ina would make things permanent."

No one had ever thought George would settle down. Even George had thought that he would never settle down, but Ina Tydings changed all that.

C H A P T E R   5

Ina Tydings was an heiress who had learned that silver spoons came with price tags and privileges. She was a Southampton blonde with blue eyes, long bones, and a year-round tan. She wore expensive, conservative clothes, tortoiseshell headbands, and drove her T-bird like Jackie Stewart at Le Mans. She was an odd combination of spoiled and practical, naive and shrewd.

"I got engaged my senior year at USC," she told George during their courtship, the pain of a sharp awakening still echoing in her soft voice as she spoke. "My fiancé, Jerry, was a pre-med student, but when he applied to med school he got turned down everywhere. When all the rejections had come in he got drunk one night and told all his friends that the turn-downs didn't really bother him. He said he was getting married anyway and he'd just as soon let me support him.

"The story got back to me. I returned the ring and he begged me to reconsider. I told him what I'd heard and at first he denied he'd said it. Then he said he'd been drunk and hadn't known what he was saying. Then he changed his story a third time and said he'd just been joking. Didn't I have a sense of humor? I concluded that there were two possibilities: either he'd really said it or he was a liar. I lost all respect for him and, of course, I never reconsidered. I also stopped dating. For a long time I thought all men were like Jerry. I thought they were all interested in me for my money.

"I joined the Peace Corps. I went to Iran for two years and taught basic health care to children in Shiraz. It was the best thing I ever did, and when I got back I found that I had begun to trust my instincts about who was a fortune hunter and who wasn't."

"And you think I'm not?" George asked. George could always say what others only thought.

"Whatever you're after," Ina answered seriously, paying attention to the instincts she now trusted, "it's not my money. That much I'm sure of."

Timing is everything and George and Ina's timing was perfect. George was thirty-one when he met Ina, just four years older than she was. He was ready to marry and settle down. She was beginning to feel panicked about her single state. They both wanted a family. Ina was every blond princess George had ever lusted after. George was every dark and handsome lover Ina had ever imagined being ravished by. He proposed on their third date. On their fourth Ina accepted.

They were married on a glorious June day in 1974 at the Tydingses' summer house on Orr's Island, Maine. After the wedding they left for the Portland airport, where they flew to Boston and then to France for a romantic honeymoon touring the wine country of Champagne. It was the perfect beginning to a marriage, and on the night they returned to New York, Ezra Tydings met them at JFK.

"I've got a surprise for you kids," Ezra said jubilantly as

they headed toward Manhattan and Ezra's car pulled to a stop in front of the Tydingses' brownstone on East Seventy-second Street between Second and Third avenues. As they got out of the car, George thought they would go into the Tydingses' house for a welcome-home celebration. Instead, Ezra led them to the house next door. Pausing on the sidewalk, he handed a set of keys to George.

"Open it!" Ezra said, gesturing to the front door. George looked at him, puzzled. "Go ahead!" Ezra urged. "It's yours! It's your wedding present!"

Stunned, George put the key in the door of the expensive house that was suddenly his.

"Isn't Daddy wonderful?" Ina asked, after they'd all shared a champagne toast to the newlyweds' new life and the beautiful new house in which they would begin it.

"Wonderful," said George, still stunned at Ezra's largesse. George and Rollie's business was just beginning to be successful after a few years of struggle. To be catapulted so suddenly into the ownership of valuable Manhattan real estate was more than he could absorb. He wasn't sure that it all hadn't happened too fast. As George struggled with his ambivalent feelings, Ina confided that she had put her father up to it.

"The more I thought about living in your place, the more I thought it just wasn't big enough," she said in her princessy way, taking it for granted the the entire world would be arranged for her pleasure and convenience. "We'll entertain. We'll have a family. Why should we be squashed together when we don't have to be? When I found out that this house was for sale, I mentioned it to Daddy. He got the idea right away."

"You mean you knew about the house all along?" George asked, suppressing a sudden impulse to slap her, furious that she had kept a secret from him. He had imagined that he and Ina would share everything the way his mother and father did, that they would make all the big decisions in their lives together—like where to live and how many children they'd have. Ina was making him feel he had no control over his own life. Between Ina and Daddy, George was beginning to feel that he was the odd man out.

"It's great, isn't it?" Ina asked, absorbed in the pleasure of the luxurious rooms and landscaped garden in back, already imagining herself the mistress of her handsome domain.

George nodded in apparent agreement. What could he say? That he was furious? That he felt castrated? George still had the old-fashioned family-style values he had been brought up with. He wanted his wife to live in a house he provided. He thought it was a husband's privilege and obligation to provide for a wife. He would have felt more like a husband in a home, even a modest one, that he had chosen and paid for himself.

Despite all of that, however, he loved the idea of living in a big, expensive, beautiful house. There was still enough of the middle-class Greek boy in him to be impressed by his sudden rise in status. Involuntarily he thought about the guys at Sigma Delta with a sharp feeling of gloating triumph. He just wished they could see him now—them with their dumb suburban houses and him with his Upper East Side brownstone. How things had changed! George's pride and his ego battled in an unwinnable war.

He was both appreciative and angry, but Ina had no such conflicts. She was thrilled with her new, luxurious house and Ezra was delighted to give his daughter and new son-in-law such a generous wedding gift. George felt he couldn't say anything without sounding ungrateful, but later that night in the comfortable bedroom of the expensive house provided by his rich father-in-law, George was not able to make love to his new wife. He blamed his limpness on fatigue, excitement, champagne, and jet lag; on everything except the anger he felt and could not express and the conflict that still struggled within him.

The night after, humiliated by the inexplicable revolt of his body, he begged off when Ina wanted to make love, saying he was exhausted. He did not sleep that night worrying that something was wrong with him. As dawn broke he figured out how to find out for sure. He telephoned a girl named Robin De Soto who had once been his secretary. She and George had fallen into bed together a few times while she'd worked for him. Fallen in and fallen out. Casually, pleasantly, insignificantly. Robin was soft and undemanding, a sexy little girl with no ambitions toward her handsome boss other than some good, wholesome screwing.

That night, the third night after his return from his honeymoon, George was unfaithful to his wife for the first time.

"I'm getting married next month," Robin had told George when he called and asked her to meet him. She didn't want to say no, but she wanted to let him know where things stood in case he had any moral objections.

"If it doesn't bother you," he said, not telling her that *he* had just gotten married. "It doesn't bother me."

Robin and George spent a few hours together in a motel on the Palisades. For Robin, a daughter of the Pill generation, it was a nice, hot episode, a spicy prewedding adventure. For George it was a kind of revenge against Ina and Ezra for making him feel like less than a man. That same night he made love to Ina the way she remembered, strongly and insatiably.

"Ecstasy! You're the best lover any woman ever had," she told him breathlessly when they were finished, rewarding George with a reassurance she didn't even know she was bestowing.

He continued to be unfaithful to Ina during the first year of their marriage, although he was careful not to let her find out or even suspect. He concealed his adulteries with kisses and flowers and attention and compliments. He was certainly one of the most romantic of husbands anywhere, ever, and to his and Ina's very great delight, their married sex life was explosively passionate. There was never another failure and George suspected that his other women were the reason why. As long as George had other women he could be the perfect lover for his wife.

"You're the sexiest man in the world," Ina told him constantly.

"Not really," he said, smiling. He traced circles around her nipples with his finger and then his tongue, recalling his afternoon's reassuringly potent performance with a pretty fabric designer. "It's just that I have inspiration most men don't. You!"

Their life, from the outside looking in, was a perfectly pieced-together jigsaw puzzle consisting of his, hers, and theirs. Hardly the typical struggling newlyweds' first home, their brownstone was photographed by *House Beautiful* and its kitchen used in an advertisement for expensive, imported cookware. The credits were very helpful to George and Rollie's business and George was driven, trying to compete with his rich and powerful father-in-law. He had a dream of making Kouras-Leland the equal of Tydings-Owen-Brennecke. Ina was no longer a vulnerable and insecure heiress ripe for the plucking, but a good wife and hostess who used her talents to help her husband's fledgling business. George was no longer a questionable outsider who hadn't made Sigma Delta; he was well connected both by talent and by marriage to the small and influential Manhattan world of architects and interior designers. His new partnership with Rollie Leland grew slowly but surely and, gradually, George felt more and more at home in the fast-paced world of New York design and architecture. There was no longer any doubt that he was a young man on the way up, and with the birth of his son, Robert, one year after he and Ina were married, he became the man he had always wanted to be.

Ezra Tydings was beside himself with pleasure. "He can have his choice," Ezra said when he visited his grandchild in the hospital. "He can be an architect or an interior designer. He can work in either the corporate division or the executive department, depending on his talents."

"Dad!" Ina said, laughing. "He's only five hours old!"

"It's never too soon to make plans," Ezra said intently. A dynast and an empire-builder, Herb Hartley's psychological twin, Ezra always had the future of Tydings-Owen-Brennecke very much on his mind.

Artemis Kouras was delighted in a much simpler way, a more directly emotional way. "Such a beautiful baby," she told George, delighted at the arrival of her tenth grandchild. "He's just as beautiful as you were!"

Nick Kouras gave George the most important benediction of all: "The man who has a son is a real man."

But it was George, more than anyone and to his own absolute amazement, who was swept off his feet. The minute he first saw Bobby and first held him, he was a goner.

"I'm in love for the first time ever," he confided to Rollie in utter astonishment, in thrall to feelings of love and protectiveness and tenderness he hadn't even known existed. "And it's my own kid! What do you think of that?"

Rollie, who had his own children, only nodded. He had known for a long time what was a brand-new revelation to George.

George was so happy that he wanted another child right away.

"Let's wait a little," Ina pleaded, still coping with diapers and feedings and visits to the pediatrician. "I need to get used to Bobby. I want time alone with him. I want time to really get to know him."

"Two would be twice as much fun," George said.

"Please," replied Ina. "Give me time."

George began to spend more and more time at home because that was where Bobby was. Now that he was a father he had nothing to prove anymore and his string of infidelities tapered off. With a son, he was confident of his own virility. Being with Bobby made him feel like a man, but being with Ina made him feel trapped.

Ina didn't say anything, but she was hurt and confused by the way George had changed. Before Bobby had been born George had been tender and romantic and passionate. He had showered her with love and caresses and kisses; now he seemed so entranced with his son that he barely seemed to remember that he had a wife. Ina had thought she was marrying a great lover, instead she found herself with an old-fashioned Greek husband and father. All he seemed interested in doing was tying her down with more babies. Ina could barely admit to herself the way she felt, but the fact was she was jealous of her own child. Her jealousy stabbed at her, an unacceptable emotion over an inappropriate object. What she never realized, because she never found out about any of George's affairs, was that her jealousy came too late, and over the wrong person.

On a visit to Denver, where she'd spent several years as a child when her father was building mile-high office buildings in the mile-high city, Ina met a boy she'd gone to grade school with, Allen Ter Horst, a Denver neighbor whose father owned a drugstore and whose mother was an alcoholic. Just as Ina had been a despised "rich kid" in school, Allen had had another cross to bear. He was the

kid the other boys ganged up on, the boy the other kids
called dumbo because of of his jug-handle ears and less-
than-impressive academic average, the boy the other kids
made fun of because his mother used to stagger down the
street in front of his house in her bathrobe, a bottle in her
hand. As a man, Allen still had the stocky build, the dirty
blond hair, and startling green eyes he'd had as a ten-year-
old. Ina bumped into him, almost literally, in the lobby of
Brown's Hotel.

"Allen Ter Horst!" she had exclaimed. "I haven't seen
you since the sixth grade!" Allen had left school to go to
another one across the city. The reason, Ina knew as well
as anyone else, was an attempt to escape the agony that
followed him as he flunked class after class and got into
fistfight after fistfight over the insults to his mother.

He looked at her blankly. "I'm sorry," he said, per-
plexed. "But I don't seem to remember you. . . ."

"Ina Tydings. We went to the Woodrow Wilson Elementary School together," Ina reminded him. "I was the one
Miss Dayle always yelled at for talking too much."

"Oh, of course," he said and the look in his eyes told
her that he wanted to get away from her. Away from his
memories? she wondered. Then, politely, he added, "How
are you? And what are you doing in Denver?"

"I'm married now and I have a son. I'm visiting my
cousin. She went to Woodrow Wilson, too. I visit once or
twice a year," she explained. "And you? What are you
doing here?"

"I live here," Allen said. "I'm a metals broker. It sounds
better than it really is," he added, always honest.

Allen had played two seasons for Milwaukee as a first
baseman until an injury to his throwing arm cut short his
promising career. Unprepared for any life outside of professional sports, he had sold insurance for a few years and,
bored, had given it up. Then he had gone back to school,
thinking about becoming a CPA, but gave that up, too,
discouraged because all the other students were younger
and smarter than he was. After that he had sold stock,
worked for a real estate broker, and, finally, began trading
futures of the copper and bauxite deposits located in the
rich hills and plateaus outside Denver for a local brokerage

firm, a job that seemed no better and no worse than any of the other jobs he had tried.

"I'm impressed," Ina said. "I can just see you shouting orders on a trading floor. You must be terrific!"

"Not terrific, but not that bad either," he said and smiled for the first time. The fact was that he had found a place on the trading floor. He was making good money and feeling good about himself. "In fact, if you have the time, why don't you come down to the exchange? I'd take you to lunch but I don't break for lunch. . . ."

He did, however, take Ina out for a drink when the exchange closed and told her the story of his life between the sixth grade and the present. It turned out that Allen Ter Horst, ex-first baseman, had a sweet, attentive nature and an openness that, compared to George's need to be in control of every situation, was refreshing.

"I may not be a superstar," he told Ina, "but once I realized I'd never be Stan Musial or a millionaire, I made peace with myself. I stopped torturing myself with other people's standards. I'm an example of the class creep who turned into a fairly happy man."

"You weren't a creep," Ina said, trying to make him feel better.

"Yes I was," he answered straightforwardly, something, Ina realized, George could never have done. "But I'm not now."

The drinks turned into dinner and, as they reminisced, Ina found herself telling Allen things she had never told anyone, not even George: about how she had felt at school when the other kids had tormented her by calling her a "rich kid" and taking her lunch money all the time "because your father can afford to give you more"; how, when she heard about Jerry's fraternity house boast, she had tried to commit suicide by swallowing a bottle of aspirin and had to be taken to the hospital to have her stomach pumped.

"You probably think I'm a terrible neurotic," she said, amazed at what she heard herself tell him.

"No," he said. He had a gentle, almost tender manner. He had suffered just like most people but, unlike George, he was able to admit it. "I understand. I've been there. I was unhappy once, too."

Ina saw Allen again the next evening and she was absolutely amazed when, after dinner, she went back with him to his apartment and they went to bed. He was a good lover, tender and relaxed. He made Ina see her husband in a new way. Unlike George, Allen did not seem to need to prove anything in bed. He did not seem to need to fuck longer and stronger than anyone else, or to hear her breathless compliments on what a wonderful lover he was. He did not seem to have winning the sexual olympics in mind. Allen just seemed to enjoy making love to a woman he cared about. Ina's evening with him was a revelation.

When Ina left Denver the next day Allen drove her to the airport.

"You'd better tell George about me," he told her as her flight was announced.

"Why?" The last thing in the world she wanted to do was tell George about Allen.

"Because I'm going to marry you."

Allen telephoned her every day that week and, that Friday night, arrived unannounced in Manhattan. George, as Allen knew, was in Chicago overseeing the installation of a new showroom in The Merchandise Mart.

"I'm serious," he told Ina over dinner. "I'm in love with you. I can't think about anything except you. I'm going to marry you and we're going to be happy."

"But I've hardly spent any time with you."

"You're going to spend the weekend with me. And isn't it wonderful?" he continued. "I don't have to meet your parents and you don't have to meet mine. We all know each other already. From the sixth grade."

"But George is coming home tomorrow. . . ."

That weekend was the worst of Ina's life. Allen and George were elaborately polite to each other and Ina was in the middle feeling miserable. She was torn between the husband to whom she felt loyal and the lover who had touched her very soul.

"He's a loser," George told her when they were alone. "What are you doing hanging around with him?"

"George, please."

"Come on, for Christ's sake. *Look* at him. He's a mess.

He doesn't know what he's doing or where he's going. He's probably a fag on top of everything else, too!'' George said, outlandishly accusing Allen of what he most feared himself.

"He's *not* gay!" Ina said, angrily defensive.

"How do *you* know?" George asked. "Have you gone to bed with him?"

The question sprang straight from George's unconscious; the look on Ina's face answered it.

"I don't believe it," George said, the betrayer betrayed, the adulterer cuckolded. "I don't believe it!"

"Well, you'd better," said Ina, "because I'm leaving you for him."

"And what about Bobby?" George said.

"I'm taking him with me," Ina said. George vowed, *"Never!"* but Ina paid no attention.

A week later, at noon on an unseasonably warm Saturday, Rollie's wife called George.

"It's Rollie," she said, sounding as if she were speaking from a great distance. "He's dead."

Within a week, George Kouras, who had struggled his way from an apartment on top of a Greek restaurant to a half-million-dollar East Side brownstone, a growing design business, a wife to be proud of, and a son who was the center of his existence, had lost them all.

C H A P T E R 6

By the late 1970s, George had a new partner and an old problem. Kouras-Leland had become Kouras-Goldberg, a firm that in three years had grown from two draftsmen and a secretary to eight draftsmen, two secretaries, and a receptionist. George and Will had moved out of their rented offices in the East Fifties and bought a brownstone on East Sixty-second Street. They gutted the handsome nineteenth-century building and completely redesigned its interior, installing an elevator and turning the three lower floors into offices, reception areas, and drafting studios. George lived in the elegant bachelor's apartment on the top floor.

"Just like my parents," he joked, thinking of the apartment he'd grown up in over the Adelphi restaurant in Tarpon Springs, the restaurant his father still owned and worked in every single day of his life. "I'm still basically a nice Greek boy who's living above the store."

George had nothing to complain about and he knew it. He and Will both drove brand-new BMWs; they both had growing stock portfolios, Caribbean vacations in February, and summer weekends in the Hamptons. Kouras-Goldberg was doing very well indeed, and in every way that mattered, George Kouras had done much, much better than the golden boys he had so envied back in the early sixties. Why then, did he feel a constant prickling of both personal and professional dissatisfaction? Why did a successful man in his mid-thirties still have the feelings of a boy not yet twenty who hadn't made the best fraternity on campus? It was a question George asked himself in the still of the night; it was a question to which he didn't have an answer.

After his divorce, George's romantic side seemed to have died. Sex had replaced love; uncomplicated sex, uninvolved sex, recreational sex, plain sex and fancy sex and sex for sex's sake. Blondes and brunettes and redheads; tall and short and slim and plump; typists and stewardesses, nurses and real estate agents, models and stockbrokers, secretaries and clerks, bank tellers and actresses blurred though his bed and his life. There were Marys and Beths, Susans and Suzannes, Lindas and Hollys, Elaines and Marguerites, Carols and Natalies, Marions and Judys, Lynnes and Barbaras. Sometimes George knew their names and sometimes he didn't and it never really made any particular difference. George rarely took anyone out more than three times because he found that his "problem," as he secretly referred to it to himself, had come back. He never had any trouble the first time he went to bed with a new woman; the first time he was as potent and strong as ever. But the second time he'd have trouble getting an erection, a failure he inevitably ascribed to fatigue or alcohol, a failure women were prepared to forgive and understand. When he didn't call a third time they tended to think that there was something the matter with them—that they weren't pretty enough, exciting enough, young enough. As long as George kept a new supply of women in his bed, he managed to perform adequately enough. But not, he was acutely aware, the way he had when he'd been twenty.

George's sexual secret was a secret he tried—vainly—to keep from himself. When he lost himself in work, he succeeded; but nights and weekends, face-to-face with himself, he couldn't quite pretend that everything was just the way it had always been. He didn't blame Ina for leaving him. He wasn't much of a man. George the lover? George the husband? It was all a bitter, empty charade, and there were times when he hated himself. George the failure, both in and out of bed, was more like the truth. Five months after the breakup with Ina, and after five months of frantic sexual activity that was always ultimately disappointing, George did something he never thought he would do: He made an appointment with a psychiatrist.

Dr. Ferdinand Liagros had been recommended by George's internist. Dr. Liagros had an office on Fifty-eighth Street just off Madison Avenue. George spent his first eighty-dollar session with Dr. Liagros talking about his sensitivity to his surroundings and how influenced he was by the rooms in which he worked and lived. George concluded the session by telling Dr. Liagros that he approved of the design of his office. He tried to make it a joke, but Dr. Liagros, who had a very slight Spanish accent and compassionate brown eyes, didn't laugh. He didn't even smile. All he said was that he would see George again the following Tuesday at four o'clock.

All in all, George went to Dr. Liagros's office eight times. He talked about having trouble sleeping; he said that sometimes he worried that he might be drinking a bit too much; he spoke of his disappointment at not having built his firm to the pinnacle reached by Tydings-Owen-Brennecke; he talked of the difficulty of meeting women he felt any real rapport with, the way he missed Bobby so terribly, his regret over the divorce; he spoke of the more-than-occasional envy he felt toward Will, who lived happily with his wife and three attractive children. But he never once, not one single time, mentioned that sometimes he had difficulty getting an erection and maintaining it.

"I'm not coming back," he told the doctor after his eighth session was over. He smiled confidently. "I met someone last night. Her name is Jade. I'm already in love."

"Love is not a cure," said Dr. Liagros.

"It is for me," said George, thinking that the difference between them was that Liagros was a scientist and he was a lover. How could Liagros possibly understand him?

"I have the feeling that, for you, love is an evasion," said the doctor.

"An evasion?" said George laughing a bit too much as he put on his coat. "What is that? Some kind of Freudian double-talk?"

"I think something's on your mind that you haven't mentioned," Liagros said, being more direct than he'd ever been with George.

"What do you want?" asked George sarcastically, buttoning his coat. "Do you expect me to tell you some bullshit that happened when I was four years old?" As George spoke a memory of the haircut flashed through his mind and, along with the memory, the horrible feeling of complete helplessness and vulnerability.

"It might be a good place to start," said the analyst quietly, ignoring George's sarcasm.

Overwhelmed with sudden panic, George fumbled with the doorknob. He couldn't get out of Liagros's office fast enough.

The instant he saw Jade again at Titian Fellowes's lower Fifth Avenue loft, George's heart went *ping!* She was the one he could talk to, the one who brought out the best in him. But their timing had been all wrong. George was ready for love, while Jade was interested in independence. What he hadn't realized was that he still had unfinished business with Ina, who had not, it turned out, married Allen Ter Horst. George had suggested the reconciliation. Part of him still cared for Ina. Most of all, he missed Bobby so much that he felt a hole had been torn from his life. Seeing Bobby, having Bobby live with him again, playing with Bobby every morning before work and every evening after work, taking Bobby to the park on weekends, showing him the animals in the zoo and buying him ice cream were precious, irreplaceable pleasures for George, filling him with a sense of almost overwhelming love that made up for every other disappointment in his life.

The rest of the reconciliation was a disaster, a replay of all the worst moments of their marriage. George and Ina fought over money, sex, and, finally, over Bobby.

"I need a new fur coat," Ina had said six weeks after she and Bobby had moved back to New York. A dark mink was what she had in mind. Her wolf parka, perfect in the West, was out of place in Manhattan. "My old one is too sporty for the city."

"I can't afford it right now. We've just had to hire more draftsmen for the Dallas job and their salaries are very expensive," said George. "Besides, it's almost spring. Why don't you wait until the fall? I'll be able to get it for you then."

Ina didn't feel like waiting. One of the privileges of being a rich girl, she felt, was that she didn't have to wait. She went to her father who told her to have Maximilian send the bill to him.

"Goddamn it, Ina. I'm your husband!" George shouted. "Can't you wait six months for the fucking coat?"

"Why should I?" replied Ina blandly. "Daddy was happy to buy it."

Furious, George grabbed the coat.

"What are you doing?" Ina screamed, as he headed for the fireplace.

"What do you think?" he snarled, holding the coat in one arm and grabbing the firescreen and throwing it aside with the other hand.

Fueled by her own rage, Ina pulled at the coat, wresting it from his one-handed grip and just barely restraining him from stuffing eighteen thousand dollars' worth of Black Willow into the open fire.

"Don't use your diaphragm," George said, right after their reconciliation. "I want to make love to you without it."

"I don't want another kid now," said Ina, guessing what was on George's mind. Defiantly she came to bed wearing her diaphragm and George, enraged, found once again that his body rebelled.

"You're no lover," Ina had said witheringly. "Even at your best, you're just a sexual athlete."

From then on George only tried to make love to her after he'd had sex with someone else, and six months later they agreed on the obvious: The reconciliation was not working out.

"Let's part as friends," George said, terribly disappointed at the failure of their reconciliation. A corner of him, a primitive but forceful corner, felt the way his father had felt when George told his parents about his divorce, the first in the Kouras family: Men, real men, didn't get divorced. They got married and they stayed married. The failure of the reconciliation made George feel worthless again. But it wasn't quite as bad as the first separation. He was older and a little more numb, but he still felt the pain.

"Let's," said Ina agreeably. "I don't hate you. I guess our breakup was as much my fault as yours."

"I'd like to see more of Bobby," George said, encouraged by her admission. Their divorce agreement allowed him to see Bobby for two weeks in the summer and one week in the winter, a provision George had bitterly fought and a provision his lawyer finally persuaded him to accept. "Three weeks a year isn't enough."

Ina shook her head.

"No," she said. "I don't want him here with you. Not in this love nest. Not where you bring your parade of conquests. I don't want Bobby to grow up like his father."

"Please, Ina," George said, almost begging, tears rising to his eyes, closer to showing real pain than she'd ever seen him. "Bobby's my son, too. I love him. Can't you understand how I feel?"

"No," Ina said flatly, used to getting what she wanted, She then returned to Denver, taking Bobby with her and leaving George to face the final failure of his marriage and the bitter loss of his only son.

The totally unexpected opportunity to have a second chance with Jade was, George realized, the chance of a lifetime. The second time around, he was less desperate and Jade was more available. The second time around he fell in love and so did she. Being with Jade erased the past and its pain and made him feel like a man in a way that no woman ever had. This time, with no Ina in the wings, Jade agreed to everything George wanted and, unknowingly, brought George face-to-face with the irreconcilable conflicts of being a man who used sex to solve every problem—until sex itself became a problem.

He wanted Jade. He wanted to be a man with her. And to do so, he needed another woman.

It was then that George met Carlys and realized that Carlys was married to Kirk Arnold, one of those golden WASPs whose rejection still, so many years later, stung. It was then that he began to have lunch with Carlys and, finally, thanks to Carlys's husband, made love to Carlys. Because she was married she could *never* be his and that guaranteed his potency with her.

When Carlys told him at the King Cole Bar that she wouldn't see him again George said that he understood. What he didn't say was that he needed Carlys, needed her to stand between him and the fears that made him less than a man with the woman he loved.

He thought that only one of two things could happen next. He could either wait or act. He could wait for Carlys to call him, or he could call her. There was, he then realized, a third alternative.

"Ada," he said long-distance, New York to Boston, a week after the meeting with Carlys at the King Cole Bar at which she said she didn't want to see him again, "the fabrics you chose are out of stock. I've picked some new ones but you're going to have to look at them and give me a decision."

George could hear the pages of a desk calendar flip. "Drop them off with Carlys," Ada said, just as George had known she would. "She's due up here on Thursday."

"Okay, Ada," said George. "Sure thing." Except that he wasn't going to drop them off with Carlys.

That Thursday, when Carlys got on the eight A.M. Boston shuttle, she was surprised to see George Kouras standing on line ahead of her.

"Ada?" she said, suddenly nervous at the sight of him. She remembered him so well, his body, his hands, his kisses. Too well. She had been afraid she'd run into him again on the shuttle and she had tried to tell herself that she was sophisticated enough to handle it. Now that it had happened she knew she couldn't. She felt her hands tremble.

"Ada," he acknowledged with a conspirator's smile. "Command performance."

They sat next to each other on the trip up, shared Eastern Airlines's coffee and Ada Hutchinson gossip and by the time they landed at Logan Carlys felt perfectly calm. George had been absolutely correct and perfectly pleasant. He never referred to the time in Carlys's apartment and he did not touch her once, not even accidentally.

"Would you like to take the six o'clock flight back?" George asked. "I could pick you up at Ada's office."

"Fine," said Carlys. "She wants me to look at the plans anyway. She wants me to begin preparing a release about Yankee Air's new offices."

Carlys felt perfectly confident and perfectly in control as she accepted George's invitation. Their one little indiscretion, she told herself, was ancient history. Besides, she told herself, this was the eighties. Sexual fidelity was as outmoded as the handwritten letter, the manual adding machine, or the rotary dial telephone and her marriage was, after all, as modern as the silicon chip.

High tech was the 1980s version of the 1880s gold rush. The infant industry spread beyond California's Silicon Valley and Route 128 outside Boston to such cities as Boise, Idaho, and Boulder, Colorado, Lake Success in New York and Stamford in Connecticut. *Time* magazine recognized the phenomenon by voting the computer "Man of the Year." Enormous opportunities opened for small, state-of-the-art assemblers, programmers, subcontractors, and systems manufacturers. Stories abounded of engineers coming up with a new wrinkle and going from a desk and a secretary to a multimillion-dollar operation with a hundred employees in a year or even less. Within two years of its founding, Osborne projected revenue of a hundred million dollars, and according to a *Wall Street Journal* story, more than 150 companies ranging from IBM to two-person, mom-and-pop outfits were making and marketing computers. Venture capital was anxious to cash in on the latest fad and an entrepreneur working from a kitchen table could hope to make a million in a year.

E-Z Tech—whose manuals were sold in bookstores, computer stores, and by mail order—rode the crest of the boom and Kirk, who had become well known for turning failure into success, turned success into a bonanza. In the first four months after Kirk had bought E-Z Tech, sales of Marian Kramer's manuals doubled and by the end of the first year had quadrupled with no end in sight as the computer boom boomed on. Less than a year after he had bought E-Z Tech for a quarter of a million dollars, Kirk turned down a flat million for it.

"There's nothing," Carlys said, in awe, "like being in the right place at the right time."

Kirk nodded but didn't smile. His success seemed to give him no pleasure. He was a cautious and brilliant businessman. He had a tiger by the tail, and he didn't want that tiger to turn. He didn't want what was happening to Osborne and Atari to happen to him. He was also, Carlys thought, a different man. A man driven not by pride but by anger. Despite his success he was still obsessed with revenge against Howie and SuperWrite. Even more, he was obsessed with Dearborn Paper and Printing. Howie had absolutely refused to make Dearborn part of Kirk's settlement.

"It's mine!" Kirk kept saying. "I found it. That bastard isn't good enough to set foot in Dearborn's parking lot! It's mine and I'm going to get it back!"

Carlys didn't understand the obsession and soon learned not to ask about it. Even the mention of the name sent Kirk into a state of almost volcanic rage.

In the spring of 1982 he was deep into negotiations with Tele Record, a manufacturer of high-quality telephone answering machines in Peachtree City, a suburb of Atlanta, and in February he told Carlys that he was definitely going to buy Tele Record. He planned to use money borrowed against his E-Z Tech stock to buy the company and merge it with E-Z Tech.

"Kirk, aren't you rich enough?" Carlys asked, feeling lost in the whirlwind of his success.

"Never!" he said. Although he didn't know it, he feared

running out of money the way his father had once feared running out of shirts. "I can never be rich enough!"

Carlys almost feared Kirk's obsession with business. She wondered if it were in some way connected with a fear that he might share the fate of his father and brother, and the thought that success was a guarantee against that fate. But she said nothing. She never told Kirk that she knew the truth about his father's death. The subject was, obviously, too painful for him even to discuss. The knowledge made her much more compassionate to Kirk, much more sympathetic to him. She knew how painful it had been to see a mother slowly die of a terrible disease; how much worse it must have been to have a parent die by his own hand. Kirk's suffering was beyond Carlys's comprehension and only now and then, when she was in a particularly melancholy mood, did she allow herself to resent him for excluding her from from such a crucial and tragic part of his past. Only now and then did she allow herself to resent the way that, as an executive wife, she had always put her husband first. Executive husbands, she was learning, always put business first.

Carlys had heard of golf widows and football widows; she had never heard of corporate widows, but that was what she was. Kirk worked fourteen-hour days. He was out of town—in Charleston, at trade shows, manufacturing plants, and distribution centers at least two or three nights a week. These days Carlys slept alone as often as she slept with her husband. She didn't blame Kirk. Kirk, she realized, hadn't changed; only their marriage had. It had survived failure. She wondered if, ironically, it would survive success.

When she shared a taxi with George back into the city Carlys wondered if he would make some kind of pass at her. He didn't. He was pleasant, he was charming, he was humorous, and he left her at her door without even a word about seeing her again. She was relieved—and disappointed.

"I told Ada that the new ticket counters are almost *too* good. They look rich and successful," she told Kirk when he got home later that evening. Smiling, she teased him, ruffling his hair. "Just like us."

He looked up from the columns of figures spread out on

the coffee table in front of him and nodded absently, preoccupied with the merger with Tele Record. He had heard her, of course, but chitchat about a new ticket counter was boring and trivial compared to a multimillion dollar deal.

"Kirk," she said suddenly, hurt by the usual faraway look in his eyes. She wanted to distract him from his work, she wanted him to pay *some* attention to her. She was starved for that attention. She, suddenly, wanted *him*. "Let's make love."

"Now?" he asked almost insultingly, as if she had suggested putting mayonnaise on ice cream.

"Now," she said, smiling. "Here."

"Here? In the living room?"

"We used to," she reminded him, taking his reading glasses off for him and holding his face between her hands and bringing her face close to his. "We used to like it, too."

"Later," he mumbled, pulling away from her, putting the glasses back on, and going back to the problems with Tele Record.

Quietly Carlys retreated, smiling wistfully to herself.

She had become, she realized, a wife. Someone to be depended on, someone to be taken for granted, someone to be loved—when her husband remembered. Carlys tried not to resent it. She told herself that that was what marriage was like: the romance faded, the excitement went, and habit set in. She didn't realize that she and Bonnie shared more than just a husband; they shared a destiny. In the beginning, just like Bonnie, Carlys just wanted someone to talk to.

C H A P T E R 7

The big stories continued to be serious and depressing: martial law still governed Poland, the Iran-Iraq war ground on in seeming stalemate, warfare continued in the Middle East, and, at home, the state of the economy was still worrisome as the unemployment rate continued a year-long upward rise. The preoccupations of the Me decade continued—the outer Me toned and tightened by Jane Fonda's workout book and the inner Me seeking to tread the paths of the *Pathfinders*.

Perhaps it was spring and spring fever, perhaps it was Carlys herself, but when George called to invite her to dinner she accepted. After all, she had her husband's permission. Kirk had been in Charleston that entire week. He had called her at the office on Tuesday to say that he wouldn't be home until Friday.

"Why don't you get some theater tickets and invite someone to keep you company?" he suggested. He knew how lonely Carlys got when he was away so much, and although he kept promising to spend more time at home, somehow something urgent always came up and the promise kept getting postponed. "I think Lansing's in town this week."

"Lansing's not my idea of a fun evening," Carlys had replied, the disappointment still evident in her voice as she faced the lonely evenings, three more than she had anticipated.

"Well, what about George?" Kirk had suggested, guiltily, remembering all of Carlys's complaints about never having any fun anymore now that he was working his twenty-five-hour days. "You seem to like him."

"I'll think about it," Carlys had said. When she had casually mentioned her second encounter with George on the Boston shuttle, Kirk had asked her if she thought George were queer. Stunned, mostly because Kirk rarely spoke about other people's sex lives, she had replied that she had never given George's sexual preferences a thought.

"I'll bet he is," Kirk had said. He remembered seeing George get out of the elevator. "He's too beautiful to be straight. Beside, most interior decorators are queer anyway."

"George is a designer," Carlys said, realizing why Kirk had so blandly invited George up to their apartment while she was still in her robe. Kirk didn't seem to pick up on her point and he dropped the subject. Obviously he felt George was a safe escort when he was out of town.

Dinner was adult, dinner was risky, dinner was serious. Dinner, above all, wasn't lunch. Lunches were safe; lunches were innocent. Dinner was different: Dinner wasn't safe; dinner wasn't innocent. Lunches needed no motivation; there was always an intention to dinner.

Carlys wondered what it would be like to have dinner with an attractive man who wasn't her husband, who wasn't a business associate, who was the kind of man who at one time in her life would never have noticed that she was alive. She also wanted to see what *she* was like: to see if she could handle a situation that simultaneously attracted her and scared her. She wanted to see if she was as sophisticated as she thought she had become. After all, she wasn't Carlys the loser anymore: She was a vice-president of a major public relations firm; she had a fabulous Upper East Side apartment, a rich and powerful husband, a fast-track Manhattan life; and once, apparently without any lasting guilt, she had made love to a man who wasn't her husband. She wanted to see if the woman and the image matched.

At lunch Le Cirque is breathlessly fashionable, a galaxy of celebrated names and faces ranging from *A* to *Z*: Arianna Stassinopoulos to Jerry Zipkin. At dinner it is conservatively fashionable, catering to an older crowd, to wealthy businessmen and jaded Eurotrash and weary politicians accompanied, mostly, by their wives. No one who had anything to hide would have dinner at Le Cirque.

"Your eyes look like emeralds," George whispered as the headwaiter seated them. He took her hand across the table and did not let it go. Jade, he knew, was having dinner with Mary Lou and Steve. She had been very secretive about some big deal they were working on and she would be out very late.

"Thank you," she said, glancing around and removing her hand from his, relieved, even though she didn't feel the slightest bit guilty, to see that there was no one she knew in the dining room.

"Kirk's crazy to leave you alone so much," he said, following her glance and looking at her until she dropped her eyes.

"The veal sounds good," she said, burying herself in the menu, wanting to ecape his intensity. "Or maybe the pasta primavera. I think it was invented here."

After they ordered Carlys began to talk nervously about

the office. He smiled and listened, allowing her to relax, as she told him crazy-Lansing stories and impossible-Sergio stories. In turn, he amused her with crazy-client and impossible-client stories and, by the time dinner was over, Carlys was having a good time, the way she always did with George. As she confidently left the restaurant, pleased with the way her Adolfo suit looked and flattered by the public attention of a man as attractive as George, she had entirely forgotten her nervousness.

"I wish we had done this sooner," she told him at ten-thirty when they stood on the corner of Park and Sixty-fifth saying good night. "I'd almost forgotten how much fun fun can be."

"I was afraid to ask."

"Afraid?" Carlys had trouble imagining that anyone could be afraid of her.

"Afraid you'd say no." George always let women know how much power they had over his happiness.

"You shouldn't be afraid of me," she said. The spring night was warm; the traffic made its dignified way down Park and Mary Lasker's yellow daffodils swayed in the islands in the middle of the avenue. Manhattan was at its expensive, glittering best, revealing, as George and Carlys stood there, why it was one of the most exciting, most alluring cities in the world.

"No?"

"Of course not," she said. "You know you can say anything you want to me.

"Really?"

"Of course."

"Then I'll say what I've wanted to say ever since that morning. What I want," he said softly, so softly that she had to lean toward him to hear, "is to be alone with you."

"No," she said smiling, trying to be nice about it. "No, really. I mean it. I meant what I said that time at the King Cole Bar. Let's just be friends. I don't want anything to happen that we'll regret."

"Nothing's going to happen that you don't want to have happen," said George. "I'd like to show you a co-op I just finished in the Sherry Netherland," he said. "The people haven't moved in yet."

Carlys looked at him carefully, unsure about whether or

not to believe him. "I promise," said George. "I won't even touch you if you don't want me to."

"Well, all right," she said. "But George, I don't want you to touch me."

"All right," he said and smiled. "It's a promise."

She smiled too, feeling a little ridiculous, and together they headed toward Fifth.

*It was a chic pied-à-terre for a London-based business-*man. The seating, upholstered in gray suede, was built-in. A black granite coffee table held a stack of financial publications. Slatted blinds at the windows made for privacy, a sleek stainless-steel kitchen looked as if not even an English muffin had ever been toasted there. An equally sleek bathroom with a built-in sink and a stall shower was totally masculine, and a bedroom furnished with a bed, two night tables, and a leather Eames chair was dim and quietly luxurious.

"He's pared his life down to the basics," Carlys said admiringly, walking around, touching the leather chairs and running her hands over the buttery textured suede on the sofas. She told herself she was safe. She remembered and believed George's promise. Still, she didn't want to sit down. She didn't want to stop walking. She didn't want to have to look at George or meet his eyes. He sensed it and didn't force her. He allowed her to continue.

"I'm always thinking about paring down," she went on. "I never get around to it. I'm afraid to give up a favorite dress. Maybe one day it'll come back into style. I can't throw away old letters or photographs and I'm incapable of getting rid of saucers whose teacups have long since broken. . . ." She went on, knowing she was talking too much and trying to force herself to stop. "I guess I'm too sentimental for the pared-down look."

"Don't change," he said, coming up next to her. "Exactly the way you are is perfect for me." He reached out and touched her hair and she shrank back so quickly she almost lost her balance.

"No! You promised!" She was terrified. She wanted to run but she couldn't. She was falling back toward the bookcase and she lost her balance.

George reached out and steadied her. Then his arms were around her and he pulled her very close.

"I promise," he murmured, his lips against her ear. "I won't touch you if you don't want me to." Even as he spoke, he stroked her hair and his lips moved to her face.

"Please don't," she said weakly.

He drew her to him, feeling the length of her body against his, the softness of her breasts, the smallness of her waist, the curve of her hips, He kissed her tenderly and then deeply, his tongue caressing her lips and then exploring her teeth and the inside of her lips, assertive but not yet insistent, judging just how far to go, calibrating his desire to her response.

"No," she said, trying to push him away, trying to resist him, trying one last time to resist herself.

"Are you sure?" he asked, his hands moving over her. "Are you *sure?*"

"No," she said, barely able to speak. "I mean yes."

"That's what I thought," he said, and he began to kiss her face and her throat and the tops of her breasts, leaving a trail of heat and wetness and desire. Deprived of will, she allowed him to guide her step by step into the bedroom.

"Yes?" he asked as he unbuttoned her blouse and moved his hands beneath her bra, caressing one breast, cupping it in his hand, freeing it from the bra and kissing its nipple.

"Yes?" he asked again. "Tell me, Carlys. Is it yes? Do you want me?"

"Yes," she whispered, almost unable to speak. "Yes."

"Yes, what?" he asked, moving away for a moment, stopping what he was doing, depriving her of his touch for an agonizing moment.

"Yes," she said, barely knowing what she was saying, wanting him to go on, wanting him never to stop. "Please."

He began again, removing her clothes and exploring her with his hands and his mouth. He caressed her throat and her shoulders and the curve of her arms, her breasts, and the place where her waist curved in. Then, moving down to her navel and the curve of her hips and her now-swollen vagina, just before he tasted her, he pulled away again for another tormenting moment. "Do you want what I want?"

"Yes," she whispered, wanting only for him to continue.

"As much as I want?" he asked, his eyes on her.

"More," she said, putting her hand on his head, guiding his mouth down toward her again, closing her eyes and existing only for his touch. "Please."

Carlys abandoned herself to him, to his hands and his mouth, his taste and his smell, to the texture of his hair and the heat of his thrusting tongue and at the moment he was about to enter her, Carlys opened her eyes to look at him and, as she did, she saw the glint of her wedding ring as her hands wrapped around his neck. Quietly, not stopping the rhythm of what they were doing, she removed it and placed it on the night table, able to abandon herself to the act of adultery, unable to confront the symbol of her marriage.

Then, opening her eyes wide, Carlys looked deeply into George's as he entered her. She wanted to feel and to memorize every precise sensation; and once he was inside her she closed her eyes and opened her mouth to his so that she was surrounded and enveloped by him. She drowned herself in him and his smell and his taste and the texture of his skin. She gave herself to him, surrendered herself to him, her memory, her past and her present. When all the sensations became unbearable and then, suddenly, exquisite, Carlys did not hear the cry that escaped her lips.

"Shhh," George said gently, holding his hand gently over her mouth.

"Did I say something?" she asked, his hand startling her back into consciousness.

"No," he said softly and kissed her. "But you were lovely, just lovely."

She was surprised when, showered and dressed, she went down into the street and nothing was different. A surly Israeli taxi driver picked her up, took her uptown, and accepted her tip without a word. Lester, the doorman, wished her a good night and so did Charley, the elevator man. No one seemed to notice that there was anything different about her. She realized as she let herself into her apartment that the irregular hours she had kept, the late-night client dinners, the cram work-sessions, the trips to Washington and Boston that often got her back home at midnight had set the stage perfectly for an illicit affair.

She shut the door behind her and saw that her collection of blue-and-white spongeware standing on a scrubbed pine hutch was exactly the way she had left it, that her log cabin quilt was arranged at the foot of the bed precisely as it had been that morning, and, when she opened the bathroom cabinet, that her toothbrush and deodorant and Janet Sartin colored astringent were in exactly the same neat order in which she had left them that morning when she'd dressed for work. She didn't know quite what she'd expected. A silent accusation in a misplaced cosmetic jar? A pointing finger in a fallen quilt? A guilty payment in a broken sponge-ware pitcher?

She brushed her teeth, washed her face, put on her nightgown, got into bed, and ran her hands down her still-tingling body. She felt extraordinarily alive and mentally lucid. Here she was, in 1982, one of those enviable women who had it all—a career she adored, a husband she loved, a lover who had said, somewhere in the night, that he couldn't live without her.

This time, Carlys did not say—or even think—*never again.*

George got home a few minutes after Carlys left him with a kiss. Jade was already there. Sitting on their bed, dressed in a pretty robe, she was simultaneously watching "Night-line," drinking a cup of herb tea, and flipping through *Vogue.*

"Will and I had a late session," he said, still aware of Carlys's touch, as he kissed Jade hello.

"You'd better get set for more!" said Jade, making it obvious she had been dying for him to get home. She was always terrible about concealing her excitement. "Remember I said I'd make it up to you the time I couldn't go to your party and meet Matty Robinson? Well, Steve and I just made a deal with Mary Lou that Savin's can have the first Stefan Hitchcock boutique here in New York! We want you to design it for us!" She paused a moment, waiting for him to tell her how wonderful her surprise was. His silence shocked her slightly. "If you'd like to, that is."

"What made you change your mind?" George asked cautiously, not about to let her off the hook so easily. "I thought you didn't want to work with me."

"That was a long time ago. I wasn't sure about our future," said Jade, telling the truth. "I didn't know if things were going to work out between us. Now that we're living together I don't feel that way anymore."

Jade wanted to make love to him, but George begged off. He just wasn't in the mood. He was excited about getting the job of designing the first Manhattan Stefan Hitchcock boutique, but he felt that Jade was playing Lady Bountiful. Maybe it was his imagination, but he thought she wanted him to show his gratitude in bed.

"Do you mind?" he asked, feeling slightly guilty. He was afraid he wouldn't be able to get hard. He told himself it was because he had just made love to Carlys, not admitting that, in the past, being with one woman had never stopped him from performing with another. On the contrary.

"I feel sort of lousy," he said. "I think I might be getting the flu."

Jade said she understood. She *always* understood. George wished she'd get mad once in a while.

C H A P T E R 8

In the beginning the affair matched Carlys's fantasy of an affair and Carlys was an innocent. An affair, as Carlys imagined it, had nothing to do with real life. An affair was time out of time, borrowed time, stolen time, unreal time. An affair was a luxury, an indulgence, something nice a woman did for herself. The beginning with George was just like her fantasy. Two hours in the late afternoon, greedily devouring each other in a rumpled bed in an anonymous hotel room; stolen lunch hours and fleeting kisses; whispered phone conversations and expensive lingerie and chilled champagne in tall Baccarat flutes.

"You have the most beautiful skin, like velvet," George would say as he kissed her and caressed her. Kirk had once said things like that. He didn't anymore. He talked about net profits, returns on investment, and dilution of stock. He seemed obsessed with E-Z Tech.

"You never talk about anything else," Carlys said, tired of hearing about the business, its problems, its potential, its future.

"What else should I talk about?" Kirk asked, impatient with her implied criticism. After all, he was doing it for *her*. *Her* money was in the company. He was making *her* rich, too. "What could be more important?"

It occurred to her to say that the fact that his wife had a lover might be more important, but of course she said nothing. She allowed her moment of childish spite to pass.

When George gave her white and yellow freesias, she kept them in her office until their fragrance faded and their fragile creamy flowers turned brown. She tried but couldn't remember the last time Kirk had brought her flowers.

When she mentioned that she loved raspberries, George remembered and fed them to her, one by one, after rinsing them in champagne. She couldn't imagine Kirk feeding her raspberries if his life depended on it.

George surprised her with a take-out dinner for two from Lutèce, which they shared in bed. Kirk hated eating in bed. He said it was uncomfortable and he complained about the crumbs.

In the beginning Carlys was surprised that she felt no guilt. Somehow, not seeing as much of George as she wanted to increased the excitement, heightened the anticipation, made the sex even more explosive, gave her the feeling that because she was denying herself so often she was in control and her secret was safe. How could she feel guilty, she asked herself, when she never got nearly as much as she wanted?

She told herself that her affair was frivolous and unimportant and the sex, in this era of sexual license, was simply a healthy and exuberant expression of fleeting attraction to another man. Monogamy, she told herself, pleased with her *mot,* was only for those who had no temptations.

She even felt virtuous in the first few weeks of her affair because it actually seemed to be good for her marriage. Her affair made her take a good look at herself and what she saw didn't always please her. Now that she had a lover she became aware of the ways in which she had been taking her husband for granted. As much as she could accuse Kirk of an unromantic attitude, she realized that the habits and routines of marriage had made her just as unromantic as he was.

She had gotten into the lazy habit of putting on her big, white terry robe the minute she came home from work and wearing it around the house. It was comfortable, but it was not very sexy. She went to Saks and bought an elegant Sanchez robe of peach moiré and a pair of chic lounging pajamas in royal blue with contrasting red trim. On Saturday mornings, she realized, she often ran right out of the house, without makeup, in jeans and a sweatshirt, to go to her gym class. She would run back to the apartment at eleven, now sweaty and disheveled, to meet Kirk and decide what to do with the rest of the day. She began to take the time to put on a thin layer of base and blusher, a quick swipe of gloss and a spray of perfume, to put on slacks and a decent silk shirt so that when she returned home at eleven she didn't look as if she'd just fallen out of bed. She realized that it had been ages since she'd told him she loved him, and so she did. And when she realized that she almost never took the initiative in sex anymore, she did that, too.

"I miss you," she told Kirk as they watched television in the small den on one of the rare evenings he was home. She moved next to him on the sofa and put her lips close to his ear. "Let's make love."

She unbuttoned his shirt and moved her hand down his body.

She made a promise to herself that her husband would never find out about her affair and so all the things she did—such as buying the new robe and putting on makeup before her Saturday morning sessions at the gym—she did casually and matter-of-factly, never drawing attention to them. She was insanely careful about not doing all the things that tip off a straying wife: she didn't change her hairdo; she didn't buy stacks of new, sexy underwear; she didn't begin to wear new perfume; and she never, not once, no matter how tempted, quoted one of her lover's witty or interesting observations to her husband. She made it a firm rule that there would be no telephone calls at home, no telltale presents, nothing in writing, no love letters or romantic notes or sentimental cards. She promised herself that she would never be seen anywhere in public with George that could not be explained by business and, above all, she solemnly vowed that she would *never* tell another living soul about her affair.

Like everyone else, she thought she could handle it.

*Being kissed by different lips was thrilling; feeling a differ*ent body, a stockier and more muscular body, stronger and more insistent, against her body was intoxicating; tasting different kisses and licking a different texture of skin and inhaling a different man's scent was electrifying. She felt infinitely desirable, her body constantly in a state of sexual arousal. With George's kisses in her mouth and the memory of his flattering words, she felt more attractive to her husband; more responsive in his bed; less hurt when, preoccupied with E-Z Tech, he sat through an entire dinner without saying a word; less annoyed when he left her at a party to fend for herself; less taken for granted when he made plans for business entertaining that included her without consulting her first.

Having a lover gave Carlys perspective. She had found that for better or for worse wasn't the problem with marriage; it was the day-in, day-out dailiness, the being taken for granted, the ordinariness of domesticity that drained the romance from a relationship. Having a lover helped. Having a lover provided the excitement she missed. Having a lover held up a flattering mirror to herself. Having a lover made her appreciate the fine qualities of her husband: his energy, his integrity, his loyalty, his consistency. Having a lover seemed to be the ideal tonic for the predictability of marriage. Having a lover made her think more of herself and other people noticed her new self-confidence.

"You look wonderful," Michelle said. "What's your secret?"

"No secret," Carlys had replied casually, thrilled by her newfound adeptness at keeping her secret a secret. Carlys had always been, after all, a woman who for many, many years had led a dull life, a woman others tended to take for granted, a woman others tended not to notice. She had never *had* a secret. Merely having one was exciting. "Just good genes and healthy living."

"You did a brilliant job handling Boone's firing," Joshua Barnes told her. T. Chet Boone was founder and president of a real estate management company that was one of Carlys's accounts. He was prickly, arrogant, impossible to get along with, and finally, despite his successes, the board voted him out. The public relations problem had been to handle the firing so that Wall Street lost no confidence in the company and she had arranged to have Boone resign to accept a public service job she'd arranged for him through Barron & Hynes's Washington contacts.

"The stock closed at a new high the week after you announced his resignation," Joshua continued, "and now Chet is talking about running for office. He thinks you're a genius."

Carlys thanked Joshua for the compliment and never told him that the solution had come to her after a sweaty session of sex with George when, feeling relaxed and drowsy, she had lingered in his bed, savoring the smell of their lovemaking on his sheets.

She decided that lying was only for emergencies. She had never been in the habit of explaining her doings or her whereabouts, and Kirk didn't notice anything different because, in the very beginning, when her affair was simply an occasional indulgence, there wasn't much different *to* notice. She thanked her hectic shedule, which gave her all sorts of reasons to keep irregular hours, and the erratic, often last-minute demands of difficult clients, which sometimes forced her to work longer than she had expected, but which also now and then gave her the sudden surprise of a free hour or two.

Time, however, was one of the problems: There was never enough. Between her job—with its meetings and emergencies, obligatory cocktail parties, and command-performance dinners—her father's increasing fragility, the gym, the hairdresser, the busy social life she shared with Kirk, and all the usual household errands, Carlys's time was not her own. She and George made love in Carlys's apartment in March. They didn't make love again until the middle of April. The next time they saw each other was ten days later and, again, eight days after that.

"Can't I see more of you?" asked George. He loved being with Carlys, but he also noticed that one woman, a married woman, a woman who could never be his, was taking the place of the many women he had had during his marriage. Jade's schedule made his affair easy. Steve, like all the Seventh Avenue designers, showed his fall line in April. March, therefore, had been hectic with getting the line ready; Market Week in April was frantic with buyers. So far, George had not had to lie to Jade except for that very first time. Busy careers and their insistence on committed independence made the beginning of his affair with Carlys effortless, both morally and in terms of simple scheduling. "Once in a while isn't enough."

"If only I had more time," Carlys said. She felt the way he felt. The fourth time they'd made love was better than the third time. The second time was better than the first. Each time demanded a next time.

"Can't you *make* more time?" he asked.

"I'll try," she said and when, in the third week of May, Kirk went to Chicago for three days to line up new banking ties in that city and Jade was in Italy for a week reviewing the new fabric offerings, she and George saw each other three evenings in a row. Then she didn't see him again for two weeks. She went back to her husband. He went back to his lover. They were two people leading two lives and feeling in complete control of them.

"Carlys, Marion Kramer and his wife are coming to New York. They want to go to the theater," Kirk said. "Would you dig up some *Dreamgirls* tickets for them and make a dinner reservation at Sardi's?"

He assumed she would do what he wanted and he was right. Carlys's priorities were strict. Her affair always came second to whatever Kirk wanted.

"White and pale yellow?" Jade suggested as she and George discussed colors for the new Savin's boutique when she got back from Italy. She had seen a new boutique in Milan, one that was a warm departure from the cool conventions of mirrors and glass, one that was a step beyond the pastels of postmodernism. She described it to George and, excited, he saw what she saw. Together they came up with a concept that wasn't his or hers, but theirs.

The boutique was a big step for both George and Jade. Savin's had committed to buying a hundred thousand dollars' worth of merchandise per season. A third of that, Jade and Steve calculated, would be profit. It meant a lot of money and a showcase in the most important retailing center in the country. For George it was a big-ticket, high-profile commission. He and Jade worked on it together, but it was Jade who put it into words: Modern but romantic.

"Just like us," George said, kissing her hair. Between the excitement of Jade and Carlys and the important commission, his doubts, most of them, most of the time, had disappeared.

Of course, they never went anywhere together. They met in hotels—arriving and leaving separately. The Waldorf, they discovered, was excellent for illicit lovers. There were entrances and exits on all four sides, through several restaurants and bars. No one seeing her enter or leave could guess where she'd come from or how long she'd been there. The Plaza, for the same reasons, became another favorite. George would usually arrive first, get the room, and call her at her office. He would let her in and they'd fling themselves at each other and breathlessly make love, perhaps have something to eat, and then make love again until eleven, when Carlys absolutely felt she ought to leave. As long as she got home by midnight she felt that no one in the building would notice a thing. She had, in the days and years before George, come home that late often enough for it not to be remarked upon.

As her affair headed into May, Carlys thought she had never felt better, had never looked better, and had never functioned better. She handled her complicated life with confidence and aplomb. People kept asking her what she had done. Had she lost weight? Had she spent a weekend at a spa? Had she had a facial? Had she done something different with her hair? Only Kirk seemed oblivious. She wondered what he'd say if he ever found out. Which, of course, he wouldn't. Still, sometimes she wondered.

C H A P T E R   9

George was the perfect lover both in bed and out. When Carlys told him that she didn't want him ever to call her at home, he told her that she didn't need to warn him. Of course he never would.

"I would never do anything to hurt you," he told her tenderly. "I'm a lover, not a destroyer."

He seemed exquisitely attuned to her moods and feelings.

"Is everything all right?" he asked gently in early June. "You seem upset."

"I am," said Carlys, and she told him about her worries about her father. Jacob Webber had fallen that Saturday night in his apartment and had been unable to get to the telephone. On Sunday, when Carlys arrived for their weekly lunch, he did not answer the doorbell, and when she finally let herself in with her own key, she found him, semiconscious, lying where he had fallen in the small hallway between his bedroom and bathroom. She had to locate the doctor who was covering for Jacob's regular doctor and get Jacob to the emergency room at Roosevelt Hospital, where an X-ray showed that he had fractured his hip.

"Thank God I found him when I did," she told Kirk when she finally reached him by phone after his Sunday morning golf game. "He was already severely dehydrated. The doctors were worried about kidney failure. . . ."

"Is he all right now?" asked Kirk.

"Yes," said Carlys. "He's full of drugs and he's sleeping."

"Then there's nothing I can do now," Kirk said. "I'll see you later this afternoon."

"But can't you come into the city now?" Carlys asked, aware that Kirk hadn't even offered to come in and simply be with her. With her father's accident, his mortality was evident. It was obvious that, one day, Jacob would die and she would be parentless. Even though taking care of her father was nothing new, Carlys felt particularly upset. "I need you."

"I told Ned Bates I'd have lunch . . ." Kirk began and then, finally giving in to Carlys, said that he'd drive right back into town. "I'll meet you at the hospital."

Kirk visited Jacob, who was glad to see him, but that evening Kirk wanted to keep a dinner date with an important bank contact and early the next morning he flew off to Kansas City to talk to a software supplier, leaving Carlys alone to deal with both the practical and emotional after-effects of her father's accident.

"I've been afraid this would happen for a long time now," she told George that Monday afternoon, happy and relieved that he could find time to meet her. She told him how upset her father's obvious frailty made her feel. "I've begged him to get a live-in companion but he refuses. All I can think about is what would have happened if he'd fallen on a Sunday night and I hadn't called until Tuesday."

"Don't torture yourself," George said, taking her into his arms after listening to her pour her heart out. He knew instinctively that she wanted comfort, not sex, and all he did was hold her. "You did all you could do."

George didn't say anything anyone else couldn't have, but the fact was he was the one who cared enough to say it, and Carlys was grateful to him for listening. She didn't blame her husband for having to leave town but, on the other hand, she didn't blame herself for turning to her lover for comfort.

George was infinitely considerate and infinitely imaginative when it came to sex. He seemed to know a thousand kisses and a thousand caresses she'd never dreamed of. He was inexhaustible, and unable to get enough of her. He knew Carlys's body better than she did, and she told him once that he had actually introduced her to it and to the pleasure it was capable of feeling.

"Oh, I didn't know," she whispered as he fondled her with his hands and his tongue. "Oh," she whispered as he excited her in ways she had never been excited, finding trigger points on her body that she hadn't known existed. "Don't stop."

"Never," he breathed.

He could bring her to orgasm after orgasm until she lay limp on his bed. She had never known that a man could make love as long and as excitingly as George could. He seemed able to control himself for the pleasure of seeing her go out of control.

"Stop. Don't," she would beg him, almost in tears. "I can't bear it anymore." And then, in the next breath, she would cling to him and beg him to continue. "Oh, please. Don't stop. I don't ever want you to stop."

She wondered sometimes whether other people had the same kind of sex that she and George had; whether others felt the same intensity, the same shattering heights and unbelievable releases. She doubted it. How could anyone else feel what *she* felt, the *way* she felt it? She tried to remember what sex had been like with Kirk in the beginning, but she couldn't recall it with any vividness, couldn't bring the memories back with any force. George and his tireless sensuality had apparently obliterated her sexual memory.

Although Carlys tried not to compare her husband and her lover, she couldn't help it. She couldn't remember the last time she and Kirk had had a real conversation, a conversation about Life with a capital *L*, about how they each felt about who they were and what they were doing. With George she did talk about Life with a capital *L*, about life and her place in it, about her job and how she felt about it, about herself, her dreams, her aspirations, her fears, and her failure. With Kirk, conversation tended to be about business, about what-they-were-doing-and-who-they-were-doing-it-with. When they didn't talk about business, they talked about the nuts-and-bolts problems of everyday life.

They talked about how long Lucy, in a post-divorce funk, was going to have to see her expensive shrink and how long they'd get the bills. Kirk would ask if the dry cleaning was back and she'd wonder if she really had to ask the Stennises back for dinner so soon. They'd been so boring, Gordon and Iris. He had drunk too much and all she had talked about was the decorator she'd hired who'd turned out to be impossible and what was she going to do about him. *Impossible!,* Iris had kept saying, *but so talented!* All her friends were green with envy over her new living room. Now it was time to do the dining room and she just didn't know if she could take his tantrums and snippy insults again. . . .

Carlys's eyes had rolled when Kirk said that they really ought to invite them over. Gordon Stennis ran a venture capital firm and Kirk had the idea of going public in the back of his mind.

"What I love about us," Carlys told George in almost-giddy relief from the unending demands and stresses of her life, "is that reality never intrudes."

George was more than just a lover; he was becoming a confidant, someone to replace Norma, who had dropped out of Carlys's life. Carlys told him things about her deepest fears and deepest feelings that she never told her husband. She and Kirk never had the time. In addition, Kirk was always extremely uncomfortable when it came to talking about feelings.

"If you had met me before I was married you'd never have looked twice," she told George, wanting him to have some idea of what she was really like. "I was a mouse, a wallflower, a real loser with men."

"I can't believe it," George had replied. "In fact I *don't* believe it."

"It was marriage that changed everything," Carlys explained. "After I got married I really grew into myself. I became the person I had always wanted to be. Did marriage change you?" By now, of course, Carlys knew quite a bit about George and *his* life.

"Not marriage," he said. "Having Bobby did, though."

"You miss him, don't you?" Carlys's heart broke for George. He had told her that he had never gotten over the devastating loss of having his child live halfway across the country. It was like having a hole torn out of his heart. He thought of Bobby every day, he said, and every day he missed him.

"All the time," he admitted with the sadness he showed whenever he mentioned his son, and although Carlys had never had a deep feeling about having children of her own, her heart went out to George.

"And you haven't been tempted to get married again?" she asked. "Are you tempted to marry Jade?"

"We're happy the way we are," he said, "as lovers and best friends. We want to keep things the way they are."

Carlys tried not to ask too many questions about Jade. She didn't want to sound jealous. She had no reason to be jealous and she reminded herself that she *wasn't*. She was simply having an affair. Still, she couldn't help it. She was curious about this other woman, about Jade.

"Does she know about me?" she finally asked after two months, unable to resist.

"Does your husband know about me?" he replied, resenting the intrusion. He had never liked discussing one woman with another. Instinctively he had never told Carlys that he and Jade were living together.

"Of course not," Carlys said.

His eyes told her that his answer was the same. She wanted to know more about him, more about Jade, more about his relationship with her. How serious was it? How long had they known each other? How had they met? She was dying of curiosity; in fact she was consumed by it. What she really wanted to know was: Who was prettier? Who was better in bed? Who made him happier? Her? Or Jade?

She managed to suppress her curiosity and told herself that the little veins of jealousy that had begun to appear and to bleed were completely irrelevant. After all, if anyone had a right to be jealous it was George. She was the married one. She was the one who was unavailable. Nevertheless, jealousy continued to stab at her, and with enormous willpower that made her proud of herself, Carlys kept her curiosity chained and her questions unasked. After all, she kept reminding herself, all she really wanted was an affair.

One night at the end of May, while making love to Kirk, Carlys began to lick his nipple with her tongue, circling it first one way, then the other. George often did that to her and it drove her into a frenzy. She hoped that if she did it to Kirk, he might get the idea and do it to her.

"Hey!" he groaned with surprise and delight, "where did you learn that?"

"*The Hite Report,*" she answered immediately, as pleased

with her glibness to her husband as she had been of her casualness with Michelle. "Where else? Now, shhh. . . ."

She telephoned George the next morning as soon as she got to her office.

"You almost got me into trouble with my husband," she teased.

"Only almost?" he teased back. "I thought I was a better lover than only 'almost'! What happened?"

"I'll never tell!" she replied, still teasing, and she never did.

Still, as soon as she hung up she felt as if she'd done something she didn't quite feel comfortable with, something she didn't really approve of. At first she thought her phone call had been in questionable taste and chastised herself for making it. Later, upon reflection, she decided that it was doing the same things in bed with her husband as she did with her lover that was objectionable. She decided right then and there upon another rule: What she did with George stayed with George. What she did with Kirk stayed with Kirk. After all, the last thing she wanted to do was make either her husband or her lover angry or jealous. All she wanted was for all of them to be happy and, as Kirk and Carlys celebrated their seventh anniversary, everyone was.

C H A P T E R   10

*A*t *the age of thirty-seven Carlys discovered desire* and desirability. She had both a husband and a lover and it was wonderful. All she wanted was more. So did her husband and so did her lover.

"Do you know what I want for dessert?" Kirk whispered ten days later. They were at an elegant Park Avenue dinner party and Kirk, seeing how other men responded to

his wife, felt a sudden inexplicable surge of possessiveness
and desire.

"What?" she asked, smiling, aware of flirting with him—
something she had forgotten to do for years until her affair
reminded her how.

"You," he said, amazed at the words that were coming
out of his mouth. Making hasty excuses they had run back
home and flung themselves on each other, something they
hadn't done since the very first year of their marriage.

"Now what?" asked Carlys dreamily after they had made
love, running her hand along her husband's long, lean back,
so much more delicate than that of her lover, who was
more stockily built.

"More of the same," he said huskily, and shuddered
deliciously under her touch.

"I can't get enough of you," George told Carlys in late
June. Carlys had left the office early and told Kirk she was
going to the gym on the way home. Then, using a devious
route through the Third Avenue entrance of Alexander's,
across Fifty-ninth Street through the side entrance of
Bloomingdale's and out the front, into a taxi, down Lex
and up Park, she had met George at the Regency. "I have
to have more of you," he said. He was inside her, moving
in and out of her slowly, holding her eyes with his as he
spoke. "I want to kidnap you and take you away with
me."

"Where would you take me?" she asked, moving with
him, keeping exactly to his rhythm, aware of their wetness
and her nipples against his skin.

"Far away," he said, still moving slowly, infinitely stretching out the pleasure, "where no one could ever find us."
Then he moved suddenly, crushing his mouth to hers,
finding her breasts with his hands and thrusting strongly
and deeply into her. "I'd fuck you and fuck you and fuck
you," he said, moving in rhythm with his words as she
wrapped her legs higher around him, wanting him to plunge
even more deeply into her.

He began to have lover's fantasies about their spending
more time together.

"I wonder what it would be like to spend the night with

you," he said. They were in the Pierre. The room faced north and had a million-dollar view of the park. Carlys and George never even glanced at it, so entranced were they with each other. "I wonder what it would be like to be able to touch you whenever I wanted, to sleep with you in my arms, and to wake up and kiss you."

"It would be wonderful," Carlys said. Wistfully she added, "But we'll never know, will we?"

"Why not?" he asked, wondering what the hell he was doing. Why was he taking these chances? Was the danger worth it? Was it *that* exciting? Was he *that* dependent on Carlys? Was he more fearful for his virility than he admitted?

"I'm married," she reminded him.

I wish we could spend a weekend together," he said over club sandwiches they had ordered up at the Warwick, knowing he was asking for trouble but unable to help himself. He kept wanting more and more of Carlys. Why couldn't enough be enough? Helplessly, sure that Jade would leave him if she ever found out, driven by a motivation he didn't understand, he plunged on. "Just one weekend. We'd go someplace beautiful. We'd walk in the woods. We'd read in front of a fire. We'd make dinner together. We'd sleep under a big, down comforter. I'd wrap you in my arms and never let you go. Can't you find an excuse?"

"No," she said regretfully. "Kirk knows I've never been busy over a weekend."

"But couldn't there be a first time?" he asked.

Wordlessly she shook her head and, gently touching his face with her fingertips, kissed him softly in sad recompense.

George's sex life with Jade, once better than ever because of Carlys, was now becoming a problem. It began to concern him on the evening of the day he had met Carlys at the Regency. Savin's had accepted the plans for the Hitchcock boutique and construction, going as smoothly as construction ever did, was well under way. He met Jade at Savin's after the store had closed to check progress. Afterward they had gone to P.J.'s for a hamburger. Jade seemed unusually animated. She told him that she and Steve had signed their first licensee that day, a manufacturer of sheets and towels. There would be more money than ever, Jade said, thrilled, because now it would be coming in from royalties, too. She joked about needing an investment counselor any day now and she talked about buying herself a fur coat and the delicious dilemma that that posed: Should it be a fisher polo coat? Or a mink trench coat? Or, possibly, a sable reefer? She was giddy with the possibilities. She also told George that she had a surprise for him.

"Guess what it is?" shs asked, almost unable to contain herself.

"What?"

She opened her purse and handed him a slip of paper. It was a receipt from New York Audio for a turntable, speakers, and a tuner in all the brands George most wanted. The amount, which had to be well into the thousands, was blanked out with a grease pencil.

"What's this?" he asked, feeling his gut tighten.

"You've been complaining about our stereo," she said. "I decided to do something about it." She smiled at him, her eyes shining, waiting to be thanked. "It's a present," she said, glowing. "From me to you with love. I've left the placement up to you," she added, wanting to make her gift absolutely perfect, "because you know exactly how you want it."

"Thank you," he said, swallowing, not telling her that *he* had planned to buy them new audio equipment but that he had put it off until the boutique was finished and Savin's had paid Kouras-Goldberg in full. "It's wonderful!" he said, trying to mean it, trying not to feel the way he had felt when Ezra Tydings had handed him the keys to an expensive brownstone and Ina had showed off a glamorous Black Willow. "Just wonderful!"

Jade held his hand on the walk home, and when they got into bed she began to kiss his face slowly and lovingly, all over, the way she always did when she wanted to make love. He returned her kisses and tried to make love to her, but couldn't.

"I guess I'm beat," he said reluctantly, moving away from her. "It's been a hell of a week."

"That's the third time this month," said Jade. She held him as she spoke, telling him with her embrace that she loved him, that she was on his side, that his problem, if there was one, was her problem, too. "Is something wrong?"

"You know goddamn well nothing's wrong!" he exploded, his voice much too loud. "Can't you just, for Christ's sake, leave me alone!"

He loved Jade, but she was beginning to be too much for him. Unlike Ina she didn't run to her father. She didn't have to run to her father—or to anyone. Jade could do whatever she wanted whenever she wanted. She didn't seem to need anything or anyone. Sometimes he wondered if she even needed him. The terrible part was that *he* needed her, personally—and professionally.

With Ina George knew that his marriage to Ezra Tydings's daughter was invaluable professionally. With Jade it was worse. She did not merely provide him with contacts. Jade gave him what she gave Steve—literally the energy and the inspiration that made the work he did with her the best work of his life. Working with Jade—on the early Hartley's store, on the showroom, on the Savin's boutique—George had finally found a distinctive style. His prior work, he knew, had been good but safe, attractive but derivative, appealing but conventional. In collaborating with Jade his work had found a form and a shape of its own. Modern but romantic, sleek but warm, restrained but luxurious—the look was distinctive and, for the first time in his professional life, George was aware that, finally, he was leading and others were following. The "Kouras-Goldberg look" that design and architectural writers described was really, and George knew it, the Jade Mullen look.

The more George realized he needed Jade, the more he realized he also needed Carlys.

"I don't even see you once a week," George told Carlys. "At least you can spare the time for me once a week."

She juggled schedules, lied to Kirk more than she wanted to, and shortcut her job. By early July she was meeting George once a week. Even that wasn't enough.

"You're addictive," George told her. "Like a drug. The more I get the more I want."

"I know," she said, burning for him. "I feel the same way."

* * *

"What do you tell Jade?" Carlys wanted to know as July came to a close and she and George were seeing each other once and sometimes twice a week. The weather burned hotter and so did their passion. The pain of his failures with Jade was assuaged by his strength with Carlys.

"Usually I don't tell her anything," he said. He didn't like to discuss Jade with Carlys. Jade was special; Jade was everything to him. Although he could be sexually unfaithful to her, he resisted any other kind of betrayal, even verbal. "She travels a lot and so do I."

"You mean that sometimes when you're in Chicago you're not?" Carlys asked.

"Precisely," he answered, smiling and tracing the curve of her breast with his finger. "And now let's change the subject."

By early August, a prisoner of pleasure, Carlys was seeing George twice a week. They made a point of never using the same hotel twice, and the only thing that bothered Carlys about her affair was that George usually asked her to make the reservations.

"Pretend you're my secretary," he advised her. "It sounds better that way.

But it didn't feel better. Carlys had managed to lie to Kirk without too much guilt, but she loathed lying to anonymous room clerks. She hated pretending to be someone she wasn't. She hated referring to George as Mr. Kouras. She hated going into unfamiliar hotels, taking the elevator to an anonymous floor, ringing a doorbell, and waiting for George to let her in. It felt shabby and sneaky and furtive.

Carlys hated the charade but counted it as the price of her indulgence because the moment she was with George, the moment they were in each other's arms, all her discomfort, all her embarrassment disappeared and she felt fully alive again in a magical transformation that seemed only to get more and more exciting.

Nevertheless, George sensed that something was bothering Carlys. He was afraid that she might be thinking of breaking it off and the thought of not having her made him panicky.

"I wish you were free," George said over and over. "I

wish I could be with you, that we could be together, that you could be mine."

He spoke so intensely, so sincerely of his yearning and his need for her, of the ways she made him happy, of the ways she meant everything to him, that soon Carlys found it painful to remind him that she was married. She found it cruel to tell a man who yearned for her, who longed for her, who told her that he'd do anything to have her, that his wishes could never come true. Nevertheless, she tried to be honest.

"I wish we could, too," she said, because sometimes she did. "But how can we?"

He looked at her with such pain that she felt she had struck him.

"I love you," he told her bitterly as the leaves began to turn. "And you're just having an affair."

As the leaves began to fall, their affair became more than just an affair and everything began to get out of control.

The Husband

"Married? Of course I'm married,
Isn't everyone?"
—KIRK ARNOLD

CHAPTER 1

THE PAST
GROSSE POINTE—PRINCETON—CHICAGO—AKRON
—MINNEAPOLIS—GRAND RAPIDS

*K*irk Arnold was all the golden WASPs George Kouras
had ever wanted to be. He had been born into the right family
at the right time in the right place. He had looks, brains, an
excess of charm, and, no soppy rich boy, he had added
earned money to inherited money. Yet Kirk Arnold was a
man with two stories. The public story was a story of a
man and his successes; the private story was a story of
a man and his losses.

He was born in the last depression year of 1934. Untouched by soup kitchens and Hoovervilles, bread lines
and boarded-up mills and factories, he grew up on a twenty-
acre estate in Grosse Pointe with every material and intellectual advantage rich and loving parents can provide.

Kirk went to Grosse Pointe Country Day school, where
he got straight A's and graduated as class valedictorian; to
Miss De Vriess' dancing class, where he wore white gloves
and learned to foxtrot; to the Grosse Pointe Country Club,
where he won the club's tennis championship year after
year. He spent summers in his family's rustic lakefront
house in Petoskey working on his tennis game, learning to
sail, necking with the "good" girls and going all the way
with the "bad" girls. At fourteen he began working summers at the family printing business, which his grandfather
had founded and of which his father was president.

When he graduated from high school Kirk was accepted
by his father's alma mater, Princeton. There he was bick-
ered by the aristocratic Cottage eating club, played on the
tennis team, became business manager of the *Daily Princetonian*, and earned honors in his economics major and

history minor. He romanced intellectual girls from Bryn Mawr, society girls from Vassar, rebellious girls from Bennington, and looked forward to a future as assured as everything else in his life: He would return to Grosse Pointe, go into the family business, marry the right kind of girl, and live the same comfortable life his parents had. None of this last was ever mentioned; it never had to be. Kirk Arnold came from a family in which the unexpected never happened.

"Take care of your brother. You have to set a good example for him," Clifford and Elyssa Arnold told Kirk when he was three and Elyssa came home with a new baby named Scott, at first a resented rival, but soon a beloved brother—Kirk's best friend, ally, confidant, and cohort in mischief. Both boys had the same parents, the same upbringing, the same advantages. Yet they were as different as day and night, as close as minutes on a clock.

Kirk was the good one, Scotty the hell-raiser. Kirk was the dependable one, Scotty the unpredictable one. Kirk was the steady one, Scotty the wild one. Scotty could get away with murder. Kirk always got caught.

Scott was chubby and freckled. He had cowlicked, unruly hair and a twinkle in his eye. Kirk was tawny and blond, a classically handsome man in the American aristocratic tradition. Scott was the rogue, Kirk the gentleman; Scott the cut-up, Kirk the square. Scott got into fights and arguments, his childhood was a combat zone of hair-raising trips to the emergency room, stitches, scraped knees, breaks, bruises, and black eyes. Kirk was a negotiator, a peacemaker, and a diplomat. Scotty talked with his fists, Kirk with words.

"If you weren't my brother, I'd think you were chicken," Scott advised Kirk, and yet it was Kirk who would one day try to kill him and, another day, save his life.

In late June of 1953 at the end of his junior year at Princeton, Kirk went home to Grosse Pointe for a two-week visit with his family before taking off for Europe with two friends from Cottage. Filled with fantasies inspired by that famous Princetonian, Fitzgerald, and his drinking pal, Hemingway, the three young men planned to go to Paris where, through a friend of a friend, they had an introduction to George Plimpton. They looked forward to sampling the romantic bohemian life, which they pictured mainly as sleeping late, drinking lots of cheap red wine, and making love to rebellious debutantes who read Sartre, discussed existentialism in Left Bank cafés, and believed in free sex.

During that two-week holiday back home Kirk tried to talk his high school girlfriend into going all the way, sold his sailboat and used the money to make a down payment on a white MG, drank too much beer with Scotty one Saturday night and festooned the country club lawns with toilet paper.

Late on the afternoon of Clifford Arnold's forty-eighth birthday, getting home from a tennis game, Kirk opened the garage door to park the MG. The impact of the carbon monoxide was like a punch in the face. He reeled backward and, gasping for oxygen, he groped his way through the poisoned air. He yanked opened the back door of his father's Cadillac and pulled the hose out of the partially opened back window. Then he saw his father. He was in the front seat, slumped across the steering wheel. The gun was still in his hand, his blood still fresh and red. Clifford Arnold had committed suicide. Always meticulous, he had left no margin for error.

"Dad!" screamed Kirk, switching off the ignition and pulling at his father's still-warm body. "Dad!"

There was no answer.

Denying the evidence of his own eyes and refusing to allow his brain to absorb its significance, Kirk flung open the big garage door. His father's head, shattered from the bullet wound, lolled to one side. Kirk pulled him out of the poisoned air of the garage. I can save him! Kirk said to himself as he tenderly placed his father's body on the grass in the clean, fresh air. If I do everything right, my father will live.

Using the kiss-of-life technique that he had learned in a Red Cross life saving class, Kirk put his mouth over his father's and forced air into his father's lungs. Five minutes went by, then ten, but Kirk didn't give up. He remembered what his teacher had said. Sometimes, he had said, it took twenty minutes or more to get a response. Don't give up!

Dad! Breathe! Twenty minutes and then thirty. Please, Dad! Please! Forty minutes and then an hour. The warmth drained from Clifford Arnold's body and the blood crusted and dried on his face, a shattered face now soaked with his son's tears. Please, Dad!

At some point Kirk screamed out loud: "Please, Dad!" There was no answer. There was no one to hear.

Kirk returned to the garage, got out the bright red plaid stadium blanket that Clifford kept in the trunk for football games at Ann Arbor, went back outside, and carefully covered his father's body. He returned to the garage again and, leaning into the car, took the note addressed to him that his father had left on the front seat, read it, and put it into his pocket. He wiped his tears away with the tail of his tennis shirt and, using the far door that connected to the servants' wing, he went inside.

Marie, the maid, was in the kitchen decorating the birthday cake with blue frosting. *Happy Birthday to Dad.* Marie had just begun tracing *Dad* with the pastry bag as Kirk rushed wordlessly through the kitchen. The sight of the red blood smeared all over his tennis whites made Marie gasp.

"Mom!" Kirk called out.

Elyssa Arnold, still in her golfing clothes, was in the dining room setting the table for the festive birthday dinner. Concentrating on her task she didn't look up. The radio was on in the kitchen and that summer's big hit "How Much Is That Doggie in the Window?" burbled through the swinging door, filling the room with a bizarrely inappropriate silliness as Marie looked in, unsure of what was happening, uncertain about what to do.

"Don't go into the garage!" Kirk was barely able to choke out the words. His tears had dried now but his heart raced erratically, stopping dead cold, starting again with a painful lurch in his chest.

"I wasn't planning to," Elyssa Arnold said absently, continuing to take the sterling butter knives out of their gray Tiffany silvercloth roll one by one. She held each up in turn to see if it needed a last-minute swipe with the polishing cloth. "I've already done all the shopping. We have everything we need."

"It's Dad," Kirk said, his voice breaking. "He's dead—"

Elyssa stared at her son, saw the blood on his face and hands and shirt. Then in horror, the meaning of the words registering, she swayed and lurched, and Kirk, instantly by her side, held her up. She turned her head away from him and supported herself with a hand on the polished and festively set dining table.

"He shot himself," Kirk said.

"Passed away." Elyssa corrected him automatically. "Say he passed away."

They were silent for a moment.

"He kept saying he would," she said in a strange, far-away voice, shaking her head in immediate, unquestioning acceptance of Kirk's words. "But I didn't believe him."

As Kirk put his arms around her she broke down. Kirk held her as she cried, trying to comfort her, completely focusing on her as a way of not thinking about himself. When she could finally control herself she looked up at Kirk.

"Tell your brother. Please tell Scotty," she said, weeping quietly now. She reached into her pocket for a Kleenex, found none, and, blinded by her tears, reached out for a napkin, and began to sob into the stiff white damask. "I can't. I can't face it. Please, Kirk. Tell Scott. Someone has to tell Scott. He's in the poolhouse."

While Marie stayed with his mother Kirk ran to the poolhouse.

Scott had just ripped open a new sack of chlorine and was measuring it out into an old, dented metal measuring cup.

"Scotts-ville?" Kirk said, using his private name for his brother. By now, completely preoccupied with his mother and his brother, Kirk was in superficial control of himself. He did not allow himself to know that he could still feel the touch of his father's inexorably cooling mouth on his own or that he could still taste his father's blood on his tongue. He cleared his throat again as Scotty looked up curiously. He was usually the one who showed up covered with blood from some scrape or another. Not Kirk. He wondered what was going on.

"What's up?"

"It's Dad," Kirk said, blinking at the transition from bright sunlight to shaded poolhouse, seeing drops of blood floating weightlessly in the air around him. "He . . . passed away."

"Passed away?" Scott repeated, the metal measuring cup suspended in stop-action. Now it was Scott who blinked rapidly several times, his pale hazel eyes suddenly unfocused. "You mean dead?"

"Yes," said Kirk. He swallowed hard, and forced the word out. "Dead."

"I don't believe it!" Scott screamed and threw the metal cup across the room. It clattered noisily along the tiled poolhouse floor, a sound Kirk thought he would never stop hearing.

"Just now. In the garage."

"You're lying!" Scott shouted.

"I found his . . . him," Kirk said. He needed to tell someone. He needed someone to talk to. He needed to pour out his pain and shock and grief. "He did it himself. Twice. He shut himself up in the garage and turned the ignition on. Then he used his gun."

Scott stared at his brother for a moment and then lunged for him. The sudden, fierce attack stunned Kirk, pushed him back until he stumbled across the open bag of chlorine.

"You bastard!" Scott screamed, coming at Kirk again, swinging ferociously at his face and body. "You bastard! It's your fault."

"Scott!" Kirk shouted, stunned, crying. "No!"

"Oh, yes!" Scott yelled, all the years of resenting Kirk crashing into his memory. Kirk, the good one. Kirk, who got the good grades, who never got into trouble, who got all the prettiest girls, who went to Princeton and was going to Europe. He was Scott, the problem. He was the one who had trouble in school, who was always being punished, who was always being asked: Why can't you be like your brother? All the hatred boiled over and Scott lashed out. "Dad wouldn't have done it if you had stayed here and helped him the way you did before. It's your fault!"

"Dad wanted me to go!" Kirk said, holding his hands up, trying to ward off Scott's punches, trying to defend himself from Scott's brutal and unfair words. "It was his idea. He bought me the ticket. He gave me the money!"

"Bullshit!" yelled Scott, moving in beneath Kirk's upraised hands and punching him in the body, and then, when

Kirk moved his hands down to protect himself, Scott swung at his face again, breaking his nose. Kirk could hear the cartilage break and feel the blood flood his nostrils, choking off the air. Suddenly he was wildly enraged. Overwhelmed by the rapid, shocking sequence of the discovery of his father's doubly successful suicide, his failure to revive him, his mother's complete breakdown, and his brother's sudden, vicious attack, Kirk totally lost control.

"Bastard!" shouted Kirk. He moved in toward Scott and began to punch wildly at him, wanting to kill him.

CHAPTER 2

The gardner, working in the nearby rose garden, heard the shouts and scuffling and broke up the fight, but not before both brothers were covered in blood and green granules of chlorine. The gardener took Kirk to the doctor where his broken nose was attended to. Scott suffered nothing worse than scratches and bruises and a black eye. Still, forever after, Scott would never forgive Kirk.

"You tried to kill me!" he said over and over during the years still to come, and in a secret part of himself Kirk knew that his brother was right. For that one split second he had wanted to kill him.

In the next days it was Kirk who took care of everything— the doctor and the funeral home, the notice for the newspaper and the arrangements for the burial, the grieving friends and employees, his devastated mother and bitter brother. Kirk comforted his mother and tried to win Scott back. He wanted Scott to be his best friend again. He needed his brother, his ally, his confidant, but Scott, drowning in some private, bitter rage, wasn't available.

"I'm sorry about the fight," said Kirk even though it was Scott who had started it.

"Fuck you," Scott snarled and, from then on, left whatever room Kirk happened to be in.

"It was your fault, you do it," Scott said when Kirk asked if Scott wanted to help pick out the clothes in which their father would be buried.

"It was your fault, you do it" was Scott's bitter reaction to everything from what cemetery should be chosen to what music, if any, should be played.

The only thing of his father's that Scott wanted was the gun.

"Why?" asked Kirk, thinking it was such a ghastly memento.

"None of your business," said Scott, who took the gun and, refusing to allow anyone to touch it, kept it on top of his bureau.

Kirk wrote and delivered the eulogy, greeted the mourners, cleaned out his father's office, and assured his employees that their jobs were secure. Following his mother's wishes, he told everyone that his father had died suddenly from a massive heart attack and saw to it that nowhere, not even on the death certificate, was suicide ever mentioned. As his father's note had requested, in the days following his discovery of his father's body, Kirk took care of his mother and his brother. He canceled his trip to Europe, met with his father's lawyer and executor, Bill Wurrant, and took care of a-thousand-and-one legal and financial details with which his mother was too distraught to deal. He tried to comfort his mother when she blamed herself for not taking her husband's threats of suicide seriously and he tried to explain to Scott that not only had his trip to Europe been their father's idea, but that he had done everything humanly possible to save their father. They did not, could not, would not listen to him. His mother still blamed herself; Scott still blamed him.

"It was your fault." Scott said with words and without words. He apportioned blame and Kirk accepted it.

On a ravishing day at the end of June, three weeks after Kirk had found his father's body, Kirk and his mother were at the breakfast table. Despite the tragedy Elyssa insisted that all the routines of everyday life be continued as if nothing had happened. Marie bustled around in the kitchen.

Toast in a silver rack stood next to a silver pot filled with hot coffee. Small porcelain dishes held honey and marmalade. Freshly squeezed orange juice waited in a frosty pitcher. Scrambled eggs cooled on three plates.

"Scott!" Elyssa called upstairs for the third time, "your breakfast is getting cold."

Elyssa turned to Kirk and sighed. Scott had always been difficult, unmanageable.

"Scott's not eating," she said in the uninflected, vaguely remote tone she had adopted since her husband's death, a death she always referred to as a heart attack. "He's lost too much weight."

"I'll go get him," Kirk said. He would never know why he did what he did, but some instinct, some terrible premonition, made him take the stairs two at a time and barge into Scott's room without knocking. The window was open, the curtains were blowing back into the room and Kirk saw Scott standing on the roof. The gun that had killed his father was in his hand.

"Scotty! Don't!" Kirk screamed and scrambled out to his brother and grabbed him from behind, hugging him around the waist.

"Leave me alone!" Scott yelled. His eyes had the same stony, furious look they had had in the poolhouse. He tried to push Kirk away from him. Scott was taller and bigger than Kirk, heavier-boned and more muscular. "Goddammit! Leave me alone!"

The two brothers grappled. Scott was stronger, but Kirk was more determined. He had seen his father die and he had been helpless. He was not going to let his brother die. This time, he wasn't helpless. He twisted Scott's wrist back painfully, forcing him to drop the gun. Kirk heard it fall to the ground with a thud. The two brothers continued to struggle, teetering back and forth on the edge of the rain gutter that ringed the roof. The gutter began to pull away from the roof with loud pops as the rivets broke under their weight.

"I said leave me alone!" Scott screamed, trying to shove Kirk back through the window.

"Never!" shouted Kirk, his arms around Scott in a crushing grip. He had refused to give up with his father, and he refused to give up with his brother. "Never!"

Back and forth the two brothers struggled, panting, determined. Suddenly Kirk's foot got trapped in the gutter, his grip on his brother momentarily loosened, and Scott pitched himself off the roof taking Kirk with him.

Kirk reached the ground first; Scott fell on top of him. Scott's injuries were limited to a broken arm and bruises. Kirk didn't die, but for weeks he wished he had. He had broken his left arm, his collar bone, and several ribs. His lungs were pierced, his left ankle shattered, and, for a while, the doctor feared that he would lose the sight in his left eye. The fall had taken Kirk into a rhododendron bush whose pointed branches brutally scratched his face, peeling off shreds of skin and severely injuring his eye, leaving a deep scar through the brow. Kirk spent six weeks in the hospital where his eye, just barely, was saved.

"I was afraid I'd be blind," he told his doctor. "I was trying to get used to the idea."

"Now you won't have to," said the doctor kindly. He smiled and expected a smile in return. Instead he got tears.

Kirk cried for the first time since he had held his father's body in his arms. He cried and cried, tears pouring out of the eye that had almost been lost. His father's life had been lost but his eye had been saved. Why? It wasn't fair. He would gladly have given his eye in exchange for his father's life.

He had lost Scott, too. Scott blamed Kirk for their father's death and he never once visited Kirk in the hospital. He would gladly have given his eye to have Scotty back, the old Scotty who had been his best friend, his ally, his cohort, his confidant, his beloved brother.

The worst injury that Kirk suffered was not a physical injury, but an injury to his soul. Scott now accused him not only of being responsible for their father's death, but also of trying to kill him and, in a secret part of himself, Kirk accepted that responsibility.

If only he had stayed home that summer and worked. . . .

If only he could take back that moment at the poolhouse when he *had* tried to kill his brother. . . .

When Kirk was released from the hospital his mother told him why Scott hadn't visited. Scott was in Covington, a psychiatric hospital in northern Michigan.

"Why?" asked Kirk, shocked. A thousand questions ran through his mind. Why had Scott tried to kill himself? Would he try again? Was Scott going to get better? Would he ever get his brother back?

"Dr. Basilynn said he was very depressed. He needs help," said Elyssa numbly. She lived on tranquilizers now, but even they did not blot out the pain of the summer's two tragedies.

"Does he think Scott will try again?" Kirk asked. He desperately wanted to know. "Does he think Scott—the old Scott—will come back again?"

"Let's not talk about it," Elyssa begged, the tears that were never very far away rising to her eyes again. "Let's talk about something pleasant."

The summer of 1953 had been a summer of two losses for Kirk Arnold—his father and his brother. It had been a summer of questions—questions that haunted him. Was whatever was wrong with his father and his brother wrong with him, too? Was he fated, one day, to do what they had done? Was he fated, one day, to try to kill himself?

Even more horrifying was another question: Would another time come when he would attack someone with the intention to kill? And, the next time, would anyone be there to stop him?

C H A P T E R   3

*I*sn't Scott Arnold the sexiest thing you've ever laid eyes on?" one of the older nurses asked Bonnie Willsey as they sorted linen. "He reminds me of James Dean." In six weeks of that summer Scott had turned from a freckle-faced hell-raiser into a lean and sullen loner.

"I think his brother is even sexier. He reminds me of John F. Kennedy," Bonnie replied, referring to the young Massachusetts senator who had just been on the cover of

Life on the occasion of his wedding to a debutante named Jacqueline Bouvier. "Only better looking."

"He thinks *you're* cute, too," teased the older nurse as Bonnie's delicate, fragile skin suddenly flushed scarlet. "I've noticed him looking at you." To tell the truth, Bonnie had noticed Kirk Arnold's interested glance, too. She often wondered what she'd say if he ever spoke to her.

Bonnie Willsey, like Kirk, had been born in 1934. Her background, though, could not have been more different from his. Her father, a Presbyterian minister, had run a mission offering shelter for the homeless and down-and-out in Chicago and her mother volunteered her time working in a South Side soup kitchen.

Bonnie grew up in a modest rectory, and she seemed to be the exception that proves the rule about PK's, as preachers' kids called themselves. Neither wild, nor rebellious, nor promiscuous, she was a mature and intelligent girl who decided in seventh grade that she wanted to devote her life to helping other people. The year she graduated from high school her yearbook entry said "Ambition: to be Florence Nightingale." She went to nursing school in Chicago and decided on a psychiatric specialty. She was a sensitive girl who knew that physical pain wasn't necessarily the worst pain. She was working at Covington as a student nurse the summer Scott Arnold was admitted.

At first Scott had refused to get out of bed in the morning, had refused to eat, had refused to talk. Except for his therapy sessions he isolated himself in his room with the cast album from *Wish You Were Here*, playing it over and over. Refusing all food and subsisting on cup after cup of black coffee, he lost twelve pounds in his first ten days at Covington.

"We're going to have to put him into the infirmary and feed him intravenously unless he starts to eat," Adam Marchant, Scott's psychiatrist, said in a staff meeting.

"He talks to me sometimes," Bonnie said. She had brown eyes and auburn hair and particularly fragile, lightly freckled skin. Her prettiness was almost Victorian in its delicacy, and she was the person on the staff closest to Scott in age. "Could I try to get him to eat?"

With Dr. Marchant's permission, Bonnie told Scott about

her favorite food: hamburgers with mayonnaise, a combination she had discovered when she'd gone with her parents to a synod meeting in California when she'd been fourteen.

"The roll has to be toasted, the hamburger has to be medium," she told Scott as they strolled the grounds—Scott slumped and gloomy in jeans and a T-shirt, Bonnie erect and clear-eyed in her crisp uniform. "With lettuce, tomato, and mayonnaise, and plenty of it."

"Mayonnaise on a hamburger? Yuck," said Scott, who liked ketchup.

"Well, what's *your* favorite food?" she challenged, putting her hands on her hips and turning to face him.

"Orange popsicles," he replied. He sensed that Bonnie really cared about his answer. She wasn't like the shrinks who asked bullshit questions and seemed satisfied with bullshit answers. "The kind with vanilla ice cream in the middle. Dad used to get them from the Good Humor man when we went to the lake for the summer. Our freezer was always filled with them."

Bonnie went into town that afternoon and stocked the Covington freezer with orange popsicles. Orange popsicles, which Scott would never again be able to look at, were all he ate for a month.

"My brother says you did more for him than the doctors did," Kirk told Bonnie the first time he ever spoke to her. They were in the common room where Bonnie was arranging magazines into neat stacks and watering the potted plants. "My brother owes you his life."

Bonnie flushed, the curse of fair-skinned people who can never hide their feelings. "It's just that I have more time to spend with the patients than the doctors do," she said modestly. "Besides, from what I hear, you're the one he owes his life to. You're the one who saved him, not me."

It was Kirk's turn to flush.

"He's my brother," Kirk said simply, as if it explained everything. Which, of course, it did.

What it didn't explain was why Scott refused to speak to Kirk except to beg him to get him out of Covington, which he referred to as a nuthouse.

"There's nothing wrong with me!" Scott insisted, angry and resentful. "All these shrinks do is ask questions. Questions, questions, questions. What the hell difference does it make? Just get me out of here!''

Kirk wanted to do what Scott asked. He wanted to make Scott happy; he wanted Scott to love him again. On the other hand, Scott had tried to kill himself and had almost succeeded. Dr. Basilynn, their family doctor in Grosse Point, had recommended that Scott get some psychiatric treatment. Kirk thought that they ought to listen to Dr. Basilynn, who had known Scott since he was a baby.

"Why don't you give it a chance?" Kirk asked Scott. "Dr. Basilynn says it can help."

"Help? Help who?" Scott asked, incensed, outraged, as if the conversation had nothing at all to do with him.

"Help you," Kirk said gently.

"Me? What do I need help for? I'm fine! I'm not crazy! Anyway, what does Basilynn know?" asked Scott, his eyes stony. "He's just an old quack."

Nothing Kirk said made any difference to Scott.

Elyssa Arnold drifted through the days in a Miltown haze. She never talked about her husband's suicide or her younger son's attempted suicide. She never talked about her feelings or what she planned to do with her life. Kirk took her to the movies and played Scrabble with her. He watched television with her and had dinner with her. They talked about everything—about Harry Truman's loud Hawaiian shirts; about Edmund Hillary, the New Zealander, and Tenzing Norkay, the Sherpa, the first men to climb Everest; about whether the new Dacron shirts really didn't need to be the ironed the way the advertisements promised. Everything, that is, except what had happened that summer.

"I don't know what we'd do without you," she told Kirk over and over that summer as he commuted between Grosse Pointe and Covington, between a bereft mother and a lost brother. "Thank God I have you to take your father's place."

Kirk, at nineteen, was no longer a boy, yet not really a man. Still, he did what he knew his father would have wanted him to do: He tried to take care of his mother and his brother. So far, there was no one to take care of him.

Kirk and Bonnie got into the habit of going for long walks on the tranquil wooded grounds of Covington and, for the first time since his father died, Kirk had someone to talk to. As they walked slowly, his movements limited by the cast on his leg and his still-painful ribs, Kirk poured out his heart to her.

"I should have known something was wrong," he told Bonnie. His voice had changed that summer: There was a huskiness which had never been there before. A huskiness that hinted at unshed tears. "My father always came down to breakfast in a suit and tie. I can remember the smell of his shaving cream. Lemony. Those weeks before he . . ." Kirk paused, searched for an acceptable word, then continued: " . . . did it, he used to come down in a bathrobe. Unshaven."

"A lot of men eat breakfast before they shave," Bonnie said. The way Kirk blamed himself upset her. His pain was becoming her pain and she didn't want him to feel it.

"Not *my* father," Kirk insisted, remembering Clifford Arnold's beautiful clothing and impeccable grooming. Until the weeks he'd come home from Princeton that June, Kirk had never seen his father with a hair out of place or without a jacket and tie. "I should have known then that something was wrong. I should have done something. Maybe I shouldn't have gone East to college. Maybe I shouldn't have gone to Princeton. Maybe I should have gone to the University of Michigan."

"Your father went to Princeton," Bonnie said. She didn't want to tell him that, from what she had heard the doctors say, Clifford Arnold would have done what he had done anyway. It was too blunt, too cruel to put into words. Still, she didn't want Kirk to take blame that wasn't his to take. "He wanted you to go there, too. You can't blame yourself," Bonnie said.

"If only I had stayed home all summer and helped out at work the way I always did," Kirk said. "Why did I have to go to Europe?"

"Your father wanted you to go to Europe," Bonnie reminded him. She was so touched by him that she had to restrain herself from reaching out to him. She wanted to comfort him, to touch the angry, red wound that ran through his eyebrow, a badge of his pain. "It was his idea."

"If only I'd taken him out to lunch, he wouldn't have

done it," Kirk said. "It was his birthday. I should have done something more. Something special. . . ."

If only, Kirk kept thinking. I should have, could have, ought to have, went the refrain that ran through his mind. Why didn't I? Why couldn't I? were the silent questions to which he could find no answers and no matter how much Bonnie tried to reassure him, he kept taking the blame.

Kirk blamed himself, pointed the finger at himself and talked to Bonnie about himself, his feelings, his guilt, his past, his shortcomings, his fear that he would never be half the man his father was, his fear that he would not be able to live up to his father's last expectations for him.

"What if I can't take care of my mother and brother?" he asked, tormented by Scott's angry rejection and his mother's cool remoteness.

"But you'll be able to," Bonnie said, reassuring him. The more she came to know Kirk, the more she admired him. He was patient with his brother. He was attentive and thoughtful toward his mother. Kirk made every other nineteen-year-old Bonnie knew seem like a child. Kirk seemed like a man, like someone who cared about others more than he cared about himself, like someone who saw life the way she did.

Hour after hour, as they walked the tranquil grounds of Covington, Kirk did something he had never done, had been brought up never to do, and that was think about himself and talk about himself. He even felt guilty about that, too.

"I'm amazed you put up with me," he told Bonnie, realizing that he had broken every rule the good manners he had been brought up with dictated. "People hate people who talk about themselves."

"I don't," she said. "It's interesting to listen to people talk about themselves."

"Really?" he asked and when she said yes, he didn't quite know whether or not to believe her. He finally decided she was just being polite.

"I love you. I won't forget you," he promised Bonnie on Scott's last day at Covington. Kirk was going to drive his brother home to Grosse Pointe and return from there, at his mother's insistence—the one decision she seemed able to

make—to Princeton to finish his last year. Scotty, who was in his senior year of high school, would go back to school and see a psychologist in Grosse Pointe. Dr. Marchant thought that a return to a familiar life might help Scotty.

Bonnie smiled and kissed him affectionately. Patients and sometimes relatives of patients regularly fell in love with staff; it was an occupational hazard and none of the staff members ever took it seriously.

"Yes you will," said Bonnie. "When people leave Covington they never want to think about it again. And they certainly don't want to be reminded of it."

"Well, I'm different," Kirk said. He had felt so hurt and sad and lonely all summer long. His father was gone; his brother was angry at him; his mother seemed so far away. He was unbearably lonely—except when he was with Bonnie. Only Bonnie seemed to understand his loss and his pain. Only Bonnie could make him feel warm again.

C H A P T E R   4

*K*irk Arnold returned to Princeton and graduated on schedule in 1954, the year *McCall's* magazine gave the world a new word—"togetherness." He had planned to move to New York where he had already been accepted into the training program at the investment banking firm of Hawes, Wainwright, and to share a Murray Hill apartment with two friends from Cottage. They would chase girls and success and enjoy a few years of bachelor life before settling down. Instead, at his mother's request, he went back home to Grosse Pointe. She wanted him to take over the family business, now being overseen by his father's executor, Bill Wurrant, and run by his father's vice-president, Gordon Marbley.

"Business has been going downhill," Elyssa told him frankly. In the year since her husband's death Elyssa Arnold had aged subtly but unmistakably. Although she was only forty-five she looked ten years older. There was a looseness in her facial skin, a deadness to her hair, an unbecoming thickening of her body. More disturbing to Kirk was the way her eyes and mouth didn't go together. There was a jarring difference between the half smile that hovered around her mouth and the glazed wounded expression in her eyes.

"Bill's honest and he certainly means well but he's mainly interested in his law practice," she told Kirk, turning to him now that Clifford was gone. Elyssa had been brought up to depend on men. With her husband gone, she turned desperately to her son. "Gordon's capable but he's not the businessman your father was. He doesn't care about the business the same way your father did—or the way you would."

Bill Wurrant had a different story to tell.

"Your father wasn't quite the businessman your mother thinks," he said. "The business was in bad shape long before your father died," he told Kirk bluntly. Bill had sandy, thinning hair and a golf-course tan. His law practice, specializing mainly in wills and estates, had made him comfortably well-off. His was a trade that thrived on care, precision, and conservatism. He was not driving a brand-new Buick and living in a nice Tudor house in Grosse Pointe because he was imaginative or because he took risks. "Your father made a number of bad decisions. Customers had already drifted away before his . . . accident. The company was too far in debt. Its assets were spread too thin."

Bill's words came as a surprise to Kirk and he resented the criticism of his father.

"Are you sure?" Kirk asked, not willing to accept Bill's assessment.

Bill nodded. "I'll show you the figures if you don't believe me."

"And what about Gordon?" Kirk asked, looking them over, surprised at the amount of debt and the faltering profits. "Dad had a lot of confidence in him."

"Gordon's a good manager, but he's no ball of fire," Bill said.

"So what should I do?" Kirk asked. He hated being

back in Grosse Pointe, driving the same roads his father had driven, breathing the same air his father had breathed. Most of all, he hated his father's house. He felt almost ill every time he drove up the driveway and parked in the garage. Every time he got into or out of his car the smell of carbon monoxide hit him like a fist. Whenever he passed the patch of grass on which he had so carefully lain his father the memory of blood nauseated him. Whenever he passed Scott's room he remembered the open window, the blowing curtains. Everything at home reminded him of loss and failure. All he wanted to do was get away.

"The most practical thing you could do is sell out," Bill advised. "Get the most you can get and go on with your life."

"How much is it worth?" Kirk asked, remembering all the times his father had turned down offers for the company, saying that he would never sell, that the business was for his children and his children's children.

"What it's worth and what you can get for it are two different things," Bill said, carefully looking over his half-moon reading glasses. He had found it prudent to prepare his clients for bad news. Clients, he had learned, did not like surprises.

"Cut the lawyer's bullshit, Bill!" Kirk said impatiently, hating the details that kept bringing back memories he wanted to forget. "Just give me a number."

"You'd probably be able to clear half a million dollars," Bill Wurrant said, using the number the accountants had come up with for the estate's tax return, a conservative but realistic number. "Invest the money. Your mother will be able to live on the income."

"At six percent," Kirk calculated rapidly, "that's thirty thousand dollars a year. My mother would have to sell the house."

"Many widows have to make adjustments," Bill said. He wasn't being heartless, simply matter-of-fact. "They just can't continue to live the same way they did when their husbands were alive."

"And what about Scott?" Kirk wanted to know. "He's going to be a freshman at the University of Michigan. How are we going to afford his tuition?"

"Can't Scott qualify for a scholarship?"

"No," said Kirk shaking his head. "Absolutely not." Scott had never been a student and in the year since his father's death his grades had plummeted. He had been lucky to get admitted to the University of Michigan. And not only was there Scott's tuition to think about but the continuing costs of psychiatric care. Scott seemed permanently angry, permanently sullen. The scrappiness, the rebelliousness, the unpredictability that had been amusing if exasperating in a child were distressing in a man. The psychologist he'd been seeing was not optimistic about a quick rebound.

For the first time in his privileged life, Kirk Arnold was faced with financial problems.

"You ought to sell, Kirk," said Bill seriously. Clifford Arnold had been more than a client—he had been a friend, and Bill only wanted to advise his surviving family of the most prudent course. "And you ought to sell now—before the company sinks any further."

"Sell?" Elyssa was aghast when Kirk told her about Bill's recommendation. "But your father wanted you boys to have the company. You know how much it meant to him to have a third generation of Arnolds in the business."

"The company's a liability," Kirk said, trying to be realistic. Bill Wurrant had shown him the balance sheets that day in his office. They made depressing reading.

"A liability?" Elyssa asked, angry, ready to defend her husband and his work. She would allow nothing to be said against him. "The company was your father's entire life! The company supported this family for two generations. It can again if you want it to!"

"I tried to save my father and I failed," said Kirk, understanding what his mother wanted him to do. The thought of living in Grosse Pointe made him sick. The fear of failing her the way he had failed his father terrified him. "What if I fail again?"

"You won't fail!" Elyssa Arnold said and clutched her son's hand, holding on to him for dear life. "You'll succeed! You can do it!"

"But I've never even worked full time," said Kirk, wanting to go to New York, wanting to start a new life free from the memories that clung to him like burrs. "You have to be realistic."

"You can do anything you set your mind to," his mother said, refusing to let him go. She needed him. Scott needed him. She would say anything, do anything to keep him. He was all she had left. He was the only one she knew would take care of her. "You got straight A's in high school. You graduated cum laude from Princeton. You were a first choice at Hawes, Wainwright. If anyone can do it, you can."

"But maybe I can't," Kirk said, trying to modify his mother's extravagant hopes. He wanted to leave and he knew how desperately she wanted him to stay. "Maybe I'm just not experienced enough, tough enough, knowledgeable enough."

What he didn't say, what he didn't even let himself think, was that the business had killed his father. What would it do to him?

*Dearborn Paper and Printing's primary business was print-*ing the owner's manuals that came with every new automobile sold. It also printed annual statements for the big Detroit motor companies, their promotional brochures and booklets. Another division published regional guides highlighting points of interest, motels, and restaurants in New England, the Mid-Atlantic States, the Rockies, the Southwest, and the Far West. The guides were given away free to motorists as a sales promotion tool by gas stations.

As Elyssa knew, as Kirk and Scott knew, Clifford Arnold had poured his life and his soul into the company Clifford's father had founded. The company, run cautiously by Kirk's grandfather, had survived the Hoover years, maintaining its position as a small and successful family business. As the forties and fifties went on, the company's profits grew and grew and Clifford Arnold turned the small and successful family business he had inherited into a medium-sized and successul family business. Nothing, it seemed, could stand in the way of ever-increasing prosperity—for America and for the Arnolds. Nothing, that is, except a mood disorder almost no one at the time had heard of called manic-depression.

As he grew richer and richer Clifford Arnold became

more and more buoyant, more and more convinced that he could make no mistake. As his business expanded he expanded, whirling like a top, faster and faster, until he finally whirled out of control. Needing more plant space, he bought a printing plant; needing greater delivery capacity, he bought a trucking company; needing more paper, he bought a paper mill. He eventually owned thousands of acres of Canadian forests for pulp, a truck manufacturing company, a chemical company that made the chemicals needed to treat pulp, and a foundry that made lead for printer's trays.

The buying was one of the early symptoms of the disease although, at the time, no one recognized it as such. So was the spending. As Clifford Arnold got richer his spending became more and more irrational. He ordered shirts by the dozen and suits by the half dozen. There were ties by the hundreds in his closet and sweaters by the stack and so many shoes that carpenters had to be brought in to build more storage shelves.

"Why?" Elyssa had asked her husband. "What do you need all this for?"

"I don't want to run out" had been his answer. "I'm afraid of running out." In the context it seemed that he was talking about clothing; in reality, as his fiftieth birthday drew near, it was life that he feared running out of.

He once bought a new Cadillac, put forty-two miles on it and turned it in, saying that he had decided he didn't like the color. The story became a family joke. The last Christmases of Clifford's life became orgies of giving, with presents piled high around the tree, stacked on chairs and sofas, filling the foyer, the dining room, and choking the den and garage. Elyssa was ashamed to have her friends over. She considered the display of wealth embarrassing.

"But I like to give," Clifford had said. "I love to give. Don't deprive me of my pleasure."

Elyssa didn't. How could she?

Clifford had the energy of three men; he needed less and less sleep. He seemed to be a superman capable of being everywhere at once, of solving problems others found resistant, of doing and being more than anyone around him. He shot off sparks and energy and ideas and there emerged, at this time, a dark side to Clifford Arnold. His temper became so short, his outbursts so abusive that employees who had worked for him for years quit.

His impatience became so extreme that he almost killed a child. Fretting and cursing at a traffic light, no longer able to tolerate the brief wait for the light to change, Clifford jammed down the accelerator of his car and missed a child on a bicycle by so little that the paint on the car fender was scratched by the buckles on the boy's book bag. Clifford was shocked and shaken by the near-miss, but no matter how he tried, he was unable to control his increasingly irritable and irascible moods. As the brilliance and the energy accelerated, picking up speed and momentum like a roller coaster on a downhill run, they began to turn in on themselves.

"Mr. Arnold, I don't think you should go ahead with that purchase of the Flint acreage," his comptroller told him. "You're overextended at the bank, the cash flow only just covers the liabilities as it is. . . ."

"And *I* think I should," Clifford had said, almost yelling. He ended his harangue by firing the man on the spot. "You're an accountant and you'll always be an accountant," he had raved. "I'm a genius and I'll always be a genius!"

Clifford went ahead and signed the paper for the purchase of a hundred-and-fifty-acre industrial park in Flint. Within six months, as his comptroller had predicted, he was unable to pay the notes. He was forced to sell a paper mill at a loss to meet the payments and, eight months later, when there was a fire in Flint, there was no insurance because, in his whirling frenzy, Clifford had never gotten around to approving the policies that still lay, unsigned, on his desk.

"It's my fault," Clifford told Elyssa. He seemed crushed, physically reduced in size and stature. Just as he had taken all the credit for his successes, he now assigned to himself all the blame for his setbacks. "All my fault."

"But it was a fire in an underground fuel storage tank. It was started by an electrical short," Elyssa answered, not understanding her husband's passionate insistence on taking the blame, not knowing how to deal with it, not even knowing that there was something that ought to be dealt

with. "That's what the fire department said. It had nothing
to do with you."

"Yes it did," Clifford insisted. "If I'd been there it
would never have happened."

"You're not God," Elyssa said, frantically trying to reach
him even as she began to realize that he was moving
further and further away. "You act as if you are, but
you're not. No one could have stopped it."

Elyssa never told Kirk what was happening and, a third
of a continent away in Princeton, he never saw it with his
own eyes.

If Clifford had been a gambler he might have been able to
stop going to the tables; if he had been an alcoholic he
might have been able to stop drinking. But he was a businessman, and he couldn't stop going to his office.

During Kirk's junior year Clifford continued to go to
Dearborn Paper and Printing every day but it was a different Clifford. His decisiveness was gone and along with it
his brilliant solutions to problems, his cheerfulness, even
his talkativeness and sudden, horrifying flares of temperament. Instead he became morose and depressed. He brooded
about the fire in Flint, castigated himself for the failure to
sign the insurance papers, and seemed afraid to take even
the most ordinary business risks. He began to talk about
suicide, but no one took him seriously.

Lithium carbonate, which most probably would have
controlled Clifford Arnold's disease, was discovered by an
obscure Austrian psychiatrist in 1949. It wasn't until 1969,
twenty years after its discovery, that it was recommended
to the Food and Drug Administration for treatment of patients suffering from violent mood shifts. Too late for Clifford, who killed himself in a depressive trough, too late for
Clifford's family, who lost a husband and father, and too
late for Kirk, who, as son and heir, inherited from beyond
the grave an impossible obligation to do everything right
that Clifford had done wrong.

"I can't bring my father back to life," he told Bonnie,
telling her about his decision as he was in the process of
making it that first summer after his father's death, "but I

can bring his company back to life. It's the least I can do for Dad. For my mother and my brother.''

Bonnie, whose parents had devoted their lives to caring about others, was moved almost to tears by Kirk's unselfishness. ''I'm so proud of you,'' she said. ''You remind me of my parents. I never thought I'd meet anyone like them. But I have.''

''You *have* to do it!'' his mother said, tears in her eyes, ''for me. For your brother. For your father.''

The last argument had been the one Kirk Arnold could not resist. Keeping the company alive would be a way of keeping his father alive. Besides, Kirk had convinced himself, it was a second chance. If he succeeded, perhaps he could make them all happy again.

In the end, of course, Kirk did not take Bill's advice. Instead, at the age of twenty-one, he named himself president of Dearborn Paper and Printing over Gordon Marbley and set about the almost impossible task of rebuilding it. If he was nervous, doubtful, or scared he never admitted it. He had been brought up to keep his problems to himself and, with his world crumbling around him, that is what he did.

With the energy of a man obsessed, Kirk threw himself into revitalizing the corpse of the business. He paid personal visits to every former, current, and potential customer, introducing himself and telling them about his plans for the company's future. He sold off the less-profitable divisions and strengthened the still-profitable ones. He brought the company's focus back to the original basics of automotive-industry printing, getting back customers that had drifted away, increasing his business with the ones who had stayed, and gradually beginning to do corporate publishing for non-automotive industry companies.

''But how do you know what to do?'' Elyssa asked, amazed at the confident way he went about reorganizing the business. She had thought he'd be good; she hadn't realized that he'd be a dynamo.

''Don't forget, I've worked for Dad since I was fourteen. I already knew quite a bit about the company,'' he said, speaking with a confidence intended to reassure her, a confidence he himself didn't yet totally feel, but one that would come with time. He was learning that the man playing a role often became that role. He was also learning that when the man inside the role disappeared, his memories disappeared, too.

"Bonnie, I love you. The last time I asked you to marry me, you told me to think it over and, if I still meant it, to ask you again," he told her in early 1955. They were walking along Lakeside Drive, the breeze from the lake fresh and strong in the early spring.

Bonnie had been amazed when Kirk had written her from Princeton, had visited her that first Thanksgiving after the summer they'd met, and had come to meet her parents over Christmas. She had thought she'd never see him again, that the rich and sophisticated girls at the Ivy League schools would make him forget all about her. After graduating from nursing school Bonnie had gone back to Chicago where she lived with her parents and worked in the psychiatric department of the Cook County Hospital. Now that Kirk was back in Grosse Pointe he visited her every weekend. Most of his friends from Princeton were getting married, and he wanted to get married, too. In 1955 everyone wanted to get married, and Kirk Arnold was no different from anyone else.

"I still mean it," he said, his arm around her as they strolled. "I meant it the last time and I mean it this time."

"But do you *really* mean it?" Bonnie just couldn't believe that he did. She couldn't believe she was smart enough, sophisticated enough, rich enough, or social enough for him. He had been born with a silver spoon; she was, literally, as poor as a church mouse.

"I really, *really* mean it." He was achingly serious. He had met her at the most vulnerable time in his life and she had helped him through it, reaching him in a way no one, not his mother or his brother wrapped up in their own grief, had been able to reach him. He was closer, intellectually and emotionally, to Bonnie than he had been to anyone. He loved her, most of all, precisely because she wasn't like all the girls he knew. She wasn't superficial, adept, glossy, social, spoiled. His father's death had changed Kirk, had made him more mature, more serious, more aware of how fragile life and happiness were. All the things he had learned since his father's death were things he admired in Bonnie.

He loved her for all the right reasons and he wanted to marry her for all the right reasons. "I love you and I want to marry you."

She took a deep breath and let it out. "I love you, too, Kirk," she replied. "And I want to marry you."

He took the orange-and-black Princeton scarf he was wearing and, with a whoop of joy that made passersby turn and stare, threw it around her and pulled her close to him.

"You'll never get away now," he told her, his face so close to hers he could feel the warmth of her fine, fragile skin. "Never."

"I'll never want to," she promised, looping the two ends of the scarf around him so they were, literally, bound together.

When Bonnie's father married them that same year the differences between them seemed so superficial as to be irrelevant. Rich boy and poor girl, altruist and businessman, sheltered daughter and too-youthful man-of-the-family were united by love and by God. Their future shone as brightly as the sun.

Four months after the wedding Bonnie became pregnant. The birth of their first child—a son, Geoffrey—took place in the same week in June in which Clifford Arnold had killed himself. The birth of his first child was an occasion for mixed feelings for Kirk. Sad memories of the past collided with joyous feelings for the present and future. He stood by his wife's bedside and, picking up his firstborn son, smiled while tears fell down his cheeks.

"You're thinking about your father?" Bonnie asked.

"Yes," he said, surprised at her intuition. "How did you know?"

"You always cry when you think about him."

"Do I?" Kirk was surprised. He hadn't known it himself.

"Yes," she said and, in looking at her husband, the mixed feelings shadowed on his handsome face, she felt a lump in her own throat.

A year later their second child, a girl, Lucy, was born.

"Birthdays are hard for you, aren't they?" Bonnie asked. On Kirk's last birthday they had had the worst fight of their marriage—a fight that started when Kirk had dropped the birthday cake Bonnie had baked and ended with his stalking out of the house and refusing to speak to her for almost a week.

Kirk nodded and swallowed hard. "They always remind me of one birthday that was also a death day."

CHAPTER 5

In the four years during which he ran Dearborn Paper and Printing Kirk brought the company back to life. His mother, unlike many widows, did not have to lower her standard of living. She continued to live on the estate Clifford Arnold had bought; she employed a maid and a gardener just the way she always had; she bought a new Cadillac every year, just the way Clifford always had. Unable to concentrate on his studies Scott dropped out of college. Kirk gave him a job at Dearborn Paper and Printing, first in sales, then in customer service, then as a plant supervisor. Scott started each new job with enthusiasm and energy that quickly turned to dissatisfaction and then anger.

"You're trying to keep me down!" he accused Kirk, blaming him now for his own unhappiness. "You want to be the big shot and I'm supposed to be grateful for a handout!"

Kirk created a vice-presidency for Scott, trying to make him happy. Scott got married for the first time when he was twenty and he and his wife lived comfortably on the salary Kirk continued to pay him whether he showed up for work or not.

"You're too good to Scott," Elyssa said. "You spoil him the way your father did."

"What am I supposed to do?" Kirk asked his mother, repeating just what Clifford had always said when faced with Scott's latest problem. "Throw him out into the street? He's my brother."

Kirk cared for Elyssa and Scott just as his father would have wanted. Not only did he do what his father had asked him to, he had turned failure into success and thereby accidentally discovered a career.

"I have a client in Akron," Bill Wurrant told Kirk one Saturday afternoon in the fall of 1958. "He owns an auto supply company and it's in bad shape. He wants to bail out but he can't find a buyer. As we were talking I suddenly thought of you. What would you think of doing for Acme Auto what you did for Dearborn Paper and Printing?"

"I don't know the first thing about the auto supply business," Kirk said. "I can't tell a spark plug from a carburetor."

"You *do* know about reviving a company. You've proved that," Bill said firmly. Bill was getting balder, thinner, richer. "Anything you needed to know about auto supplies you could learn in a day. Before you turn me down, let me tell you a little about the company. Where it's been, where it stands now. . . ."

Kirk listened, his interest piqued. Dearborn Paper and Printing had been doing so well that Gordon Marbley now ran the day-to-day operations. Success was making Kirk restless. Success wasn't nearly as interesting as the problems of failure. Running a business was boring in comparison to saving one. The more he thought about going to Akron, the more he liked the idea.

"You're confusing saving a business with saving a life," Bonnie said when Kirk told her. She foresaw a replay of the exhaustion to which he had driven himself when Dearborn had been in need of saving. "You think as long as you can save a business, you might be able to rewrite history and save your father's life."

"Come on!" said Kirk. "You don't believe that psychological horseshit, do you?"

"Yes," she said, reminding him that she had spent years working with psychiatrists and studying the ins and outs of the human personality. "In your case, I do."

Kirk shrugged and paid no attention to her. He appointed Gordon Marbley president of Dearborn Paper and Printing and went to Akron as a temporary vice-president of Acme Auto, finally, he thought, escaping the memories that Grosse Pointe held.

*   *   *

"What about us?" Bonnie asked, *thrown by Kirk's sudden* announcement. Every time the synod had assigned her father to a new church Bonnie and her mother had automatically moved along with him. "Where do we fit in?"

"I'll stay in Akron during the week," Kirk said. He was anxious to get away from Grosse Pointe. He was looking forward to escaping his mother's constant phone calls asking for his advice about everything from what kind of sandwiches to serve her bridge club to whether or not she ought to give the maid a raise. He was looking forward to relief from Scott's anger and resentment, from Scott's constant marital and financial problems that he was expected to solve. Most of all, he was looking forward to getting away from himself and the memories that seemed as fresh as ever every time he went to his father's house. "I'll come home weekends."

"But that's not a marriage," said Bonnie. Her own parents had eaten dinner together nearly every night of their lives. Without ever consciously thinking about it Bonnie had assumed she and Kirk would to the same. "And what about the children? They'll miss you terribly."

Geoffrey was five; Lucy, four. Geoffrey, elegantly long-boned like his father, counted the minutes every afternoon until his Kirk came home; Lucy, all blond curls and sunny smiles, had been a daddy's girl from the day she'd been born.

"It's only temporary," Kirk assured her, not even beginning to understand Bonnie's sharp sense of being left behind. When he and Scott had been growing up Clifford had often been away on business. In Kirk's family Clifford's absences had been taken for granted. Daddy being away on business was simply the way things were. "Just until I get Acme back on course."

"You want to get away from your family, don't you?" Bonnie asked suddenly.

"Of course not!" exploded Kirk. He wanted to get away from Grosse Pointe. That was all.

Bonnie didn't quite believe him.

They had been married only five years and already Bonnie was beginning to think that Kirk should have married one of the rich girls he'd gone with before they'd met at Covington. Bonnie didn't know how to give dinner parties—

and she didn't care. Bonnie didn't know how to handle a maid—and she didn't want to learn. Bonnie didn't know how to smile and be nice to business associates whose drinking, dirty jokes, and obsession with money offended her—and she didn't think that knowing how was anything worth knowing. Kirk and Bonnie had come from different worlds and the differences were just beginning to show. Bonnie was beginning to realize that being a successful businessman's wife was something that didn't interest her.

Kirk thought no more about the conversation but that night when he moved toward Bonnie in bed, wanting to make love to her, she pushed him away and turned her back to him.

"Temporary" turned out to be from that moment on—and it was the beginning of a pattern. It was the second time Kirk brilliantly reorganized and revitalized a failing business.

Kirk spent Mondays through Fridays in Akron, where Acme was located. He lived and breathed Acme and its problems. It was all he thought about and all he talked about.

"I'm sure glad Acme's a company and not a woman," Bonnie said more than once when Kirk got home for weekends. She was teasing but, then again, she wasn't. She was lonely and unhappy and she felt guilty and disloyal for blaming Kirk for her unhappiness. "You talk about that company as if you were in love with it."

"How could anyone be in love with a company?" Kirk asked, taking her literally, sensing that she was referring to deeper feelings, which he was unwilling to confront. Later he would decide that Bonnie had a point. Whenever he threw himself into a new company and its problems he lavished on it the care and attention of a man passionately in love. As soon as the problems were solved and the crisis over Kirk fell out of love—until the next company and the next set of problems came along. He was gradually becoming a man who reserved his strongest emotions for things that couldn't love him back, for things that couldn't hurt and abandon him the way his father and brother had hurt and abandoned him.

* * *

As uncomfortable as Kirk Arnold was with putting feelings into words, he was adept and effective in business. As soon as Acme began to show reduced inventories, an increased cash flow, and promised next quarter profits, Kirk began to lose interest.

"Acme doesn't need me anymore," he told Bill. "Have you got any more losers I can turn into winners?"

Bill introduced Kirk to Joseph Metzer, the president of Sandol, a Minneapolis company whose name had once been synonymous with home sewing machines.

"Can you do for us what you did for them?" Joe Metzer asked after outlining Sandol's problems with competition, foreign imports, and the decrease in home sewing.

"I can try," Kirk said. He went to Sandol with the title of vice-president, oversaw the reorganization of the company, turned its red ink to black, and on his twenty-sixth birthday got fired for his troubles.

"Fired?" Kirk said, stunned at Joe Metzer's words.

"You heard me," Joe said. He was stocky and dark, a tough man with hard eyes. "You did the job I hired you for. Now get out!"

Kirk went back to his office and, using the lamp on his desk, smashed all the windows in his office and left the building.

He got into his car, slammed the door, floored the accelerator, and roared out of the parking lot for the last time. He ran all the red lights and, when he got on the expressway, aimed his car like a bullet, driving like a kamikaze pilot. On his way throught an underpass he ran the car off the road and smashed it into a cement sign stanchion. He felt his head snap forward with the impact of the crash and heard the shattering of glass. The next thing he heard was the scream of a police siren.

"You're lucky you got out of this alive," said the state trooper who pulled Kirk from the wreck. The weather was clear, the traffic was light, and yet he had totaled his brand-new Buick and almost killed himself.

"You mean Joe Metzer is lucky he got out of this alive," Kirk replied, realizing that at the moment his car went out of control that he had been thinking about killing Joe. The trooper looked confused.

"Joe Metzer?" he asked, glancing into the front seat of Kirk's car. "Was there a passenger?"

Kirk Arnold shook his head. His forehead was bleeding where it had smashed against the steering wheel and his ribs were cracked. The cop put him into the squad car and drove him to the hospital. "No passenger," Kirk repeated.

"Then who's Joe Metzer?"

"The cocksucker who just fired me," said Kirk.

"Listen, mister," said the cop, "a lot of people get fired. It's no reason to damn near kill yourself."

"Sure," said Kirk bitterly. "A lot of people get fired. A lot of people don't get fired on their birthday."

That night Bonnie brought Kirk his birthday cake in the hospital. Kirk refused to eat it and when Bonnie left he gave it to the night nurse. Puzzled, she didn't know what to do with it.

"Just get it out of my sight," he said, and angry tears poured down his face. He hated birthdays.

"Joe hired me to tell him what he was doing wrong and when I did it, he hated me for it. He just waited until I got him out of the red and then he fired me. He wanted to do it all along," Kirk told Bill Wurrant the next day when Bill visited him in the hospital. Nevertheless, it was Joe Metzer who recommended Kirk Arnold for his next job.

In swift course, using the talents he had discovered working for the company his father had left him and refining them in other corporate situations, Kirk Arnold turned around a small Gary, Indiana, steel mill; directed the reorganization of a regional bank in Lake Forest, Illinois; and, at the request of a colleague of Bill Wurrant, accepted an assignment with a furniture company in Grand Rapids. It was in Grand Rapids that Kirk Arnold fell in love for the first time during his marriage. This time, though, it wasn't only the company he loved, but the woman who owned it.

Susan Morlake was tall, blond, blue-eyed, beautiful, and smart. She was also rich. Morlake Reproductions had been founded by her grandfather, a Welsh cabinetmaker, and expanded by her father. Upon her father's death half the company stock had gone to Susan and half to her mother. Susan's mother, Bessie, in her sixties, was a woman who liked her garden, her collection of porcelain cats, and the Grand Rapids library, of which she was a trustee. Of her husband's and father-in-law's business she knew virtually nothing. Susan, on the other hand, an only child, had loved the company, the smell of wood shavings and glue, the sound of saws and chisels, the bolts of colorful upholstery fabrics, and the comparative quiet of the office area with its busy clatter of typewriters and cheerful ring of telephones for as long as she could remember.

"Can I be president one day?" she asked her father when she was twelve-going-on-twenty-five, a gorgeous, animated, and irresistible child.

"Girls can't be presidents," her father told her affectionately. "You can be a president's wife."

Susan did just that—sort of. She married a Phoenix stockbroker, stayed married for four years, divorced him, and moved back to Grand Rapids. The year was 1963 and Susan had news for her father.

"Women can too be presidents," she told him, putting a copy of *The Feminine Mystique* on his desk. "But even though I'll be a 'nepot' I'm willing to work my way up."

Rodney Morlake had never been able to resist his daughter and he couldn't resist her now. Starting with the lowly spot in the mail room Susan began to learn about the furniture business. She learned about purchasing, billing, shipping, and, in the highlight of her year, accompanied her father to the big show in High Point, North Carolina, where all the manufacturers showed their new lines to the press and the trade. When Rodney died unexpectedly of a heart attack the following year Susan found herself in the peculiar position of being low woman on the totem pole and, together with her mother, also an heiress. If she wanted to be president of the company all she had to do was give herself the job. The problem was that she didn't know enough and she was smart enough to realize it.

"What should I do?" she asked Cecil McCormick, a lawyer and lifelong friend of her father's, who was on the board. Cecil advised her to rely on the board.

She sought advice from Broderick Laurents, a rich GM dealer and also a board member. Brod suggested she hire an outside president to replace her father.

"Help!" she cried to Bessie, who spoke to Leon Nash,

an old beau from before her marriage with whom she'd kept in touch over the years. Leon was a banker and he had a lawyer friend, Bill Wurrant, who knew this fellow who had an outstanding record in helping companies facing crises.

"I understand your experience is in rescuing companies that are in trouble," Susan told Kirk at their first meeting. "I'm not sure if you'll be interested in Morlake Reproductions. We're not in trouble but if I don't make the right moves we will be. Do you think you might be interested in a situation that isn't in crisis?"

He looked at her and smiled. She noticed the scar that ran through his left eyebrow and decided that it gave him a distinctly swashbuckling look.

"There's always a first time," he said, thinking of how much Susan reminded him of the Ivy League girls he'd once chased. Blond, longlegged, and beautiful, she was the kind of girl he'd grown up with, the kind of girl his parents had always thought he'd marry—the kind of woman *he* was now beginning to think he should have married.

Kirk spent eighteen months at Morlake and it was eighteen months of firsts. It was the first time he'd worked with a woman who was an equal, the first time he'd talked about his father in years, and the first time Bonnie worried seriously about her marriage.

"My father was in perfect health," Susan told Kirk during the first week he spent in Grand Rapids learning all about the company, its past and present, with Susan as his guide. "In fact he'd even been to his doctor the week before for a checkup. He came home and joked that the doctor had said we'd be stuck with him for another fifty years. Four days later he dropped dead. He got up to change the channel on the television set, fell to the floor, and that was it. There was no sign that anything was wrong. He just died. The doctor called it massive heart failure."

"That's exactly what happened to my father," Kirk said, at that instant borrowing Rodney Morlake's biography for his own father. As he uttered the words an enormous wave of relief washed over him. In Susan's eyes he was normal, just like other people. And in his own eyes he felt that way, too, suddenly freed from the shadow of his father's death, freed from the deep, dark feeling that he was destined one day to repeat his father's act. "He was perfectly healthy up until the day he died," Kirk said, feeling comfortable, for the first time in years, with himself, with his past. "Only forty-eight."

"For a long time I was afraid I'd die," Susan went on, confiding in Kirk. "I thought one minute I'd be here and the next I wouldn't. I was afraid all the time, but I gradually got over it."

"I know what you mean," he said, smiling compassionately, incredibly relieved to hear that someone else felt the way he had felt, relieved that he wasn't the only one, and relieved that he wasn't crazy.

*In the beginning Kirk and Susan rarely talked about any-*thing but business. They discussed inventories, orders, a proposed new line of furniture adapted from the currently fashionable Danish Modern, shipping, credit problems, and advertising plans. Kirk was surprised at how clear-minded and decisive Susan was; she was impressed at how knowledgeable about everything from billings to balance sheets he was.

"I didn't think women were interested in business," he told Susan after their first three months. The only women Kirk had ever met in business were secretaries or bookkeepers; in 1964 female executives were rare and the stereotype was that they were masculine, bitchy, or indecisive. The fact that Susan was none of those was a surprise—and an education—to him.

"That's what my father thought, too," she said. "The fact is that I seem to be much better at business than I was at marriage."

"I wonder," mused Kirk, making a rare introspective remark, "if that's what my wife thinks about me."

Susan looked at him curiously; whatever she thought of his remark, she kept to herself.

"Morlake Reproductions this, Morlake Reproductions that," Bonnie said in exasperation a year after Kirk had begun spending more time in Grand Rapids than he did in Grosse

Pointe. "I'm getting tired of hearing about it. Isn't it about time you found a new company to fall in love with?"

"You sound like a jealous wife," Kirk said.

"I know," Bonnie admitted. "It's just that I miss you. We're married but most of the time I live alone."

"Everyone can't be like your parents, together all the time," Kirk said. The amount of traveling he had to do for business was a longtime problem between them, one that seemed to have no solution, at least while the children were young.

"Maybe I'll have an affair," Bonnie said lightly. "Like the rest of the bored wives around here."

"I assume you're teasing," Kirk replied, stung both by Bonnie's words and by his own guilty thoughts about Susan.

"Of course I'm teasing," she said, but they both wondered if she really was.

C H A P T E R 6

The first time Susan and Kirk went to bed together they blamed it on alcohol. During the Grand Rapids market week, Morlake Reproductions gave a cocktail party for the trade and press to introduce a new line of Danish Modern designs. Susan, who was strictly a one-old-fashioned-on-Saturday-night drinker, sipped Scotch on the rocks nervously as she talked to buyers and reporters about the new line. Kirk, who made a point of never drinking on business occasions, did not drink at all during the party. Afterward he and Susan went to dinner, something they did often when work stretched late into the evening. He ordered a bottle of champagne.

"Champagne?" she asked, surprised.

"Absolutely," he said, as elated as she had ever seen him. His blue eyes seemed bluer; his tawny hair tawnier, its gold highlights a purer gold. "The party was a big success. Morlake used to be known strictly as a traditional house. With this new Danish line the trade now thinks of it as an across-the-board vendor. The combination of Morlake's reputation for quality and reliability plus an up-to-date line makes it a real competitor. The orders are going to show it, too. Three months from now Morlake will be selling to outlets that never even looked at the line before.''

"Really?'' asked Susan, thinking of her father.

"Absolutely,'' Kirk said, toasting the success he promised, making it real with the clink of their glasses.

"My father would be so proud,'' said Susan. "Gee, I miss him. I wish he were here.''

"I know what you mean,'' Kirk said. "Every time I sense that I've turned the corner with a company I think of my father. I'd give anything for him to know.''

They finished the champagne and Kirk ordered a second.

"I'm already sort of high,'' Susan confessed, covering her glass with the palm of her hand. "I'd better not have any more.''

"Do you mean I'm going to have to finish this all by myself?'' he asked in mock alarm.

"I guess so,'' she giggled. "What a fate!''

At ten o'clock they were the only people left in the restaurant; at ten-thirty they stood on Grand Rapids' deserted Main Street.

"If we were in New York I'd take you to the Stork Club,'' Kirk said, feeling expansive.

"If we were in New York I'd let you,'' she said, imagining how exciting it would be to enter the Stork Club with a man as handsome as Kirk Arnold. "But since we're not in New York why don't we just pretend we're at the Stork Club?''

He turned to her, bowed slightly from the waist, and, extending his hand, said, "Would you care to dance?''

There, under the traffic light that turned from green to red and back to green, they danced a sedate foxtrot, then a mock-sexy mambo, and finally, cheek to cheek, a whirling waltz that seemed to lead right to Susan's house.

"How did we get here?'' she asked, as they stood at her front door while she fumbled for the key. "My car's in the driveway but I don't remember driving it.''

"You can't be that drunk,'' he said, feeling slightly giddy himself. "You stopped drinking hours ago and you've had a big dinner plus coffee.''

"Then," she said, turning and putting her arms around him, "I must be drunk on you."

They woke in her bed the next morning, awkward and embarrassed, and during the next week they self-consciously confined their conversation strictly to business. Although he desperately tried not to, Kirk couldn't help but compare sex with Susan to sex with Bonnie.

Sex and money are said to be the main sticking points in marriage. The Arnolds never had a problem with money: Kirk always earned more than enough and Bonnie was totally unmaterialistic. Sex was something else. After the very early years of marriage Bonnie and Kirk seemed to be totally out of synch. When the children were young it was Bonnie who wanted sex—and found that her husband was preoccupied with business.

"We hardly make love anymore," Bonnie had said several months after she had turned her back on her husband in bed. Geoff was four then, Lucy was three. Bonnie thought she might like another child. "We haven't made love in over a month."

"Has it been that long?" Kirk asked surprised. He had lost track.

"Yes," said Bonnie unhappily. Kirk was always tired, he no longer seemed interested in her, and she felt very uncomfortable bringing up the subject. She didn't know how to talk about sex—not even with her husband. "It's been over a month."

They made love that night, but for a while it was usually Bonnie who made the first move. Later, when the children were older and Kirk was prospering in his career, it was he who wanted sex.

"Bonnie," he said, "let's go away for the weekend. Just the two of us. My mother will take the kids."

"But we can't go away. Not this weekend. Lucy has a science fair on Saturday and Geoff is on the JV baseball team," Bonnie would say. "I don't see how we can disappoint them."

Eventually sex more or less withered away; both husband and wife regretted it; yet, despite genuine attempts, neither knew quite how to restore the sexual excitement of their early years together. Without ever saying so, each blamed the other. Bonnie thought that Kirk put his business first. Kirk thought that she put the children first. Meanwhile, Bonnie and Kirk looked at the people around them. They saw husbands and wives who fought about money and in-laws and how to raise the children. They saw married people who drank too much and criticized each other in public and flaunted their infidelities. Then they looked at themselves and counted their blessings and told themselves that things would change, things would get better.

"I think about you all the time," Kirk confessed to Susan Morlake late one afternoon after the factory had closed and they were alone in the office. "I can't help myself."

"You're married," Susan said, obviously upset. She, too, had thought of Kirk constantly, remembering what it had been like with him and how she had felt. "I don't want to get involved with a married man. It's too painful."

"Do you want me to stay away from you?" he asked.

She swallowed hard. "Yes," she said.

But despite their resolutions they couldn't stay away from each other.

Their affair brought with it all the pleasures and pain of adultery—the excitement, the heightened eroticism, the guilt, the lying, the sense of shabbiness alternating with the sense that their love was destined to be. Neither of them knew what would happen nor even what they *wanted* to have happen. Kirk had a wife he still loved and to whom he felt loyal; Susan had been through one divorce in her past, and to become involved in another, particularly where small children were involved, was too disturbing even to contemplate. The image of herself as a homewrecker almost made her ill. In the end, the impossible decision about their future was taken out of their hands when Kirk's reputation spread beyond the Midwest.

The treasurer of Morlake Reproductions had a daughter whose boyfriend was a feature writer on the *Chicago Sun-Times*.

"This Kirk Arnold would make a good profile for the business page. 'Corporate Miracle Worker,' " the young man told his girlfriend's father over a Sunday dinner, already seeing the headline. "I think I'll give him a call. I'd like to interview him."

The first article about Kirk Arnold appeared in 1968 under the young man's by-line. The *Sun-Times* article led to a call from *Businessweek* and an article appeared in that magazine in 1969.

One week after the *Businessweek* article appeared, Kirk got a call from Joshua Hynes.

"You're a miracle worker?" he asked over the telephone. "I can tell you that over here at Barron & Hynes we sure as hell need a miracle."

Kirk listened to Joshua Hynes's story with interest. In later years Kirk would paraphrase Tolstoy to a reporter: "All successful companies are successful in the same ways," Kirk said. "All unsuccessful companies are unsuccessful in different ways." Kirk considered it his job to find out what had gone wrong with a company and find ways to fix it. He would eventually be acknowledged as virtually a genius at it. He never, however, seemed to realize that his marriage was going wrong although the signs, the most dramatic of which was his affair with Susan, were all around him.

"Manhattan?" Susan asked when Kirk told her about the offer.

Kirk nodded sadly. "It's an incredible offer."

"I think you should accept it," Susan said, involuntary tears coming to her eyes.

"To put the distance between us?" he asked, astonished at how much pain he felt at the thought of being separated from her.

She nodded, the lump in her throat making it impossible for her to speak. She broke down and wept.

"I hate it!" she cried. "I hate it!"

"What?" he asked, holding her. "What do you hate?"

"Being a goddamn martyr," she sobbed.

Reluctantly Kirk finally decided that Susan was right. So far Bonnie had no idea about his affair but he couldn't count on keeping it a secret forever. It *would* be better to get away. The deceptions of adultery were not for him. He knew he was being a coward, but he wanted to get out before he got further in. Going to Manhattan, putting distance between him and Susan and their increasingly intense relationship, was one solution. Kirk left Grand Rapids feeling torn, leaving someone he loved, suffering still another loss. He permitted himself no regrets.

"Manhattan?" Bonnie asked, appalled, when he told her about the offer. "I don't want to move to Manhattan."

Bonnie's idea of Manhattan was of an evil, dark, and glittering city. Her images were based on FBI crime statistics that showed New York leading the nation, headlines about garbage and taxi strikes, Cosa Nostra gangsters gunning each other down in public, reports of a school crisis so severe that many families left the city for nearby suburbs, and films like *Midnight Cowboy* with its striking images of sleazy streets and mean lives. She imagined men with needles in their arms on streets piled high with rotting garbage.

"We can't live there," she said bitterly. "What kind of a life could we have there?"

"Wonderful!" said Kirk, whose images of the city consisted of the corner of Fifth-seventh and Fifth, where Tiffany faces Van Cleef and Arpels, the glittering lights of Broadway with excited throngs lined up to see the latest hits, the restrained luxury of the Four Seasons restaurant and the opulence of Sutton Place. "There's theater and restaurants and movies and ballet. There's department stores and museums and galleries. There's a hundred and fifty different kinds of cheese at Zabar's and a thousand different bottles of wine at Sherry-Lehmann. You can have anything you want anytime you want it."

"I don't want to go. I don't want to drag the children there," said Bonnie, more stubborn than Kirk had ever heard her. "It's big and dirty and dangerous."

"But Bonnie," he began, not understanding how a woman who would go into Detroit's inner city to work at a drug and alcoholism counseling clinic could fear Manhattan. "Manhattan is where the big boys are. It's what I've been working for. For both of us."

She looked at him and in that moment she knew her mother had been right. She and Kirk had come from different worlds—different worlds that kept her from being the kind of wife she wanted to be and that made him into the kind of husband she no longer knew how to love. She had decided to tell him that he should go to New York without her when a two A.M. telephone call from Dr. Basilynn made her reconsider and decide to stay with Kirk a little while longer.

"It's Scott," Dr. Basilynn said when Kirk picked up the phone.

"Scott?" asked Kirk, waking from a deep sleep. "What happened?"

"He's dead," said Dr. Basilynn, going into the details. "He shot himself."

There was a long, terrible pause.

"I'm sorry, Kirk. I'm sorry."

"Scott," Kirk said simply, turning to Bonnie as he hung up the telephone. The blood drained from his face. "He's dead. He shot himself with Dad's gun."

With that, he choked, no longer able to speak. He began to sob—long, dry, heaving, noiseless sobs that left him gasping for air. Bonnie took him into her arms and tried to comfort him.

"Poor Scott, poor Kirk," Bonnie said, cradling her husband in her arms, her heart going out to him. She held him as he gasped for breath. She stroked his head and his back and wondered when his agony would be over. She tried to think of the right words, words that would be comforting yet still true, as she held her sobbing husband in her arms. There weren't any.

She went to New York with him and they each gave up a dream. Kirk gave up his dream of a Fifth Avenue apartment for a pleasant house in Armonk, and Bonnie gave up her dream of going back to school and stayed with a husband who needed her.

On the day Bonnie and Kirk left for New York Elyssa Arnold gave Kirk the gun his father and brother had used.

"I thought you might want it," she told him, holding it out to him. It was wrapped in a blue-and-white striped towel.

Kirk was speechless, appalled. It was the last thing he wanted. He didn't know what to say, and not knowing what else to do he accepted the unwanted memento and packed it away with his belongings. It stayed there in the carton with his textbooks from Princeton and his diploma until the day, years later, that Carlys unpacked it.

CHAPTER 7

No one who knew Kirk and Bonnie Arnold understood their marriage. They were different people from different worlds and all that outsiders saw were the differences. Kirk was handsome, charming, and sophisticated. He was a worldly man; his ambitions were worldly ambitions and his values were worldly values. Bonnie looked and dressed more like a university student than the wife of a successful businessman and the mother of two grown children. Her delicate skin went without makeup and she wore peasant dresses trimmed with rickrack and silver jewelry. Her beautiful long auburn hair, now lightly streaked with gray, fell in a single braid down her back. With her clothes and semibohemian style, Bonnie made a point of being different. She was an idealist and an altruist, her ambitions were idealistic ones and her values altruistic ones.

No one who knew Kirk and Bonnie knew their story; everyone who knew them wondered why they were together. Everyone thought they understood what Bonnie saw in Kirk; no one understood what he saw in her. Bonnie sensed the condescension and in the beginning she reacted to it by trying to ignore it.

"You're so lucky to be married to him," women would tell Bonnie, making it perfectly obvious that they wondered what someone as wonderful as Kirk saw in someone as mousy as her. "He's so handsome, so successful, so charming."

"Yes, I am lucky. Kirk is wonderful," Bonnie said loyally, trying not to be hurt by their insensitivity. She wondered what people who envied her so much would say if they knew how empty the marriage had become. Kirk had retreated into a shell since Scott's death, and just as Elyssa never mentioned her husband, Kirk refused to talk about his brother. He threw himself into his work with a single-minded ferocity even greater than that which he had poured into Dearborn Paper and Printing. Bonnie was afraid for Kirk. She felt he was a man holding himself on a fine edge just this side of an explosion.

Sunday, bloody Sunday. If Saturday night can be the lone-liest night of the week, then Sunday afternoon can be the emptiest afternoon of the week. It was for Bonnie Arnold. She was from a family of ministers, educators, and social workers. In Bonnie's childhood home Sunday afternoons, after church, had been filled with people sharing a big Sunday dinner, gathering around the piano singing songs, and, later, playing Monopoly and Sorry. Bonnie had loved Sunday afternoons. She had been part of a happy family of parents and child connected by love, part of a happy, extended family of friends and congregation members enveloping her with warmth and affection.

Now, in the nineteenth year of her marriage, Sunday afternoons stretched away silently and endlessly. Not for Kirk the simple pleasures of friends and family and a shared Sunday dinner; not for Kirk the unsophisticated amusements of board games and long walks. On Sunday afternoons Kirk worked, making Sundays indistinguishable from Tuesdays. For years Bonnie had felt chilled and lonely and left out. When she had complained Kirk hadn't understood. Kirk had grown up in a big house with servants, entertaining was formal and choreographed, no one dropped in, no acquaintances shared a simple meal or the pleasures of cleaning up afterward in a big, warm kitchen. Bonnie endured the chill and the loneliness for a long time. She endured them out of loyalty to the husband she loved, she endured them because she had married for better or for worse, she endured them for the children, she endured them because she kept hoping Sunday afternoons would change. But they hadn't and Bonnie had finally done something about her loneliness, her emptiness, the almost unbearable stillness of Sunday afternoons that had come to symbolize the emptiness of her marriage.

In 1972 Bonnie, her mothering years over, had returned to unfinished business: She entered the nearby University of Connecticut and completed her master's in psychiatric nursing. That summer of empty Sunday afternoons, the summer of 1974, was the summer of Watergate, the summer of the eighteen-minute gap in the White House tapes, of Erlichman and Haldeman, of Rebozo and Colson, of Magruder and Mitchell and Rosemary Wood. In the time between, the marriage fell apart.

Disillusion was in the air and there were those who decided not to give in to it. Michael Bennett would say later in an interview that he got the idea for *A Chorus Line* as an antidote to the cynicism of the Watergate scandals. Bonnie Arnold's reaction was similar. She, too, wanted something to believe in. As the Watergate scandals broadened and widened, as Richard Nixon became the first United States president to resign from office, she felt, as Michael Bennett had, an insistent need for an antidote. For Bonnie it would be going back to work. She could no longer ignore the condescension she heard in other women's voices as they told her how wonderful Kirk was while they looked pityingly at her simple clothes and unmadeup face. She could no longer bear the way Kirk didn't even notice her when she came into a room. Bonnie, who had never been selfish, now realized that it was up to her to save herself.

Silverbranch was a fine private psychiatric hospital in nearby Stamford and Bonnie, with her newly minted degree and earlier work experience, was welcomed to the staff. Returning to her earliest interest—helping others—stimulated a part of Bonnie that had been dormant during her years of domesticity. The more she could help others, the more she wanted to. Service to others had been, after all, the tradition in Bonnie's family. For Bonnie, who had felt alien in Kirk's world of business and businessmen, going to work was like going home. She had hoped that work, *her* kind of work, would restore her to herself, and it did. What she never dreamed was that, at forty-two, an age that no longer seemed old but suddenly, finally, adult, she would once again fall in love.

Bonnie wanted to tell her husband, but paralyzed by guilt and remorse and the still-strong ties of loyalty, she could not find the words.

"This Carlys Webber you keep talking about, is she nice?" Bonnie asked one Sunday afternoon in the winter of 1973. Bonnie wanted to talk about love, about herself, and about

what had happened to their marriage. Instead she talked about a woman she had never even met—a woman whose name her husband kept repeating. "This Carlys Webber? Is she pretty?"

Kirk and Bonnie were alone in the big, white clapboard house. Even the stereo didn't seem able to fill the echoing emptiness of the Sunday afternoons they spent alone with each other. Their children were grown and living away from home. Geoff, now eighteen, was a baby-boom baby who had traded his father's handmade three-piece suits for jeans and work shirts. He had dropped out of college after his freshman year and was living in a craft commune in northern Michigan where he was apprenticed to a weaver. Lucy, seventeen now, was following in her brother's footsteps. She was a freshman at Princeton where, despite a good set of brains, she was apparently majoring in astrology, TM, vegetarianism, and the I Ching. Kirk loved his children, but their values, their aspirations, and their references were a mystery to him.

"Carlys? Nice? Pretty?" Kirk replied absentmindedly from behind *Barron's,* wondering with a sudden, uncomfortable stab of guilt why Bonnie was asking about Carlys. "Yes, she is. What makes you ask?"

"You talk about her all the time," Bonnie observed in a carefully neutral voice. Bonnie's extremely fair, sensitive skin betrayed all her emotions. If Kirk had looked at her carefully he would have noticed an unusual pallor to her skin that made her pale freckles seem to stand out, a paleness that was a sign of anxiety. But he didn't look at her carefully. She was his wife. He had lived with her for too many years to really see her.

"I do?" Kirk was surprised. He hadn't realized it. He *had* been aware of how careful he had once been not to mention Susan Morlake except in the most casual way. The difference was that he had been sleeping with Susan; he had never even kissed Carlys.

"All the time," Bonnie said and dropped the subject as abruptly and mysteriously as she had opened it. Carlys Webber wasn't what she wanted to talk about. She wanted to talk about her marriage and she didn't have the courage. She still felt affection for Kirk, a wistful, residual affection, a loyalty born of habit and respect. Kirk thought he under-

stood the way she felt, but emotions made him uncomfortable and he barricaded himself against his feelings behind
Barron's stock tables.

"This Carlys Webber," Bonnie said *several months later,*
although Kirk had begun to make a point of not talking
about Carlys any more than he talked about Howie or
Molly Mundees. "I think she's in love with you."

It was Sunday afternoon again and Bonnie had been in
the kitchen baking the oatmeal cookies she'd begun to
make every Sunday and throw away, untouched, every
Saturday. It never occurred to Kirk to wonder about Bonnie's sudden passion for baking. Bonnie's own theory, she
told herself with a sudden, unexpected lump in her throat,
was that she was cooking her marriage away.

"You don't sound upset," he said, wondering why not.
Unaccustomed to putting his feelings into words, Kirk didn't
attempt to do so now.

"I'm not," said Bonnie. "After all, you're a very handsome man. I'm sure a lot of women are attracted to you.
Why shouldn't this Carlys Webber be one of them?"

For a moment Kirk thought that Bonnie sounded as if
she *wanted* him to be attracted to Carlys. The idea was so
outlandish that he dismissed it the moment it crossed his
mind.

"She doesn't love me," he said firmly. "And I don't
love her in case you're worried about it."

Bonnie said nothing.

Though the rich brown sugary smell of the cookies wafted
through the house, it did nothing to fill the emptiness of the
rooms in which they lived, emptiness that was destroying
Bonnie and that Kirk, totally preoccupied with the problems at SuperWrite, didn't seem to notice.

"How old is she?" Bonnie wanted to know *several weeks*
later, coming into the den from the kitchen. She wore an
apron and Kirk realized at that moment just how much he
hated to see his wife in an apron. He remembered his
mother in evening clothes, dressed for tennis or golf or a
charity committee meeting. He even remembered her wearing dungarees, bathrobes, sailing slickers, furs, and bathing

suits, but he'd never seen his mother in an apron in his entire life.

"Who?" Kirk asked from behind the Sunday *Times* business section. A Yankees–Red Sox game unfolded on the television set and fudge brownies were baking despite the ninety-degree heat.

Winter had turned into spring and spring had turned into summer and the gulf between Kirk and Bonnie had widened. Bonnie was waiting for Kirk to notice, but Kirk stayed buried in his work. Her lover wanted to marry her and she wanted to marry him. All she had to do was tell her husband, and she couldn't do it.

"Carlys Webber," Bonnie said, as if it were perfectly obvious.

"I don't know," said Kirk guardedly. "Why the hell do you keep asking me about Carlys?"

"No reason in particular," said Bonnie suddenly, irrationally, almost on the verge of tears.

"Then stop it," he said, annoyed.

Bonnie dropped it, wondering why she kept talking about Carlys Webber when all she wanted to talk about was herself.

Bonnie remembered the time, years earlier, when, in an attempt to save her marriage, she had persuaded Kirk to see a marriage counselor with her. He had agreed on one condition—that on one visit they would talk about a subject she would choose and that on the next they would discuss a subject he would choose. She had, foolishly she realized now, agreed to his terms. She had wanted to discuss his obliviousness to her feelings; he had denied it, pointing out that he was considerate, faithful, a good provider, and a concerned father. The subject he had chosen was her hostility to his work. The sessions, arbitrated by the counselor, had turned into debates that Kirk had won with logic and that never got anywhere near the emotions Bonnie had wanted to probe. When Kirk said he felt that marriage counseling was a waste of valuable time and money, Bonnie, defeated, could only agree. Bonnie's own attempts to reach her husband had failed, marriage counseling had failed, and, in the end, the marriage had failed. All she had to do was tell him. It was the one thing she still couldn't do. Not quite. Not yet.

That next Sunday, the eighth of September, the last of the empty husband-and-wife Sunday afternoons and the day Gerald Ford granted Richard Nixon a full and absolute pardon, it was Kirk's turn to ask a question.

"Why do you keep asking me about Carlys Webber?" he wanted to know. All afternoon long he had felt terribly anxious. He had followed Bonnie from room to room, not wanting to let her out of his sight. They now sat in the den, the smell of banana bread filling the room. "I almost get the feeling you *want* me to fall in love with her."

Bonnie switched off "60 Minutes" and looked at her husband. A wash of tears suddenly blurred her eyes.

"I just want you to be happy," Bonnie said, having trouble getting the words out.

"I *am* happy," said Kirk, aware of her tears, noticing that her fair skin, always a barometer of her emotions, suddenly became blotchy. "I'm happy with you. *We're* happy." He paused, suddenly afraid of where the conversation was leading. Then he plunged on, a man in an out-of-control vehicle, scared almost to death, unable to stop himself. "Aren't we?"

And that was when she told him that she wanted to leave him.

What Bonnie told her husband was that there was someone else. His name was Norman Dean. He was a psychiatrist, and his father had been a clergyman, too—a Methodist minister just like Bonnie's father. He'd spent time in Northern Ireland treating the psychic victims of civil war, the ones whose wounds were beyond bandages and surgery. He was going back to Northern Ireland and Bonnie wanted to go with him.

"I want to be with him," Bonnie concluded, simply, all emotion having been washed away over the previous year during which she had struggled with herself, torn between a husband she still loved and to whom she felt loyal, and a lover whose interests were her interests, whose passions were her passions, whose values were her values, whose world was her world. "I want a divorce."

"But I thought we were happy," Kirk said, dazed, Bonnie's words hitting him with the impact of a slap in the face.

"*You* were happy," she replied. "I was lonely."

At first Kirk refused to accept the fact that his wife wanted a divorce. He replied to her words with tears—the tears he had held back all his life. Tears too long unshed for his father, for Scott, tears for Susan streamed silently down his face as the pain of every loss echoed and re-echoed through the long closed-off vaults of his memory.

For three weeks, refusing to submit helplessly to another loss, he turned himself inside out trying to persuade Bonnie to change her mind. Propelled by the anguish of still another crucial loss he begged her to tell him what he had done wrong, and promised to change. He threw himself at her, asking her to take a vacation with him, they'd go anywhere in the world she wanted to go. He pleaded with her not to leave him. He would be alone. He could not face being alone. He could not face another loss. Still, she did not relent. He threatened to cut her off without money, but it was a desperate and empty threat because money had never meant anything to her. Panicked, he was reduced to begging his children to plead with their mother not to leave him.

Bonnie remained firm in her wish for a divorce, and as the days and weeks went by Kirk began to realize that the pain he felt at the prospect of losing her was, in fact, the pain he had experienced—but never allowed himself to feel—over the loss of his father and his brother. Gradually he realized that the divorce was not the worst of the losses he had faced but simply a trigger that freshened the memories of others. Because his affair with Susan had given him an indication of what marriage *might* be with a woman who was interested in all the things he was interested in, who shared his values and aspirations, he did not go as far as he could have gone to save his marriage. He did not tell Bonnie that he loved her because he didn't and for a long time now, he realized, hadn't.

A month after Bonnie asked for a divorce Kirk Arnold left his marriage of twenty years with two suitcases full of clothes and a half dozen cartons of personal possessions that were put into storage. He had suffered another almost unbearable loss and he had no one to talk to except a woman he'd never kissed, a woman named Carlys Webber.

C H A P T E R 8

*J*ade and Kirk. Kirk and Jade. Husband and lover. They had never met; they never would. They both began to feel uneasy at the same time. Jade expressed her doubts and was relieved when she allowed George to talk her out of them. Kirk, who had learned that feelings were frightening, refused to admit his suspicions—even to himself. He told himself that everything was fine, just the way it always had been—until it was too late.

When George and Jade bought their Sixty-fifth Street apart-ment in February Jade assumed they'd move in right away. She was stunned when George asked for time to design the renovations, and more time for the construction.

"Four, five months, at least," he said.

"Four or five months!" she exclaimed. Four or five more months of living in his apartment on top of each other, snarling and snapping at each other and apologizing and making up? It seemed like an invitation to disaster. "Shouldn't we move in right away and do the construction while we're living there?"

"If you think we're on each other's nerves now," he said, "wait until there are painters, plumbers, plasterers, and electricians underfoot."

Jade realized that he had a good point, but she was beginning to feel uneasy. He had dragged his feet about finding an apartment. Now that they had, he was dragging them about moving in. When she said that she had the feeling that he was having second—and maybe third and fourth—thoughts about their relationship, though, he told her that she was being paranoid.

Jade's feeling that something was going wrong increased when, by the middle of March, George hadn't yet said anything about renting a house for the summer. Their house—the house Jade thought of as "their house," the one with the view of Mecox Bay—would be gone unless they made the commitment. Jade had assumed all along that they'd rent it again this summer the way they had the year before and the year before that. Now she was beginning to wonder.

"The broker needs to know if we want it again," she told George in the third week of March. "She called me twice this week."

"Tell her we'll get back to her," George said casually. Then he sprang another surprise on her: "I'd like to go to East Hampton and see what's available there."

"East Hampton?" Jade asked, confused. George had always put down East Hampton as being too nouveau. Dean & DeLuca on Newtown Lane? she recalled him saying. Next thing, there'll be a McDonald's and a subway stop! "I thought Bridgehampton was your favorite Hampton."

"It is," he said. "But that doesn't mean we shouldn't take a look at the East Hampton rentals."

George never got around to driving out to East Hampton. He had a dozen reasons: he was busy at the office; he had to go out of town; he was taking Bobby to Bermuda.

"I have the feeling you don't want a house this summer," Jade said and George denied it.

"Of course I do," he said, but he did nothing about finding one. Jade hated putting pressure on him, hating being put in the position of being a nag, of sounding like a wife. Even when she'd been married, she thought ironically, she'd never sounded like a wife. She had never had to ask George about doing something in the past. He had always wanted the same things she'd wanted at the same time. Now he seemed to be going one way while she was going another.

"Unless we sign the lease and make a deposit," Jade said, "we're going to end up without a house this summer."

George seemed not to care and on the beautiful April day the broker called to tell Jade that "their house" had been rented to someone else, Jade came down with the first cold she'd had in years. She was sneezing and coughing, her nose ran like a faucet and tears dripped from her eyes. She couldn't breathe and her throat felt as if someone had rubbed it with sandpaper.

"I feel like a Dristan commercial," she tried to joke through her misery. "Only nothing helps." She sneezed again and blew her already-red nose with her millionth Kleenex of the day.

George brought her a huge bunch of forsythia and, after he'd put it in a vase and set it on the table in the corner of the bedroom, sat down on the edge of the bed and took her hand.

"I don't understand it," she sniffled, feeling weepy and depressed, hating to be confined to her bed on a beautiful spring day. A vaporizer, nasal spray, cough syrup, and aspirin overflowed on her night table and a wastebasket full of soggy tissues stood by the bed. "I *never* get sick."

"Don't you know what the shrinks say about colds? They say that colds are repressed weeping," George said. Consciously, he was teasing. Unconsciously, he was telling her that she was crying and that she had a reason to cry. He had just begun sleeping with Carlys and part of him realized it was a desperate way to prove himself. He hated himself for failing with Jade and he knew he would continue to sleep with Carlys. He was afraid that if he didn't he would continue to fail with Jade and she would leave him. No longer would he be able to blame the too-small living space for their problems. All Jade knew was that her lover said one thing and did another, and that she didn't know what to think.

"What do you know about what shrinks say?" Jade demanded, her flare of annoyance making her forget her cold for the moment. "About colds or anything else?"

"I went to one once," George said with a superior smile. "That's why I'm such a glorious specimen."

Jade stuck her tongue out and threw a wad of soggy Kleenex at him. He laughed, then, despite her contagious condition, they made love.

"Fevered and feverishly," she commented to George when they were done and she felt once again that everything was fine, that everything was the way it had always been. "You were wonderful."

"You weren't so bad yourself," he smiled. "For a beginner. . . ."

He went into the kitchen to make her some tea, aware of Jade's suspicions, afraid that she'd leave if she found out about Carlys but unable to stop. The horror was that he needed them both—Carlys *and* Jade. Jade was the one he couldn't resist. Carlys was the one who made him potent.

Two days later Jade's cold was better and she got out of bed and went to work. She tried to put her unease behind her, but she was depressed because for the first time in two summers she and George had no plans. He talked about going to Maine and Nantucket for long weekends instead of renting a house, and he insisted that he loved her and wanted to live with her and she had no reason not to believe him. Why shouldn't she? He had never lied to her before.

They moved into their beautiful new apartment in July and George's irritability seemed to disappear, their sex life flourished, and the next weeks seemed almost like a honeymoon. George's difficulties seemed to have vanished.

"Ecstasy,"Jade told him after they'd made love in every room, a project that had taken several enjoyable days.

"Aren't you glad we waited?" he asked, thinking that now he could take Carlys to his old apartment. "Don't you feel that this is the real beginning for us?"

Jade nodded.

"And we'll live happily ever after, won't we?" Jade couldn't resist asking. She hated to sound possessive and old-fashioned, but she couldn't help herself. Despite the independence she insisted on, she also wanted reassurance.

"Happily ever after," he confirmed, and the way he said it convinced her that he meant it.

One week after they'd officially moved in together Jade wanted to do something special to mark the anniversary. She went to Madderlake, George's favorite florist, and sent him an extravagantly beautiful tiger-spotted orchid.

"Do you want to enclose a card?" asked the salesman.

Jade hesitated, then she had a brilliant idea.

"No," she said, smiling. "Let him guess which of his girlfriends sent it!"

That summer was the summer before Kirk's forty-eighth birthday, the birthday he had always dreaded, the birthday on which his father had taken his own life. Rescuing companies the way he had once rescued his father's company seemed to be a thing of the past. He even admitted to himself that Bonnie might have been right, that maybe her psychological horseshit wasn't such horseshit, after all. He was finished with compulsively recapitulating what he had done once out of grief and guilt.

He had then gone from one failing company to another, a one-man rescue squad, never staying long enough to enjoy success. Despite Bonnie's observation, he had never admitted what he had been doing—blindly reliving the aftermath of his father's death in a vain attempt to change the outcome—until Carlys had pointed it out to him. Thanks to her, thanks to E-Z Tech, he told himself, he was finally free. Instead of dreading his forty-eighth birthday he now felt that it would be the beginning of the second half of a rich and satisfying life. He knew that he owed his present happiness, his present success to his wife. Without Carlys, without her encouragement and insight, without her professional advice and personal support—both emotional and financial—none of it would have happened. He appreciated it, but he never expressed his appreciation in words. He was uncomfortable with words but not with gestures. He decided to surprise Carlys with a trip.

"Do you remember Iris Stennis?" he asked in July. He had been spending more and more time in Charleston. He felt guilty about neglecting Carlys yet he was glad that she was the kind of independent woman who didn't need him the way Bonnie had.

"How could I forget?" Carlys rolled her eyes. "The Lady with the Decorator!"

"Her sister owns a villa in Cap d'Antibes," Kirk said in the tone of voice that Carlys knew preceded a happy surprise. "She's spending the summer in Southampton with Iris and she's renting the villa—to us!"

"A villa? In Cap d'Antibes? How jet setty!" Carlys

remembered the old Carlys who would have swum the Atlantic to spend even one night in a villa. The new Carlys, the Carlys who had a lover, didn't want to go. She didn't want to spend a second away from George that she didn't have to.

"We have it for two weeks," said Kirk.

"I love it!" Carlys exclaimed. "I'll have to clear it with Joshua, though." She smiled even as she hoped that Joshua would object and she wouldn't have to go. She loved Kirk but she had to have George. She didn't know how she could stand being away from him.

"If Joshua gives you a hard time," Kirk promised, "I'll talk to him myself."

"Two whole weeks?" George asked. *"In Europe? You* mean I won't even be able to talk to you on the telephone?"

Carlys shook her head. The expression on George's face ripped at her, tearing her apart. It both scared and excited her to have that much power over someone.

"I'm afraid not," she said softly. They were at the Regency, in bed, lying side by side, their arms and legs intertwined. He moved and she felt him take his leg away from between hers.

"Don't," she whispered, trying to restrain him. "Put your leg back. I liked it there."

"I like you *here,*" said George, rolling onto his back, dislodging her head from its resting place on his shoulder. "I *need* you here."

He and Jade had just moved into the apartment on Sixty-fifth Street. George needed Carlys. He needed her so that he could be a man with Jade.

"But you knew right from the beginning," said Carlys hopelessly, "that I had other obligations."

"I didn't know right from the beginning," he said, mocking her cruelly, "that I was going to fall in love with you."

On the day that Carlys left for France, on an impulse, she sent George a copy of *How to Make Your First Million.* As a joke, she autographed it: "L & K, Lansing."

Her first gift, their first private joke. They were becoming more than casual lovers indulging a physical attraction. They were making connections, becoming a couple.

* * *

The Villa Soleil shared the same peninsula with the Hotel du Cap, the hotel where Fitzgerald stayed, where Greek millionaires encamp for the summer, where Garbo rested and Dietrich showed her famous legs by the pool. The villa was set in a grove of pine and cypress trees and its terraces, shaded by yellow-and-white striped awnings, overlooked the warm, clear dark blue of the Mediterranean. A romantic, shaded path, nestling beneath the trees, led down to a series of large, flat stones, perfect for sunning and sea bathing. The servants, an elderly couple from Languedoc, served hot, flaky croissants in the morning and cool poached fish for lunch. For dinner Kirk wanted to try every three-star restaurant in the area.

"I want to taste the bouillabaisse at Chez Tetou, the *brioche de foie gras* at L'Oasis, and *anything* at the Quatre Murs," he said after burying himself in the Gault-Millau.

"You'll get fat," Carlys warned.

"You won't," he said, noticing that she didn't seem to have much of an appetite. In fact, he thought, she had lost weight in the past six months. Not that it wasn't very becoming.

That week Jade found a copy of a book called How to Make Your First Million *on George's night table.* The book, Jade remembered vaguely, had been a best-seller a few years ago. She opened it and found, on the first page, a handwritten dedication: "L & K, Lansing."

"I didn't know you knew Lansing Coons," Jade said, wondering where on earth George had met Lansing Coons. George had never expressed one syllable of interest in the stock market or in getting rich. In fact he had always explained his lavish spending by saying that he wanted to leave the world the same way he came into it: naked and penniless.

"I don't," George said casually. He was a wonderful liar because he always stuck vaguely to the truth. "Not really."

"Then why is he dedicating his book to you with L and K?" Jade asked. "Love and Kisses?"

George shrugged. "It's a joke," he said, taking the book from her and putting it away in the bookcases that lined a wall of the living room. "Now, what do you want to do for dinner?"

Jade did not mention the incident again. She also did not forget it. George had never thanked her for the orchid although she knew he received it. She remembered her flippant words at Madderlake and thought that, perhaps, her unconscious knew something she didn't. Now with the book and its mysterious inscription she was beginning to wonder if George was doing to her what he had done to Ina. She wondered if George was having an affair. She began to watch him carefully, not even beginning to know what she would do if he were. She had once gone too far to try to save a relationship. She did not know how far she would be willing to go a second time. She waited and she watched, and although she couldn't help it, she felt herself pull away from him, slightly, almost imperceptibly, but definitely.

"Are you all right?" Kirk asked Carlys at the end of their first week in France. "Do you have the flu or something?"

"I'm fine," she said with a smile that didn't seem like her smile. They were on their way down to the rocks where they usually spent the morning sunbathing and swimming.

"You don't *seem* all right," he said, wishing she'd take off the sunglasses that hid her eyes. It wasn't like him to persist in a conversation about anything as vague as feelings and Carlys was immediately on guard.

"You've barely had an appetite," he continued. "The other day you passed up a chance to go shopping in Nice and last night, at the casino, you acted as if you couldn't wait to leave." What Kirk didn't say but what was also on his mind was that she seemed preoccupied, distracted. She even seemed different in bed. She didn't seem like the wife he knew, the woman he was used to.

"Those people were stupefyingly boring," Carlys said, needing to explain herself. Kirk sensed something, she realized. She was sure that nothing showed but she had to be careful. "She was a gold digger and he was a dirty old man. I couldn't *wait* to get away from them." They'd gone to Cannes with friends of Iris Stennis's sister, a retired English scrap metals baron and his twenty-year-old mistress. He was a pompous bigot and she, dripping with diamonds and rubies, hung on his every word and, bite by bite, fed him his dinner and pretended to "burp" him when he was finished. Carlys had loathed them.

"Well," admitted Kirk, who could be much more tolerant than she, "they *were* a bit outrageous."

"A bit?" asked Carlys, taking his hand and laughing. "They were the *definition* of outrageous!"

They walked down to the water, hand in hand, making plans for the rest of the day and Carlys was sure she'd carried off her moment of icy fear beautifully.

Still, Kirk couldn't get rid of the feeling that something was bothering Carlys. She didn't want to go sightseeing. Most afternoons she begged off, saying that she preferred to read the big batch of current best-sellers she'd brought along. She called her office every day and Kirk almost had the feeling that she wanted a crisis, was looking for an excuse to go home early, but when he asked her about it she denied it.

"Why would I want to leave paradise?" she asked, gesturing at the terrace with its luxuriously comfortable furniture and expansive view of the pines and the sea. "It would take wild horses to drag me away."

Yet he couldn't get over the idea that she seemed preoccupied.

"Carlys, are you worried about something?" Kirk asked. "Is there something on your mind?"

"Not really," she said. Kirk's solicitousness disturbed her. It stirred her guilt and she looked at him closely, wondering if he suspected. She couldn't tell. His face had that unrevealing, upper-class expression she had been so attracted to from the beginning. "Well," she admitted, telling him about something that really did worry her, "Tom is a big problem. He pretends to like me but I know he undermines me behind my back. But it's nothing, just office politics."

"As long as it isn't me," Kirk said. "As long as I haven't done something to make you unhappy. . . ."

She looked at him and tears sprang to her eyes.

"You? You do something to make me unhappy?" she said, going to him and throwing her arms around him. "Oh, my God, no!"

He held her in his arms and from that moment on Carlys seemed like the Carlys he knew. Office politics were something Kirk could understand.

C H A P T E R   9

*The telephone on Carlys's desk was ringing the mo*ment she stepped into her office on Monday morning.

"Other people go crazy without their shrinks in August. I went crazy without you," said George, his voice tender and intense. "When can I see you? Right now? Instantly? Sooner?"

Instantly? He wanted to see her instantly! *She* wanted to see *him* instantly. She had missed *him* so much when she'd been away that *she* had gone crazy. All she had wanted, all she had thought of, was being in his arms, feeling his lips on hers, his hands on her body, her body on fire.

"I can't," she said, desolate, wanting to meet him more than anything in the world. She remembered leaving her office to meet Kirk once, years ago, before they were married, before he was her husband, before he was her lover. She had gone that time because she had nothing to lose. She wanted to do the same thing again but she couldn't. She was a different Carlys now. She had something to hide and everything to lose.

"Can't?" he asked. He sounded as if her words had crushed him.

"Not now," she answered, and went on to explain what her first day at work would be like: Joshua wanted to see her; so did Lansing. There was a copy meeting followed by a cable television operator's presentation. She was having lunch with Ada followed by a meeting with everyone who worked on the Yankee Air account and, after that, a first meeting with a new client. After *that* she was meeting Kirk at a cocktail party for metropolitan area computer dealers. All of that didn't even include the two overstuffed envelopes of correspondence that had piled up in her absence or the stack of pink telephone messages all labeled IMPORTANT, IMMEDIATE, or URGENT.

"Today!" George said urgently. "If you don't, I'm going to come up there and get you!"

He hung up, leaving her flattered by his intensity and afraid of his threat. Would he be crazy enough to come to her office? What would she tell people? How would she explain who he was? Her heart pounded as she sat there numbly with the telephone still in her hand, momentarily unable to think, unable to move. The sound of his voice had been as arousing as the touch of his hands. She was aware that desire made her breasts feel suddenly, exquisitely, painful with yearning and that heat blazed between her legs where they were crossed in her chair. However much he wanted her, she wanted him. As she sat there motionless, in thrall to a rush of intense physical desire, the phone rang a second time.

"Sergio," her secretary announced, and Carlys sighed and picked up the phone.

"Cincinnati!" He whispered his outrage into the phone. "What kind of idiots run your media department anyway? They've booked me on a Cincinnati talk show! Local! Not even syndicated!"

The mere thought of it caused Sergio to run out of words, though only temporarily. Carlys could hear the sucking noises of the filter in the background. Sergio was at home in Sands Point talking to her from the inflatable raft in his swimming pool. As he spewed out his outrage, Carlys realized she had never been swimming with George. She wondered if he was a good swimmer. She had wondered the same thing while she swam in the Mediterranean with her husband. Her mental infidelities made her feel almost guiltier than her physical infidelities, yet she couldn't control them.

"Carlys, you tell them that Sergio Maliterno does *not* go to Cincinnati," he continued in his creepy whisper, a superstar in a supersnit. "Furthermore . . ."

She had a five-minute conference in the hall with Joshua, who had heard over drinks at the Yale Club that the big Eastern Airlines account might be coming loose.

"Carlys, you have a great track record with both Ava and Mid-Atlantic," Joshua said, speaking conspiratorially so that no lurking spies could overhear his hot scoop. "How do you think we ought to go about getting it?"

"Getting what?" she asked, still thinking about George.

"Eastern, for Christ's sake!" Joshua exclaimed. He was annoyed at Carlys for taking time off. He was annoyed at her for not paying attention. He was annoyed at her because, lately, she didn't seem to spend one thousand percent of her time and energy thinking about her work. Tom had pointed it out over the past few months and Joshua was beginning to agree with him. He wasn't paying Carlys Arnold a six-figure salary for her to run off to France and then come back in a fog.

"Come on, Carlys, you're back from vacation! This is Madison Avenue. Not Cap d'Antibes! Get with it! I want some ideas from you by this afternoon!" he finished and stalked off down the hall.

She sat through the executive committee meeting half hearing talk about new accounts and old accounts, about accounts that might be in trouble and accounts that might be coming loose from other agencies. She vaguely listened to bickering about whether or not the ladies' room needed a new sofa and whether the receptionists ought to be required to fill in for the switchboard operators at lunchtime. She sort of heard the saga of the broken Coke machines that had apparently almost caused the clerical staff to walk out en masse the previous Friday and the eternal squabbling over procedures for reserving the conference rooms. As the words swirled and eddied around her, she worried that George might be barging into her office at that very moment, making their private business public. She remembered what George had said and the way he'd said it and the way she had physically reacted to it. She was aware again of the ache in her breasts and the heat between her legs. With a start she realized Joshua was talking to her.

"What's the problem with you and Sergio?" he was asking.

"No problem," said Carlys, not quite knowing what he was talking about.

"He said that you hung up on him."

Carlys explained that she'd listened to Sergio's complaints and told him that she'd have his promotional tour rescheduled. She had been brief with him, but polite. She had *not* hung up on him. Joshua listened to her explanation and seemed to accept it, but the skepticism on his face told another story.

Carlys got back from lunch at two-thirty, the meeting on the Yankee Air account was over at three-forty-five. The meeting with the new client was scheduled for four-thirty. If she rescheduled it for later in the week, she'd be able to meet George for an hour before she was due to meet Kirk at the computer retailers' reception.

"Oh, my God, how I missed you! I thought I would die. You look beautiful!" he said, taking her into his arms. It was just a quarter to five and the late August sun slanted into the ordinary room, the golden light turning it extraordinary. "Just wonderful and beautiful and exquisite."

He kissed her hungrily, his hands avidly roaming over her body. She sank into him, her body close against his, feeling his hardness, his warmth, his hunger.

They were in a cozy room in the Algonquin, the traffic noise from Forty-fourth Street reminding them of the busy city below. He kissed her mouth and her eyes and her face and her hair and she shut her eyes and felt she was melting into him. He took his mouth away from hers for a moment and, holding her by the shoulder, looked at her again.

"Not just wonderful. Not just beautiful. Not just exquisite. But the most alluring woman who ever lived. Carlys, I counted the days until you came back. No, the hours, the minutes. The seconds. . . ."

She smiled and touched his face, his lips, his eyes and took his hand to her mouth and kissed its back and then its palm and then, one by one, its fingers. George could make the most extravagant declarations of love sound like simple statements of inevitable fact.

"It was all I could do not to call you the minute I got back," she said. "I just wanted to hear your voice."

"I wish you had," he replied. "I would have done anything to hear your voice."

She smiled and took off the linen jacket she'd bought in Nice and threw it on the chair. Holding his eyes with hers, she began to unbutton her blouse, aware of how much he wanted her and of how much pleasure she was giving him. Thrilled by her sexual power she flung her blouse over the jacket and stepped out of her skirt and panty hose. Still holding his eyes with hers, completely naked now, she stepped toward him and he held his arms out to her.

He was so hungry for her, so hard and so excited, and she was so anxious for him, so starved and so hot, that they fell on the bed and tore at each other so wildly that they were finished almost the instant they'd begun. Breathless, their hearts pounding, they looked deep into each other's eyes and began immediately to make love again, shamelessly and demandingly and unself-consciously, until they exploded in a second shattering, simultaneous climax.

"Welcome home," he whispered with a lover's smile, his face close over hers, when he caught his breath again.

"I missed you," she said, stroking his thick, dark hair.

"I know," he said lovingly. "I missed you, too. Thank you for the book and the orchid. They made me feel close to you even though you were gone."

"Orchid?" she asked.

"It had no card," he said, smoothly covering the skipped beat of his heart. "It came the same time the book did. I guess it was from a client."

"Wish it *had* been from me," Carlys said. "I wish I'd thought of sending you an orchid."

Quietly they lay in each other's arms for a delicious while, savoring the nearness of each other, kissing and stroking each other, comfortable with one another's bodies.

"Topless?" he asked, caressing her suntanned breasts and kissing them.

"The French, you know," she said. "I wanted to fit in."

He smiled and kissed her nipples.

"Your nipples are the same color as your skin," he said. "It's sexy. And a bikini bottom," he noticed, tracing the skimpy white outline around her buttocks and triangle with his fingertips. He caught her pubic hairs in his fingers and, holding her still, kissed his way down from her breasts to her navel, leaving a hot trail of pleasure. He moved his hand down between her legs, feeling her moistness and the residue of his own wetness.

"Oh, please," she sighed, writhing on the bed. "I want you in me."

"Not yet," he said. "Wait. I want you to want me more."

He kissed her slowly, intimately.

"Now," she begged, her hands on his shoulders, trying to draw him up to her.

"In a minute," he said, and using his mouth and his fingers brought her to the edge of climax, until the sensations she felt were almost unbearable. Then, when she was just about to explode, he put his mouth, still wet with his taste and hers mingled together, on hers, plunging his tongue deeply into her at the same instant that he plunged into her so deeply that she felt him in the very center of her being.

Carlys left the Algonquin in an erotic daze, late for her appointment with Kirk, worried about getting a taxi. She did not notice Ray Mundees, who saw her as she waited for the doorman to get her a cab. He was staying at the Harvard Club and wondered what the hell she was doing coming out of a midtown hotel in the middle of the afternoon.

Almost half an hour late, Carlys entered the smoke-filled noisy, private room upstairs at 21 where the assembled computer salesmen were having their party.

"Sorry," she apologized to Kirk. "I was held up at the office."

"Carlys, you look great!" said Sid Hatton, a Staten Island dealer. "What the hell have you been doing to yourself?"

"Going to the French Riviera with my handsome husband," she replied, glorying in her tantalizing secret. She and George had made love, bingeing on each other, until the very last second and Carlys had had no time for a shower. Her panty hose were wet from their lovemaking and the hair at the base of her neck was still sweaty with their passion. She took Kirk by the hand and squeezed it suggestively.

"Later?" she whispered when they had an unobserved split-second together.

"Later," he agreed, aware of how much sexier Carlys seemed lately and observing that other men, men like Sid Hatton, noticed it, too. He was proud to have such an attractive wife. He was also, he realized, jealous. He put aside his stab of jealousy as he and Carlys began to work the room together.

That night George finally thanked Jade for the orchid.

"It's beautiful," he said, coming out of the shower. Lately Jade thought he seemed to be showering *all* the time. She wondered what his recent fetish about cleanliness was all about. "I've been meaning to thank you but I kept forgetting. It must be old age."

Jade smiled wryly.

She didn't believe him, though she knew what he meant about old age. They were both in their mid-thirties, and age was definitely beginning to show. She had noticed uncharacteristic dark circles under her eyes lately and her gums seemed tender and swollen. As they turned off the light she made a mental note to make an appointment with her dentist.

C H A P T E R 10

hat summer had seemed full and promising, a season of riches and satisfaction. That fall was an autumn of dissonance. Prophetically, black was the color of the season in fashion and death was in the headlines. There were the deaths of Ingrid Bergman and Grace Kelly—women a generation had grown up admiring. A series of sinister and mysterious deaths in the Midwest were traced to cyanide-filled Tylenol capsules and temporarily terrified a nation. Brilliant careers crashed during the squalid Martin-Marietta–Bendix takeover battle when renewed whispers about William Agee and Mary Cunningham reminded Carlys of her own tainted departure from SuperWrite. John DeLorean, once the shining hope of the decaying auto industry, was arrested on drug charges. Solidarity was banned and in protest, shipworkers in Gdansk, led by Lech Walesa, went on strike. There were weeks of rioting in Poland, the president of Lebanon was assassinated, and anti-Semitic bombings sprayed the streets of Paris with glass and blood. The tone of the news had turned from bright to somber and Carlys's own mood had shifted from confidence to restlessness.

Now that they had come back from France, Carlys's discontent with Kirk sharpened. Now that they had returned from vacation, love was something Kirk seemed to have put away with the suntan lotion and bathing suits. When people told her, as they so often did, how dynamic Kirk was, when they told her how exciting it must be to be married to such a dynamo, Carlys smiled and replied that yes, Kirk was wonderful and that being married to him was everything a woman could hope for. She didn't know she was saying the same things Bonnie had once said. Like Bonnie, she wasn't lying, but she was leaving out part of the truth.

She didn't tell them about the price tag that came with success like Kirk's. She didn't mention the evenings he came home so tired and drained that he couldn't eat dinner or the glamorous dinner parties that ended with his falling asleep in the taxi on the way home. She never said anything about his fourteen-hour weekend sleeping bouts after a hectic week, about the way one drink sometimes seemed to knock him out or about his irritability with what he considered to be unimportant details. She never complained about how much time he spent away and how, even when he was there, he wasn't. And, of course, she never told anyone that Kirk's interest in sex was far down on his list of priorities and that his performance was routine and perfunctory.

She didn't mention that Kirk didn't have much time for his family and that he took it for granted that she would stand in for him. She was the one who listened to Lucy's endless romantic crises and Geoffrey's latest plans to make a million without compromising his principles. She was the one who wrote to Kirk's mother keeping her informed of her son's latest triumphs, and she, of course, was the one who continued to visit her father, pay his bills, see to it that he ate properly, and supervised the live-in companions that his frailty now required.

Of course she didn't talk about their intimate life. She didn't say that it hurt her, despite her efforts not to be hurt, when Kirk seemed to take her totally for granted and the way he seemed to have time for everyone and everything except her. She didn't say that, except for their conversations about business, Kirk had little time or patience with the personal problems affecting his family or hers.

"You handle it" was his annoyed response to her concerns about Lucy and Geoffrey.

"You call," he said when she mentioned that it had been a long time since he'd spoken to his mother.

"You'll just have to find someone else," he said when she told him that she learned that her father's companion had been letting him sleep in urine-stained sheets.

You do it. You take care of it—it was a refrain that echoed her childhood. Her husband was treating her the way her father had, and although Carlys realized that she was an adult now and not a child, she still resented it. Her resentment made her vulnerable to her fantasies and to George's words. She felt guilty about it, but now when her husband made love to her, she began to pretend that it was her lover.

She felt even guiltier about the way she compared her husband and her lover, sometimes preferring one and at other times preferring the other. She had crossed the line of thinking her affair a luxury; she began to think of it as a necessity. She now accepted it as an essential part of her complicated but satisfying life.

When she told George about her worries about her father, she found herself wishing Kirk were as understanding about her concerns as George. When she told Kirk about her problems at the office, she wished George were as knowledgeable about the ins and outs of business as Kirk. When she was with Kirk, she sometimes wished she were with George. When she was with George, she sometimes wished she were with Kirk. Sometimes she thought she loved them both. Sometimes she thought she loved neither.

There were the terrific times when she made love to George and then made love to Kirk and felt doubly loved.

"I can't get enough of a good thing," she told Kirk and he thought she meant him.

"I can't get enough of a good thing," she told George and he thought she meant him.

So taken was she at times with her own sexual allure that she wondered what it would be like to have another lover, a third man and maybe even a fourth. She had a different way of looking at men now, confident and perhaps a bit challenging. She had always wondered what it would be like to be one of the girls who always had flocks of boy-friends and now she knew. It was wonderful. It made her love herself as much as they seemed to love her. The good times, though, were canceled by the bad times.

There were the terrible times when she felt she was cheating both her husband and her lover. The terrible times when she lied to them both, when she stole time from one to give to the other.

"I'm going to have my hair done on the way home from work," she told Kirk. "I'll be late," she said and went off to meet George.

"Cellini is having a reception for its store managers across the country. They're showing the new line and I have to go," she told George. "It's a command performance," she said and went off with Kirk to a cocktail party to introduce the press to a new line of software manuals.

She didn't feel wonderful then. She didn't feel desirable or alluring. She felt like a cheater. She felt that she was living her life slinking into dark corners. She was cheating both her husband and her lover. Most of all, though, she was cheating herself. How could she love either of them when she didn't even love herself?

Carlys wished she had someone to talk to. When she had begun her affair she had decided not to tell anyone about it. She still thought she was wise not to have spoken, but silence, like success, had a price tag. Because she confided in no one her secret occupied more and more of her time, more and more of her energy, more and more of her fantasy life. Telling no one made her affair loom larger and larger until she began to think of nothing else. She remembered their past meetings, the words George whispered to her, the touches and kisses and caresses. She made up lies and lived deceptions, constantly balancing her secret life against her public life, her love affair against her marriage.

She began to wonder whether she'd ever leave her husband for her lover, whether she'd choose her romance over her marriage.

She began to be afraid of how much she thought about George and how much she lived for their meetings. She had gotten away with her double life for six months and she was beginning to think she had been overly cautious. She wanted to spend more time with George and her rigid list of priorities—husband, father, job, lover—disintegrated like so many shattered commandments.

"I want to go to your apartment," she told George in late September, the idle words seemingly unrehearsed although the thought behind them had been growing over the summer. Now that she knew him better she wanted to see his apartment. She wanted to see what the place he lived in said about him.

"I'd love you to," he said, "but I thought you preferred hotels. You said you thought they were safer."

"I was too cautious," Carlys said.

His apartment was like he was: uncluttered, romantic, sensuous, deceptively simple. Neutral linen covered the built-in seating, a wall of bookshelves held art books and baskets of fabric samples. An Eames chair was clearly masculine and the large glass coffee table held only a stoneware bowl of matches from what seemed to be every restaurant in the city—the sign of a man whose private life was a life led in public. The stainless-steel kitchen reminded Carlys of the galley in an airliner and the bedroom, carpeted and darkly shaded, held only a bed and two night tables. A wall of storage faced a television set and a small bathroom with a stall shower led off the bedroom. Nothing betrayed the presence of a woman: no makeup in the bathroom, no nightgown hanging from a hook, no patterned potholders in the kitchen.

The uncompromising spareness of the apartment comforted Carlys. Although she knew that George had a girlfriend, it made her feel that she was the most important woman in his life. She couldn't help thinking that if George's girlfriend didn't even keep a toothbrush or a bottle of hand lotion in his apartment she couldn't be very important to him.

"Room for one," Carlys commented, thinking of her collection of blue-and-white spongeware, the family photographs that lined the tables, and the Shaker baskets she bought whenever she wanted to treat herself. "My clutter would drive you crazy."

"Nothing about you would drive me crazy," George said, smiling and taking her into his arms. They made love in his bed.

"All the comforts of home," Carlys said afterward as they sipped white wine kept cold in his refrigerator, and from then on they always met in his apartment.

Even so, Carlys was still relatively careful. Only rarely, when it was raining or when she was desperately pressed for time, did she take a taxi right to George's building. Most times, though, she went into Bloomingdale's on the Lexington Avenue side, crossed the main floor, went out the Third Avenue exit and walked the few blocks to George's. Other times, using the multiple entrances of Alexander's, she did the same thing. Sometimes she got out of her taxi on Second Avenue and walked west; other times she took the subway, got out at the Fifty-ninth Street stop and walked east. Even though she felt sure that no one suspected a thing, she still took the basic precautions—most of the time.

Barney Gelber was a celebrity dentist whose father had also been a celebrity dentist. Inscribed photographs of film and stage stars, well-known politicians, and famous dancers hung on the walls of his waiting room. Jade always teased him that she was probably his only nonfamous patient.

"My gums have been terribly swollen lately," she said as she arranged herself in his reclining chair and the nurse clipped the towel around her neck. "I guess it's imminent old age."

Barney Gelber smiled and said, as dentists always do, "Let's take a look."

He examined her mouth carefully, first with a mirror, then with a variety of instruments. When he was done prodding and poking, he took the mirror again and this time, very carefully, examined her gums. Every time he touched them with any pressure Jade flinched. As he examined her, she examined him. From close up Jade studied his even, pleasant features, good skin, and green eyes. Even more, she studied the changing expressions on Barney Gelber's face. They seemed to her to change from casual confidence to concern.

"Is anything wrong?" Jade asked when he'd taken his fingers out of her mouth and she could talk. His examination had taken a lot longer than Jade had anticipated and she began to worry.

"Not that I can see," he said carefully. "I'd like to take a few X-rays, though."

With awful fantasies of a mouthful of false teeth and a lifetime of denture cleansers Jade went into the X-ray room and the technician X-rayed her mouth. She went back into Barney Gelber's office and waited until the film was developed. Dr. Gelber held the film up to the light and examined it carefully, again taking much longer than Jade had imagined.

"Is everything all right?" she asked anxiously. Doctors' silences always brought out her paranoia.

Barney Gelber looked at her. His kind eyes and pleasant face held an uncertain expression.

"I can't see any dental reason for the swelling and tenderness, although they're obviously there," he said. "It's possible you have a virus of some kind or perhaps some kind of general infection. I think you ought to check it out with your doctor."

"No false teeth?" Jade asked, suddenly relieved.

"Not for a few years," Barney Gelber smiled. "But, please, make an appointment with your doctor. Don't let this go untreated. It doesn't look like it's going to go away by itself."

Jade promised that she would. She'd probably have to take some antibiotics and suffer an upset stomach for a week. She hated antibiotics. They made her feel bloated and miserable. Still, she took Dr. Gelber's advice and made an appointment with her internist. Unavoidably, because she was off to the Milan-Paris-London circuit, the appointment had to be put off for two weeks.

One of the hardest things about having an extramarital affair, Carlys discovered, was trying to remember all the things she'd done *before* her affair. How often had she had her hair cut? How often had she come home with full shopping bags after a stop at Saks on the way home from work? How often had she gone to her gym? How often had she mentioned a purely social lunch with Michelle or an impromptu visit to her father? When had she done the grocery shopping? She tried to remember and tried to make her life look as normal as possible even though some of her "lunches" were afternoons with George and once in a while her Saturday "gym class" was two hours with her lover.

She thought she did a good job, but sometimes she slipped up.

"I thought you just *had* your hair cut," Kirk said when Carlys said she couldn't meet him and Marion Kramer for drinks.

"I did," she said, thinking quickly. She had arranged to meet George and she had used the haircut as an excuse, forgetting she had used it just two weeks before. "Rosemary couldn't give me an appointment for color last time. So I made it for Thursday."

Kirk let it drop, obviously convinced. After all, she sounded convincing even to herself. When she saw George that Thursday, their lovemaking was even more passionate than usual. The lying, the subterfuge, gambling and winning, playing with fire, the glamorous sense of living a real-life thriller only added to the wild excitement.

"Let's spend a weekend together," George said as she dressed to leave. October had just arrived. Jade was off to Europe for an early look at spring ready-to-wear. "I don't want to let you go. I never get enough of you. Just a weekend. Just two days and two nights. We've never spent a night together. You've never slept in my arms." He kept touching her as she dressed, reluctant to let her go.

"I can't," she said. "I've never spent a weekend away from Kirk."

Even as she explained why she couldn't go she began to wonder how she could arrange it.

"Cincinnati?" Kirk asked, incredulous. "For a weekend?"

Carlys shrugged. "Sergio refuses to go unless I go with him. You know what he's like."

"Fuck him!" Kirk exploded. His feeling that Carlys was different had returned more strongly than ever, and although he could find no rational reason for it he felt angry and irritated with her. "Don't go. I don't want you to go."

"*I* don't want me to go," Carlys laughed. "But what can I do?"

"Tell him to go to hell," Kirk said angrily. Then, calming down, "Tell him to go by himself. He's a big boy."

"I've been through this with him," Carlys sighed. "With him *and* with Joshua. It's part of the job."

Carlys went to Cincinnati. Cincinnati was the Inn at Saw Mill Farm in West Dover, Vermont, where, except for meals, she and George did not leave their luxurious room for the entire weekend.

"Again," George said as he left her early Sunday evening. "Soon. Please?"

"No," said Carlys, afraid she'd gone too far. Kirk had barely spoken to her after she'd told him she would be away for the weekend. "It was too much of a chance. Kirk was angry."

"Please," insisted George. "You did it once. You can do it again."

That next Saturday when Carlys got to the gym, Dierdre told her that her husband had called. Carlys felt an instant tense knot in the pit of her stomach.

"He wants you to call him at home as soon as you arrive," Dierdre said. It wasn't the first time Mr. Arnold had called. He had also called two weeks before. That time Mrs. Arnold had canceled at the last minute and when she told him, Mr. Arnold had sounded surprised and told her not to bother to give Mrs. Arnold the message.

Carlys thanked Dierdre and tried to smile. Kirk had never called her at the gym before. Was he checking up on her? Did he suspect something? Her hand shook as she dialed her own number.

"Let's have lunch," Kirk said. "I'll meet you at Mortimer's at one."

"What a terrific idea!" Carlys said. "I'd love to!"

Carlys hung up, relief washing over her. As she changed

into her leotards, she noticed that her hands were ice cold. They were still shaking when she began the warm-ups.

In Paris, trying on sweaters at Sonia Rykiel's rue Grenelle boutique, Jade noticed that her hair seemed disgustingly oily even though she'd shampooed it that morning. She also noticed that, under her makeup, her face was blotchy and broken out. She peered at herself more closely in the mirror and saw that she couldn't blame the unflattering dressing room lighting. There was a sprinkling of pimples across her cheeks and chin. She hadn't had a pimple since she'd been fifteen and she wondered what was going on. Geriatric acne? She'd never heard of it.

Joke or no joke, Jade didn't feel right. She didn't feel like herself. Lately her hair had been impossible to manage, her skin was a mess, and her legs seemed numb, as if they didn't quite belong to her. She had gotten her period just before she left for Paris and she still had it although it was spotty and peculiar, not that that meant much, her periods had always been unpredictable. Still, she had the feeling something was going haywire. It was probably the reason she had been feeling so emotional before she'd left for Paris.

On the night before she left she finally told George what was on her mind.

"That book," Jade said, bringing it up again. George's explanation had not been convincing. "L and K? Love and kisses? I just can't imagine someone like Lansing Coons signing a book L and K to another man."

"I told you it was a joke," said George, sounding irritated. "Don't you believe me?"

"And the plant? said Jade. Her half-formed doubts were tormenting her with their shadowy elusiveness. "I was joking when I told the man at Madderlake that I wanted you to guess which of your girlfriends it was from. Maybe it wasn't such a joke."

"So you think I have other girlfriends?" George asked. "Is that what's on your mind?"

Jade nodded.

"Well, I don't have another girlfriend," he lied. Then, looking deeply into her eyes, he told her the truth. "There's only you, Jade. You're the only one who matters to me."

"You're sure?" she asked in a rare moment of insecurity. She hated to sound unsure. She didn't want to be clingy or possessive or demanding of reassurance. She had, she thought, put all those adolescent emotions behind her.

"I love you," he said, and it *was* the truth. "Don't you believe me?"

"Of course I do," she said, and she did. She knew, deep down, that whatever else George might do, he did love her and she pushed her doubts aside and went off to Europe, hoping that she was doing the right thing.

After a passionate night George took her to the airport, something he'd never done.

"I wish you didn't have to go," he said, waiting with her in the First Class lounge. He had bought her an armful of magazines and paperbacks and a white rose, and had kissed her so deeply in the departure lounge that she had been embarrassed. George had called her every single morning and evening in Milan, Paris, London. He told her how much he missed her.

"My arms are empty without you," he said, his voice as intimate and near as if he'd been in the next room. "I have a thousand kisses—all for you."

Alone in the dressing room, a pile of sweaters and skirts on the chair, Jade remembered his words and his hands. She nodded. Whatever else was going on, she did believe that he loved her.

CHAPTER 11

*G*uilt *was no longer a pin dot. Guilt had begun to* spread and stain. Guilt shadowed Carlys's thoughts and feelings until it became a self-made prison, a prison she carried with her everywhere she went. The more she tried to assuage her guilt, the more it trapped her. As her erotic links to her lover grew stronger, her guilt toward her husband grew greater and sex, which she once told herself was natural and healthy, now seemed mired in guilt and furtiveness. The nightmare was that the guiltier she felt toward her husband, the more exciting the sex became with her lover. She began to take crazy chances. She was lying to everyone: to her husband, to her lover, to her secretary, to her boss, to her father, to her friends. She was stealing time: time from her job, time from her marriage, time from herself. She was burning on a shorter and shorter fuse, and all she was aware of was the heightened, almost unbearable excitement of being in her lover's arms.

It was up to her, Carlys told herself as she got more deeply involved with George, more afraid of the risks she was taking, more afraid that everything was getting out of control, to make sure that Kirk suspected nothing. As her affair began to frighten her with its intensity, she turned to her marriage with its security, and its very routine, for reassurance.

In mid-October she asked Kirk's secretary to schedule a free evening for him. She paid a scalper a fortune for a pair of tickets to *Cats*. She bought a new dress, a short, lacy black confection from Saks and, to go with it, some sexy, strappy sandals from Maud Frizon. She made a dinner reservation at Carolina. She asked Kirk's driver if he would work that evening.

"I've done everything," she told Kirk, when she told him about her surprise, "except to arrange with God for it not to rain."

As it turned out Kirk had a late afternoon meeting down on Wall Street. He had no time to come home and relax and change; instead he met Carlys at the theater. He thought she looked beautiful and he loved the perfume she was wearing. Chloe. He didn't tell her, though. She already knew that he thought she was beautiful. He didn't say anything about the perfume either. After all, he bought it for her every year, twice a year: at Chrismas and for her birthday.

He couldn't concentrate on the play. His mind kept drifting to business and, strangely, to Bonnie. He had filed Bonnie away just as he had filed away the rest of his past: He almost never thought about her. He didn't like to. She reminded him of all the losses that had scarred him: the loss of his father, his brother, and, finally, the failure of his first marriage. Still, as the T. S. Eliot words and the Andrew Lloyd Webber score drifted in and out of his awareness, he kept thinking of his first wife. Not of the early, busy years but of their last year together. He didn't know why, but he kept trying to remember the signs of her adultery. All he could recall was that she always seemed to be in the kitchen, cooking. Thank God, Carlys never cooked. In the dark theater, he reached out and took her hand, something he rarely did anymore. Touched and pleased, almost grateful for his affection, she squeezed his fingers.

"You were so preoccupied you barely heard a word," Carlys commented over crab cakes and ribs barbecued over a mesquite wood fire. She knew that he was negotiating to produce manuals for Apple's new Macintosh. It would be a major coup and she knew he was anxious about it. She had sensed that he was preoccupied at the theater; she assumed it was over business. It was the preferable assumption, the logical assumption. Kirk saved his emotions and his energies for his career, something of which he was proud. Like his father, he liked to say, he was a hard-headed businessman. He didn't believe in wasting his time or energy on frivolities. Thinking or talking about feelings—particularly disquieting ones—was a frivolity. "How are the talks with Apple going?"

"Fine," he said absently. He kept wondering how a man could tell if his wife was being unfaithful. The suspicion had finally come to him the weekend Carlys had returned from Cincinnati and he had found a matchbook from the Inn at Sawmill Farm in Vermont. He didn't mention it. Instead he waited to see if she would say something, to see if he would find another, more conclusive clue. In the meantime he kept the matchbook in his briefcase.

"Then what's the matter?"

"Nothing."

"Something," she pressed. "It has to be something."

"We're happy, aren't we?" he said suddenly, unexpectedly.

"Of course," said Carlys, her throat dry. She took his hand across the table. Just as Kirk had once asked Bonnie a question to which he did not want the true answer, Carlys was unable to stop herself. "What makes you ask?"

He shrugged uncomfortably. He did not want to have this conversation. He did not know why he had started it. He retreated into safety and control. He smiled and made a joke of it: "Just a yearly checkup, I guess."

They finished dinner, the awkwardness between them dissolving as they talked about business, his and hers. Kirk was so preoccupied with his own sense of relief that he didn't even notice hers.

They had stepped close to the edge of a cliff and, at the last moment, pulled back.

On her return to New York from Paris Jade remembered her departure. Between George's passionate kisses and trans-Atlantic phone calls she half-expected him to meet her plane. She looked for him as she disembarked and as she cleared customs. When she got home the apartment was empty and when she looked for a note from George there was none. Had she been right? Had he lied to her? Was there someone else? Her emotions were like a seesaw, going up and down. Her period had lasted three days, disappeared for five, and then unexpectedly returned, a spotty discharge instead of a regular flow. Jade was filled with doubts and she began to worry about something she'd always taken for granted—her good health.

She called George's office, but he was out. Jade wondered if he'd left her, told herself she was crazy, and began to unpack, stacking the Charvet shirts she'd bought for him on his side of the bed. When she was just about done she heard his key in the front door.

"I missed you," he said, taking her into his arms, and holding her as if he were starved for her. "You don't know how much I missed you."

"I missed *you*," she said. It was true. "I thought about you every day."

No matter how hectic the days were—and the showings of the collections, always late, ran from morning to early evening, followed by cocktail parties and dinners and visits to the latest discos—Jade constantly found herself thinking of George. She wondered what he'd think of this boutique, that restaurant. She wished he were there to share the frenzy, the glitz, the moments of unintentional humor, the frequent displays of temperament, the egos, the shoving and the pushing, the jealousies over who got which seats, the mad rush backstage to congratulate the designer afterward, the anxiety to share a success, the desperation to flee a failure. She wanted him to enjoy with her the excitement of a new look or a new trend, and, once in a while, those perfect moments when the right model and the right outfit, perfectly accessorized and perfectly presented, took everyone's breath away and reminded people what the circus was all about in the first place. "I wish you could come with me—just once."

"Maybe next time," he whispered, his lips on her face, his mouth close to her ear.

This time, as every time he saw her, he was aware of how wildly attracted he was to her. There was no one like Jade. No one looked like her, no one had her two-steps-to-the-left sense of humor, no one saw things exactly the way he did as much as she did. "We've never been to Europe together."

"I've brought Europe to you," she said. "Go look on the bed."

"The only thing I want to see on my bed is you," he said with a comic leer, taking her by the hand and leading her into their room, noticing that, even through her sweater, her breasts seemed fuller. He felt indescribably aroused, and as Jade melted into his arms she thought, as she had so many times in the past, that the only thing better for romance than being apart was being together again.

Kirk's phone call to the gym had scared Carlys. His questioning at Carolina scared her even more. Kirk had always made a point of never getting angry; She feared what he might do if he *did* get angry. Carlys had always sensed that there were unexpressed passions in Kirk—they attracted her and they frightened her. She remembered how he had once smashed every glass in the kitchen. It was a side of him she had never seen before—or since. It was a side of him she hoped she'd never see again.

In October, during an unseasonable cold snap, she met George late one afternoon at his apartment, the way she always did, waiting until everyone was gone and his office was empty.

"A weekend is all I'm asking," George said after they'd made love. "You did it once. You can do it again."

"No, I can't," she said. His intensity, once flattering, now frightened her. She had wanted an affair, not an obsession. "I'm afraid that Kirk suspects something. He was furious the time I told him I had to go to Cincinnati. I can't get away with it again."

"So what am I supposed to do?" George asked cruelly, even though he held her gently and his voice was tender in her ear. Even as she turned him down he felt himself get hard again. "Wait around for the crumbs of time you can throw me?"

They were lying in bed, their arms wrapped around each other, a moment for intimate conversation, not for a struggle. Carlys got up. She felt she needed to get away from him, at least physically. She didn't want to have this conversation while she was in bed next to him, feeling his erection against her thigh. Without thinking she got up and walked over to his closet. It was chilly in the room and she wanted a robe. She opened the closet door thinking she'd borrow his.

"It's empty!" she said, shocked. It took her a moment to understand and then she did. She turned and looked at him. "You don't live here," she said, comprehending. "You're living somewhere else. With someone else. With Jade."

He nodded.

"How could you?" she asked, stunned at how hurt she was, at how betrayed she felt, at the extent to which she felt sullied and cheated. "How *could* you?"

"How could I what?" he asked. His tone was reasonable and tender. "You're married, Carlys. What do you want? Do you think you can keep me on hold? Waiting for your convenience?"

"But I didn't know. You never said. . . ."

"I don't owe you explanations," he said, getting out of bed and coming over to her, touching her. He was still kind, but he was tearing her heart out. She pulled away from his touch and sat down on the bed for a moment, desolate and empty, conflicting emotions pulling her apart. She didn't know what to say. What *could* she say? There was nothing to say.

Without a word she began to dress.

"I'm in over my head," she said finally, feeling as if she were sobering up from a terrible sick binge, as if she were seeing reality for the first time in months. She looked at the harsh and tawdry facts: a wife cheating on her husband, a lover cheating on his beloved. She saw a woman she didn't recognize, a woman she didn't want to be. She saw a man she didn't want to be with. A man who used women. A woman who let herself be used. She wanted to erase it, to obliterate it. She shook her head. "I don't want to see you anymore. I can't handle it."

He took her hand and when she pulled it away, he took it a second time.

"I'm not going to do anything you don't want me to do," he promised. She had heard those words before and had believed them. But now she realized that all along he had been doing what she didn't want him to do—with her consent. She caught a glimpse of herself in a mirrored door and she thought she saw a stranger, a woman she didn't recognize in an unfamiliar room with a man she barely knew. Who was she, she asked herself, and what was she doing here? "Carlys, are you sure you mean it?"

"Yes," she said, taking her hand away. "I'm sure."

She was afraid he'd try to persuade her to stay but he didn't. Profoundly ashamed of herself she went to the door, let herself out, and did not look back. Pain, humiliation, and relief flayed at her as she told herself that it was all over and that she had somehow gotten away with it.

C H A P T E R   12

*J*ade was nervous the minute she walked into Dr. Lionel's examining room. The feeling that something was wrong with her had not lessened, but intensified. She was still staining. Her hair was still oily and impossible to manage. Her skin seemed to have changed in color and even in texture—it seemed both darker and coarser. She felt she had trouble moving—she felt heavy although she had gained no weight and her legs still seemed numb and unresponsive. She had recalled the Cancer Society advertisements that ran in the back of magazines and, going down the checklist, realized she had several of the warning signs. Her worries about her health pushed her worries about George into the background. She went to Dr. Lionel expecting him to tell her that she was being a hypochondriac and advise her to take some vitamins. But he had done nothing of the kind. He had performed a careful head-to-toe physical and, when he was done, sent her to a gynecologist.

"I want you to get a complete gynecological exam," he told her. "And don't wait."

While Jade sat in his office he called her gynecologist and asked him to see her right away.

"Is something wrong?" Jade asked just before leaving Dr. Lionel's office.

"That's why we're checking you so carefully," he replied in that maddening don't-worry-we'll-take-care-of-you way doctors have.

Now that the affair was over Carlys felt enormously relieved—relieved that she had gotten away with it, that Kirk hadn't found out. Relieved to be free of the anxiety and guilt that had weighed her down. She was relieved to go back to normal, and the life that had once seemed a little dull was now gloriously welcome.

She hadn't counted on George. She had forgotten his persistence. She had forgotten the way her saying no meant nothing to him. He began to call her every day at the office. He didn't make the mistake of begging her to see him. Instead he told her how much he missed her.

"I think about you all the time," he told her. "I passed by Lutèce today. Do you remember the lunch we had there? The one Ada paid for?"

"Whenever it rains, I think about you," he told her one rainy day. "Remember how it poured the night we met?"

"Please don't call me," Carlys said.

"Why not?" he asked.

"It's too painful," she said.

"You mean you miss me, too?" he asked.

"Please," she replied, trying to make him understand that she meant it, that she wasn't playing games. "I don't want you to call me anymore. It's over."

She told her secretary to tell Mr. Kouras that she was out or unavailable or in a meeting whenever he called.

"Of course, Mrs. Arnold," said Lisa. Every day for the next three days George called, and every time he called Lisa told him that Mrs. Arnold was in a meeting.

"He told me to tell you that he'd call you at home tonight," Lisa told Carlys that afternoon.

Carlys went into her office, closed the door, and dialed the number herself.

"You told me once that I didn't have to ask you not to call me at home," Carlys reminded him, horrified at the thought of having to have a conversation with George while Kirk was in the room. "Don't you remember?"

"Of course I remember," he said. "But we were having an affair then. I understood. Now we're not even seeing each other anymore. Why can't I call you at home?"

"Because I don't want you to," Carlys said.

"But I miss you," he said, throwing himself on her mercy. "I miss the sound of your voice."

"Just don't call me!" begged Carlys, almost hysterical. "Please."

It took a while, but Jade finally got the words out in Dr. Fishbein's cozy beige and leather book-lined office. He had examined her carefully, and if he had drawn any conclusions he had kept them to himself.

"What's wrong?" she asked.

"I'm not sure," he said. "That's why I want to do some tests."

"What kind of tests?" asked Jade, scared, her throat tight and her stomach in knots.

"I'm going to send you for a mammogram and, of course, we'll do a Pap test."

"Pap test?" That was the test for cancer. Jade had known there was something terribly wrong all along. She felt her insides clench.

Dr. Fishbein nodded, then responded to the worry on her face. "Jade, try not to worry. Let *me* worry."

He knew, of course, that that was easier said than done.

Yet, at this moment, he was doing the most he possibly could.

"You'll let me know the minute you have the results?" she asked, feeling doomed, wondering whether she had years or months left and wondering what she was going to tell George, Steve, her mother. She didn't want people to feel sorry for her. She didn't want people to feel they had to tiptoe around her.

"Of course I will," he said. "I'll call you the minute I get word from the lab."

Jade realized that he was being kind but it didn't help. For every hour from that moment on she walked around with a constant lump in her throat. She noticed each sunset, wondering how many more she'd see. She savored each cup of coffee as if it might be her last. She straightened all her drawers and scrubbed down the kitchen as if in preparation for an important visitor. She went to her lawyer and made a will.

"I saw my lawyer today," she told George. "I made a will."

"A will?" he asked, surprised. "Aren't you a little young for that?"

"It pays to be safe," she said. She hadn't told him about her visit to Dr. Fishbein. She was afraid he wouldn't want to touch her if he thought she had cancer. More than ever, she needed him to hold her, to touch her. More than ever, she needed the comfort of his arms. "I left everything to you."

"Jade, don't be grim!" he said. Talk of death upset him.

"Hold me," she said, feeling suddenly weepy, holding out her arms to him.

Four days later, on an unseasonably warm morning in early November as Carlys left for work, the doorman smiled and pointed to the horse and carriage standing in front of the building. The driver was a young man, blond and virile and handsome, an actor perhaps, driving a horse and buggy as a way to make money until he got his big break.

"Mrs. Arnold?" he asked. He had an actor's voice, mellow and smooth. He read from the order slip. "Mr. Kouras asked me to pick you up and take you to work. He told me to be sure to drive you through the park."

Carlys glanced at the driver, then looked back at the doorman, who was watching with interest. She swallowed hard and smiled at the doorman and allowed the driver to help her into the carriage.

She was furious at George. Why couldn't he accept her word that everything was over between them? What if Kirk had come downstairs with her? What did the doorman think? What if one of the neighbors had overheard?

She wanted it to be over. Please God, she prayed, let it be over. She wanted to be free. She wanted to go back to her life.

She neither called nor wrote George to thank him. She did something she had never done in her life—nothing. She let his gesture go unacknowledged. She wanted him out of her life.

George was sure Carlys would at least phone to thank him. After all, even if he said so himself, sending a horse and carriage to someone's front door in the middle of Manhattan was memorable and romantic, and Carlys was the kind of woman who was always punctilious about such things as *please* and *thank you.* When, after three days, she didn't phone, George phoned her.

"Mr. Kouras called when you were in your meeting," Lisa told Carlys. "He said he'd call back. What should I tell him?"

"Tell him," Carlys began, but then thought for a moment. "Tell him that I received it and that I appreciate it. Thank him for me, would you please?" Carlys thought she was handling the situation perfectly. She was being polite but she wasn't getting involved. She wondered what Lisa thought. She hoped she thought that George Kouras was just another business acquaintance. Her guilt, which had evaporated in the vast ocean of relief she had once felt, now returned, stronger, more devastating than ever. Guilt was now combined with fear—fear of George, of what he might do. The persistence, the recklessness that had once seemed romantic were now terrifying. Fear and guilt had spread until they now touched the most casual encounters of her day, leaving her almost incapable of thinking, almost incapable of functioning.

"What the hell's the matter with you?" Joshua had demanded. She had lost two clients in a row.

"Nothing," she had said and made excuses for her failure.

"I'm not paying you to screw up," he warned.

That evening when she and Kirk were watching television, the telephone rang and Carlys, afraid to answer but more afraid not to, picked it up.

"Carlys," George said tenderly, his voice coming at her through the phone like a caress. "I wanted to do something I thought you'd like, but you haven't even spoken to me. You had your secretary call. Are you angry with me?"

"No, of course not," she said, turning away from Kirk, unable to allow him to see her face, thinking that her world was shattering. She wondered if her voice sounded normal. What was normal? She couldn't remember. She choked back fury at George for calling at the same time that she tried to ignore her uncontrollable excitement. Her knees felt wobbly, her breath caught in her chest, her lungs didn't seem to get enough air, and her heart pounded. She tried to remember what she sounded like when she was talking to a client. Was she as terse? "I think it was very . . . appropriate." There, she thought, that sounded normal.

"Then should I do it again? I'd like to make you happy," he said, his voice enveloping her in tenderness and danger.

"No," she said. Kirk looked up from the TV and studied Carlys, who had turned so he couldn't see her face. "Once was enough. Thank you," she said and hung up, almost dropping the receiver.

"Who was that?" Kirk asked.

"Lansing," she said brusquely, aware only of her racing heart and shortness of breath. They seemed so obvious, she was sure that Kirk would notice them, too.

"What's the matter?" Kirk asked. "You sound annoyed."

"He's a pain!" said Carlys, switching off the light on her side of the bed and punching at her pillow. "Why the hell does he need to bother me at this hour?" She rolled over and put her baby pillow over her head to block out the light from the television set. Kirk looked at her and wondered what was bothering her. She never went to sleep at eleven o'clock, and he had never heard her so irritated with a client. It just wasn't like her.

It also wasn't like her to lie. He'd run into Ray Mundees

at 21 and Ray had mentioned that he'd seen Carlys leave the Algonquin a few weeks ago at five-thirty as he was entering the Harvard Club. Kirk wondered just what Carlys was doing at the Algonquin at five-thirty. She always said she hated its dark rooms and self-consciously literary and theatrical shabbiness. He'd met her at 21 at six-fifteen. She'd been late. She'd said she'd gotten tied up at the office. Why hadn't she mentioned being at the Algonquin? And the other day the doorman had said something about Mrs. Arnold going to work in a horse and carriage. What was that all about? Why hadn't she mentioned it? What was she hiding from him? He remembered Bonnie. He suddenly remembered the details: she had cut her hair; she had lost weight; she had, after years of disinterest, wanted to make love to him. He had noticed but he had thought nothing of it. He had ignored his intuition, and he had lost her.

"Carlys?"

"Yes?"

"Are you seeing someone? Are you having an affair?"

She took the pillow away and sat up and switched on the lights. She looked at her husband and told him the truth: "No," she said. "I'm not."

He looked at her again. "Are you sure there isn't something you're not telling me?"

With that, she exploded. "How dare you ask me that? Have *I* kept something from you? What about you?" she demanded, facing him finally with her anger and resentment. "You lied to me about your father. You lied to me about being an only child. I know all about Scott."

The blood drained from Kirk's face. He was furious, but he kept his voice low, concealing his rage. "How did you find out?"

"From Geoff," she said, ignoring the sinister pseudocalm that had come over Kirk. "I was so worried about you. I was afraid you'd hurt yourself. Or maybe someone else. Maybe even me. I had to speak to someone. I finally called Geoff. He told me everything about your father, about Scott and Covington. Talk about secrets, Kirk! Don't accuse me of keeping secrets. Not ever! I even know about Dearborn."

"How did you find out about that?" he asked. That

quiet, angry voice was much more frightening than screaming or shouting could ever have been.

"From your mother," said Carlys. "You don't talk to
me. So I have to talk to other people. I know everything,
Kirk! All the secrets you kept from me. All the secrets that
made me feel that you excluded me from everything that
was most important to you! Don't you *dare* accuse me of
keeping things from you. Don't you *dare*!"

Still pale, his eyes stony, he had no response to her
accusations. There was one. He retreated into his charac-
teristic silence and let her think that he believed her.

She had lied too many times. She had lied about being
late. She had lied—by omission—about the horse and carriage. Ray had seen her coming out of the Algonquin. She
had been different ever since the summer, both in bed and
out. The first time he'd called her at the gym she hadn't
been there although she'd said she was taking the six-thirty
class and would be home late. There were just too many
things that didn't add up; too many things that didn't make
sense—things like the matchbook from an inn in Vermont
that was still in his briefcase.

The next day at the office, Carlys telephoned George.

"Don't ever do that again!" she said the moment she
heard his voice. Her own shook with emotion. Kirk had
barely spoken to her that morning. Wordlessly, he had left
the apartment. His accusations made her feel scared and
guilty. His refusal to reply to hers left her angry and rebellious. "Never!"

George's response was to send to her office, with his
apologies, a glorious basket of forced paperwhites. To pre-
vent him from calling her at home again she telephoned to
thank him.

"It was very nice of you," she said. She sounded both
sincere and formal. "They're beautiful."

"I had hoped you'd like them," he replied, his voice a
lover's voice. "I love to give you beautiful things. It makes
me happy."

Bonnie had left him, and Kirk had let her go, but Carlys
was not Bonnie. This time the pain was not an echo of
other pain. This time the thought of another loss, the loss

of Carlys, was more than he could bear. He loved her more than he had ever loved anyone, and he would not let her go. He would do anything and everything to keep her, even if he had to destroy himself and her to do it. He felt very rational as he called a corporate detective he knew and asked him to recommend someone. The man recommended John Plandome, who was discreet, reliable, and expensive. John Plandome, used to husbands with wandering wives and wives with unfaithful husbands, understood completely.

"I'd like a copy of her personal telephone book," he said, "a photograph, and her office address."

George sent an antique sterling silver letter opener from James Robinson's to Carlys's office. It was the perfect, discreet lover's gift, something for the office that would not invite questions or excite curiosity. It did, however, interest John Plandome, who had gotten friendly with the head of Barron & Hynes's mailroom.

Feeling like she was walking on a mine field, Carlys returned the gift in person. She didn't want to risk angering George with an impersonal messenger; she didn't want to write a note; she didn't want to put anything in writing. She went to George's office in the middle of the day when there were people around, when she would not be vulnerable to him, when no one would suspect a thing. Because her visit was innocent, she took a taxi to George's front door. John Plandome, in a Dodge Dart, double parked across the street.

"Didn't you like it?" he asked her. He seemed crushed but Carlys tried to ignore it. Ever since the call she had watched Kirk, trying to determine if he'd been suspicious or if he'd accepted her excuse about Lansing. He never referred to his suspicions again. He tortured her with his silence and she tortured herself with uncertainty.

"Of course I like it," she said, afraid to anger George, afraid that he'd show up at her apartment, call her again when Kirk was there, or do something that would shatter her marriage and her life. George had told Carlys early in their affair that when he was in love he would stop at nothing to conquer his loved one. She remembered thinking at the time how romantic it was. Now, it terrified her.

"Then see me again," he begged. "Please. Just the two of us. Just once. . . ."

There were people around: draftsmen; receptionists; Will, his office door open, at his drawing board, was looking at them curiously. She didn't want to risk a scene.

Even as she agreed she knew she should never have said yes.

John Plandome went to James Robinson and, on a pretext, obtained the name and address of the purchaser of the silver letter opener. It was the same name and the same address as the building in which Mrs. Arnold had spent an hour in the middle of the afternoon.

"George Kouras," he told Kirk and gave him George's office address.

Kirk nodded. George Kouras. A man he had once let into the apartment he shared with his wife while she was still undressed, still in her nightgown and robe. Kirk made a note of the address and when he got home he went to the closet and got out the gun that had killed his father and his brother.

She knew she would make love to him again. She had never imagined that George would be unable to.

"It's never happened before!" he said, his voice strangled, trying desperately to excite himself, the old anguish coming back more brutally than ever before, making him feel inadequate and worthless. Sex had once been a drug and now the drug no longer healed. "I know I can do it. Just give me a minute. I know I can!"

"Maybe it's better this way," Carlys said, relieved.

"No!" he said, his voice choked and desperate. "I need you!"

"Please, George. Let's just end it," said Carlys, glimpsing an ending, a way out. "I think it's come to its own end anyway."

"Why *can't* we go on?" he asked pathetically, not a lover but a man in anguish. He was now terrified that Jade was thinking of leaving him. She had been withdrawn, barely responsive. It was obvious that something important was on her mind; he kept thinking that any moment she would tell him that she no longer wanted him, and that his world would crash. "Why can't we go on just the way we have been?"

Carlys said no every way she could think of. At first she was as kind as he was. She didn't want to fight with him or to hurt him. She didn't want him to ruin her life. She just wanted to leave him.

"Why not?" George kept wanting to know. "You know I want you more than Kirk does."

He was beginning to get insistent. Carlys regretted telling him as much as she had—that her marriage wasn't as romantic as it had once been, that sex with her husband had become routine, disappointing.

"*I* love you," George insisted. "*He's* just your roommate."

"Please, George," Carlys said. "Don't talk about him that way."

"*You* did," he said with a sudden flash of cruelty.

"I'm sorry, George," Carlys said, shaking. She felt overwhelmed with shame and fear. "It's over. That's all. It's nothing you did or said. I can't handle it anymore. I don't want to risk my marriage. It was a terrible mistake and I'm sorry if I hurt you. I regret it, but it's over. It has to be."

She picked up her bag, wanting to end the conversation, wanting to get out of his apartment for the last time. Its walls were beginning to press in on her, and George's demands were beginning to suffocate her.

"Good-bye," she said at the door, turning toward him one last time in a gesture of appeasement. "Please don't be angry."

She shut the door behind her and never heard the buzzer. When no one answered George assumed one of the draftsmen had gone out for coffee and forgotten his key. It happened all the time and George automatically buzzed back.

Jade absolutely did not believe Dr. Fishbein and that is exactly what she told him.

"Jade Mullen!" he chided, although he certainly understood why she refused to believe him. "If you don't believe me, maybe you'll believe the lab report," he said and pushed it across his desk toward her. She looked at it and blinked.

"Really?" she said, still incredulous, laughing and crying at the same time. She was thirty-five, two doctors had told her that she'd never be able to conceive. She had absolutely, totally given up on the idea of ever having children and now this man *and* this lab report were telling her that she was pregnant. She simply couldn't believe it.

"Really!" he said and smiled. "The chances that you could have conceived must have been a million to one but you did. All I can say is that this baby realy wants to be born!"

The first thing Jade did when she left his office was head toward Lexington Avenue. She was giddily, hysterically happy. She knew now why she had been so up and down. She now understood all the puzzling physical symptoms that Dr. Fishbein had explained weren't all *that* unusual during the early weeks of pregnancy.

As she turned the corner of Third into Sixty-second Street, Jade smiled and hugged herself, cuddling the precious life she carried. When she got into the lobby, she buzzed and told George she was on her way up.

Carlys stood in the small foyer waiting for the elevator, a small European-style one, and when it arrived, she opened the door and blindly walked into her husband.

"Kirk!"

They stared at each other in shock as George opened the door, expecting Jade. Kirk reached into the Tiffany bag and withdrew the gun as the three of them froze and Jade, too excited and impatient to wait for the elevator, came up the stairs and turned the corner. She smiled at George but then saw Carlys and instantly understood. She opened her mouth to say something but no sound came out.

As he pointed the gun at George Kirk Arnold's face seemed as white as the scar that ran through his left eyebrow. He was about to murder his wife's lover when suddenly he seemed to change his mind. Slowly, he turned the gun until it came to rest on his own temple, and pulled the trigger.

CHAPTER 13

It all happened in a fraction of a second although, in retrospect, the moment seemed to go on forever. At the time, it happened so fast that Carlys didn't even think.

"No!" she screamed, as she saw Kirk move the gun up to his right temple. She hurled herself at her husband, grabbing at his arm, and forcing it down and away from his head as George leapt toward Kirk, throwing him off balance. The gun waved wildly as Kirk fell toward the floor and the roar of the explosion filled the small foyer silencing everything. Their heartbeats stopped, and so did their thoughts.

Stunned, Kirk looked at his hand as if it were the hand of a stranger. He still held the gun.

"Give it to me," Carlys said, holding out her hand for the gun, still acting automatically, without thought. Silently he handed it to her and she almost pushed him into the elevator and got in behind him. In shock they rode to the ground floor and went out onto the street where Kirk hailed a taxi.

"Eleven East Seventy-ninth Street," he told the driver as he got in behind Carlys and shut the door of the cab. He leaned back in the seat and, as he did, his suit jacket opened and Carlys saw the blood pumping through his white shirt plastering it to his body.

"Driver!" she screamed as Kirk suddenly moaned and slumped forward, clutching his abdomen with his arms. "New York Hospital. Emergency entrance."

"Jade!" George screamed, rushing over to her. She lay slumped on the floor. "Jade?" he asked, touching her. She didn't answer. She didn't move. He couldn't tell if she was breathing.

George looked up at Will and a draftsman who had run up the stairs when they heard the gunshot.

"What happened?" Will asked, out of breath.

"I'm not sure," George said, white with shock. "I don't know what happened to the bullet. I don't know if she's hit or not."

Jade was still lying motionless on the floor, face down. She didn't seem to be alive.

Together, George and Will carefully turned her over.

The doctor's name was Eric Resch. He was very young, too young to be dealing with life and death. Kirk was taken to the operating room immediately and Eric Resch told Carlys that Kirk's condition was critical. He had lost a great deal of blood, there were severe abdominal injuries, his vital signs were erratic. None of the doctor's words told Carlys what she wanted to know.

"Is he going to be all right?" she asked, aware of the peculiar feeling of emotional numbness. She knew she was panicked, knew she was desperate, knew her world was coming to an end, and yet she felt nothing. At least she thought she felt nothing, although her mouth was dry and her throat so constricted she could barely speak. Her heart pounded so wildly that she gasped for breath. "Is he going to live?"

Eric Resch didn't answer. He didn't have to. The expression in his clear, blue eyes told Carlys that he didn't know. What he could tell her was that the police were being called.

"The police?"

"It's the law," he said. "We have to report all gunshot wounds."

As they moved her Jade sighed and the noise seemed almost shattering in the strange silence of the foyer. She was breathing. Thank God, thought George. She's alive. Her eyelashes fluttered and she opened her eyes.

"What happened?" she asked bewildered, not even sure of where she was. Vaguely she wondered what she was doing on the floor. "What's the funny smell?"

The smell was cordite.

"So now you know," George said. He couldn't look at her.

"Now I know," she said.

"Do you hate me?" he asked, desperate to know. He *had* to know. What would he do if she left him? What would become of him?

She turned away. How could she answer his question when she didn't know the answer herself. Then she felt the wetness between her legs and screamed. She remembered another time, another place, another man, another miscarriage.

"Please!" she said, between the wrenching spasms of pain. "Call Dr. Fishbein." Then waiting for the next spasm to pass and catching her breath, she said: "You'd better take me to the hospital."

The first call Carlys made was to her lawyer.

"Kirk's been arrested," she told Judith, repeating the new phrase that haunted her: Bedside arraignment. "Please come."

Then she called Joshua.

"Kirk's had an accident," she said. "Please, Joshua. Pull all the strings Barron & Hynes can pull. I want to keep it out of the papers."

Dr. Resch came down from the operating room.

"We've removed the bullet," he said, his face betraying no emotion, only fatigue and wariness.

"And?" asked Carlys.

"And we still don't know," he said. "He's in intensive care."

The bullet had been removed from the base of his spine where it had lodged and Kirk was unconscious, his vital signs fluttering unsteadily.

Carlys left the hospital only to attend to another emergency.

At ten o'clock that morning Howie Mundees, a hale and hearty seventy-one, was pulling out of the driveway of his Locust Valley home when a car coming in the other direction smashed head-on into Howie's Buick, killing Howie instantly. The driver of the other car walked away. Or, rather, staggered. The police learned he was drunk and he had been drinking since the night before. The alcohol level in his blood was so high that he was in a state approaching coma. The police also discovered, checking their computerized records, that he had been arrested four times previously for drunk driving.

"Please," said Molly on the phone, for once sounding

her age. "Miriam's under sedation. Please, Carlys, could you take care of the funeral?"

Not knowing if Kirk would live or die and unable to do anything to tip the scales, Carlys arranged Howie Mundees's funeral.

After he examined her Dr. Fishbein said that Jade would be all right.

"But I don't know about the baby," he said, taking off his glasses and rubbing the place on his nose where they dug in and hurt. "I don't know if we're going to be able to save it or not."

"Baby!" said George, stunned. "Baby? What baby?"

"She's pregnant," said Dr. Fishbein, putting the glasses back on and blinking momentarily. "Didn't you know?"

George shook his head.

"She never told me," he said and finally broke down. He sobbed with joy and shock and horror at his own almost insane recklessness with the woman who meant everything to him.

In her room Jade lay in bed, afraid to move, afraid almost to breathe, afraid to do anything that might harm her baby. Hers and George's. Dr. Fishbein had been blunt. He just didn't know if the baby could be saved or not.

"It's going to be born," Jade said with almost superhuman ferocity. "I know it!"

Dr. Fishbein wasn't so sure.

"I know I have a hell of a nerve to ask a favor of you," Molly told Carlys when Carlys returned her call from a booth in the waiting room. It was the afternoon of the funeral and Kirk was still in intensive care, the green blips on a video monitor the only indication of life. Molly sounded more like an old lady than a woman who had spent her life desperately wishing she had been born a man.

"What favor?" Carlys asked remotely. She had, of course, told no one about Kirk. Judith had solved the legal dilemma with the police brilliantly while Joshua had seen to it that nothing appeared in the newspapers.

"Faith and I have come to a decision," she said. "We're two little old ladies now. Howie's gone. Ray has found a happy niche handling the family's investments. There's no family left anymore at the company. We've decided that we want to sell SuperWrite," Molly declared. "Carlys, we'd like to sell it to Kirk. Do you think he'd be interested?"

"Interested?" Carlys repeated. She didn't know if he'd live or die. As she tried to think of what to say someone tapped on the glass door of the phone booth. It was Dr. Resch. He nodded and smiled and gave her the "thumbs-up" sign.

Carlys almost fainted with relief. Leaving Molly hanging on, bewildered, Carlys flung down the telephone; racing after Dr. Resch she followed him to Kirk's room. How could she have done it? she had asked herself a thousand times in the past week. How could she have risked her marriage? How could she have been so willfully, so stupidly self-indulgent? How *could* she have thought that she'd get away with it?

She looked cautiously into the room. Kirk was awake. He looked thin and pale, even the gold in his hair seemed dimmed. She walked in, going to the side of his bed, ready to face his anger, his outrage, his betrayal.

"You were wrong to do what you did," he said softly in his curiously husky voice.

"Yes," she said quietly, already weeping, bracing herself for her punishment, for his bitter, accusing words, words to which she had no defense. "I was wrong."

"So was I," he said with a sudden sob, holding out his arms.

E P I L O G U E

June 1983:
Wives and Others

*J*ade and George's son was born, ironically, on the same date as Carlys's and Kirk Arnold's eighth anniversary.

"I'm going to name him Chris," she told her mother. Chris was the name of Heidi's oldest boy, Jade's godchild. "But things are going to be different for Chris and me than they were for us."

Dorothy Mullen nodded. Jade was thirty-six; Dorothy had been eighteen at the time she'd first been pregnant. Jade was free to make her own decisions; Dorothy had still been living with her parents. Jade could afford help and nice dresses and good schools—all the things Dorothy hadn't been able to afford. The times were different. Marriage wasn't the only possibility for a woman anymore. Manhattan was different from Auburn and George Kouras was different from Arnold Mullen. George had been with Jade right along; he had been at the hospital when his child had been born.

"Marry me," he had said when he first saw his son.

"No," said Jade. She was over her anger, over her bitterness, although for a while she had refused to see or to speak to George. She had asked him to move out of their apartment and he had. She was living alone now, and so was George. The odd thing was that they suddenly began to see more of each other than they had when they had been living together. "You're a lover, George. Not a husband. Not a domestic creature."

"I'll keep proposing," he said.

She smiled, her dazzling, thousand-watt smile. 'And I'll keep saying no."

It was George's turn to smile. He knew, as he had always known, that a woman's "no" never meant anything. He'd keep asking until he got her to change her mind. One way or another he'd get her for his own.

He didn't know that Jade would continue to say no. And he didn't know, although she did, that keeping a certain distance between them was the key to their relationship. Jade would not have a husband, but then, she didn't want one. Chris, though, would have a father and she would have a lover. It was hardly conventional but, as Jade reminded herself, being conventional had only gotten her into trouble. Being unconventional had always been the key to her happiness.

In the next months Kirk and Carlys talked more than they ever had since they had first fallen in love. Now, without the narcotic of romance, they talked against a background of reality. Carlys spoke of too little love, too little affection, and a desperate need for his attention. When he hadn't given it, she had turned, starving, to someone else. He spoke, for the first time since he had talked with Bonnie at Covington, about a past burdened with violent losses and silent rages; about the penalties of secrecy; about a family who never mentioned the dead and tried to bury the past.

Kirk Arnold had never consciously thought about marriage, about what it might mean or be. He had simply assumed, as most men of his generation had assumed, that marriage was in the background of a successful man's life. What was in the foreground, what provided identity, respect, rewards, pleasure, and status, was a man's career. Kirk had put both his wives—and both his marriages—into a compartment that was isolated from the rest of his life, the career that interested and involved him more than anything. Ironically, his affair with Susan Morlake helped him understand Carlys's affair.

"You must have felt just as lonely as I did," he admitted.

The purchase of SuperWrite by E-Z Tech, a complicated transaction involving transfers of stock and cash, agreements about royalties and dividends and future earnings, turned Kirk Arnold from a successful businessman into a tycoon and Carlys's idea of using Kirk as the spokesman for the company he had created turned him into a celebrity.

"It's not SuperWrite," he told Carlys when the papers had all been signed and everything was official. "It was Dearborn Paper and Printing I cared about."

"I know," she said tenderly. She knew that, to Kirk, Dearborn Paper and Printing was a symbol of his father, and having it was a way of keeping his father alive and close to him.

"I guess I should have told you," he said, acknowledging her angry accusations for the first time. He looked ashamed, and avoided her eyes. There were so many ways, he now realized, in which he had built walls between them, walls that had driven her away from him.

She nodded, not belaboring the subject.

"No more secrets?" was all she asked.

"No more secrets," he replied.

* * *

In June Kirk and Carlys gave a big party to celebrate two events: the changing of SuperWrite's name to Clifford Industries, in memory of Kirk's father, and their eighth anniversary.

"You two are so happy," said Joshua, noticing the way they spoke to each other and touched each other. "You act like you're on a permanent honeymoon. What's your secret?"

"We have no secrets," Kirk said as he glanced at Carlys, no longer hiding any of his feelings for her. "Not anymore."

They had had so much stacked against them, her past with too little love and his past with too much loss and too many secrets, and yet, somehow, they had won.

As much as anyone ever can.

SUPERIOR FICTION *from the* FINEST CONTEMPORARY AUTHORS